ACCLAIM FOR MELISSA TAGG

MUIR HARBOR SERIES

"An extremely charming tale with a twist and mystery. Tagg is at her best with this one, mining the depths of family and love. A shining novel not to be missed."
  -**Rachel Hauck**, *New York Times* Bestselling Author

"With complex characters, a swoony romance, and a charming seaside town you can't help but fall in love with, Melissa Tagg delivers once again!"
  -**Courtney Walsh**, *New York Times* Bestselling Author

"In *Autumn by the Sea*, award-winning author Melissa Tagg shows us how a family is held together by love, not by sharing a last name or heritage. The story has everything readers want: an engaging romance, a keep-you-guessing mystery, and intriguing characters. Written with Tagg's trademark humor, book one in the Muir Harbor series made me eager for what comes next."
  -**Beth K. Vogt**, Christy Award-winning author

"This story about finding a place to belong is pure perfection and loveliness from start to finish. Not only is it set in a gorgeous seaside village, but both Neil and Sydney's journeys tugged at my heartstrings and did not let go till the end. Filled with Tagg's signature blend of romance, charming quirk, and emotional depth, *Autumn by the Sea* is definitely one for your keeper shelf."
  -**Lindsay Harrel**, author of *The Inn at Walker Beach*

MAPLE VALLEY SERIES

"Powerful. I've always loved Melissa Tagg's stories, but this one is something special. Lyrical, yes. Enchanting, of course. But her story about a broken man meeting an equally broken woman and their journey to healing touched unexpected places in my heart. An absolutely beautiful, compelling read."

-**Susan May Warren**, *USA Today* bestselling, award-winning author

"This book . . . so many feelings, so much love for this friends-to-more-story. I loved all the emotions these characters brought out while finding their happy ending . . . Truly an inspiring read."

-**RelzReviewz.com**

WALKER FAMILY SERIES

"Tagg crafts a beautiful romance filled with humor, mystery, and heartfelt emotion . . . Tagg's moving story beautifully explores themes of redemption and the nature of home."

-**Publisher's Weekly**, for *All This Time*

"Bear and Raegan are endearing and intriguing characters, and readers can't help but fall in love with them. A doozy of a first kiss is completely worth the wait, and even a little suspense is skillfully worked into the plot—in case pulses weren't already racing. (They were.)"

-**RT Book Reviews**, 4½ Stars TOP PICK! for *All This Time*

"Tagg excels at creating wholesome romances featuring strong young career women, gentle humor, and an unobtrusive but heartfelt infusion of faith."

-**Booklist**, for *From the Start*

BOOKS BY MELISSA TAGG

MUIR HARBOR SERIES

Autumn by the Sea

A Seaside Wonder

Wedding at Sea (coming in 2023)

MAPLE VALLEY SERIES

Now and Then and Always

Some Bright Someday

WALKER FAMILY SERIES

Three Little Words (prequel e-novella)

From the Start

Like Never Before

Keep Holding On

All This Time

ENCHANTED CHRISTMAS COLLECTION

One Enchanted Christmas

One Enchanted Eve

One Enchanted Noël

WHERE LOVE BEGINS SERIES

Made to Last

Here to Stay

A MUIR HARBOR NOVEL

MELISSA TAGG

For my grandpa

January 7, 1969

*D*ear Maggie,

    I should probably start by confessing the chances that I'll actually send this letter are slim. I don't even know your street address. And we only just met. A man doesn't send a love letter to a woman after one chance encounter.

    Though, for the record, I don't believe my brother and I happening upon you at the chapel on the cliff was chance at all. Maybe someday the world will shipwreck my simple faith. Maybe age or experience will dull what today feels like an everlasting glow. But for now, I'm still an unspoiled believer, unwilling to credit to coincidence what my soul insists is from the Divine.

    And make no mistake, this IS a love letter.

    Even if it remains unread for years to come, it begs to be written regardless. I've never kept a journal, never felt the need to chronicle my life—perhaps because there hasn't been much to chronicle so far. But after meeting you, well . . . it seems there's been a writer in me all along, just waiting for something worth writing about.

    Someone, that is. Someone with the prettiest hazel eyes I've ever seen. To think, when I first stepped foot in Muir Harbor, I thought

1

the blustery seaside would be the most beautiful thing I'd lay my eyes on during my family's short trip! But no—it's you. I'm crazy about your red hair and your funny laugh and your kindness. (I told you this was a love letter.)

I know we're young, Maggie. I know we only talked for a few hours this afternoon (and let's be honest, my brother did most of the talking). I know this timing is awful. I ship out soon. Who knows when I'll return. Or if . . .

But I also know I've never met anyone like you. I feel like I could tell you anything. And everything. And maybe I will tonight at the pier. I might even say something impetuous and impossible and true. Something like, I love you, Maggie Muir.

Yes, I just might.

For now, I simply needed to write these words, I guess. To lay my heart on the line in letter form and maybe, hopefully, build up the courage to do so in person. I have a feeling I'm going to need a lot of courage in the coming weeks and months.

But then, I guess love and bravery go hand in hand. Love is the bravery to show up and be seen and known . . . to see, truly see, and to know in return. And bravery, I think, must stem from a bone-deep knowing of a love worth fighting for.

So I'll see you tonight, Maggie Muir. At the pier. (I hope you dress warm. It might snow.)

Until then,

R

Augusta, Maine
November 2, 2018

*I*f not for the proprietor's name on the little shop's window, Philip might never have thought of it again.

Of the letter he'd found all those years ago, faded and crinkled. Of his teenage curiosity and confusion at the unfamiliar name scribbled in Grandfather's tight handwriting. The same name that had rasped from white lips, not even a whisper, that very summer night in the hospital. *Maggie Muir. Maggie Muir. Maggie Muir.* At the time, he'd honestly thought it might be a deathbed confession.

Except Grandfather hadn't died on that long-ago night. No. Almost two decades later and the man was as stoic and alive as ever back at the house Philip had avoided for so long. Until the phone call that had summoned him back six months ago . . .

The one that'd changed everything.

A late-autumn breeze came sweeping in, wrapping Philip in a chill that hinted at the coming winter and rooted his feet to the sidewalk outside of—he glanced up, taking in the artsy sign above the storefront windows—Bits & Pieces.

An antique shop, perhaps, considering the assembly of

trunks and chairs and what looked like an old shutter, painted and repurposed into a wall shelf, on display behind the glass.

He barely spared the items a second look before his gaze scooted down once more.

Proprietor: Indi Muir.

Unusual first name, sure, but it was the last name that set the years-old memories to unspooling—the letter, Grandfather's collapse, *Maggie Muir*—and what else could he do but follow the threads through the little shop's front door?

Philip stopped just inside, the bell overhead trilling as the scents of cedar and stain—and hmm, vanilla?—enveloped him. Good grief, the place was crammed full. Not with people but with things. Just tons and tons of things. More chairs. Accent tables. Vintage lamps. So many knickknacks his eyes didn't know where to land.

And color—it was like a rainbow had fallen from the sky and melted all over everything in the room. Wasn't just an antique store, it seemed, but some sort of restoration shop where old stuff was given new life. Furniture reupholstered or stripped and stained or repainted. He'd watched enough HGTV with Holland to know that was shiplap on the walls. Not original, certainly, because a building this old would have plaster walls and—

His thoughts cut off as the sound of voices drifted from a back room. First, a man, his words too mumbled and low to make out, and then . . .

"You can't possibly be serious, Ben. You just . . . you can't. I don't understand."

How could a tone sound so lilting and melodic even as it sagged with distress? Was that Proprietor Indi Muir speaking? He angled around a waist-high bookcase, the male's muffled response lost to him. As it should be because he hadn't come in here to eavesdrop.

But what *had* he come in here to do? Find the owner and —what? Interrogate her about her last name? *I know this is a total long shot, Ms. Muir, but I'm just wondering if you might have a relative named Maggie Muir. Apparently my grandfather once knew someone by that name and I have all these questions.*

Right. As if he'd managed even once in his entire thirty-four years to get out a single intelligent word to a pretty woman.

Not that he knew what Indi Muir looked like. The voice *sounded* pretty, that was all. But he didn't even know if it belonged to Indi Muir. Could belong to anyone and he . . .

Well, he'd apparently finally gone off the deep end. Because here he was awkwardly standing around thinking about how he couldn't talk to women when he was supposed to be getting ready for a stuffy dinner party with a bunch of faculty members who still saw him as a kid. Never mind his twelve years of teaching back in Seattle or his spot at the table at every history department meeting.

Grandpa's old spot.

Grandpa? Where had *that* come from?

Grandpa had stopped being Grandpa the day of Dad's funeral when he'd presented Philip with his first tie and told him to sit up straight in church. By the time they'd gone down to the basement of St. Mary's for tasteless sandwiches and finger Jell-o after the service, the older man had morphed into Grandfather and he'd been Grandfather ever since.

Shouldn't be here. Really shouldn't be here.

And yet, his feet carried him closer to the back of the shop, where a green-and-white-flowered curtain covered a doorway he assumed must lead into a stockroom or break room or whatever sort of room a store like this had need of.

"Just hear me out, Indi. I'm not trying to hurt you."

Ah, so it *was* Indi Muir talking to the man. Ben, she'd called him, hadn't she?

5

"If that's the case, then I'd really hate to see what actually trying to hurt me would look like. Because I can't think of a single thing that could be worse than this."

"I can." The man's voice raised a notch. "Going through with something I know isn't right would be worse. Walking down an aisle when I'm not ready to make those kinds of vows would be worse."

"The bride walks down the aisle, Ben, not the groom."

Sudden understanding at what he was hearing thumped through him. He took a step backward, but the moan of old hardwoods creaked underfoot and he froze. The couple currently on their way to not being a couple had to know someone was here now, right? If they hadn't heard his steps, surely they'd heard the bell over the door when he entered.

And yet, the man—Ben—carried on. "Can't you see I'm trying to do the honorable thing? I could've dragged this out. I could've kept pretending."

"So you were pretending when you proposed? When you told me you loved me and wanted to spend the rest of your life with me?"

He shouldn't be listening to this. Shouldn't have even come in the store, not when the chances were next to none that this Muir he was eavesdropping on was even slightly connected to his grandfather's Muir. After all, that letter he'd discovered in Grandpa's study, the one addressed to a Maggie Muir in Muir Harbor, Maine, was almost fifty years old.

Grandpa. Again.

Well, if the man he'd known as Grandfather had ever sounded anywhere near as soft and affable as the man who'd written that letter, the warmer title might've fit.

Affable. Ha! The writer of that note had been downright lovesick.

And he just couldn't square it. Couldn't for the life of him imagine author and professor Ray Camden writing anything so wordy and tender. Either Grandfather had changed, hardened through the years, or he wasn't the man Philip had known his whole life. Probably both.

Then again, maybe he hadn't been the one to write that letter at all. But it'd been signed with an *R* and he could've sworn it was in Grandfather's handwriting. Besides, if he hadn't written it, why had Philip found it in the man's desk?

Or, shoot, probably the real question was how on earth he still remembered it so clearly. Or why it even mattered. Or what concoction of impulse and unreality made him think just because the owner of this store shared a last name with someone from Grandfather's past, she'd be able to offer any insight at all into a man who'd always been a mystery to Philip, even though he'd spent the bulk of his childhood living in Grandfather's house.

And now he was living there again. The last thing he'd ever wanted. But it wasn't as if he'd been drowning in options last spring. He'd signed the paperwork, he'd made the commitment. Holland needed him.

" . . . deliberately choosing to misunderstand me." The man's voice lifted another decibel. "It's not that I don't love you. I just don't want to marry you."

"Is that supposed to make me feel better?" For the first time, a tremble entered the woman's tone.

Indi, her name is Indi.

He liked it. Liked the rhythm of it paired with her last name. *Indi Muir.* It was the kind of name that waltzed off the tongue—or, well, would waltz, he assumed, if he ever had a reason to say it out loud. Or maybe not. If he tried to say it to *her*, if she was anywhere near as pretty as her voice and her name, he'd stumble over the syllables like a toddler just learning to walk. Er, talk.

But what reason would he ever have to say the woman's

full name out loud to her face anyway? How weird would that be?

And why was he still standing here? *You're an idiot, man. Get out.*

Philip turned on his heel. He'd pretend he'd never seen that name on the front window. Or if his resurrected curiosity over that old letter got the best of him, he'd settle for Googling. Yes, he'd Google Maggie Muir and Muir Harbor and maybe even Indi Muir, just for the heck of it. Goodness knew he could use the distraction after all the heaviness of the past six months, all the ways he was failing Holland.

"Please don't walk away, Indi."

"You're the one who's walking away. I'm just ending this conversation before it gets any worse."

Philip bumped into a dresser, heart picking up speed as realization whooshed in. The voices were growing closer and now he could hear steps. They were going to rush through that curtain any second, weren't they? And he didn't have a chance of reaching the front door before they saw him, not with a maze of furniture complicating his path, and when they spotted him, they'd know he'd overheard them because his cheeks would turn red. Because they always, *always* did. Because he was Philip West, forever incapable of anything even slightly close to a poker face.

All this flew through his muddled brain in the milliseconds before he made the decision.

A stupid, stupid decision.

Even as he scolded himself, his legs scurried, carrying him around the dresser and toward the oversized wardrobe next to it. He yanked on the ivory knob and flung himself inside.

Dark crowded around him the moment he tugged the door closed, and then, the voices again. And footsteps. More creaking of the floorboards.

An absurd move, maybe, but at least he'd made it inside in the nick of time. They hadn't spotted him. If they had, someone would've yanked the door open by now. And then he'd have no choice but to dig a hole and bury himself alive. Or move to Bolivia, maybe. Certainly never set foot in this shop again.

"I don't want to hear any more. Please, just leave."

He inhaled, the smell of varnish nearly overpowering, a tiny sliver of light slanting in between the wardrobe doors. Hopefully he wouldn't have to stay in here too long. Hopefully after Ben-the-dumper took his leave, Indi Muir would return to the backroom. Hopefully he could sneak out undetected.

Hopefully she'd be okay.

The voices grew muffled again. They must be nearing the front of the shop. Seconds later, he heard the jingle of the bell over the door and clamped his lips to keep his sigh of relief from giving him away.

He strained to listen for her footsteps, for any telltale sound or lack thereof to let him know he was safe to make his escape. *Not long now.* Any minute and he'd be back outside in the cold Maine air and he could pretend he'd never let a wayward whim get him into a scrape like this and—

The wardrobe door pitched open, light flooding in, stealing every last startled thought from his clearly malfunctioning brain save one:

She *was* as pretty as her voice.

And then, exactly as he knew it would, the name tripped instead of waltzed as it slipped nonsensically free.

"I-Indi Muir?"

Wait, the creeper in the closet knew her name?

And what in the world was he doing in there? Why hadn't she heard the bell when he entered Bits & Pieces?

And how—*how?*—was Indi ever going to tell her family about Bennington Foster's graceless exit from her life? Another failed relationship. Another broken engagement. At least she hadn't been the one to call it off this time. But did that make it better or worse?

Better, please let it be better. She'd wrecked so much the last time.

The man in front of her cleared his throat, and Indi's grip tightened on the shoe she'd pulled off just before yanking on the wardrobe door. One dumb compliment from Ben a month ago about how much he liked her in heels and she'd felt obligated to wear them more often than she would've otherwise. But for once, those spiky extra three inches might come in handy—that is, if the stranger wedged into the antique wardrobe proved dangerous.

She huffed, blowing a dislodged curl away from her forehead. "You looking for Narnia or something?"

The man lifted one hand and then stared at it as if he didn't know what to do with it now that it was in the air, eventually settling for running it over the front of his rumpled white oxford. His navy blue tie hung loose, a sign he'd fidgeted with it one too many times.

"Narnia. Ha. That's, uh, very . . . funny. I-I loved those books as a kid."

"So did I. Especially the one where—" What was she doing? Her fiancé had just dumped her and a weirdo was hiding in a wardrobe she couldn't manage to sell, and she was making small talk?

The man's eyes were trained on her shoe. "A-are you going to hit me with that?"

"Maybe. If the situation warrants." Or she could just throw

it at him. Gosh, why hadn't she thought to do that to Ben? She should've plucked off her shoe and chucked it at him the moment she'd realized where that backroom conversation was headed.

"I don't think it will. Warrant it, I mean."

"You don't think it will? Or you know it won't? You're not a very confident criminal, are you?"

"I'm not a criminal at all." He straightened and bumped his head on the top of the wardrobe, then winced.

Honestly, any other day and Indi might laugh at the peculiarity of this. But if she let out a squeak of laughter now, there was no guaranteeing it wouldn't turn into a sob in the next moment. Dumped. Just like that. Before her family had even had a chance to meet her fiancé.

"I'm not a criminal," he said again. "I-I only hid in this thing. I didn't attempt to steal it."

"Well, I wish you would. It takes up way too much floor space."

The man just stared at her for stilted seconds before finally opening his mouth again. "I suppose I should explain. Not that I have much of an explanation. Nothing that makes any sense, that is. You see . . . I . . . when I heard . . . when I realized . . ." He shook his head, clearly frustrated at his inability to finish the sentence.

"Oh brother, you might as well come out." She lowered her shoe and stepped backward, the movement uneven considering her one bare foot.

The man cleared his throat. Again. Smoothed down his tie. Again. And finally, he stepped free of the wardrobe.

Holy buckets. The man was . . . he was . . . tall, for one thing. But also far more handsome than a nutcase who hid in antique furniture had any right to be. She'd never seen eyes that color of gray—rich and deep and frankly, remarkable. His mussed dark hair had the slightest bit of silver at his temples, which only increased his attractiveness, even though it had to be premature. Because the rest of his appearance told her he couldn't have more than a few years on her. Even the tiniest gap between his two front teeth was somehow charming, and how was it possible she could tell he had dimples even though he wasn't smiling?

Definitely not smiling. Oh no, that was pure embarrassment on his face, his cheeks almost as red as the fabric she'd chosen for the tufted chaise nearby. The chaise she probably would've dropped onto by now for a good old-fashioned cry if she hadn't happened to catch a glimpse of this man disappearing into the wardrobe just as she came barreling through the storeroom curtain.

"It's not that I don't love you. I just don't want to marry you."

Goodness, she'd said almost the exact same thing to Trey eleven years ago. Had he, like her, forgotten how to breathe the moment after hearing those words? Had the shock of it made him too go numb?

The numbness probably wouldn't last, though. Oh no, at some point, the emotion would crash in and then the panic as she imagined telling Maggie and Neil and Lilian. *I guess I'm not getting married, after all.*

She couldn't stand the thought. Dreaded the sympathy and the worry and worse, the very real possibility that they might not be surprised at all.

Why did her gaze have to pick that moment to land on the mirror with the gilded bronze frame on the opposite wall? The last thing she wanted to see was her own reflection—messy light brown curls having long since tumbled free from her ponytail, pale skin, and evidence of the paltry tears she'd allowed back in the storeroom in the red rimming her eyes. Lovely.

"For what it's worth, he's obviously a buffoon."

Her attention darted back to the man. Still here. Somewhere in her cluttered thoughts, she'd assumed he would simply slink away after finally coming out of the wardrobe. But no, he was still standing there watching her. His hair was even more tousled now. He must've run his fingers through it when she wasn't looking. What had he just said?

"I-I didn't mean to overhear. I'm truly sorry I did. And that I hid like that."

Oh. *Oh.* Was that why he was blushing? Not because he'd made the zany decision to hide in a wardrobe, but because he'd overheard her complete humiliation?

Something clicked inside her then. Some sort of emotional survival instinct that demanded she lift her chin and straighten her shoulders. But that was hard to do with one shoe on and one shoe off. So she shook off the left heel and squared her posture, tipping her head to look the tall stranger from the closet right in his ridiculously appealing gray eyes. "What can I help you with today?"

He blinked, cleared his throat for the third time. "Um . . . I-I don't . . . what?"

If there was one bright spot in this awful, horrid day, it was the amusement that managed to wiggle in at his obvious discomfort. "You must've come in here for something. Are you looking for a particular piece? Or just browsing?" Maybe he was on the hunt for a gift for someone—a girlfriend or wife, mom or sister. She didn't get many male customers.

She didn't get many customers at all. Not here at her Augusta store. At least her original shop back in Muir Harbor was thriving. But replicating that same feat here in a bigger city was a hurdle she couldn't seem to clear. She'd been so sure opening a second store was the right move. But if things didn't pick up soon, her broken engagement wouldn't be the only thing she'd have to confess to her family.

She needed to make a sale today. Just one measly sale and maybe then she could convince herself everything was going to be okay. "I'm running a special this week," she blurted, pushing a tendril behind her ear. "Thirty-five percent off all furniture."

One corner of the man's mouth rose at the same time as he lifted his hand to rub the back of his neck. "You really want to get rid of this wardrobe, don't you?"

A whole sentence without stammering, and darn it, she was right about the dimples. "Got a truck? I can help you load it right now. I'm stronger than I look."

Those gray eyes peered at her for a moment. "I don't doubt it, Indi Muir."

It was the second time he'd said her full name, and for the second time, she wondered how in the world he knew it. And seriously, what was he doing here? Who was he? What sort of person eavesdropped on a breakup and hid in a closet and then just . . . stayed? She opened her mouth, ready to bullet one question after another at him, even if it did cost her a sale.

But the blare of her phone stole her opportunity. *Ben?* She whipped it from the pocket of her jeans, gaze immediately connecting with the screen.

Not Ben. Her sister's name and photo lit up the screen. Rude, perhaps, to answer it when she was with a potential customer. But Lilian usually texted, rarely called. Which meant this might be important. Besides, did the man from the wardrobe really count as a customer at this point?

She tucked her phone to her ear. "Hey, Lil."

"You have to come home. Right now. No, not home. The hospital. They're taking her to the hospital. She's already in the ambulance."

Her sister's words tumbled over each other, and Indi's grasp on her phone tightened. "What? Slow down." Was that panic in Lilian's voice? Lilian *never* panicked. *Home. Hospital. Ambulance. She . . . who?*

Her breath left her lungs as Maggie's face filled her mind.

"It's Maggie," Lilian confirmed. "She collapsed. Neil doesn't think she was breathing and . . . you have to come, Indi. *Now.*"

"O-okay. I will. I'll be there as soon as I can."

Lilian was talking again—but Indi couldn't register the words. Not with the fear coiling inside her, not with the sound of a siren in the background of the call. *Not Maggie. Please, God. You can't take her from us. You can't take her from me.*

"A-are you okay?"

She whirled to face the man from the wardrobe again. When had Lilian ended the call? When had Indi stuffed her phone back in her pocket?

When had she given the tears permission to finally escape? "I . . . I . . . Maggie."

The man's jaw dropped. "Maggie? Maggie Muir?"

She should probably wonder why he was looking at her like that, gray eyes wide. She should wonder why he'd just said Maggie's name in the same peculiar tone he'd said hers earlier. She should wonder all over again who he was and what he was doing here.

She should *move.* Grab her heels, her purse, her car keys. Get to Maggie as soon as she could. Because Maggie could be . . . might already be . . . *no.* She shoved on a shoe even as she scoured the store for her purse. She'd left it behind the cash register counter, hadn't she?

"By the way, you never said which Narnia book was your favorite."

What? The man's face was blurry through her onslaught of tears. She struggled to slip on the second shoe, her whole body trembling.

"You started to say earlier, but then you cut off."

He moved closer to her, the concern in his expression breaking through her clouded vision. *He's trying to calm you* down. *The strange, blushing man from the wardrobe is trying to help.*

She sniffled, then took a ragged breath. "*The Magician's Nephew*. That's my favorite."

"Mine too. I've always loved a good origin story." He reached up to pull his tie free and held it out to her. When she didn't take it, he nudged it closer. "It's the closest thing I have to a handkerchief."

Understanding mingled with disbelief. "I can't blow my nose on your tie."

"You really can. I don't like it. I hate wearing the thing."

He was . . . he was . . . she didn't know what he was. She only knew she had to leave. *Now.* Another sob wracked her body as she bolted toward the counter and reached for her purse. She had her keys out in seconds. She needed to lock up before she left. Turn the *Open* sign to *Closed*. And oh, the lights—

"I'm not sure you should be driving."

"I have to go. I'm sorry. It's a family emergency. I have to get to the hospital. If you're really interested in the wardrobe, I can hold it for you."

"I-it's just . . . you're shaking. You've already had one shock and now . . . I just don't think it's safe."

She slung her purse over her shoulder. "I don't have a choice. It's not as if I can walk. Muir Harbor's almost an hour away." The words scrambled from her as she wound her way to the front door.

"Muir Harbor?"

There was that tone again. But she didn't care anymore. And if he wouldn't leave, fine, he could just stay here. He could make off with every last piece of furniture in the place if he wanted. She had to get to Maggie . . . had to see her before—

"I can drive you."

She stopped at the front door, streaming tears nowhere close to slowing. "What?"

"I know you must think I'm bananas—hiding in that closet like I did. And I know you have no reason to trust me." He cleared his throat. Fourth time. "But I'm a safe driver. I can get you to the hospital in one piece."

He was right. She had no reason to trust him.

But he was also right that she was shaking and crying and probably in no shape to drive. She swiped the back of one hand over her eyes. *Should've accepted his tie.* "You're a complete stranger."

"My name's Philip West. I'm thirty-four. I'm a history professor. I teach at Thornhill College here in Augusta. More importantly, I've never had so much as a speeding ticket."

And *The Magician's Nephew* was his favorite Narnia book. Why that fact should be the one that pushed her over the edge, she didn't know. And it didn't matter. All that mattered was getting to Maggie.

Maggie, who'd given her everything.

"Okay, Philip." She handed him her keys. "But we're taking my car."

2

"*What* do you mean you don't know if you're going to make it?"

One hand tight around the steering wheel of Indi Muir's small SUV, Philip winced at the censure in Connor's tone. He was tempted to end the call and drop his phone into the console. A real nuisance sometimes—the fact that his best friend was now one of his colleagues.

One who'd expected to see Philip at this evening's Thornhill faculty dinner party. They'd made plans to be miserable through the whole thing together.

Philip's gaze strayed from the empty stretch of highway in front of him to the few final wisps of hazy gold and orange feathering through the darkening sky. Shadows curled in and around the thick covering of trees on one side of the road, their tips cresting and dipping with the rise and fall of the hilly landscape.

He'd been in this car with Indi for almost half an hour and she hadn't spoken once. Only the blare of his phone a minute ago had broken the uneasy silence between them.

"It's bad enough you're late," Connor went on. "If you don't show up at all—"

"I told you. It couldn't be helped."

Or maybe it could've. Maybe he could've left Indi Muir alone and in tears, never mind how she'd gone from one heartbreak to another in a matter of minutes or that she'd been about to get behind the wheel while appearing to be on the brink of a breakdown. But in addition to throwing chivalry to the wind, walking away would've meant ignoring the realization that she *did* know a Maggie Muir.

Maggie Muir of Muir Harbor, Maine.

The woman they were hurrying to get to *had* to be the one from Grandfather's letter. Which meant there *was* something to the whim that'd propelled Philip into that antique store, something crazy and uncanny and impossible to ignore.

So, no, it couldn't be helped that he was here in this car right now instead of back in Augusta at a stodgy party, trying to fit in with a bunch of faculty members who hadn't seemed entirely pleased at the dean's decision to hire Philip after Grandfather's abrupt retirement.

Truth was, half the time Philip wasn't pleased about it either. If not for his fifteen-year-old half sister, he probably would've run back to Seattle straight from Mom's funeral in May. Away from Grandfather's cold, cavernous house. Away from the grief. Away from the memories, waiting like hazy specters around every corner.

Away from the sorrow in Holland's eyes. Worse, the flickers of accusation that broke through every now and then when she looked at him.

He shook his head, his fingers clenching around the steering wheel. At least he didn't need to worry about his sister this evening. She was at a sleepover at a friend's house. He'd been trying to convince himself all week Holland had agreed to go because she was beginning to heal, not just as a means of getting away from him.

Connor's voice jutted in again. "Phil—"

"I'm sorry. I really am. Maybe I can still make it." If he broke the speed limit the rest of the way to Muir Harbor and back.

Except this was Indi's car, and he hadn't given a single thought to how he was supposed to return to Augusta after delivering her to the hospital. And he didn't have his glasses. He was fine without them during the day, but once the sky went pitch-black, which wasn't far off, he wouldn't have any business being on the road.

Connor sighed. "Look, I know parties like this aren't your thing. They're not mine either. But you haven't been at Thornhill all that long and—"

"Not true. I practically grew up there." He'd spent half his childhood running through the hallways of the ancient buildings dotting the small college's property. Had always preferred the noise of students' voices and steps to the hollow silence of Grandfather's house.

"But you're new to the faculty. There are expectations. Some of Thornhill's biggest funders are here tonight."

Yes, and Philip was smart enough to know the dean hadn't added him to the history department roster solely because of his own teaching credentials, but because of his status as Ray Camden's grandson. Along with having been a fixture at Thornhill for decades, Grandfather was also a best-selling novelist, which meant he was the closest thing the college had to a celebrity.

But after Mom had died in the spring, Grandfather had announced his retirement from teaching and holed himself away. Which meant it was Philip's job to be his stand-in, to mix and mingle with the wealthy alumni at tonight's dinner.

Which he would've, no matter how much it grated on him, if he hadn't happened to walk past Bits & Pieces. Hadn't seen Indi Muir's name. Hadn't suddenly remembered that old letter and let his questions about Grandfather's past get the better of him. "I'll try to get there, okay?"

"And what am I supposed to tell everyone in the meantime?"

"Tell them . . ." He glanced at Indi, faded tear tracks still staining her cheeks. At least she wasn't trembling any longer. "Something came up."

"Word to the wise, vague doesn't go over well with this crowd."

"Fine. Tell them I believe in being fashionably late. Tell them I hate caviar, so I'm waiting to show up until there's a good chance it's gone."

A faint sound came from the seat next to him—a chuckle? More like a snort, but considering it was the first peep he'd heard from his passenger, it was something.

"Gotta go, Connor. I'll check in later."

His friend let out another long sigh before ending the call, and Philip abandoned his phone to the console, letting his head drop against the headrest.

"You had plans tonight."

Indi's feeble whisper drew his gaze. She'd pulled a band from her hair earlier, freeing the last of her riot of curls. She wore the band on her wrist now, along with a collection of beaded bracelets every bit as colorful as the rest of her ensemble—a denim jacket, sleeves just a tad too short, over a flowy sort of dress that reminded him of a patchwork quilt.

"I'm sorry," she added.

"You don't have to be sorry." No stammer. He deserved a pat on the back.

Although, if getting a single sentence out stammer-free to a pretty woman counted as some kind of monumental achievement, his ability to function at the dinner party was questionable, at best. Why was it Philip could stand up in front of a classroom and speak without a hitch, but when forced into conversation with a female his age, he suddenly had all the verbal eloquence of a turnip?

Then again, maybe there wouldn't have been any single women at that party. This was Thornhill they were talking about. Most of the faculty resembled Gandalf the Grey.

"Is something funny?"

He glanced over again. Indi's green eyes were trained on him.

"You smiled. Why?"

Sheesh, she was direct. "I . . . well . . ." He shifted, his seat belt lancing into his chest. "S-sorry." So much for no stammering.

"Now you're the one who doesn't need to be sorry. You don't have to apologize for smiling. You can smile all you want. It's a nice smile. I've always liked dimples. Ben has dimples, too. Or, well, just one, and his isn't nearly as pronounced as yours. Honestly, if I put the two of you side by side, I'd call yours the more handsome smile. So maybe it's good he called the whole thing off. Because a girl should think her fiancé's smile is more handsome than anyone else's, shouldn't she?"

She'd gone from silent to downright chatty, and wait a second, had she just called him handsome?

"Now I've gone and embarrassed you."

Great, his warming cheeks had given him away. And not for the first time tonight.

"Anyhow, don't you think a girl should think her fiancé's smile is the best smile?"

He cleared his throat. "I . . . I—"

"I'm trying to distract myself, if that's not obvious. I don't usually talk about grinning this much, dimples or no. Although, for the record, you just did it again. Grinned, I mean. And you never answered my question about why you smiled in the first place."

There was a forlorn undercurrent beneath her chatter. This woman was a total stranger to him, but he'd have to be a stone statue not to feel for her. He'd have to be like . . .

Grandfather.

Except not the Grandfather who'd written that letter. That man, all softness and sentiment, was also a stranger to him. That man would know what to say to Indi now.

"I . . . I guess I was smiling because . . . because you're right, I did have plans tonight but I can't find it in me to regret missing them. I don't like formal dinner parties. I don't like small talk. It makes me twitchy."

"And I suppose I can attribute your second grin to my inane rambling."

"No." He guided the car along a curve. "You can attribute it to you calling me handsome. Women don't generally go around saying things like that to me."

"I didn't call you handsome. I called your smile handsome."

"Well . . . okay."

"Anyhow, all the women you know must be blind."

A laugh pushed free. A laugh he probably should've reined in. Because this poor woman was in the middle of a crisis. He hadn't entirely pieced together who Maggie Muir was to her —other than a relative, obviously—or what exactly had happened, but he knew it was bad. If Indi's panicked state back at the store hadn't told him as much, the way she'd held her phone in a vise grip ever since would've.

And as for him . . .

This *wasn't* him. He didn't chase impulses into antique stores. He didn't miss dinner parties, no matter how much he dreaded them. He didn't hide in wardrobes or make spontaneous offers to drive strangers to hospitals.

And he didn't laugh when he knew he shouldn't.

"Philip!"

Indi's shriek yanked his focus into sharp, shocking clarity as movement outside his windshield barreled into his view. A deer, its eyes glowing in the dark, racing across the road in front of them, but not quickly enough.

Instinct took over as he jerked the wheel and Indi yelped again.

The car jolted, its headlights scrambling over the shadowed landscape as Indi jostled in her seat, both knees bumping into the glove compartment. She clamped her lips together to keep from screeching a third time, her muddled gaze losing sight of the deer.

The squeal of the tires gave way to a jouncing that sent her purse and phone flying from her lap. Until, finally, a thud. And a thump—her head, knocking against the corner of her passenger-side door. Then, a sudden, pounding silence.

The ditch. They'd landed in the ditch.

"Indi. Are you okay? Are you hurt?" Philip cut the engine, jerked free of his seat belt, and twisted to face her. "I'm so sorry. I shouldn't have swerved like that."

"But the deer—"

"I should've braked instead."

"No time." Her hands shook as she unclicked her seat belt.

"I didn't realize we were coming up on another curve. Are you hurt anywhere?" Philip leaned toward her. "I heard something hit. Was that your head? I could kick myself. Here I insist it's not safe for you to drive when you're upset and then I go and land us in a ditch."

She bent, reaching for her purse, heart still sprinting even as a strange calm settled over her. In the grand scheme of this day, a near-collision wasn't exactly at the top of her list of worries. "It's fine. I'm not hurt. You're not hurt. The deer's still alive." She turned to him. "I just need to get to the hospital."

He stared at her for a moment, the dim all around them not enough to hide his obvious concern. But finally, he nodded and faced the wheel once more, reaching to turn the ignition. The engine rumbled to life. "At least there were no other cars around. That's something to be grateful for." He shifted into reverse.

But her SUV didn't budge.

She watched as Philip's brow wrinkled and he pressed the pedal again. The vehicle only shuddered, engine growling, wheels spinning uselessly. Apology rimmed his eyes as he looked her way, his huff of frustration sending strands of hair billowing over his forehead. "I'll take a look." He was out of the car in a dash.

Leaving her alone with the whoosh of cold air from his hastily opened and closed door. And the worry that refused to taper. *Maggie.* Her mother—not biologically, but in all the ways that mattered most. *In the hospital. Not breathing.*

No, she couldn't do this. Couldn't keep sitting here as she had for the past forty minutes, replaying every busy day leading up to today, deriding herself for not spending more time with Maggie. Wishing she hadn't let the stores take over her life for months—years, really—and more recently, Bennington.

Goodness, she'd been engaged to Ben for two weeks now and Maggie hadn't even met him. Maggie had been so eager to get to know him, but every time Indi had tried to arrange an introduction, Ben had been stuck in Augusta, over-whelmed with work.

Or maybe it wasn't work. Maybe it was doubt in their rela-tionship. Maybe it was some kind of knowing what was coming.

Maybe, somewhere in the course of their whirlwind relationship, Ben had seen just a little too deep. Realized that in marrying her, he'd be forever complicating his life. Tying himself to a mess. *Indi Muir—the Messy Muir.* The one who could never undo her worst decision and all the emptiness it'd left behind.

Indi wrenched free of the car before the despair crawling up her throat had the chance to choke her. The moment her feet hit the ground, a stinging wind hurled against her, capturing the hem of her dress and twisting it around her legs. She tugged her jean jacket closed with one hand, burrowing her chin in its collar as she moved to join Philip at the front of the vehicle.

"One of your headlights is out." He pointed. "And there's a tiny dent. I'm so sorry."

"I don't care about the car. I really don't. I just want to know if we can make it to Muir Harbor."

"I think we can. We're only stuck in a muddy spot. Why don't you get in the driver's seat? I'll push."

He was already bunching up his sleeves to his elbows, the tie he'd offered her earlier in lieu of a handkerchief now hanging loose and unknotted around his neck. On another day she'd make a joke about how this stranger wasn't dressed for something like this. Probably tease him too, accuse him of driving into the ditch just to avoid that dinner party. The one with the caviar and the small talk that made him twitchy.

But fear and fatigue and another frosty gust kept her words trapped inside. Instead, she rounded the car, plopped into his seat, and started the engine. At the knock on her window a second later, she hit the button to lower it.

Philip leaned down, goosebumps lifting the hair on his arms. "Don't be afraid to gun it if you have to."

She nodded but he didn't move.

"Indi, I—"

"Please don't apologize again. We're wasting time."

"I wasn't going to. I . . . I thought—"

"Philip." There was no keeping the exasperation from her voice.

"Of course. Wasting time. I shouldn't . . . I was just going to offer to pray. F-for Maggie. And you. And the car."

"What? Oh, um—"

"But I can pray while I push." His words released in a rush and a moment later he disappeared from outside the window, reappearing at the front of the car, placing his hands on the hood, giving her a nod.

Her fingers gripped the wheel. Philip had wanted to *pray.* Philip, who she didn't know from Adam.

Philip, who'd called Ben a buffoon and offered his tie as a tissue. Who'd thrown off his evening's plans to drive her to a seaside town an hour away. Who blushed and stammered and who, even now, was braced against her vehicle, ready to most likely be splattered with mud as he pushed.

Who in the world are you, Philip West?

She pressed the pedal, eyes glued to the profile traced by the glow of her headlights and then, as her gaze trailed down, his straining arms.

She gasped as the car jerked, her grip on the wheel tightening. Philip stumbled forward a couple of steps as she steered the car backward, her focus jutting to the rearview mirror to make sure there weren't any cars coming from behind. She angled the vehicle onto the highway's shoulder and shifted into park.

And then there was Philip at her still-open window, grinning down at her. "Just that quick and we did it. Do you trust me to drive the rest of the way or should I hop in the passenger seat?"

"Y-you can drive." He'd passed his stutter on to her, it

seemed. She reached for her door handle, but he beat her to it, opening the door, waiting for her to step out.

She slid from the seat, too many thoughts bumping into each other. *Ben. Maggie. Hospital. Deer.*

Philip. With his sleeves still rolled up, the wind having a field day with his hair. But why were his eyes narrowing? Why was he staring at her forehead?

"You *are* hurt." He lifted one hand and brushed away a strand of hair.

A shiver wriggled up her back. "What?"

"I knew I heard something hit. It was your head. There's a little blood." He tugged his tie free and lifted it to her forehead before she could mutter a protest. "Just a tiny cut, I think. Does it hurt?"

"N-no. I hadn't even realized . . ." Her voice trailed off as chilly night air, tinged with the faint scent of cologne, wrapped around her. A nervous laugh slipped free. "You really don't like that tie, d-do you?" Was it the cold or the sheer strangeness of this situation sending another shudder through her?

Or maybe the utter gentleness of his touch, the kindness in another dimpled grin. "I really don't. It's nice of you to give me a reason to retire the thing." He lowered the tie and pressed it into her hand. "Your teeth are chattering. Let's go, we need to get you to the hospital. And I think that might be your phone ringing in the car."

She blinked, ears perking to the sound of the muffled ringing. She raced to the other side of the car, dropped into her seat, and bent, swiping her hand over the floor mat while Philip took his place behind the wheel. Her palm finally connected with the phone as Philip pulled onto the highway. "Lilian?" *Please let it be good news, God. Please let Maggie—*

"Are you almost here?"

Were they? She drove this road at least twice a week, splitting her time between Augusta and Muir Harbor. Shouldn't she know where she was right now? "We'll be there soon."

"They have to do an emergency surgery. It was—is—her heart. They had to call the surgeon at home, but he's on his way here. They'll be taking her back within the next half hour, I think."

"I have to see her first. I . . . I have to . . ."

"I don't know if there's going to be time. They want to get her into surgery as quickly as possible. If it goes well, they'll be able to avoid doing a bypass later and—"

"Lil." She couldn't get out her sister's full name. Couldn't even begin to voice the question she needed to ask most.

But Lilian heard her unsaid words all the same. "Dr. Lakeman said he expects a positive outcome." Her sister's voice had gone soft. "He said . . . he said if she can make it through surgery, then her chances are good."

If not for the *if* lodged into that last sentence, Indi might be able to stop balling Philip's tie in her hand. *Positive outcome. Chances are good.* Those were the words she needed to focus on.

She let out a breath. "I just really want to see her before they take her into surgery." Tears filled her eyes all over again as the car rumbled beneath her. Had Philip just sped up?

"Maybe you'll beat the surgeon. Have Bennington drop you off at the emergency entrance before parking."

Bennington? Her gaze swept to Philip. *Oh.* Indi had said *we* and Lilian had thought . . .

She'd thought incorrectly. But now wasn't the time to spill the news of her broken engagement. The call ended moments later and she lowered her phone to her lap, blinking to keep her tears at bay. She'd cried enough tonight. No more.

"Do you mind if I ask who Maggie is? Family, I assume?"

Philip's quiet question stilled her. "She's my mother."

"Oh." He paused. "But you call her by her first name?"

"I'm adopted. My siblings were older when they came to live with Maggie, so they never called her Mom. I'm the youngest and by the time I could talk, I'd heard Lilian—my sister—calling her Maggie for so long that's what I called her too. She's old enough to be my grandmother, actually." She was rambling again.

"I see."

He didn't, couldn't—not fully, anyway. Because Maggie was unlike anyone else. She'd been through so much in her life. First the death of her fiancé in Vietnam decades back, then the loss of her first daughter to a tragic accident twenty-eight years ago. And then there was the missing granddaughter Maggie had been searching for ever since.

But in the midst of her personal pain, Maggie had taken in three orphans from three different backgrounds and loved them without reserve.

"How's your head?" Philip's voice cut in again.

She traced the edge of his tie, now thoroughly mussed, with her thumb. "It's fine."

"And, um, the rest of you? You've not had the best of evenings."

Massive understatement, that. They passed a sign for Muir Harbor. Only ten miles. "My sister thinks you're Ben, by the way. When I said *we* on the phone, she just assumed."

The man had to be sharp enough not to miss her obvious ducking of his question. But he had the grace not to press her. "Don't know if I like being mistaken for him. After all, he only has one dimple."

It was the second time he'd made her laugh since they'd gone into the ditch. Which really shouldn't be possible, not with such a storm of emotions swirling around inside of her.

"You said siblings—plural. There's Lilian and . . ."

"There's one other sibling in addition to Lil. Neil. He's the oldest. Same age as you, actually." Hadn't Philip said he was thirty-four back at the store? Although how she remembered it considering the state she'd been in, she didn't know. "I'm twenty-eight, in case you're wondering." He wasn't, surely. If anything, the man had to be wondering whether her anxious babbling had its limits. "Anyway, Neil's Scottish—came to the States as a teen, but still has an accent that totally throws people when they first meet him."

"And you grew up in Muir Harbor?"

She nodded. "On a blueberry farm right on the coast. Maggie's ancestors founded the town. And the farm. She grew up there. Maggie is . . . she's . . ." Her voice cracked. So much for sounding normal. Holding it together.

She squeezed her eyes closed.

"Indi, I'm going to get you there in time. I promise."

She opened her eyes to find Philip's gaze resting on her again. He returned his focus to the road a moment later, but goodness, how could the briefest shared look with a stranger feel so fortifying?

You should've let him pray earlier. Had he meant it when he'd said he'd pray while he pushed the car? Probably. Nice as he was, he'd most likely been praying this whole time.

Maybe, hopefully, his were the kind of prayers God listened to.

The engine rumbled as Philip sped up again.

⸻

She'd left her purse.

Philip watched in the rearview mirror as Indi huddled into her jacket while she jogged toward the hospital's emergency entrance, her dress whipping around her ankles.

He hadn't planned to go in. He'd dropped Indi off in front of the entrance, then figured he'd park her car and call an

Uber. He had no place barging in on Indi's family. Her siblings would be waiting for her. The sister who'd called. The brother with the accent.

And anyway, he'd spent enough time in a hospital earlier this year.

Well, no, not *enough* time. Not considering Mom had waited until the last minute to call him. Waited until the treatments weren't working anymore. Treatments he hadn't known a thing about. For a cancer he hadn't known a thing about.

His fingers closed around Indi's ring of keys, the one for her car jabbing into his palm.

Her keys. Her purse. He supposed he could hide her purse under a seat, leave her keys under a floor mat.

But she'd looked so small and alone just now, right before being swallowed up by the hospital's revolving door. And, darn it, what if she got in there and couldn't find her family members? What if she needed . . . something? Someone?

He towed himself from the car, tugging Indi's purse with him, cold night air foreboding as it scraped over him. Just the thought of walking into the fluorescent lights ahead of him sent unease creeping down his spine and shambling back up again. But he hadn't brought Indi this far to abandon her now. He'd follow her in, deliver her purse and keys, make sure she found her family.

Then hightail it back to Augusta and whatever was left of that dumb dinner party.

As soon as he emerged into the waiting area, his gaze landed on Indi as she rushed into the embrace of a man with dark hair and bristled cheeks, worry evident in the circles under his eyes.

"Lil's in with her now. Room 113." The man's gentle voice was tinged with a Scottish burr. So this was Neil, the brother. "Only two people can be in with her at a time." The man peeled what must be a visitor's badge from his shirt. "It's just down the hall and to the right. There's a nurses' station on the way if you can't—"

"I'll find it." Indi slapped her brother's badge on her coat upside down, but just as she began to move past him, she caught sight of Philip. "Oh, Neil. That's . . ."

Recognition lit Neil's eyes. Recognition that didn't make sense considering Indi hadn't finished her sentence. Hadn't said Philip's name or explained his presence. Instead, as if she simply didn't have the energy for any more of an introduction, she turned and disappeared down a hallway. As for Neil, he spared Philip only the briefest glance before moving past him to the revolving door.

Huh.

The cloying, overly familiar antiseptic smell wrapped around him as he turned toward a check-in desk. Maybe he should leave Indi's purse there. Yes, that's what he'd do. Then he could leave, escape these awful fluorescent lights and the memory of Mom—

"You should head back with her."

He turned at the voice. A woman with short blond hair stood at the corner Indi had disappeared around. Was she talking to him?

"I-I'm sorry?"

"Really, she's on the brink of breaking down," the blond-haired woman said. "She shouldn't be alone. I'd go back in with her, but someone needs to call Wilder."

Was he supposed to know who Wilder was? And why was she looking at Philip as if she knew him? Same way Neil just had . . .

Oh. Lilian. The sister. The one who'd assumed earlier on the phone that he was Indi's fiancé. *Ex-fiancé.* Apparently she still assumed it. Had Neil, as well? Wait, that would mean . . . had Indi's family never met her fiancé?

33

"I'm glad you were with her when she got the call. I hated the thought of her driving here on her own. I'm Lil, by the way. Nice to finally meet you."

"U-um, nice to meet you, too, b-but I'm not—"

"Room 113."

"But—"

Lilian already had her phone to her ear as she passed him, moving to a waiting room chair. He shook his head and turned, letting his legs carry him around the corner and down the corridor . . .

Until there she was, standing in front of an open door, her arms wrapped around her torso.

"Indi?"

She whipped her head in his direction, blinking, the tears he knew she'd tried so hard to contain on the drive here now spilling down her cheeks.

"Philip, I . . . I'm sorry. I meant to tell you to take my car back to Augusta. I should've . . . why are you . . ." She dropped her arms as he reached her, gaze falling to her purse. "Oh."

"This is Maggie's room?" He glanced past her into the room, a monitor blocking his view of the patient in the bed.

"Yes, but I suddenly don't want to go in. The moment I do, this all becomes real."

The dull thud in the back of his skull was a plea, begging him to escape the hospital before it turned into an all-out killer headache. Before the memories . . . sitting beside Mom's bed in a whitewashed room, wishing she'd wake up so he could ask her why she'd waited so long to call.

But he couldn't just leave Indi. He reached for her hand. "Come on, I'll go in with you."

He kept his steps soft as they walked in, Indi's chilled fingers still encased in his, his gaze moving to the woman in the bed as they neared. Her eyes were closed, her skin pallid, white hair splayed, just enough hint of color left to suggest it'd once been a vibrant red.

Maggie Muir.

Grandfather's Maggie.

No, Indi's Maggie. Indi, who'd already had her heart stomped on today and who clearly loved this woman with everything in her.

She let go of his hand and dropped into the lone chair beside the bed. She swiped the back of her palm over her eyes, taking a ragged breath. The monitor near the bed beeped and voices drifted outside the room. Somewhere down the hall, a janitor pushed a mop bucket, its wheels grumbling against the floor.

He *knew* these sounds. Knew this overwrought weight that came with the waiting, the wondering . . . the one horrible *what-if* that drowned out all the others.

What if this is goodbye?

His stomach clenched. Dad, gone. Mom, gone.

And Holland . . . sometimes he wondered if she was gone, too. Because in six months of being his half sister's legal guardian, he wasn't sure he'd seen a single spark of light in her eyes. Oh, she was living and breathing and going about her teenage life. But most days, she looked as numb as . . . as he felt.

And it wasn't as if Grandfather was any help. He kept to himself most days, holed up in his office. They were a wreck of a family, falling apart at the seams.

The complete opposite of what he'd seen of Indi's family so far. The way Neil had hugged Indi, Lilian's concern that she not be alone . . .

"I can't lose her."

Indi's aching voice reached for him over the pounding in his head. She dropped her face to Maggie's hand, her tears staining the white sheet below. Instinct lowered him to a crouch beside her. He let Indi's purse topple to the floor as he gripped the armrest of her chair with one palm, the other falling to her knee.

"Should I go get Lilian? She said something about calling someone. Wilder, I think."

Indi lifted her head. "Good, I'm glad someone's calling him." Her voice was shaky. "Although I would've thought Neil would . . . Wilder's his best friend. Basically like another sibling."

He didn't need the explanation, but maybe Indi needed to explain. Another attempt at distraction. And yet, with Maggie right here in front of them, soundless and still, he had a feeling there wasn't a distraction in the world that would do any good just now.

"I'm not sure where your brother went. I saw him leave—"

Indi's gasp stole his next words and his gaze jerked upward.

Maggie had opened her eyes. Hazel, blinking, attempting to focus . . .

Then looking at *him*.

"R-r . . ." The voice, reedy and thin, rose from the bed. "R-r-r . . ."

He sucked in a breath as his hand dropped from Indi's knee.

"Maggie? Can you hear me?" Indi leaned forward, wrapping both of her palms around Maggie's.

"Indiana Joy. You're here." Barely a whisper.

"Yes. I'm right here. I came as soon as Lil called. I only wish I'd gotten here faster. You're going to be having surgery soon. We'll be waiting here the whole time. We all love you so much and . . . oh my goodness, I should probably tell someone you're awake."

He couldn't look away from the tenderness in Maggie's eyes. Why was she still staring at him?

Indi wrenched herself from her chair. "I'll be right back. I'll get a nurse."

No, he should be the one doing that. Indi shouldn't have to leave Maggie's side. He spun around to stop her—

"You look so much like him."

He turned, slowly, gaze returning to the woman in the bed. He moved closer.

"You look like . . ." She swallowed and her eyes closed.

He looked like who? *Grandfather?* Somewhere between Augusta and Muir Harbor, he'd pushed his curiosity about that old letter to the back of his mind. Probably around the time that deer had jumped out at him. Or, no, earlier—when Indi had looked at him with her red-rimmed eyes and called his smile handsome. But now . . .

Maggie gave a raspy cough and opened her eyes again. "You look like . . . like Robert."

Her voice had grown fainter, a distance feathering through her hazel eyes. *Robert?* Who was that? Not Grandfather, obviously. Not Ray Camden.

It doesn't matter now. This woman almost died tonight. She's minutes away from heart surgery. You shouldn't be here.

"If I don't . . . if I don't make it . . . be good to Indi."

He could swear his heart thudded to a halt. "Oh, but . . . I-I should tell you who I—"

"I know who you are." She smiled then. It was strained and shaky and small, but definitely a smile. Definitely meant for someone other than him.

But he didn't have a chance to correct her. This time, when Maggie Muir's eyes fluttered closed, they didn't open again.

3

*J*ndi had no memory whatsoever of the moment when Philip's poor, battered tie had found its way back into her hand.

But it had and she held it now, balled up in her fist, as she paced the waiting room. Maybe she'd stuffed it in her jacket pocket before arriving at the hospital. Maybe Philip had delivered it to her along with her keys and purse, pressed it into her hand sometime after Maggie had been wheeled away to the OR two hours ago. Or perhaps three.

She didn't know. Time had stopped in its tracks tonight. Just up and froze, along with her ability to think clearly. Her brain was so crowded with worry and fear, she couldn't even keep up a conversation.

Which was why she was over here paving a trail from one end of the room to the other instead of huddled up with Lilian and Wilder, whispering as they tapped away on their phones, reading up on angioplasties and recovery times and who knew what all. They weren't even arguing—a miracle, really, considering how little patience her sister generally had for the man. Wilder Monroe might be Neil's best friend, but he was also the closest thing Lil had to a nemesis. Except apparently the trauma of the night temporarily eradicated all that.

As for Neil, he'd returned to the hospital an hour ago after running back to the farm for a short time. She didn't know why. Another conversation she simply hadn't had the energy for. He was off looking for a vending machine now.

Which left her alone.

Well, no. There was Philip. Sprawled in a waiting room chair, long limbs stretching in front of him, eyes closed and his head resting against the beige wall behind him. Earlier, while they'd shared a bag of peanut M&Ms, she'd tried to talk him into taking her car back to Augusta.

"Maybe later," he'd said.

But now later was here—and so was he. Still. And there was absolutely no rational reason why his sleeping presence should feel so strangely comforting. Just like there was no reason she should suddenly have the urge to sit in the chair beside him and rest her head on his shoulder.

No reason, surely, other than she was exhausted. Physically depleted, emotionally wrecked, and—

An eerie cry drifted from beyond her rattled thoughts. Faint, feeble. Beckoning.

She paused mid-step, her gaze moving past Philip, toward the hallway beyond the waiting room. Not the one that'd led to Maggie's door, but another . . .

There it was again. A high-pitched cry. A baby.

She blinked against the sharp lights overhead, a shiver creeping through her as she turned toward the muffled sound. Was the ER waiting room somewhere near the obstetrics wing? Was the nursery nearby?

Please, not the nursery.

She shook her head, a tremble working its way from her chest through the rest of her. No, the OB wing was on the other side of the hospital altogether.

39

Another cry, and when had her legs started moving? She'd already passed Philip, started down a deserted corridor. Seconds became minutes, time finally ticking once more as she walked.

She turned another corner. Down another hallway. Past more doors. The overhead lights were dimmer in here, silence crowding the narrow space save the faraway wail still hovering in the air.

Yes, a baby. Unmistakable. Echoes like slithering, inescapable whispers.

Her jean jacket slid off one shoulder as her steps slowed until she stopped altogether, breath held captive in her lungs, fear tangling with memories she never allowed in. *Never.*

She wasn't hearing this. This was her mind playing tricks. Had to be.

"Indi?"

Her breath released in a whoosh as she spun.

Lilian.

Her sister moved toward her. "You all right? You look like you've just seen a ghost."

No, she hadn't seen one. But maybe she'd heard one. The past, coming to haunt her. Preying on her fear for Maggie, taking advantage of the hospital setting. Resurrecting the old nightmares she used to have in those first few years after . . .

Another shudder wracked her. But at least she couldn't hear the hushed cry anymore. It'd evaporated with Lilian's appearance.

She pulled her jacket up over her shoulder with one hand, Philip's tie now dangling from her other. "I-I'm fine. Just needed to move."

"A nurse came to give us an update right as you disappeared."

"What? What'd she say—"

"Not much, but it's good. They're finishing up now.

Maggie made it through. Come on, I want to ask the nurse some questions if she hasn't gone back yet."

"Lil." Indi reached for her sister's arm, after hours of pacing, her feet suddenly refusing to move now. "She made it through?"

Lilian stilled, the relief-filled assurance in her eyes like an embrace. "She made it through."

Indi all but hurled herself against her sister, needing the physical contact nearly as much as she needed air. *She's going to be okay. Maggie's going to be just fine.*

This night and all its terror was nearly over. She blinked back more tears. "I have cried so many times tonight. I don't know how I can have any tears left." Her voice cracked.

Lilian squeezed her tight before releasing her. Leaving one arm intact around Indi's waist, Lilian steered her back the way they'd come. "Wish you'd been in the room when the nurse came in. Wilder jumped up when he spotted her, spilled a whole can of soda in the process. Typical. I thought Neil might pass out from relief when she told us the good news. Of course, he probably won't rest easy until he's seen Maggie for himself. I doubt he'll leave the hospital until tomorrow, though he was saying something about the rest of us going back to the house to get some sleep when I left to come find you. Sounds like they don't expect Maggie to wake up for a few hours at least."

They turned a corner. "Oh, and if you're wondering, Ben's still out like a light."

Ben. Ben!

Right. Lilian still thought . . . and Neil too . . . and probably Wilder, for that matter. She'd been in such a fog earlier she hadn't bothered to correct anyone and now . . .

Her gaze immediately found Philip as they emerged into the waiting room. His shirt hopelessly wrinkled. One hand stuffed in his pocket. Long lashes resting against his cheeks.

Lilian lowered her arm. "He seems nice."

Nice? The word didn't come close. "I . . . I guess I should wake him up."

Lilian elbowed her. "Yeah, and then maybe you can finally make a proper introduction. I'm obviously going to have to interrogate him at some point."

"Lil—"

"He's your fiancé and I'm a lawyer and cross-examination is my love language. You know this. But considering the night we've all had, I'm willing to wait until morning."

He's not my fiancé.

She needed to say the words out loud. Explain the situation.

But instead, fingers still curled around Philip's tie, she leaned close to Lilian for another side-hug, then made her way to Philip's sleeping form. She lowered beside him, suddenly impatient to tell him the good news as she tugged on his shirtsleeve, lightly, just enough to rouse him.

He opened his eyes, blinked once, twice. Focused. And then must've read the news on her face. Because a light glinted in his gray irises as his voice lifted. "Maggie's all right?"

All she could do was nod. And return his drowsy, dimpled smile with one of her own.

He stretched his arms, his legs, letting out a sigh as his gaze traveled the room. She watched with him as Lilian began bulleting one question after another at a nurse, as Neil and Wilder hugged, their palms slapping against each other's backs. And then, moments later, as Lilian set the nurse free and snapped at Wilder about the spilled soda still puddled on the floor nearby.

Ah, there was the Lilian she knew and loved.

"I guess I should get going." Philip combed his fingers

through his hair. "I hope there's a late-night Uber driver around here."

"Hate to tell you, Philip, but this is Muir Harbor. We're a tiny town. The closest thing we have to Uber is Freddie Watkins and his old station wagon. And considering the man's pushing ninety, I don't think he's taking taxi calls at this time of night. My offer still stands, though—you can take my car." She folded his tie as she spoke. "But not until morning. You need to get some more sleep."

"Then if you could give me a ride to a hotel—"

"Don't be silly. You can come out to the farm. I think the rest of us will be heading home soon." *Home.* The only thing that could make her feel almost as good as seeing Maggie awake and alert and alive.

Sleepiness still clung to Philip's features as he shrugged and stood. "Bet you didn't think when you found me in that wardrobe you'd be bringing me home tonight. But . . . is it me you're bringing home? Or does your family still think—"

"Yes, they still think you're Ben."

He gave her another heavy-lidded grin. "Ben the Buffoon."

"You shouldn't call him that. You don't even know him."

"I know he only has one dimple. A travesty."

"You're funny when you're sleepy, Philip West." Add it to the incredibly small list of things she knew about this man. She reached for her coat from the back of a chair, stuffed Philip's tie in her purse.

"Hey."

She slung her purse over her shoulder, then stilled at the alertness in Philip's expression now.

"I-I know I shouldn't have been there . . . earlier, at your store, I mean. I shouldn't have overheard . . . but I did overhear so—"

"Can we not talk about it? Please?" Too much had happened since her unceremonious dumping hours ago, and she just needed to be happy and relieved for a little bit. Maggie had made it through surgery. Maggie was going to be okay. That was more important than anything else.

So she wouldn't think about her broken engagement now. Wouldn't think about Ben. That could wait. Just like telling her family about the end of her engagement could wait. Which meant maybe letting them keep assuming whatever they wanted about Philip's identity wasn't such a bad idea. For now.

Yes, she'd set them straight some other time. Like tomorrow morning, after they'd all had a chance to rest. After the exhaustion of this night had worn off.

Later. She'd explain everything . . . later.

* * *

A cascade of sunlight, beams of dancing dust particles, met Philip's bleary gaze as he opened one eye and then the other. His muscles pinched in protest as he rolled from his side to his back, the cushions underneath him shifting—not his familiar mattress, no bedsheets.

Where in blazes . . . ?

He bolted upward, sluggish confusion dissolving as remembrance crashed in. Muir Harbor—that's where he was. On a couch, covered with an afghan, in a farmhouse so close to the sea, he'd gone to sleep listening to its tussle with the rocky shore.

He lowered back onto an embroidered throw pillow. Good grief, when had he last slept this well? He'd slumbered like a baby in the hours since Indi had driven them away from the hospital in the middle of the night, never mind the soreness in his back and shoulders now.

Or his rumpled clothes and unbrushed teeth and the

sudden awareness that he was in *Maggie Muir's* house. What had once been just a random name tucked into his memory, a haphazard bit of mystery from his grandfather's past, was now a living, breathing person to him. He'd actually met her and—

His phone pealed into the morning quiet, muffled by a cushion but still loud enough to startle him into jerking so hard he tumbled from the couch. He landed with a thud, the tasseled rug that covered the hardwood floor bunching underneath him. Peachy. If his thumping fall didn't wake the whole house, his still-blaring phone would.

Which, come to think of it, had the potential to be more than a little awkward. He'd been too bushed last night to give much thought to the fact that Indi's siblings still thought it was her fiancé crashing on their couch. But this morning, in the light of day . . . well, all things considered, it might be best to avoid any solo encounters with the family.

He scrambled to his knees, stuffing one arm under a cushion until he found the phone. He gave a groggy "Hello" as he pulled himself to the couch once more.

"You stood up my husband last night."

Tabby. Right. He probably should've predicted this call. "Morning to you, too." He lifted one hand to rub the back of his neck.

Connor's wife gave a snort. "I'm not in the mood for manners this morning, Phil. Not when I was supposed to be enjoying a good book and a bubble bath last night and instead, I got a call from my poor husband who was dying of boredom at a dinner party because his buddy didn't show up. I'm so annoyingly in love with that man you know what I did? I changed into a stupid dress and went to that stupid party and sat in *your* stupid empty seat."

He managed a laugh, though he kept it to a low volume. "I'm sorry my absence messed up your bath time, but it really couldn't be helped." He let his gaze wander the room, taking in details he'd missed last night. The nicked but polished cedar planks of the floor. Two overstuffed off-white chairs across from the couch. A rocking chair in the corner, and next to it, a quilt rack packed with blankets.

Overhead, creaking footsteps let him know he wasn't the only one awake. What time was it anyway?

"So is there a purpose for this call other than chastising me?" He rose from the couch, drawn to the gaping window at the front of the room and its stunning view. On the other side of the glass, a grassy lawn gave way to the craggy shoreline that bordered an endless expanse of wild blue. This was the view Indi had grown up with? He'd only spent one night here —just a few hours, really—and already, reluctance clogged his throat at the thought of leaving.

But he had to. Holland would be home from her sleepover by noon and he should be there. Which meant he should find out if one of those voices reaching through the register nearby belonged to Indi and see about borrowing her car to return to Augusta.

"Fine, we'll return to the topic of how you're going to make up for last night another time. Because, no, it's not the only reason I called."

Shoot, her long exhale didn't bode well.

"Ray missed another deadline."

He leaned his elbow against the glass pane, buried his fingers in his hair. Cold skimmed off the window in waves. "Oh."

"Look, I know it's not your job to keep your grandfather on task. But this was his second deadline extension. I'm not sure how much longer I can stall his editor."

If he had to guess, he'd say there were probably more days than not Tabby wasn't sure how much longer she could put up with being Grandfather's literary agent at all. But then, if it weren't for her job, she might never have met Philip. Who might never have introduced her to his best friend. First and only time in his life he'd ever played matchmaker.

"The man's a repeat *New York Times* bestseller, isn't he? His publisher's not going to drop him. I know it's probably frustrating working with him—"

"Frustrating?" Tabby snorted. "Phil, why do you think I was so desperately in need of a bubble bath last night?"

"Sore muscles? Good hygiene?"

"He doesn't return my calls anymore. I doubt he reads my emails. I don't even know if he's *trying* to write this book."

His sigh fogged the glass in front of him. But when the fog cleared, his gaze snagged on a huddled form nestled in a quilt in one of the white Adirondack chairs on the lawn. Wait, was that . . . *Indi?* Yes, the curls fluttering in the morning breeze gave her away.

A sheen of frost covered the grass. Had she slept out there?

She couldn't have. It's way too cold.

He pushed away from the window and crossed the room, the voices from upstairs growing louder. "I'm sorry, Tab. I wish I could help somehow. But I'm not exactly close to the man. We might live in the same house, but I hardly see Grandfather." And besides, Philip had his hands full trying to figure out how in the world to connect with Holland.

His teenage half sister didn't seem to appreciate the fact that he'd given up his job and his condo and his life in Seattle to move back to Maine last spring. To be . . . whatever it is she needed him to be in the wake of Mom's death.

He swallowed and shook his head before the grief or regret or guilt or most likely all three had even the slightest chance of elbowing in. No time for that now. He scanned the room for his shoes. Found them by the rocking chair. He shoved his feet into them, not bothering to bend down and tie the laces. He patted his back pocket—good, he had his wallet. Now to go outside before he encountered anyone in Indi's family, make sure Indi didn't have frostbite or something, then ask about her car keys. Or about that ninety-year-old with the station wagon she'd mentioned last night.

"I know he's had a hard year." Tabby's tone softened. "And you have, too."

"Don't worry about me. I'm fine." Or he would be. As long as he made it home before Holland. And found some way to shake off the strangeness of the past half-day since he'd first stepped into that little shop of Indi's.

Except, as he moved into the hallway, his gaze bobbing over the open staircase and the picture frames cramming the wall, the coat tree near the front door fairly sagging with its mountain of jackets and scarves, he wasn't so sure he wanted to shake off any of this.

Because this house, what he'd seen of it so far anyway, was homey and peaceful—so different from Grandfather's. That seaside view outside the living room window was beckoning and beautiful. Even last night at the hospital, he'd felt somehow *right* in Maggie's room. As if he was meant to be there.

Maggie's hospital murmurs came back to him again now. *"You look like . . . like Robert."*

At some point in the wee hours of the morning, after walking into this house, right before he'd drifted off to sleep, understanding had settled around the edges of his mind. That old letter, the one he'd found almost twenty years ago . . . its tone hadn't sounded like Grandfather because Grandfather hadn't written it.

His *brother* had. Robert Camden. Philip's great-uncle. A man he'd never met and knew very little about, but apparently resembled.

That had to be it. The letter had only been signed with an

R, after all. And sure, he'd thought it was Grandfather's handwriting, but it wasn't that odd for one family member's writing to resemble another's, right?

Felt a little deflating, to be honest. A mystery solved without an intriguing climax. Of course, there was still the question of why Grandfather had it in his possession. *Maybe he kept it to remember his brother by.* But even that bit of sentiment didn't fit with the Ray Camden he knew.

Tabby's voice pulled him back. "You don't get to tell me not to worry about you, Phil. Not when, despite my annoyance, I know you wouldn't have stood up Connor last night without a good reason."

"We're back to that again?" He stopped in the entryway and lifted a small frame from an antique table, gaze brushing over each face—Indi and her siblings posed around Maggie. Maggie was younger in this photo, hair a radiant red, same hazel eyes he'd seen last night.

"I just want to know everything's okay. With you *and* your grandfather."

"I'll try to talk to him, okay? I can't promise it'll do any good, but I'll try." At the sound of thumping steps overhead, he replaced the frame and glanced toward the staircase. Any minute now, Neil or Lilian might come down those stairs. They'd seemed nice enough last night, but the minute one of them called him Ben, he'd surely start stuttering and stammering, hemming and hawing.

And he just didn't really care to know how that scenario might end.

"Uh, listen, Tab—can I let you go?" He pulled open the front door, the tinkling of wind chimes nearly lost to the whoosh of windswept waves as he stepped onto the porch. A burly chill bounded over him.

"Why do you suddenly sound panicked?"

He hurried down the porch steps. "Um, well, it's possible I've gotten myself into a sort of, er, situation."

"What kind of situation?"

"I guess you could call it a case of mistaken identity. One involving a fake engagement."

Had she just spit out her coffee? "What'd you do, wander onto the set of a Hallmark movie? Where are you, anyway?"

He stopped a few feet in front of the porch, tipped his gaze and took in the rest of the house—its quaint yellow siding and white gingerbread eaves like something out of a storybook. "I'm in Muir Harbor. Technically, just outside of it. On a farm. On the coast."

"What the heck, Philip? Why?"

He started across the lawn, sights set on Indi's hair still whipping in the wind. "Fill you in later."

"No way. You can't just mention a fake engagement and not give me the details. I'm your best friend."

He laughed despite the autumn cold scraping over him. "Connor's my best friend."

"Same difference. Two shall become one and all that."

He reached Indi's lawn chair, felt the corners of his mouth lift at the sight of one slippered foot sticking out from underneath the quilt. She looked cold, but not frozen solid. Had she come out to watch the sunrise or something?

"Tab, I really have to go. I'll tell you everything later, I promise." After he got himself out of this weird situation. Got back to Augusta. Back to his normal life.

Where the air *didn't* smell of sea salt and pine. Where there was no cozy house or sweeping view, complete with frothy whitecaps collapsing against a rugged shoreline. No strange sense of peace curling around him.

He let out a long breath and before Tabby could argue, he ended the call. He slipped his phone into his pocket, then reached down, giving Indi's shoulder a light squeeze and shake. "Indi?"

Her only movement was a slight tightening of her grip on one corner of the blanket. For Pete's sake, her fingernails were practically blue. Why hadn't the woman thought to grab a coat?

Why hadn't he? He shook Indi's shoulder again. "Hey, really sorry to wake you but—"

"Go away, Neil."

"It's not Neil."

Finally, she opened her eyes, squinting against the sunlight at first, then widening her stare as surprise and then realization feathered through her green eyes. "Oh. *Oh.*" She sat up with a jolt. "H-hi. Good morn—" She attempted to stand as she spoke, but her feet were tangled in the quilt.

Philip's arms shot out to steady her before she stumbled backward, the blanket pooling on the ground. He got a mouthful of her hair as a hefty gale gusted over them, billowing her purple pajama top.

Not until he was sure she was steady on her feet did he drop his hands from her shoulders, fighting a grin and a laugh and the ridiculous urge to catalog this moment in his mind for later. Something to remember and enjoy days from now—no, only hours—when he was back to being the Philip West he was supposed to be.

Rather than the Philip West who'd awoken in a place he didn't know, but didn't want to leave.

⊱⋅•⋅⊰

Considering Maggie had almost died last night—*died*—on the same evening Ben had dumped her, it really shouldn't

51

matter one whit that an attractive man had found her sleeping outside looking like . . .

Like whatever it was she must look like in oversized pajamas and fuzzy slippers and hair so tangled it'd probably make a perfectly good bird habitat.

Indi bent to pluck her quilt from the ground and wrapped it around her torso, partially because it was a little too close to mortifying being around the man while wearing purple flannel pajamas, but mostly to escape the dancing light in Philip's slate-gray eyes. "You're laughing at me."

"I'm not."

She cinched the blanket under her arms in front of her. "You're grinning. Which is almost the same thing."

"You called my grin handsome last night."

So she had. So it was. But that was entirely beside the point. "Yes, well, I was distraught last night. Is there a reason you're here?"

"Here as in . . . here? I-I mean, at your house? You wouldn't let me go home. You insisted I come here and get some sleep before—"

"I mean *here*. Standing on the lawn on the coldest morning this autumn so far. Without a coat." And yes, she knew how ridiculous that sounded coming from the woman wearing a blanket.

But she'd needed to come out this morning. She'd needed the crisp air and bright sun to chase away yesterday's lingering shadows. Maggie and Ben and that eerie crying she'd heard in the hospital corridor. The same crying that had come back to her in a dream overnight. Just like . . . before.

Philip combed his fingers through his hair. "I wanted to make sure you hadn't slept out here all night." He glanced over his shoulder toward the house. "And, well, I don't know if you remember, but I'm pretty sure everyone back there is still under the impression that I'm—"

"Oh my goodness." Her blanket fell down one side as she slapped her palm over her mouth. "They all think you're Ben." Because, yes, in her exhaustion the previous night, she'd somehow thought it was completely reasonable to let their mistaken assumptions go uncorrected.

"Yeah." He shrugged. "Which wouldn't be so bad except I'm a terrible actor. I auditioned for a production of *Willy Wonka* when I was in fifth grade. Wasn't even good enough to land a role as an Oompa-Loompa. Thus, why I practically ran out of your house a minute ago in an attempt to avoid seeing anyone."

Her palms started sweating. "*Did* you see anyone?"

Philip shook his head. "No, but—"

"Good." She hiked up the quilt, knotted it around her torso, and grabbed hold of his arm. "Then there's still time for you to leave before they start asking questions."

"Questions?"

"Yes, like when's the wedding and where are we going on the honeymoon and how many kids are we thinking of having." Her blanket tripped her for the second time. But this time she steadied herself against Philip, pulling him toward the house.

"I've always thought four was a nice number."

"Philip!" She pushed her hair out of her face with the hand that wasn't still gripping a fistful of the man's shirtsleeve. "You don't understand. My sister's a lawyer. From the moment I told everyone I was engaged—to a man they've never met, no less—she's been waiting to get you on the proverbial stand. I mean him. I mean Ben."

"Well, I've got a question of my own."

She stopped at the porch steps and dropped his arm. "Okay, shoot."

"If you want me to leave so badly, why are you dragging me back to the house?"

He was still trying not to laugh, wasn't he? Trying, but completely failing to hide his amusement. She really must look a wreck. "I'm glad this is so entertaining for you. And for your information, I was going to get my car keys. I was going to loan you my car so you could get back home."

"And save you from having to make an uncomfortable introduction."

"Exactly."

"I don't suppose it's occurred to you to just explain there was a simple misunderstanding?" He paused when she didn't answer, too much knowing gliding into his eyes. "Oh. You're not ready to tell them about the buffoon."

It shouldn't be possible—that this same man who'd stammered and blushed and had barely been able to finish a full sentence when he'd stumbled out of that silly wardrobe yesterday could almost eke a smile from her now just by calling Ben a buffoon. When she was cold and bedraggled and flustered and . . .

Fine. She was *fine.*

Really. Because Maggie had pulled through last night. Because she was home, in this place she loved, with the people she loved. And as for Ben . . . she'd get over him. She'd get over the buffoon.

She climbed a porch step. "Correct, I'm not ready to tell them the engagement's off. But the other problem with telling my siblings you're not Ben is that then I'll have to tell them who you *are.* Which is basically a stranger. A stranger I got into a car with. Who I let sleep on our couch last night. Doesn't entirely speak well of me. And when you're already the flighty youngest sibling . . ." She shrugged and climbed another step.

"I didn't make off with any fancy china or silverware in the middle of the night. That should count for something." Philip's steps sounded behind her. "And just for the record, flighty isn't at all the first adjective I would've thought of to describe you."

"Well." She halted on the top step, turning to face him. "You don't really know me."

"I guess that's true." Philip had stopped one stair below her, bringing him eye level with her, and huh, that almost looked like regret filling his expression.

Regret over what? That he didn't know her? Nonsense. The poor man had likely been asking himself what he'd gotten himself into every hour since he'd first met her. He probably couldn't wait to get out of here.

"Anyway, once you hit the road, we'll both be spared a slew of awkward questions. Not that I'm trying to throw you out. I'm just . . ."

"Trying to end our accidental charade," he finished for her.

"Right." Oh, she felt like a heel. After all he'd done for her, she was practically tossing him out the door. "Do you want some coffee first for the road?" It was the least she could offer. She could probably even scrounge up one of Maggie's blueberry muffins. "We've got plenty of closets you could hide in while I fill a travel mug for you."

He laughed. "Very funny. No, I'll leave. Go get your keys. I can wait out here."

She turned to the door but stopped, angling to face him once more. "Philip . . . everything you did last night, driving me to Muir Harbor, staying at the hospital all that time . . . why? You didn't even know me."

The morning breeze sifted through his hair, plastering his rumpled shirt to his tall frame. He reached up to rub the back of his neck, then shrugged as his arm came back down. "I, um . . . I know what it's like not to make it in time. My mom, last spring . . ."

He looked away, words he hadn't said settling in and around the ones he had.

Oh. Oh, Philip. "That's . . . I'm so—"

"It's okay."

It wasn't. She could tell by the way his posture had gone rigid, the way he stuffed both hands in his pockets. The fact that he still hadn't looked back at her.

But she could also tell he'd wished back his words the moment he'd uttered them. Which meant the polite thing to do now was turn away, reach for the doorknob. Let this nice man go home.

But the moment her fingers closed around the knob, the door opened without her help, the unexpectedness of it jerking her forward and then sending her faltering backward. She landed with her back against Philip's chest, one of his arms instantly hooking around her waist, her *oomph* colliding with his as her blanket dropped to the porch floor.

Neil stood on the threshold, eyebrows raised.

Surprise must have rendered Philip as motionless as she was, his hand still splayed on her stomach, the warmth of him doing as much to heat her cheeks as her own embarrassment.

"Neil, h-hi."

Neil crossed his arms, eyeing Philip's hand placement.

She wrenched away. "We were just . . . he was . . . I'm . . . Are you going to the hospital? Can I come with?"

Neil eyed her pajamas. "Dressed like that?"

Philip stepped to her side. "The blanket completes the ensemble."

She sent him a glare. Or maybe a grin. Who even knew with the way her nerves had picked that moment to go into a tizzy? Probably because of the way Neil was now looking at Philip.

Or maybe the way Philip was looking at her. Amusement. Kindness. A smidge of embarrassment.

Finally, Neil broke the nervous silence. "Sure, you can ride to the hospital with me." He glanced to Philip again. "You coming?"

"Uh, unfortunately, I need to get back to Augusta."

"He's going to take my car." She reached for Philip's hand and tugged him past Neil, over the threshold, closing the door behind them before Neil could say another word.

"Well, that wasn't awkward at all." Philip chuckled.

She moved to the coat tree, reaching for the jean jacket she'd worn last night. "If by not awkward you mean tragically uncomfortable, I completely agree." She pulled her keys from her coat's pocket, along with something else.

She turned back to Philip and held out the crumpled ball of blue fabric. "Can't let you forget this." His tie, a shabby mess.

"Huh, I was kind of hoping never to see it again. I wasn't lying about not liking it."

"If it's any consolation, it's in no condition to be worn." She handed it over, along with her keys, then glanced outside. Good, Neil had abandoned the porch. He stood out on the driveway by his truck now. And was that Wilder with him? Since when had he gotten here? "If you don't mind leaving my car in the spot behind my store, that'd be great. There's a little mail slot by the back door you can shove the keys in. Someone will give me a ride back eventually." She opened the front door once more and stepped onto the porch. "Thank you, by the way. For everything. Driving me to the hospital and staying and . . . and going along with a case of mistaken identity. Truly, thank you."

"My pleasure." He held out his palm.

She placed her hand in his. "Really? It was your pleasure pushing my car out of a ditch, sitting in a hospital waiting room for hours, and sleeping on a couch at least a foot too short for you?"

"You got me out of that dinner party, remember?" He gripped her hand and grinned as he shook it.

"I also contributed to the demise of your tie. Don't forget that."

"I won't. I doubt I'll ever forget anything about last night."

He let go of her hand just as a seaside breeze captured the wind chimes. *Neither will I.*

4

Two Months Later
Friday, January 4

*I*f Mr. Batunde hadn't been the nicest landlord Indi could've hoped for, she might've flinched under the weight of his sympathy as she signed the paperwork, officially declining the renewal of her lease.

Or wilted in embarrassment when she handed him the key to her Augusta shop.

Well, no, not her shop anymore.

The older man slipped the key into the pocket of his blazer, his kind smile almost making up for the pity in his eyes. Or maybe not so much pity as apology. "Sure wish I could lower the lease amount. I would if I could." He leaned against the counter spanning one wall of the store's backroom. Empty—the counter, the room, all of it.

"Oh no, Mr. Batunde, I would never expect that."

"You've been my tenant for a year—and a star one, at that. I think you can call me Olu now."

Did a shop owner who hadn't managed to turn much more than a minimal profit even a single month since opening day really count as a star tenant? No, a star tenant would've found a way to draw in foot traffic, especially during the holidays. A star tenant would've re-upped her lease.

A star tenant definitely wouldn't be closing her doors only eleven months in.

But she didn't really have a choice, did she? Her Bits & Pieces Augusta location had been running on financial fumes for too long. With her lease up for renewal, she either needed to make some kind of drastic change to improve business quickly or end the venture altogether.

Don't think of it as an ending. Think of it as a beginning.

It's what she'd been telling herself for days now, weeks. Closing her second location meant she could begin spending more time in Muir Harbor, more time with Maggie and her siblings. She could make up for all those months last year when she'd constantly been running back and forth between home and here, running two stores at once. Make up for all the weeks she'd been distracted by a shiny new relationship followed by a whirlwind engagement.

And then a just-as-hasty breakup.

Goodness, she'd been standing here in this very spot when Ben . . .

Nope. Nope, nope, nope. Not going there now. Not with poor Mr. Batunde—Olu—looking so uncomfortably remorseful, he might actually offer her this building for free any minute now, and how awful would that be?

And anyway, she was over it. Over Ben. He hadn't really broken her heart or anything. Just bruised it a little. Nothing like she'd done to Trey—

"Hope you know I was rooting for you," Olu's voice cut in, saving her from another train of thought she had no desire to board.

"I know you were." The man had stopped by the store once a month since she'd opened early last year and never left before buying something to take home to his wife. She just wished he hadn't been her sole loyal customer in this town. Oh, she'd known owning a store in a big city wouldn't be the same as in her little hometown hamlet. She just hadn't expected it to be so . . . discouraging.

But this wasn't all bad. It really wasn't. She could focus on her flagship store now. She could spend more time on what she loved—creating the inventory that filled its shelves. And she could help out at the farm, too. Neil had been keeping Muir Farm afloat pretty much singlehandedly for years. She could play a bigger role now.

Olu folded the signed paperwork and stuffed it in the same pocket as her key. *His* key. "It's that darn bypass. Rerouted all the traffic around downtown instead of through it. Truth be told, I'm thinking of selling off this old place. I'd have held on to her if you were sticking around, but now . . . dunno. Might be time to let her go." He stuck out one hand. "It's been a pleasure doing business with you, Indi. I wish you the best."

She made herself smile as she shook his hand. Found the words to thank him. Had to blink back tears when he asked if she'd like a few minutes in the building alone. And then he was gone, out the back door.

And it was just her and the quiet and the subtle smell of gingerbread and cinnamon sticks, somehow lingering despite the fact that she'd packed up the Christmas decorations a week ago. Before packing up everything else, too.

Including the curtain that used to separate the backroom from the main store floor. She slipped through the opening now, the morning's peach-hued sunlight pouring in the tall glass windows up front, spilling over the bare wood floor, reaching to the spot where that huge, old wardrobe once stood.

Not for the first time since that autumn evening in

November, Philip West's face filled her mind. His kind, gray eyes and twin dimples, his ever-tousled hair.

She'd thought about contacting him once or twice over the past two months. Had even looked him up on Thornhill College's website—which was how she now knew his middle initial was B. *Philip B. West.* She'd wanted to find his email address on the site so she could thank him for filling her car with gas before returning it to her shop. But then she couldn't help remembering how he'd witnessed her complete humiliation after Ben had walked out. How he'd seen her fall apart over Maggie.

How he'd grinned when he'd spotted her ridiculous purple pajamas the next morning.

Really, a girl could handle only so much humiliation.

She wrapped her arms around herself now, gaze gliding over the floor she'd swept yesterday. She'd turned the heat down last night before leaving with her last carload of boxes, which meant she could almost see her breath in the chill of the empty building now. Usually she liked this—the embrace of a delicious, crisp cold wrapping around her, the kind that made her think of winter evenings when she was a kid, huddled in front of the farmhouse fireplace back when money had been especially tight. Of course, she hadn't known about the money part then, nor of Maggie's worries about utility bills or keeping Muir Farm operational.

All she'd known was the warmth of home and the delight of a brawny wind hurling itself against the house. Everything had seemed so simple then. Safe, uncomplicated.

Before senior year and Trey and . . . choices she could never undo.

Her fingers curled around the front of her sweater dress, clenching at its waistline as she reversed course and headed for the back. Olu had been kind to offer her a couple of minutes to say goodbye, but she'd never been that great at goodbyes. Generally made a mess of them, truth be told.

It was why she'd skipped the one that should've mattered most.

A shiver clambered through her, and then another, leaving cracks along the way, crannies just waiting to be filled with the same old sorrow, the same old regret—

A jarring jingle of bells stopped her in her tracks. She whirled. "Sorry, we're closed." *For good.* Wait, was that—? "Neil?"

Her brother stopped just inside the front door as he jabbed one thumb over his shoulder. "Sign still says *Open.*"

"What in the world are you doing here?"

His cheeks were ruddy under a layer of bristle. He wore his usual faded Levi's and probably a flannel shirt, too, underneath his light jacket. Usually by this time of year, they'd all be bundling up in thick, fleece-lined coats, but this winter had been ridiculously mild so far—cold, yes, but not frigid. Not a speck of snow, not even on Christmas. Far as she knew, Indi was the only one disappointed by that fact.

Neil moved toward her in long strides. "Thought maybe you could use some company on the drive back."

"But my car, your truck—"

"Wilder dropped me off. You don't mind me hitching a ride home with you, do you?" He unzipped his coat. Sure enough, blue plaid peeked out from underneath. It was as familiar as his deep voice, his accent always a little stronger when he was doing that thing he did so often—caring. Wearing his big-brother heart right on his flannel sleeves.

"Neil." She dropped her shoulders. "It's the day before your wedding."

"I know that."

"You didn't have to come."

"I know I didn't. But I wanted to. I would've driven with

you this morning, but you were already gone by the time I got back to the house."

Yes, because she'd timed her departure purposely—after Lilian left for her law office, before Neil finished his morning chores. Of course, she hadn't been as successful at avoiding Maggie. But then, Maggie had seemed to sense she hadn't wanted to talk about the fact that this was her last business trip to Augusta. She'd sent her off with a simple hug and a travel mug filled with coffee.

That was Maggie—ever intuitive. Maybe somehow more so after her stint in the hospital. Hard as these past couple of months had been, that was one blessing Indi hadn't over-looked—Maggie's recovery. She'd been home from the hospital in a matter of days, up and about in a week's time. Had even hosted a huge community Thanksgiving gathering just a few weeks later.

"Anyway, getting Wilder to bring me to Augusta had its pros. Gave me the opportunity to grill him about his best man speech, make sure he's not planning to bring up anything that might send Sydney running away."

As if that would ever happen. Neil's fiancé was just as hopelessly smitten with him as he was with her.

More than that, Sydney Rose had changed Neil's life the day she showed up at Muir Farm last year. There'd been a short while when they'd all hoped, even believed, Sydney might be Maggie's granddaughter, who'd been missing ever since the tragic car accident that had killed Maggie's oldest adopted daughter over twenty-eight years ago. A toddler at the time, the granddaughter's body had never been found.

And Maggie had never stopped hoping.

In the end, though, while Sydney hadn't turned out to be Maggie's granddaughter, she had turned out to be the love of Neil's life. And Indi's sole focus for the rest of this weekend would be making sure they had the wedding reception of their dreams.

"Did you also give Wilder a stern warning about staying on Lil's good side just for a day?" she said now. "For the sake of a peaceful wedding and all?"

"I'm not sure that's possible." Neil laughed and leaned down to give her a hug. "I'm sorry about the store closing. You okay?"

She nodded against his shoulder before stepping back.

"Really?"

"Really. Just let me run upstairs and grab my stuff and then we can head out." That was something she wouldn't miss —staying here in Augusta several days each week, sleeping in the small studio apartment upstairs instead of her bedroom at home.

Neil followed her through the backroom and up the narrow stairs that led to the apartment. "Place looks different," he said, entering the hollow space behind her. "How does it look even smaller without furniture?"

She grabbed her purse from a window ledge and turned to him. Neil had helped her move a few belongings into the apartment a year ago. And now he was helping her leave, refusing to let her make the final trek from Augusta back to the farm alone. "I'm lucky to have you for a brother, you know that?"

He harrumphed. "Actually, I do."

"Sydney's lucky, too." She pulled on her jacket. "Although, just for the record, if you two weren't so adorable, you'd be unbearable."

Neil grimaced. "Don't really love being called adorable by my little sister."

"Well, then don't walk around so lovesick and moon-eyed all the time."

"I am not moon-eyed."

"You are the very definition of moon-eyed."

He rolled his eyes and turned back to the stairs.

"Hey, Neil, wait. Can I ask you something?"

"If it's about my love life, then no."

She zipped up her jacket. "Not about that. Though it's nice that you finally have one. Gives hope to the rest of us single people."

His grin dissolved in an instant. And oh, shoot, there was that look. The same one she'd been seeing off and on for weeks now—worry, concern, probably a little curiosity too. And it wasn't only Neil. Maggie, Lil, Wilder, even Sydney— they'd all taken turns wearing the expression ever since she'd finally told them about Ben and the broken engagement.

"I was joking, Neil. Please don't give me the *I'm worried about you* look."

"But—"

"The barn. I wanted to ask you about the barn. The small one. Specifically, the loft." Confusion clouded his eyes at her abrupt change of topic but she barreled through before he could stop her. "What would you think of me using it as a workshop?"

His forehead wrinkled. "You have a workshop above your other store."

Yes, and the space put this dinky apartment to shame. The second floor over her Muir Harbor shop was big and bright, with exposed beams and an expansive window that over-looked the harbor. She could lose herself for hours up there— sewing new cushion coverings, sanding old furniture. "I know, but I was thinking I could turn it into . . . something. I haven't decided what yet. Maybe an apartment like this. Or a space another business could lease. Or maybe even an addi-tion to my store—a coffee shop or gallery. Something that could bring in an additional income."

He rubbed his chin. "I know you had a rough go of it here, but isn't business good in Muir Harbor?"

"Good enough, yes. But I heard you and Maggie talking about medical bills the other day. The health insurance company is being a pain and money's been tight with the farm for a long time—"

"Indi, no."

"You and Syd are having a small wedding to save money."

"We *want* a small wedding."

"You're starting a whole Airbnb business on the side to bring in extra income." The man had built a luxury treehouse, of all things, last autumn. His fiancé had created a website and they were already taking spring reservations. "Why can't I contribute, too? I've got this huge space in a prime location in town and I'm not using it for something worthwhile."

"One, your workshop is worthwhile. Two, the farm's not your responsibility."

"I live there, don't I?"

Neil stuffed both hands in his jacket pockets, quiet for a moment as he studied her. And then, "Aren't you ever going to talk about it?"

Not this. Not again. She whirled away from him.

"You were *engaged*, Indi. And now . . . you're not. And that's a big thing. But it doesn't seem like you're dealing with it. Instead, you're talking about starting a side gig? Look, if you won't talk to me, at least talk to Maggie or Lil or even Syd. You need to tell someone what you're thinking or how you're feeling or—"

"How I'm feeling is *fine*." She about-faced, her hands landing on her hips. "It was a whirlwind engagement. Probably never should've happened in the first place. It's not like it was with Trey." Surprise flickered in Neil's expression. Probably because she rarely brought up Trey, usually avoided all mention of her first engagement. But desperate times called for desperate measures. "I barely even knew Ben. We'd only dated for six weeks. I never should've accepted the proposal."

He folded his arms. "Have you talked to him at all?"

"He's texted a couple of times." Neither of which she'd responded to. "Called once." She hadn't answered. He hadn't left a message.

"You're really okay?"

"I'm really okay." As long as she stayed busy. As long as she didn't have to have any more conversations like this.

"And if I don't believe you?"

The blare of her phone saved her from answering. She pulled it from her coat pocket and glanced down. A caller from Florida? She didn't recognize the number but was tempted to answer anyway. A sales pitch from a telemarketer would suit her just fine right now if it meant escaping Neil's questioning.

But she knew her brother. She could stall but it wouldn't matter. He'd just bring this up again on the drive home. So she squared her shoulders and willed assurance into her tone. "I love you, Neil. I love you for coming here and caring. But I need you to hear me. I'm fine. I'm over Ben. I'm at peace with the store closing. I'm not falling apart." *I'm not messy, complicated Indi Muir.* Not anymore.

"I just want to help."

"Then give me the okay to use the barn loft. That's what would help me. Tell me you'll help haul my unfinished inventory there when you're back from your honeymoon."

His smile was brief. A little sad. "Kind of miss the days when you called it art."

"Huh?"

"You used to call your work art. Now you call it inventory." He placed his arm around her shoulder. "Come on. Let's go home."

Philip curled the concert program in his hands as he zeroed in on two empty seats halfway to the front. The small auditorium smelled of aged stone and someone's overly flowery perfume. The strains of tuning instruments reached out from behind the velvet curtain serving as a backdrop to the chairs and music stands on stage.

Not exactly how he relished spending a Friday evening, but Holland deserved to have someone in the audience watching her. Even if she'd made it clear she couldn't care less if he showed up.

Eight months. Nearly eight months since Mom had died. Somehow he'd thought things might be better by now, even just a little.

He plopped into a cushioned chair, its faded burgundy and high-pitched squeak attesting to its age. With his awkward height, he barely fit in the thing. It'd be all he could do not to knock his knees into the chair in front of him for the next hour or more. *Oh, please don't let this thing go longer than an hour.*

The hinges of the chair beside him moaned as Connor lowered. "Have to say, when you said you'd get me out of the house while Tabby's out of town, I was thinking pizza at Mulroney's. Wasn't expecting a high school concert."

"Not a high school concert. This is a legit orchestra, mostly made up of adults. Holland's the youngest, by far." And not only was she first-chair, she was also tonight's star soloist.

It was the only thing she seemed to care about these days —her violin, rehearsals, hours of practice in her room at Grandfather's. An undeniable prodigy, his sister. The instructor she'd been working with since she was all of four years old was convinced she was destined for Julliard.

"Hey." Connor elbowed him. "Thanks, by the way."

He nodded. "For dragging you to this thing? Of course. Tabby will be happy I made you come. By the end of tonight, you'll know your Bach from your Beethoven and you can impress her with your newly cultured self."

Connor cast him a sidelong glance. "You know what I mean."

Yes, he did. Knew that when Connor had texted him earlier asking if he had plans for the evening, his friend had been looking for company. Connor had needed a distraction —like Indi Muir on that drive to Muir Harbor back in November.

Absently, his hand rose to his chest where his tie would've been if he was wearing one. Had Indi ever found the wrinkled tie he'd left in her glove compartment? He hoped so. Hoped it'd made her laugh.

He flattened his program against his leg, refusing to let himself count how many arrangements they'd be sitting through in the next who-knew-how-long. "Tabby comes back from her trip with her sisters tomorrow?"

Connor nodded.

"You can stay with us if you want tonight. Lord knows Grandfather's house has enough empty guest rooms. We can even swing by Mulroney's and grab a couple large pepperonis on the way back." Maybe he could convince Holland to join them. Though a fifteen-year-old girl probably had little desire to hang out with the bachelor brother she'd made a sport of avoiding and his married friend.

He just wished he could figure out *why* Holland avoided him so much. Not just avoided, downright resented. Sure, he didn't know his sister all that well. He'd already been nineteen when she'd been born, after all. By that point in his life, so much distance had crept into his relationship with Mom, he'd tended to look for excuses to stay in his dorm at Thornhill instead of come home on breaks.

But when he had, especially when she'd been a toddler, Holland had adored him. She'd soaked up his attention, their relationship more like uncle and niece than half siblings. And in future years, when he returned from Seattle for the occasional holiday, she'd still seemed to like him well enough.

These days, though, she barely tolerated him.

If he could just figure out how to break through to her. Convince her, somehow, that he cared. That he might even be able to help her in her grief.

I understand, Holl. I lost a parent, too.

Difference was, he'd lost Mom years ago.

"It's better this way, Philip. I promise. You'll be happier here with your grandpa. You'll still see me plenty." How was it he could still feel the stunning effect of those words? First, the disbelief. Then, the shock. Later, for too many weeks that turned into months that turned into years, the sheer rejection. It was always there, glomming on to what was left of his childhood.

"You all right, man?"

He followed Connor's gaze to the program in his fist. Now crumpled. "Uh, yeah, fine."

"Well, thanks for the slumber party invite, but I'll pass. Just, uh . . . just had to get through this evening, and when my sponsor didn't call back right away . . ." Connor shook his head and splayed his hands over his knees. "This many years sober, and it's tempting to think it can't pull you back."

"Any reason tonight's particularly rough?" The seat in front of him tipped back as a man settled in.

Connor shrugged. "The holidays are always difficult, especially for Tab. All her siblings have kids. All my siblings have kids. Kills me to see her trying so hard to pretend she's not hurting, to know I can't fix this. Then her best friend tells her she's pregnant at our New Year's party, and as much as she loves her sisters, I have a feeling this trip is having its hard moments for her and . . . I guess it all just kind of crashed in on me tonight."

"Man, I'm really sorry. Wish I could do something to help."

But he was doing a bad enough job helping Holland. He'd known Christmas would be tough. It's why he'd spent way too much on gifts and ordered enough food to feed half the congregation at St. Mary's.

But Holland hadn't wanted to go to church on Christmas Eve, had barely picked at her food on Christmas Day. And though she'd politely thanked him for the new iPad and the books and the violin charm to go on the hand-me-down bracelet of Mom's she wore day in and day out, there'd been an impenetrable wall between them. A cavern of emotional distance he just couldn't figure out how to cross.

He was failing. Every day. And it was eating away at him.

"You are helping." Connor's words cut in as the orchestra conductor strode onto the stage. "You got me out of the house. You got me here." He paused. "Ever consider doing the same thing for yourself? Holland?"

"What?" His knee jabbed into the chair in front of him. At the frown from its occupant, he muttered an apology.

"Get out of your grandfather's house for a while. I know it hasn't been easy. Why not get away? Holland's homeschooled, isn't she?"

Yes, had been for years at her violin instructor's suggestion. The man had convinced Mom Holland's musical gift needed more of her time and attention. So she did online schoolwork in the mornings and devoted her afternoons to practice.

"And you're not teaching during J-term," Connor went on. "So get away for a while. Take a trip somewhere. Take Holland. Maybe it'd help you, I don't know, bond or something."

It wasn't a terrible idea. His lack of classes during the college's short January term, during which students took brief one-credit courses or went on service trips, meant he wasn't due back at Thornhill for the spring semester until the end of January. But where would they go? And what were the chances he could convince Holland to come along?

"Then maybe while you're away," Connor added, "you can free up enough mental space to consider Tabby's idea."

Philip could feel the frown take over his face. "Don't tell me she sicced you on me."

"It's not the worst idea ever."

By idea, of course Connor meant Tabby's latest outlandish brainchild. Her suggestion that Philip help Grandfather finish his current manuscript. Playing ghostwriter to the great Ray Camden—yeah, of all the turns his life had taken in the past year, that was one he planned to walk right on past, thank you very much. He might've written his fair share of research papers and historical journal articles over the years, but he wasn't a novelist and, more than that, he wasn't Grandfather's favorite person.

"We were college roomies, West, don't forget. I still remember the days when you wanted to be a writer. It was always a bit of a toss-up which side would win out—your history nerd side or your wordsmith side."

"Yeah, well, the history nerd side came out on top." He could appreciate Tabby's frustration with Grandfather's lack of progress on his latest book, but he'd learned long ago not to interfere in the man's life.

"By the way, that New Year's party I mentioned? Tabby was annoyed you didn't show."

Of course she was. "Let me guess—because I wasn't there to meet whatever single woman she had waiting for me?"

"Fine, yes, Tab had a very nice lady waiting to meet you."

"I don't need a very nice lady." The curtain at the back of

the stage rippled as musicians began filing into the auditorium and taking their seats.

"Right. Because you've already got one camped out in your head. Exactly where she's been for two months now."

Philip jerked his gaze to his friend. "Indi Muir is not in my head."

"The fact that you knew exactly who I was referring to says everything."

"It says nothing." Except that he'd obviously mentioned Indi and Muir Harbor and the pull of that old yellow farmhouse by the sea one too many times since that night in November.

But he hadn't been able to help it. Perhaps that short-lived trip should've been little more than a blip in his memory, but instead it'd somehow become the one bright spot in his autumn. His entire last year.

After so many months of numbness after Mom's death and the move back to Augusta, he'd *felt* something at that little farm.

"I'm just saying, you have no idea the kind of restraint it's taken for me not to tell Tabby she can stop playing matchmaker because shy, bookish Philip West finally has the first crush of his life."

He shifted, accidentally knocking into the chair in front of him again. "Are you *trying* to insult me?" He scanned the stage for Holland's white-blond hair. Almost every musician had taken a seat by now. Where was she? Did the star soloist come out last?

"Shy and bookish are not insults. Not according to my wife. She says it makes you endearing."

"I don't want to be endearing and I don't want to be having this conversation." What he wanted to do was get through this concert without bruising both knees and earning another glare from the man seated in front of him.

What he wanted was to find Holland out in the lobby afterward and compliment her and search her face for any glimmer, no matter how meager, that she was going to be okay. That somewhere underneath the loss and grief of the past year, she was still the Holland he'd once known.

That he was still the uncle-like brother she'd once loved.

That he could be for Holland what he'd long-ago wished for himself. What he'd needed when he'd been the one stranded at Grandfather's house. A safe harbor when it felt like everything he'd ever known was lost at sea.

A silence fell over the auditorium as the lights dimmed and the conductor rapped his stick against his podium. The musicians lifted their bows and instruments.

Wait, they weren't starting, were they?

"I don't see Holland," Connor whispered.

Philip leaned forward, knees thumping the row in front of him again. He didn't bother apologizing this time, didn't even hear whatever it was the man said. Not with confusion pooling in his stomach, setting it to churning.

He stood. Someone behind him hissed a reprimand but he couldn't make himself sit.

Where was Holland?

5

*H*olland all but flung herself over the threshold, through the mammoth door leading into the near-dark of Grandfather's house. Heavy hinges creaking, the door whooshed over the polished floor, the gaping opening ushering in a wailing gale.

And a blast of cold that clambered over Philip as he followed his blustering sister into the entryway. "Holland—"

"I said I was sorry." Strands of chin-length wet hair were plastered to her pale cheeks, her clothes matted to her thin form. The dim, tawny light of the sconces on opposite walls was just enough to make out the defiant set to her jaw, the pinched stubbornness of her pressed lips.

"You were swimming. In your clothes. In a rec center you'd broken into with a boy. On a night when you were supposed to be performing on stage."

Her wet shoes slurped against the floor as she headed toward the open staircase that spilled into the expansive foyer. "I don't need a play-by-play. I was there."

"Do you have any idea how worried I was? When I realized the conductor was starting the concert without you, I was ready to panic-dial every hospital in a fifty-mile radius. If that cop hadn't called when he did—"

"But he did and I'm fine and the rec center director isn't even pressing charges, so there's no reason to freak out now." She was nearly to the stairs.

But he crossed the foyer in three long strides, jutted one arm in front of her. Fingers clenched around the ornate iron banister, he leveled her with the closest thing he had to a parental glower until she had the decency to look up at him.

"I need to know why you did it, Holl. I need to know why you didn't show up for the concert you've spent weeks practicing for. I need to know . . ." He could feel himself withering right in front of her. The arm he'd used to bar her way sagged. "I need to know what I'm doing wrong. I'm trying here. I've been trying for months."

"And I wish you'd stop. I don't need you attempting to bond with me or connect with me or be my guidance counselor. Being my legal guardian doesn't make you my father."

"I'm your *brother*."

"Barely."

At that lone, hurled word, he dropped his arm from the banister.

"Look, I get that what I did tonight was stupid. But Jordan —he's just a dumb guy. I swear, nothing happened. We swam, we got caught, that's it."

"That's not it. You also missed your concert."

"Well, maybe I'm sick of my whole life revolving around an instrument. I hate how much time I've given to that thing. I hate how much time I missed with—"

She clamped her lips together, wrenching her gaze away.

Oh, Holland. He reached out to touch her arm, but she jerked out of his reach and started up the stairs, wet shoes leaving prints on the carpet. "I want to be alone."

Should he let her go? Follow her? He didn't know how to

do this. She was right. He wasn't her father. He wasn't her uncle. He wasn't even her friend. He turned away, scraping his fingers through his hair.

The sound of her steps faded. Had she stopped or—

"I want to go live with my dad."

Holland's voice was so soft behind him, her words didn't even register at first.

And she must've realized it because there was more force in her tone the second time. "I want to go to Texas. I want to live with Dad."

The front door was still open, sharp air slicing in with every howl of the wind. He turned to face her again, tipping his head to where she stood halfway up the stairs. "Mom wouldn't want you to go to Texas. Bryce hasn't been a part of your life in twelve years."

He shouldn't have said it so bluntly. Hated how it made her flinch.

"That doesn't mean he can't be a part of it now." She set her jaw and stared him down.

Defeat sludged through every inch of his body as his step-father's face filled his mind. Or at least, what blurry image remained in his memory. Dark hair, matching goatee. The man Mom had married not long after Dad died had never taken much of an interest in Philip, certainly hadn't made space for him in his small apartment.

Which was why Mom had left him here, in this oversized mausoleum, when he was seven. Where, years later, Mom had eventually come back to live again, too, three-year-old Holland in tow, after she and Bryce had divorced.

"Holl—"

"I want to go to Texas." She whirled away and raced up the stairs.

He needed to stop her. Needed to say something to erase the idea from her head. To explain why it was impossible.

Bryce hadn't even bothered coming back for Mom's funeral last spring. Why did Holland think Philip had uprooted his whole life, moved back to Maine?

What started as a sigh plummeted into a groan as he dropped to the staircase, bending his knees in front of him.

"I know it's a lot to ask, Philip. But she's going to need you when I'm gone. The paperwork's all ready."

His last conversation with Mom—over the phone. Why had she waited so long to tell him about the cancer? Had she thought he wouldn't come?

The slamming of Holland's door echoed from the second floor. And then, after a moment of pulsing silence, the sound of another door latching. *Grandfather.* How much of his argument with Holland had the man just heard?

He pushed to his feet, crossed the foyer to close the front door, then turned to the tapered hallway that reached toward the back of the house. Deep burgundy covered the walls, the darkness punctured only by a thin yellow sliver from underneath the door at the end of the hall. Clipped steps and seconds later, he stopped outside Grandfather's closed-off study.

Every day of the eight months since he'd returned to this house, he'd avoided this room where so many of his worst memories had happened. Where, when he was six, Grandfather had explained why he'd been pulled out of school and delivered here. *"There was an accident, Philip. Your father . . ."*

Where, not all that long later, Mom had knelt in front of him, telling him he'd be staying here after she went to live with her new husband.

And where, last spring after the funeral, Grandfather had insisted he move back in. *"Holland shouldn't be uprooted at a time like this. She's used to living here. She needs a sense of normalcy."*

Well, if tonight was any indication, normalcy hadn't done a thing to help her.

He took a breath and pushed the door open. Instantly, the smell of pipe tobacco shrouded him, along with a trapped staleness that spoke of how often Grandfather barred himself in the wood-paneled room. A pale glow from a lone lamp highlighted the layer of dust covering the cherrywood desk.

And, of course, there was Grandfather in his usual spot. In a chair by the window, sights locked on the bare splinter of light from the streetlamp outside visible between heavy drapes. His silver hair had nearly thinned into nothingness since Mom's funeral.

"How much of that did you hear?"

No response. No surprise.

"Did you hear her say she wants to go live with Bryce?"

Grandfather didn't so much as stir in his chair.

"I could use some help here. You know Holland better than I do."

Finally, Grandfather turned his head. "Is that my fault?"

The old man's piercing stare, his gray eyes rimmed with blue half-moons, pinned Philip to his spot beside the desk. *Why?* Why was it always like this?

This right here was why he'd been so enamored by that little slice of time he'd spent in Muir Harbor. He'd thought it was the farmhouse or the coastal scenery, but no, it was glimpsing Indi Muir with her family. It was seeing her glistening love for Maggie, the hugs she'd shared with her siblings. It was hearing the way Maggie had said Indi's name —*Indiana Joy*— in those few hallowed seconds when she'd opened her eyes in her hospital room.

That family had love in abundance. They had a kind of closeness he'd almost forgotten was possible. He'd had it once—back when Dad was alive. But after he'd died, everything had changed.

"We can't keep going on like this, Grandfather." Philip was suffocating here and Holland needed . . . something. He just wished he knew what.

"Get away for a while." Connor's words from earlier stole in. *"Take a trip somewhere. Take Holland. Maybe it'd help."*

Maybe Connor had the right idea.

His gaze dropped to a framed photo on Grandfather's desk. Faded, sepia tones—two men in uniform. Grandfather and his brother, Robert. Once, decades ago, he'd asked Grandfather about the photo. About his brother, about his own time in Vietnam.

The man had refused to open up. Just like he'd refused anything more than a growl of annoyance when Philip had approached him with that love letter he'd found almost twenty years ago. What would he say now if Philip told him he'd actually seen the woman from that letter? Been to her town, even slept in her house?

He'd probably say nothing. After all, now Philip knew it wasn't Grandfather who'd written the letter, anyway.

And clearly it wouldn't be Grandfather who helped him help Holland. He turned his back on the older man and stalked to the study door. He'd have to do it on his own. Figure something out . . . on his own.

Just as well. He had plenty of practice being on his own.

───※───

The night air felt fragile somehow, a crystalline moon tucked into black velvet, the morning's mild temps lost to a brittle breeze that wisped its way in and around the bare branches of Muir Farm's backyard trees.

Indi knelt near an open outlet at the back of the house, her fingers nearly numb after hours of decorating for tomorrow evening's outdoor reception.

Well, not entirely outdoor. A white marquee tent took up half the lawn space. A crew of church ladies had been here earlier, setting up tables and chairs inside the rented tent, arranging the centerpieces Indi had designed, shaking their heads and laughing at the idea of an outside wedding reception in the dead of winter, never mind the portable heaters that would warm the space tomorrow night.

Personally, Indi loved the idea. Loved Neil and Sydney for thinking of something so magical. So . . . *them*. This farm had brought them together. It was only fitting they celebrate right here.

Of course, Wilder Monroe might object to the idea that the farm had brought them together. After taking on the mantle of his late father's private investigation agency, Wilder had been the one to track down Sydney in Chicago last fall and haul her back to Muir Farm on the hunch she was Maggie's missing granddaughter. His hunch might not have panned out, but he loved taking credit for Neil and Sydney's happy ending all the same.

Indi scooted closer to the outlet and lifted a green extension cord—a little too noticeable against the brown grass underfoot, but it was better than Harbor Hardware's only other option of neon orange.

"Will you be annoyed if I admit I have a slight fear that the second you plug in that cord, it'll blow a fuse and we'll see sparks?"

She glanced up to see Maggie standing on the back steps, the light of the kitchen window brushing her white hair into a halo of sorts, her favorite sunshine-yellow shawl around her shoulders.

Indi chuckled. "It won't annoy me unless it turns out your fear is warranted." Hanging a thousand twinkle lights, she could handle. Morphing their farmyard into a winter wonderland, easy-peasy. But messing with the fuse box in their dank cobweb-filled basement—not really her expertise. "Cross your fingers."

She jabbed the plug into the outlet and a breath later, a fairytale glow careened from every direction. From the icicle lights tracing the edges of the reception tent. From the twinkle lights wrapped around the trees and the lanterns dangling from their branches.

Maggie walked down the steps, her white tennis shoes crunching over the grass as she turned a slow circle. "Oh, Indi, this is . . . it's gorgeous. No, it's enchanting. Completely and entirely enchanting."

The gentle awe in her voice was a blanket of warmth, folding itself around Indi until the last of her leftover angst from this morning—the pang of closing the store, the uncomfortable turn her conversation with Neil had taken—simply slipped away.

This was a weekend for celebration. For joy. Neil and Sydney were starting a new life together.

And in a way, she was, too. No more second store pulling her away from this place she loved. No more living in two towns part-time. No more being so preoccupied by her own life that she missed what was happening here. Like the signs that had led up to Maggie's heart attack. Or the financial struggles facing the farm.

She could help pick up the slack. And whatever Neil thought about her plan to produce an income from the space over her Muir Harbor store, she knew the idea had promise. She just needed to empty out the second floor, move all her supplies and extra inventory, start fixing the place up, and surely at some point, a more concrete vision for the space would come to her.

"You used to call your work art. Now you call it inventory."

As if beckoned by the echo of Neil's words, her brother's collie, Captain, came loping from the grove. The cluster of trees behind the marquee tent separated the house from the main farm grounds where the machine shed and barns and a smattering of other buildings gave way to the blueberry barrens that stretched into the distance. Captain reached her, his panted breaths filling her ear as she ruffled his fur before standing.

Maggie pulled her shawl closer around her shoulders. "I think it's safe to say your brother owes you one. And Sydney, too." She moved to Indi's side, reaching out to squeeze her arm. "I just hope this isn't too hard for you."

Decorating for one wedding, Maggie meant, with her own so recently called off.

But it wasn't so recently. Two whole months plus two days—that's how long it'd been since Ben walked out of her life.

Then again, Maggie and the rest of her family weren't necessarily entirely caught up on the timeline. Because, well, Indi hadn't necessarily entirely told them the full story. She hadn't even spilled the news of her broken engagement until early December, a full month after Ben had dumped her. She hadn't wanted to bring it up in those first days of Maggie's recovery. But the days had quickly turned into weeks and suddenly it'd been Thanksgiving and Neil had proposed to Sydney and of course she hadn't wanted to do anything to spoil their happiness and . . .

Okay, fine, she'd been a coward about the whole thing. When she did finally tell everyone, she'd been purposely vague about the details. So vague they all still thought the man they'd met the night of Maggie's heart attack was Ben.

Funny, considering that what little she knew of Philip B. West convinced her he was most likely Bennington Foster's opposite in just about every way. Ben had been all smoothness and pure flirtatious charm. She could admit to enjoying the lengths he'd gone to impress her in their short courtship —fancy dinners at nice restaurants, a horse-drawn carriage ride through one of Augusta's picturesque neighborhoods.

But could he name his favorite Narnia book?

Probably not.

Just like Philip, with his blushing and stammering, probably hadn't uttered a single flirty sentence in his life.

"You're smiling. That's a good sign, I guess."

Oh, right, Maggie. Who was worried preparations for Neil's wedding were taking a toll on her. "I'm really good, Maggie. More than good. I'm beyond happy for Neil and Syd."

Maggie slipped one arm free of her shawl and slid it around Indi's waist. "I just hope you know it's okay if you're not feeling great. It's okay if you're struggling with this."

It was this morning's conversation with Neil all over again. But she was better prepared for it tonight. Maybe it was the moonlight or the gentle breeze. Maybe it was the magic of the decorated backyard.

Probably it was the woman beside her. Everything kind and compassionate. *Alive.* Not just physically, but alive inside, too. They'd all noticed it since Maggie's surgery—the new lightness in her hazel eyes, the wider smiles. It was as if the heart attack had caused her to somehow shake off the weighty remnants of her painful past.

She didn't talk as much anymore about the search for her granddaughter, even though Indi knew Wilder's investigation was still ongoing. Lately, she didn't regularly walk to that stretch of seaside sand and rocks either, to the spot where it'd happened—the accident that had taken Diana Muir's life.

Indi had never really known what to make of Maggie's steadfast belief that her granddaughter was still out there somewhere. She studied Maggie's face now, looking for any signs that all the wedding preparations might have taken a toll on her. She'd ask, except she knew exactly what Maggie's response would be. *"I'm sixty-five, not one-hundred-and-five. Between my cardiac rehabilitation routine and all the annoyingly healthy food I've been eating, I'm probably in the best shape of my life. I can handle making a wedding cake, silly girl."*

"Are *you* struggling? I mean, with Neil flying the coop and all?"

Maggie laughed. "I don't think he's technically flying the coop. All he's doing is moving up a floor."

Yes, because he'd spent all of December turning the farmhouse attic into a gorgeous master suite with its own bathroom. Something he'd been able to afford thanks to an early wedding gift from Sydney's birth father.

Speaking of Neil, he'd probably be showing up here sometime soon. Wilder had insisted on throwing him a bachelor party—as if the two of them alone, hanging out on Wilder's houseboat and watching *Star Wars*, counted as a bachelor party—but Neil was sensible enough not to stay up late the night before his big day. She'd rather him not see the decorations until tomorrow.

She scratched Captain's ears then returned to the outlet. But before she could kneel, her phone vibrated in her pocket. She dug it out. Huh. Same number as this morning. Who would be calling her from Florida? She shrugged and let the screen go dark, then met Maggie's eyes under the glow of the backyard lights.

"Come in soon, all right, dear? It's getting colder."

She nodded, letting her gaze float over her handiwork once more as Maggie climbed the cement steps and let herself into the house. *Enchanting.* It really was. The lights, the crisp air tinged with a sea-salt brine, the moon. She'd hope for glittering stars tomorrow night. Snow would be even better.

She knelt beside the outlet and pulled the extension cord free, then blinked against the sudden veil of darkness as her phone dinged once more. A text this time. Probably Lil, working late as usual, asking if she needed to pick up any last-minute decorations or food supplies on her way home.

Or that same number again. The Florida one. Curious, she tapped the message open with one finger, cold air trekking down to her lungs as she inhaled.

Until, at the sight of the name in the first sentence, she stopped breathing altogether.

Hey, it's Trey. You didn't answer my calls so . . . I hope it's okay to text. Got this number from Lil. Can we talk sometime? Soon? It's important.

"Holland? You still awake?"

Philip stood outside his sister's bedroom door, the second floor of Grandfather's house as too-quiet as ever. He would've thought with a teenager in the place, there'd at least be some loud, thumping music every now and then. Maybe the drone of the TV.

But other than Holland's violin practice, this place echoed with silence.

The tray he balanced with one hand jostled as he rapped on her door again. "Holl? I brought a peace offering. Hot chocolate."

Punishing seconds stretched, long enough he eventually leaned against the wallpaper-covered wall, his sigh leaking into the hushed hallway, a line of closed doors blocking off unused rooms, save Grandfather's at one far end and his own at the other.

Not that the room he slept in each night had ever really felt like his. Certainly hadn't ever beckoned him back.

Finally, just when he was about to give up, the door inched open. He shifted, cocoa sloshing over the edges of both mugs. Holland eyed him through the crack in her door. "I'll take a mug and the Reddi-wip can."

"The idea was sort of that you'd let me in?" He shouldn't have said it like a question. At some point or another, he probably needed to start being firm with her. Putting his foot down. Right? "Can't let you hog the whipped cream."

"Fine."

She actually opened her door then. Stepped aside and gave him a look that said, *Coming in or what?*

"Gotta say, Holl, I really wish I'd known Reddi-wip was the key to your heart a little earlier."

Okay, so maybe expecting her to crack a smile was a little much. But she'd opened her door. She'd let him in. He'd take it.

He set the tray on the desk along one wall, handed her a mug that was somehow still steaming even after she'd kept him waiting in the hallway. He raised the can of whipped cream and lifted his eyebrow. At her nod, he squirted a generous helping into a swirl.

"Thanks." She moved to her bed and sat, crossing her legs, her plaid pajama pants nearly blending into the colorful quilt he recognized as the one that used to cover Mom's bed.

Made him think of that blanket Indi Muir had worn around the farmhouse yard that day last fall. The one she'd tripped over and dragged along the browning grass.

Now *there* was a place that beckoned him back. That charming farm. The little town nearby. He'd driven through Muir Harbor on his way back to Augusta that November morning, past the line of docks at the pier, through the quaint downtown. It's how he'd learned Indi had another store in her hometown.

He topped off his own mug with a squirt of whipped

cream, then lowered into the swivel chair at her desk and glanced around the room. It was very . . . minimalist. White walls, white curtains, white rug. At least the quilt provided some color. And the blue lampshade on her bedside stand.

His focus scooted down to the framed photo perched next to the lamp. A selfie—Mom and Holland, all smiles despite the tube in Mom's nose and a scarf hiding her bald head.

He took a drink of his hot chocolate, not caring if it burned his throat. *You came in here for a reason. Talk to her.* "Holland—"

"Look, I get that you're probably weirded out that I was with a guy tonight. But I swear to you, it was no big deal. If I hadn't been in such a bad mood, I never would've gone along with him."

She hadn't said so many words to him at once in months. "Um, I was just going to ask if you like the cocoa."

"Oh." She took a sip. "You used a packet of powdered hot chocolate and water."

"Well, yeah. That's how you make it."

"The pros melt actual chocolate and use hot milk and nutmeg and stuff. And real whipped cream." Her hair had dried into strands that framed her face, only the slightest wave. Not like the ringlets she'd had as a toddler. No more chubby cheeks either. A light sprinkling of freckles covered her nose and high cheekbones.

He couldn't help another glance at the photo, an old memory resurrecting from an abandoned place in the back of his mind. Sitting on a couch that belonged in the seventies with its orange-and-yellow-striped pattern. Dad setting a tray on the coffee table. Three mugs. A Disney movie on the TV.

An old Sunday night tradition that died when Dad did. "Did Mom make it that way for you?"

Holland eyed him over the rim of her mug, took a long swallow, then set the cup on her bedside stand, blocking the photo. She moved farther back on her mattress and crossed her legs. "You don't have to do this. You don't have to try to, I don't know, connect with me or whatever. Nothing happened tonight. Nothing. I promise."

He cupped his hands around his mug. "You broke into a rec center. I wouldn't exactly call that nothing."

"If you need to ground me or something, even though I'm your half sister, not your kid, fine, go for it. I'll take it. I won't argue. Then can we talk about me going to live with my dad? Please?"

He forced himself not to sputter as he swallowed. "Why were you in a bad mood tonight?"

"I don't want to—"

"I'm not trying to connect with you. I just want an explanation. I think I deserve it after getting a call from the police that about gave me an aneurysm."

She grabbed her pillow from the end of her bed and hugged it to her torso. Didn't say a word.

He'd made it this far. He could wait her out.

She sighed, flopping back against the wall behind her bed. "Mom pretty much begged me to audition for the orchestra last year. I wasn't going to do it. She was sick and . . . I didn't want to spend all that time in rehearsals when . . ."

Oh, Holland. He could feel his heart lurch against his rib cage, his own grief battling with sorrow at the thought of what Holland must've been feeling tonight.

And she'd been so alone in it. He hadn't known. Just like he hadn't known what Mom and Holland had been dealing with for months before Mom had finally called. *God, I don't know how to do this. I don't know what she needs.*

"Holland—"

"There's no point in talking about this. Like I said, if you want to punish me, just do it."

Frustration simmered in his stomach, souring the hot

liquid he'd swallowed, burning until he couldn't help himself any longer. He set his mug on the tray and stood. "I'm not going to punish you."

"What?"

He crossed the room and opened Holland's closet, hoping he'd find—yes. He pulled a duffel bag from her top shelf.

"So privacy isn't a thing around here anymore?" She jumped off her bed. "You're scrounging around my closet now?"

He dropped the bag at the foot of her bed. Her forehead wrinkled as her gaze wrenched from the bag to him.

"Pack enough for two weeks. If the duffel's not enough, I'm pretty sure there's extra suitcases in the hallway closet."

"What? Are you crazy? Wait . . . did you already call my dad? Am I going to—"

"You're not going to Texas."

"Then where—"

"I don't know where we're going, but you and I, we're getting out of here. I don't have any J-term classes and you can do schoolwork anywhere, so we're going . . ." He plucked her half-emptied mug from her bedside stand. "Somewhere."

"You're freaking me out right now."

"Consider it payback for freaking me out earlier."

"I'm not packing a bag."

"Fine. We'll get whatever you need when we get there."

"Get. Where?"

"I already said, I don't . . ." His words trailed as the answer found him just that quick. So simple. So obvious. They wouldn't even need plane tickets.

Hadn't he wanted to return to Muir Harbor every single day since that windy morning in November? Hadn't he just minutes ago been thinking about the place for the second time tonight? Hadn't he asked himself a dozen times why he'd felt something there he'd never once felt here?

Peace.

He'd felt peace. Maybe even hope. Didn't know why, he just had. And wasn't that exactly what he was desperate to give Holland? Some semblance of hope to heal the grief he knew was lurking somewhere underneath the hard shell she tried so hard to keep in place.

"Just give me two weeks, Holl. We'll get out of here. We'll spend some time together. We'll be . . . a family. Can you just try? Can you give me that much?" Because in return, he'd give her everything, if he could. Anything to bridge this gap between them.

You're the only family I have left, Holland.

Not exactly true. There was still the brooding man downstairs. But Grandfather had pushed Philip away long ago. *Sorry, Tab. Even if I wanted to ghostwrite the man's book, he clearly doesn't want me in his life.*

Holland propped her hands on her waist. "And if I cooperate with this crazy plan of yours, if I give you two weeks, then what?"

He took a breath and used the only bargaining chip he had. "We'll contact your dad after the two weeks are up. If that's still what you want."

6

"*T*here you are, Indi Muir. I hear you're responsible for all of this."

Indi halted only a few steps inside the marquee tent, the unzipped doorway behind her letting in a flurry of cool air and a tumbling knot of gnarled leaves as Cecil Atwater, long-time editor of the *Muir Harbor Gazette*, flagged her down.

Voices and laughter and music pealed through the tent, flecks of twinkling light and flickering candles draping everything in a festive glimmer. And outside, winter's twilight was a chorus of pastels lilting in and around a swell of pillowy clouds. Between the ceremony at the church in town and the happiness filling the tent now, the hum of the portable heaters a perfect backdrop, Neil's wedding could only be categorized as perfect.

If only Indi could bring herself to enjoy any of it.

No, that wasn't true. She'd enjoyed watching her big brother blink back tears as he'd recited his vows an hour ago. She'd enjoyed the look of pure delight on both his and Sydney's faces when they'd gotten their first peeks at the whimsical backyard scene.

And maybe she'd enjoy the rest of the night, too, if she could make herself forget about the phone she'd left up in her bedroom. The text from Trey. The one she'd never answered.

The one she never would've received at all if Lilian, apparently, hadn't given him the number. All day she'd been waiting for the opportunity to confront her sister and ask her what in the world had possessed her to pass on contact information to a man Indi had honestly thought she'd never see again.

But pinning Lilian down had been next to impossible. Lilian had appointed herself Neil and Sydney's wedding coordinator and, thus, had been a roadrunner all day. The longest she'd stood in one place was up at the front of the church beside Indi. But Indi could hardly confront her there.

Which meant she'd have to confront her here. If she could just manage to find her. Well, and sidestep Cecil. But the longtime newspaperman had his usual notebook in hand as he reached her.

"Don't tell me you're working tonight, Mr. Atwater."

Cecil chuckled. "I'm afraid weddings are front-page, above-the-fold news around these parts, as you well know."

Indi reached for a glass of champagne from the dessert table, her hands plenty warm thanks not only to the heaters huffing away in all four corners of the tent, but also the thick, black fingerless gloves that matched the leggings and fur-lined boots she wore under her navy blue bridesmaid dress. She'd needed a splash of color to make up for the subdued hues, so earlier, when she'd traded her heels for the boots in between the wedding and the reception, she'd also added a mustard-colored scarf made of chunky yarn.

Come to think of it, maybe that's where Lilian was—back at the house adding a warmer layer.

"Can you confirm a few facts for me?" Cecil plucked a

pencil from behind his ear. "You're responsible for tonight's décor?"

"Uh, well, yes—"

"You must've spent hours on the centerpieces. Where'd you get all the mason jars?"

Each centerpiece was its own creation, a mix of jars and floating tea lights surrounded by clusters of evergreen and sparkling fake snow Indi had meticulously applied. "Um, we kind of have a big supply around here. You know, with all the jams and jellies Maggie makes."

"Can I quote you on that?"

On Muir Farm's supply of mason jars? Poor Cecil really was scraping the bottom of the barrel. "Sure, I guess."

"And, say, I've been thinking about doing another article on the old missing Muir granddaughter case. Now that everyone knows Sydney isn't Maggie's granddaughter, I assume the investigation is back to square one?"

Questions about jars and decorations, she could handle. But kind as Cecil was, much as he and his newspaper were a fixture in this town, their whole family had tired of seeing the Muir name in headlines through the years. "Actually, Cecil—"

"Oh, hold on a sec." Cecil waved at someone behind her. "Peyton, come over here. Indi, you haven't met my nephew yet, have you? I finally convinced him to move up from Georgia in the fall."

A man who looked to be in his mid-thirties moved to Cecil's side. He held a camera and wore a warm grin nearly identical to Cecil's. Between his sandy blond hair parted at the side and his blazer and bow tie, he had a debonair look to him. And maybe a familiar look, too.

"Indi Muir, meet Peyton. Peyton, meet Indi."

"Ah, another Muir." The man held out his free hand. "Sister to the groom, yes? I met the other one a minute ago."

Lil? Good, that meant she was around here somewhere.

"Nice to meet you. Although, I think maybe we've met before. You used to visit Cecil in the summers, didn't you?"

Peyton's brown eyes brightened. "You remember?"

"Visitors stand out in Muir Harbor. But also, I remember that." She pointed to his bow tie. "You were the only kid I'd ever seen wear a bow tie to church."

Peyton laughed as Cecil spoke. "You do have a good memory. Yes, my sister, God rest her soul, used to send Peyton up to visit me for a few weeks each summer."

Peyton's grin dimmed. "After she died, Dad wasn't inclined to send me as often."

"But we stayed in touch." Cecil pushed his glasses up again. "And now he's the official *Gazette* photographer. I can no longer claim the newspaper is a one-man operation. Imagine that. Anyhow, I'm glad you've met both Muir sisters, my boy. I do believe both are single so—"

"Indi, can I steal you away for a second?"

Indi could hug her new sister-in-law. She spun toward Sydney, but not before catching Peyton's apologetic nod and half-smile. "Yes, please. Nice chatting, Cecil," she said over her shoulder. "Peyton, nice to meet you." Only when they'd moved away did she lean closer to Sydney. "Whatever you need, I'm grateful for your timing. I think you just saved me from a matchmaking attempt." Not to mention, Cecil's probing questions.

"Really?" Sydney glanced behind them. "The guy with the bow tie?"

"Don't look!"

"Oh, he's pretty handsome. He's no Neil, but then, who is? Hmm, he's got a camera. Which probably means he's artsy and creative and that should totally be your type, shouldn't it? Or is it too soon to be talking about your type? You know, after stupid Ben took a hike."

Indi did hug her new sister-in-law then.

"What was that for?"

"For not tiptoeing around things. Now what did you need?"

"Only to say thank you. For all of this." Sydney swept her hand in front of her, the sparkle of a diamond ring—once Maggie's—nearly a perfect match for the glimmer in her eyes. Her red waves were gathered to one side, spilling over her shoulder and painted with brushes of gold from the lights overhead. Since the ceremony, she'd added a white faux fur cape over her stunning dress, complete with a fluffy hood hanging loose behind her. "Much as I loved the idea of a wintry backyard reception, I couldn't really picture it. But this . . . it's just beautiful."

"*You're* beautiful. Neil couldn't take his eyes off you the entire ceremony."

"That's kind of expected on the groom's part, isn't it? It would've been weird if he'd been looking at anyone else, yeah? Except for the pastor maybe."

"Take the compliment, Syd." The hem of Indi's dress fluttered around her knees as a boisterous laugh sounded from across the tent. Her gaze followed the sound, landing on Tatum Carter, Sydney's grandfather, sitting next to Maggie on a piano bench at the end of one table.

Was it really only last fall their families had become linked through the discovery that Sydney was a Carter? As in Carter Farms, largest blueberry farm in the region. Tatum Carter owned half the land from here to Augusta, had actually been gunning to buy Muir Farm for a while. Both Maggie and Neil had turned him down flat.

But considering how he was laughing with Maggie now, all that must be water under the bridge.

"I can't believe it sometimes." Sydney's attention had flitted to her grandfather and Maggie, too. "I came to Maine on the crazy hope of finding just one family member.

Instead, I got not one family, but two—and a husband, to boot."

"I think said husband is looking for you." Indi pointed to where Neil was finishing off a piece of cake, his impatient gaze scouring the tent while well-wishing townspeople crowded around him.

Sydney chuckled. "That man really can't stand being the center of attention. Excuse me, but it appears I need to go save my favorite Scot."

Indi gulped a drink of her champagne as Sydney moved away, the bubbles burning the back of her throat just as she spotted it—a flash of blue satin. *Finally.* Lil, in a bridesmaid dress that matched Indi's, moving across the tent at a clipped pace.

Not just moving. Skulking, her heels poking into the soft ground as she carried . . . a pair of old boots? Her short hair bounced around her chin, framing the scowl on her face.

Indi abandoned her champagne flute and started after Lilian, a slow, wry smile finding its way to her face as she realized where Lilian was headed. Toward Wilder—who else? —sitting at a middle table, relaxed and chatting and right in the path of Lilian's ire. What had the man done to raise her sister's hackles now?

Wilder's face split into a grin when he saw Lilian coming, dark eyes sparking. Twenty years the guy had been hanging around Muir Farm, practically an honorary member of the family, and not once had he seemed put off by Lilian's dislike of him.

"Evening, Miss Muir," he drawled as Lilian reached him. "Nice party."

"Wilder Monroe, my bedroom is and always has been off-limits to you."

Indi halted mere feet behind Lilian, surprise choking the laugh that gurgled in her throat.

Wilder held up one hand. "Now, Lil—"

"Don't *Now, Lil* me. Neil and Maggie and everyone else might not care if you go roaming around our house, conveniently and constantly stopping by right at mealtimes, staying in our guest room or on the couch when your dumb houseboat can't handle a little thunderstorm—"

"I love my dumb houseboat, thank you very much."

"—but my room is not open territory."

Wilder's grin only widened. "I'm perfectly aware of that."

"Then would you mind telling me why I found *your* dirty old boots sitting by *my* bed?" She thrust them at his chest.

Wilder rose from his seat, straightening to his full height at least a half-foot taller than Lilian. "I don't mind telling you at all. They're my father's old boots. I happen to be a little attached to them." He spoke with embellished patience. "But as I'm sure you can tell, they're beat up and Neil told me one time you were able to work some magic with an old pair of his—something about stitching in a new sole. He offered your services. I expect he's the one who put them in your room."

Was it just Indi's imagination or did her sister seem to shrink some? She tucked a piece of golden blond hair behind her ear. "Oh."

"Now if you'll excuse me, I'd like to try a piece of Maggie's cake." He looked past Lilian. "Oh, hey, Indi. Good job on the decorations."

Lilian glanced over her shoulder, her gaze connecting with Indi's.

Don't laugh. Don't you dare laugh or she'll kill you.

Or maybe not, because her sister's sharp glare was already pinned once more on Wilder's retreating back. "I really can't stand that man."

Indi scooted to her sister's side. "I think everyone's aware of that fact at this point."

"I was that loud?"

"It's not so much the volume as the daggers in your eyes."

Lilian huffed and set the boots on a nearby chair. "He just expects me to play cobbler, does he? I should toss those filthy things in the Atlantic."

No, not even Lilian would do something that cruel. They were all aware of how much Wilder still missed his dad, even three years after his death. Lilian would rant and rave at the man in person, but she'd most likely have the boots mended by Monday.

"So . . . when were you going to tell me you talked to Trey?"

Lilian turned—slowly—to face her. "Oh. He called you, then?"

"And texted."

The text played over in her mind again, just as it had a thousand times since last night. *Can we talk sometime? Soon? It's important.* What could they possibly have to talk about after all this time?

Only one thing came to mind. And she couldn't talk to him about that. About . . . her.

Lilian shifted her weight from one heel to the other. "I'm sorry I didn't tell you—"

"I don't want an apology. I want an explanation."

"He's the one you need to talk to. Not me."

She could see it—Lilian's walls going up. This was her lawyer's stance, a frustratingly impenetrable position that was equal parts offense and defense. "So you know why he's trying to get ahold of me?"

Lilian sighed. "Please, just—"

"Eleven years, Lil. I've spent eleven years trying not to think about him. Trying not to think about . . ." All she'd given up. Letting go of Trey had been one thing, the right thing. But the rest of it had left a yawning chasm inside of her. Even now, after all these years, the longing hadn't gone away. Or the pain. The regret.

No. *No.* She couldn't do this now. She should've waited to talk to Lil about it. Or better yet, she should've deleted Trey's text and pretended she'd never seen it.

Her runaway thoughts slowed and disappeared as her sights landed on a tall man ducking through the tent's zippered opening. The low lighting partially shadowed him, but not so much she couldn't make out his height, his dark hair, a hint of silver at the temples.

It can't be . . .

She blinked once, twice. And then he shifted just slightly and the waning light of dusk reached in from outside and caught in his gray eyes.

Philip.

———◆———◆———

Philip knew the moment Indi Muir spotted him. He felt her gaze and read her shock and he *knew.*

This had been a mistake. Showing up here—in her town, at her house, crashing a wedding reception—definitely not the kind of thing a sane person would do.

A sane person would've stayed back at the sole available hotel room Muir Harbor had to offer, never mind the way Holland had flopped onto the only bed the second they walked in the room, started flipping channels until she found one of her beloved home renovation shows, content to ignore him just as she had on the drive down to Muir Harbor.

A sane person would've been able to talk her into taking a walk around the quaint downtown or out to the harbor instead of making a promise to track down some fast food, Holland's *"Don't hurry back"* all but pushing him out the door.

And if, in his search for food, a sane person had happened to see a wedding party spilling out of a church, had happened to recognize Indi and her siblings in the group, he might've settled for waving. You know, instead of making three right turns and letting his Honda fall into the line of cars making their way out to the farm. Not that he'd known this was where they were all headed but—

Okay, seriously, a sane person definitely wouldn't just stand here staring at Indi.

A sane person . . . would flee.

He jerked around, pushing through the tent's wind-whipped canvas door, blindly letting his feet carry him across the backyard.

"Philip!" Indi's voice pummeled him from behind.

He veered toward the house, pathetically and ridiculously desperate to be out of her sight. *Running. You're actually running away from her. Pathetic.* His breath feathered white in front of him and he slowed. He gulped in a swath of cold air and halted completely, bending over his knees as a pair of boots stomped past him and stopped in front of him, blocking his path.

"It *is* you."

He straightened in time to see Indi's hands flying to her waist, a breeze rife with the brackish scent of the sea lifting her curls and tugging at the edges of her scarf.

"What in heaven's name are you doing here?"

Wow, he'd remembered her eyes were green. But he hadn't noticed last time he was here just *how* green. Even in the shadows of sunset, they shone a liquid, luminous emerald.

An emerald that sparked with vexation.

He was never, ever listening to Connor again.

Connor only said to take a trip. He never specified Muir Harbor. And he certainly hadn't suggested waltzing on out to Muir Farm as if he belonged here or something.

Fine, that part had been Philip's own little bit of brilliance. "S-sorry to just show up like this but—"

"Indi, why'd you take off?"

Philip didn't have time to place the female voice coming around the side of the tent—Indi's sister, maybe?—not with Indi reacting first, pure panic in her eyes. She grabbed ahold of the front of his coat and hauled him to a door at the back of the farmhouse. She yanked on his arm and towed him inside.

Ah, thank the Lord for warmth. It curled around him as he stumbled inside, and oh, he hadn't seen this room last time he was here. The kitchen—walls a buttery yellow, white cupboards wrapping around the room, and a collection of plants crowding the window over the sink. It smelled like a bakery. Or like . . . like Christmas. Like the kinds of holidays he'd once had back when Dad was alive. Before he and Mom had gone to live with Grandfather.

From the kitchen, Indi led him into a long, narrow dining room, an old oak table taking up most of the space and an antique hutch spanning almost an entire wall. Through an arched opening, he caught a glimpse of the living room where he'd slept the last time he was here. Hey, they still had a Christmas tree up.

Not one year of living in Grandfather's house had they had a tree. Until this past year, that is. He'd put one up for Holland's sake. Not that it seemed to matter to her.

"Why are you here?" Indi hissed, poking one finger at his chest.

Right, focus. "Well . . . I . . . y-you see—" He cleared his throat. "T-that is—"

"Great, we're back to the same Philip from the wardrobe who couldn't get a full sentence out if his life depended on it."

And there was another thing he hadn't noticed last time he was here—how uncannily charming Indi Muir was when she was frazzled. Or fine, maybe he had noticed it, but she'd been in crisis mode then, fresh off a broken engagement, and it wouldn't have been proper to acknowledge it.

Probably wasn't proper now, either. But a man could only overlook so much for so long. She was pretty and she was charming and she was . . . glaring at him.

"Maybe if you wouldn't interrupt me, I could get a full sentence out." He stepped backward, bumping into the dining room table.

Her grimace only deepened. Indi had called his smile handsome two months ago, but gosh, if his smile was half as magnetic as her frown, then he should've had women throwing themselves at his feet his entire life, shy and bookish or not.

Indi yanked her scarf away from her neck. "Fine. No more interruptions. Take as many full sentences as you need to tell me what the heck you're doing here."

"O-okay. The thing is . . . I . . ." *For Pete's sake, spit it out.* "I just want you to know I'm not completely nuts." Wait. Not what he'd meant to say. And yet, at the utter disbelief on Indi's face, he had to defend himself. "I know you saw me hide in a wardrobe when we first met. And I eavesdropped on your breakup. Now I'm here again, totally out of the blue, and I just ran away from you—"

"Not really helping your case here."

"But I'm generally a very normal, typically very boring person." He was making a wreck of this. But how was he supposed to explain his presence here in a way that made any kind of sense at all? Especially with a charming and flustered Indi Muir staring him down?

Wait a second, why *was* she so flustered? Yes, his showing up here was peculiar, but why had she looked so alarmed a minute ago? "Indi?" He peered at her until the pieces started arranging themselves. "Does your family still think . . . do they not know . . ."

The sound of the kitchen's screen door slapping against its frame cut in.

Apprehension took over Indi's face all over again. This time, she grabbed his hand and lunged for the staircase at the front of the house, garland wrapped around the banister, and what else could he do but barrel up the steps after her?

"You shouldn't be here, Philip," she whisper-barked at the top and dropped his hand.

He glanced behind her—narrow hallway, beige walls with a lilac-print wallpaper border at the top, a line of closed doors.

No, not all closed. The second one was open a few inches.

He looked back to Indi. "Why shouldn't I be here? Did you never tell your family who I am?"

Gone was the irritation in her green eyes. In its place was a chagrin that tugged on his amusement.

"So they still think I'm the buffoon. And if they see me they'll assume we're . . . what? Together?"

She pulled a clip from behind her head and let her hair fall around her shoulders. "No, I told them the engagement was over. I just . . ." She winced. "Left out a few details."

"Kind of important ones." Voices drifted from down below.

"Well, excuse me, Philip, but I didn't think we'd be seeing you again. I didn't exactly expect you to show up here tonight. And I'm still waiting to hear why you're—"

She was interrupted by the creaking of a bedroom door, the one already open. Indi whirled around at the exact moment a figure dressed in black sprinted from the room. Indi's gasp filled the small hallway.

Philip didn't have more than a second to think before the

charging form knocked into him, shoving him into the wall. Indi's voice rang out. "Stop—who—why were you in my—?"

Philip lunged after the intruder but he was too late. The man surged past Indi. She managed to grab hold of his arm, but instead of slowing, the man jerked, pulling Indi after him as he tore down the steps, wrenching away in time to race ahead and out the front door.

While Indi tumbled the rest of the way down the staircase, landing in a clump at the bottom.

*C*haos erupted around Indi—frantic voices and flashes of movement, a sharp wind gushing through the front door, banging it against the wall.

And thumping footsteps that had to belong to Philip. He reached Indi's side at the same moment as she attempted to sit up.

"Wait." He touched her arm. "Don't move too much until you're sure nothing's broken."

Oh goodness, she could hear the echoes of every bump of her fall and she could taste blood. She must've bit her tongue. But broken bones? No, she'd be feeling much more than some indistinct throbbing right now if that were the case. "I think I'm okay."

"Indi, what on earth happened?"

She looked up into frightened hazel eyes. *Maggie.* Had she seen the whole thing? Probably. She'd heard Maggie's voice drifting up from downstairs just before the man in black had raced from her room.

My bedroom. Someone was in my bedroom.

More hurried steps sounded, clattering through the house.

"Maggie? Indi? What's going on?" Lilian appeared, and just behind her, Wilder.

Indi opened her mouth, but Philip spoke first, his tone calm and precise. "Someone was upstairs in one of the rooms. He pushed me aside and then . . ." Apology brimmed in his stormy gray eyes as he motioned to the open front door.

Wilder spared Philip only the briefest glance before springing across the entryway and out the door.

"Are you hurt, dear?" Maggie moved close, her wide eyes darting between Indi and Philip. Did she recognize Philip? Did she remember those brief seconds in the hospital when she'd opened her eyes to see him?

"I'm fine."

At Maggie's side, Lilian folded her arms, her narrowed gaze zeroed in on Philip.

Not that he noticed. His fingers still rested around Indi's elbow, his scrutiny a mix of gentle and firm as she squirmed. "You fell down half a flight of stairs. Take a second before moving."

"We had a prowler in the house. We shouldn't just be sitting here. We should be helping Wilder look. Plus, there's still a reception going on." She scrambled upward. Or tried to, but she faltered the moment she put weight on her ankle, her wince betraying her.

In an instant, Philip was on his feet, one arm circling her waist. "Stubborn woman, you *are* hurt."

"I'm not hurt and I'm not stubborn and—" Her ankle buckled as she attempted to pull away from Philip and she couldn't help another flinch.

His arm around her held steady. "It's your right one, isn't it? We need to get your boot off. Get some ice on your ankle. It could be sprained."

"I've had a sprained ankle before, Phi—" She clamped her lips together, her eyes shooting to Maggie and Lilian, a remembrance that started out rickety, due to the fall, no doubt, slowly solidifying until her heart began racing all over again. She couldn't call him Philip. Because they didn't know this man as Philip West.

To Lilian—and Maggie, if she remembered him from the hospital—this was still Bennington Foster. Which explained the death glare. Lilian thought she was staring down the guy who'd dumped her sister. Oh for pity's sake, how could this night possibly be any worse?

You could've actually broken your ankle. That would've been worse. Or she could've been knocked unconscious, she supposed. Philip could've ended up in a physical altercation with that man in black, and that wouldn't have been good because something told her he wasn't the brawling type.

Though that was some solid strength bracing her against him just now. And why did he smell so good? It was annoying.

His fingers brushed her shoulder. "Come on, let's get you sitting down and your ankle elevated."

"It's *fine*. Trust me, I know what a sprained ankle feels like and this isn't it." She'd probably only bruised it on a stair.

"Well, I know what a person in pain looks like, so could you just humor me, Indi?" He gave a huff of exasperation, but if she wasn't mistaken, there was a shimmer of amusement in the man's eyes.

Really? At a time like this? And why wasn't he stammering anymore? "I'll sit when you tell me what you're doing here."

The man had the audacity to chuckle, but before he could reply, Maggie stepped up and patted Indi's arm, the one not currently ensconced under Philip's shoulder. "Dear, I think you should listen to your . . . ex?"

So Maggie did remember him. One corner of Philip's mouth lifted now. "Yes, Indi. You should listen to your ex." The other corner quirked.

She was going to throttle him. She was going to interrogate him until he told her what he was doing here, demand an explanation for where his stammering had gone, and then throttle him.

Just as soon as she was sure she could walk

Maggie squeezed her arm. "I'll go get an ice pack from the kitchen. We'll get you settled and then you need to tell us exactly what happened." She looked up at Philip. "Can you get her to the living room?"

"I can get myself to the living room."

Philip ignored her entirely. "Sure. I can do that."

Maggie didn't turn to the kitchen just yet. "It's so nice to meet you, Ben. Again, that is. I have a vague memory of you being in my hospital room. That did happen, yes?"

"Uh, yes. You . . . you said I looked like someone. Robert."

"I did? Well, you do. It's those gray eyes. Robert was my fiancé decades ago. I've never met anyone with eyes like his. Not until you." Maggie gave him a soft smile, before turning one more look of concern on Indi. "I'll be right back with that ice pack."

As soon as Maggie turned, Philip leaned down. "I'd ask if you can walk, but I don't really trust you to answer honestly."

Whatever retort was on the tip of her tongue melted the moment he swept her into his arms and crossed the entryway.

"Philip!" Her squeal drew a laugh from him, his chest rumbling against her, as he carried her into the living room. "Put me down."

"I'm going to. As soon as I get to the couch. Or do you prefer one of the chairs?"

"I prefer that you stop manhandling me." There was that irritatingly good smell again. Like coconut and some kind of sandalwood or teakwood or . . . something. How was she supposed to know one masculine wood scent from another?

She just knew it was confounding. And unnerving, too. Almost as unnerving as . . .

As the shock on Lilian's face as she stared at Indi over Philip's shoulder. *Oh dear.* Oh dear, had she just—

Philip lowered her to the couch, bending his head to her ear, clearly aware of her near-panic. His voice was low and close. Too close. "Yep, you just called me Philip in front of your sister. But don't worry. I'm going to come to your rescue again and I won't even have to lie to do it." He straightened and turned to her sister. "My first name's Philip. Middle name's Ben. I'm pretty easygoing as far as which one I go by."

He dropped onto the couch beside her and patted her knee, then started untying her boot.

And she couldn't decide whether to elbow his side or breathe a sigh of relief at the lack of follow-up questions from Lilian. The only saving grace, surely, was the fact that they had much bigger things to deal with at the moment.

Philip B. West. B for Ben. Of all the blasted coincidences.

"I should call the police." Lilian pulled out her phone and lowered to the arm of a chair. "Unless—are you sure it wasn't just one of the party guests? Maybe someone wandered up there looking for the bathroom."

"He was in my room." She let Philip pull her boot free.

"And he practically flung her down the stairs." There was an edge to Philip's voice.

"Wasn't just Indi's room," Neil said, halfway down the staircase, visible through the opening to the entryway. "Someone went through my room and Lilian's too."

Since when had Neil come in the house? He must've run upstairs while Philip had lugged her in here. Had he been hovering behind Maggie and Lilian before? If so, she couldn't believe he hadn't shoved his way to her and gone into instant overprotective brother mode the second she landed in a heap.

He probably saw Philip get to me first. Just like they all had.

Just like they'd all seen him pick her up and carry her in here. She didn't even want to know what they must be thinking about why he was here.

A groan escaped her lips as she took off her other boot.

Philip's palm dropped to her knee. "Your ankle? Or did you hurt something else?"

"It's not that." Her ankle hurt, sure, but it wasn't that bad. The truth—she had to tell her family the truth. Set them straight on Philip's identity before they started asking her if she was getting back together with this man she'd never been with in the first place.

But Wilder burst in before she could utter a word, and Maggie wasn't far behind, a bag of frozen corn in her hand. "I couldn't find an ice pack," she said. "But I think this'll do."

Breathing hard, Wilder flopped into the same chair where Lilian perched. She scowled and moved from its arm to the recliner next to him. "He's long gone," Wilder panted. "A car was racing down the lane by the time I got outside. My jeep is blocked in, so I couldn't have gone after him if I wanted to." He cast a look around the room, his iron gaze heavy with meaning. "Gray sedan."

Lilian gave a sharp inhale. What, did a gray sedan mean something to her? And why had Neil crossed his arms the moment the words were out of Wilder's mouth?

For once, when Lilian looked at Wilder, it wasn't irritation in her ice-blue eyes but wary understanding. "You think it's happening again, don't you?"

Happening again? "What's happening again?" And why did Maggie wear the same look of . . . *knowing* as the rest of them?

Neil leaned against Lilian's chair, expelling a sigh of resignation as his eyes found Indi's. "Back in October, Lil and I started noticing some strange things happening around here. A gray car idling in our driveway one night. Footprints in the yard that didn't belong to any of us. And then someone made a mess of my treehouse."

His treehouse? Who outside of the family would've even known that place existed? It was tucked away in a grove at the edge of a far field. And as for footprints, that wasn't that weird. The farm had visitors all the time.

"Someone had a heyday in the machine shed just after Thanksgiving, too," Neil added.

Lilian leaned forward. "But then nothing happened in December and we thought it was over."

We. As in, everyone in this room. Except for Philip. Except for her. "Why didn't I know about this?"

"We weren't trying to be secretive." Lilian laced her fingers over her knees. "You just . . . you weren't here very much in the fall. We knew you had a lot going on—juggling the stores, getting engaged, and then, um . . ." She glanced to Philip.

And then getting un-engaged.

At Indi's jerk, the bag of corn slipped from her ankle and landed on the coffee table. She tried to rein in her runaway frustration but it was impossible with everyone now staring at her. With Philip sitting next to her. With that pang in her back and her wrist throbbing.

Okay, so maybe she was a little more injured than she'd realized. Tears pricked her eyes.

"Indi." Philip's voice was low.

"I'm fine," she whispered.

"You're lying."

The couch cushion seemed to swallow her, her bleary gaze trekking from face to face, some masochistic need to confirm they'd all known about this. They'd all chosen not to fill her in.

Because once again, her life had been a mess.

And, oh, she knew that's not what she should be upset about right now. She should be upset that someone had invaded their home tonight. She should be upset that someone, very possibly the same person, had been trespassing on their property repeatedly.

Wilder stood. "Neil, you should get back to Sydney and all the guests out back. I'm going to go take a look around upstairs, but someone needs to call the police. I got pics of the tire tracks, so at least there's that. Wish I'd gotten a look at the license plate, but there was too much dust kicking up."

"I'll call," Lilian said as Wilder disappeared up the staircase, her eyes darting between Indi and Philip. "Hope you were planning to stick around for a while, Ben. You two are the main eyewitnesses so—"

"He's not Ben." The words slipped out, low, almost dark. Probably because of the vibrating soreness in her ankle. The leftover shock of plummeting down the stairs.

They all knew. They purposely didn't tell me . . .

Wilder's footsteps thumped overhead.

Lilian held her phone in midair. "What did you just say?"

"He's not Ben. His name's Philip—"

"I heard the explanation already. It's Philip Ben—"

"No, he's not. I mean, yes, that's his name." Frustration, humiliation, guilt—all of it thudded through her at once. "He's not Ben. He's not the man I was going to marry."

"But he came to the hospital with you. He slept on our couch. You told us—"

"I never said he was Ben. I just . . . never corrected you when you assumed he was."

Her sister's jaw dropped, and for all Indi knew, Maggie and Neil's faces mirrored Lil's. But Indi didn't look around to find out. Abruptly, she shoved her boots back on and stood.

"Indi, your ankle—"

She was moving before Philip could finish his sentence— out of the room, out of the house.

"Indi, wait."

Philip pushed through the farmhouse's door, his steps rattling the porch's weathered boards. Indi was already limping toward the outcropping of gray-brown rocks that traced the coast out front. How could she move so fast with an injured ankle?

The night air coiled around him as he clambered down the porch steps and rushed after her, the wind carrying the faint strains of music from the backyard reception, along with an icy-cold that tunneled down the collar of his jacket.

Indi wasn't wearing a coat at all, just like that morning he'd found her asleep on an Adirondack chair. But it was at least twenty degrees cooler tonight than it'd been then.

"Indi!"

She picked her way across the uneven shoreline, her fur-lined boots not fit for such rocky ground. With a groan, he tugged his phone from his pocket and tapped out a text to Holland. He'd been gone over an hour now, hadn't he? *Sorry it's taking me so long. Everything okay? Be back soon.*

He hurried to catch up to Indi, releasing a huff as his fingers finally brushed her arm.

"Indi, your ankle—"

She whirled to face him, her dress whipping in the wind. "Why are you here, Philip? In my town, at my house—why?" She swiped one hand over her eyes, then hugged her arms to herself.

And he had to fight the urge to steady her with his palms. The same rugged gusts driving deep-blue waters against craggy rocks mere feet away seemed as if they could knock Indi over with ease. Yet, she stood her ground, her frown hardening as she awaited an explanation he didn't know how to give.

He'd thought about this last night, after leaving Holland's bedroom and loading up his suitcase. He'd lain in bed and considered the possibility of running into Indi in Muir Harbor and rehearsed what he might say to her. But any words he'd thought of then were now entirely adrift at sea.

Or merely lost to the chaos and confusion of the past ten minutes. Was this really what she wanted to talk about just now—why he was here instead of what had just happened? What she'd just learned? Watching her tumble down the stairs had been horrible enough, but seeing the way she'd sunk lower and lower into the couch as her family filled her in on all that had happened at the farm had almost been worse.

"Philip." Her teeth chattered around his name.

He shrugged off his jacket and slipped it around her shoulders, ignoring the growing impatience in her stare. "Can we at least sit? I know, I know, your ankle is fine, but indulge me."

She was the one to huff in irritation now, but she acquiesced, moving a few feet away and dropping onto a sandy patch of ground. She tipped her gaze to him. "Happy?"

He lowered beside her. "Delighted." Although if he'd known she was going to give in that easily, he would've suggested they go back to the house. Already his cheeks and nose felt like ice. And either he was imagining things or a few tiny flurries swirled in the air around them.

At least he'd worn a thick sweater tonight. He let himself look ahead, absorb the unending view stretching in front of him. A pale shaft of moonlight squeezed through the clouds, dancing over churning waves. His phone beeped and he glanced at Holland's reply.

I'm fine. Take your time. But get extra fries.

He sighed and pocketed his phone, Indi's edginess practically radiating next to him. "Sorry. That was my sister. Holland. She's why I'm here."

Indi slipped her arms into the sleeves of his coat with an expression that said *finally.* "Your sister."

"Half sister, actually. She's fifteen. I'm her legal guardian. And I'm, uh, not exactly killing it in the role."

"Oh, yes, when you were here before, you mentioned your mom . . ."

He nodded. "It's not been the easiest eight months. I thought maybe if we could get out of town, go somewhere, have some fun . . . I don't know. I just . . . I didn't know what else to do."

Indi was quiet for a moment. "Fifteen. That's so young. To lose a parent, I mean."

"I know." Just like he knew bringing Holland here was a long shot. It'd made sense in his head last night, though. Spend two weeks with Holland somewhere, anywhere that wasn't Grandfather's house, and maybe they could find their footing somehow.

Yet, Holland had brought up Bryce twice just in the one-hour drive to Muir Harbor. It'd been all he could do to give vague responses, sidestep the reality that if her father had had any interest in actually *being* a father, he wouldn't have walked out on her over a decade ago.

And then Mom wouldn't have needed to talk to a lawyer when she'd known she was dying. Wouldn't have had all the paperwork in order for Philip to step in as guardian.

Whitish-gold stars peeked through the eventide. And, yes, those *were* snowflakes. Sparse and small. Not enough to cover the ground.

Not enough.

"Coming here, it was a whim," he finally went on. "A last-ditch effort, I guess. But when I was here in November, there was just something about this place. I hardly even saw much of the town then, but it felt . . . I don't know . . . a little bewitching or something. And I know that sounds ridiculous but—"

"No, it doesn't." Indi tucked her hands into his coat pockets. "Muir Harbor's special. A little on the eccentric side, but special. And peaceful. It's a good place to rest."

Rest, that sounded nice. *God, I'm so . . . tired.*

Because these past eight months had been like trying to walk through layers of mud, the weight dragging his steps, coating his soul. Because he'd been awake half the night last night picturing Holland's bereft eyes. *"I'm sick of my whole life revolving around an instrument . . . I hate how much time I missed with . . ."*

Mom. It was the closest his sister had come to mentioning their mother in so long. The closest she'd come to giving him a glimpse into her pain. It was why he hadn't argued when she hadn't packed her violin. Maybe she needed to get away from her instrument in the same way he needed to get away from Grandfather's house.

"Where's Holland now?"

"Back at the hotel." Only one in town as far as he could tell. An old-looking building called The Lodge. "She's watching HGTV. She's obsessed with home reno shows. The hotel only had one open room, so we're sharing. Only one bed, too, so I guess I'll be getting cozy on the floor tonight. Anyway, we both needed space after the drive."

"Right. The Barrington family reunion is this weekend. They're probably taking up all the rooms at The Lodge that weren't already used up by wedding guests." Indi glanced over at him, wearing the nearest thing to a smile he'd seen since she'd crashed down the stairs. "Small town. We all sorta know what's going on everywhere at all times."

At that last sentence, her expression fell. And suddenly they were right back on that couch in the living room, Indi sagging into its cushions. Not everyone knew what was going on at all times. She hadn't known what was going on around her own house.

He didn't have to know her well to sense what that realization had done to her. Her family might've thought they were doing her a favor in leaving her out of it until now, but if they still thought that after the way she'd deflated while they talked, well, then those were some serious blinders her family members were wearing.

Or they weren't the idyllic, close-knit family he'd thought. What a disappointment that'd be.

"I'm really sorry for showing up tonight, Indi. With everything your family's dealing with at the moment, the last thing you needed was me appearing on your doorstep and making everything worse. I really didn't intend to crash a wedding reception. But I saw you come out of the church and, I don't know, I got impulsive or something."

Splotches of red stained Indi's cheeks and her teeth chattered, the ghost of another grin reappearing. "I've never heard you say so many sentences in a row without stammering."

He watched the wind lift her hair again, then glanced at her ankle. "You should really be icing that." Definitely shouldn't still be wearing those boots. "And I should be getting back to Holland."

He stood and reached one hand toward her. He helped her to her feet before turning his gaze to the farmhouse. Gosh, he really would've loved to linger here longer. Watch the ocean dance from the warmth of the living room. Talk to Maggie, ask her about Robert, the great-uncle he'd never known. Maybe even join that reception out back.

"Hey, it's snowing."

At the soft note of wonder in Indi's voice, he turned away from the house. "Barely."

She shrugged. "It's something, though. I've been waiting

119

all winter for a good snow. I thought the forecast was hopeless for tonight, but I'll take flurries over nothing at all."

She'd been tossed down a staircase tonight. She'd found out her family had been keeping something serious from her. And, oh yeah, there was that confession about his identity she'd been forced into.

And yet, she stood in front of him on the wind-and-water-chiseled shore, swallowed up in his coat, finally really smiling now. Because of a few snowflakes.

And then, "Is your middle name really Ben?"

"Uh . . . yes. B-Benjamin, actually. Close enough to Bennington, yes? C-can you walk back all right?" Why was he stuttering again?

She folded her arms, his sleeves flopping over her hands. "If you're thinking about picking me up again—"

"I'm not." He was. He reeled a smile of his own from somewhere underneath his regret over leaving. "I really should get back to Holland."

Indi stared at him for a moment, moonlight splashing in her eyes, then nodded as she slipped off his coat and handed it over. "And then you can bring her here."

—————•—— ——•—————

The wind flung itself against the house as if desperate to charge its way inside—claw through the walls and rattle the windows until the glass panes gave way. Those few flurries a couple of hours ago had never amounted to much, but they'd left a ferocious squall in their wake.

Indi leaned over the daybed in the spare room at the end of the hall, keeping the bulk of her weight on her good ankle as she stretched a cotton sheet over the mattress.

And tried to ignore Lilian's drilling stare from the doorway.

"What in the world were you thinking?"

She tucked the sheet around both bottom corners before straightening. "I know, I know, the hoodie looks ridiculous with my dress." But she'd been cold after those long minutes out on the shore earlier and the chill had only reached deeper while she'd dutifully iced her ankle after coming back inside. Considering the wedding reception was still technically underway out back, she hadn't ditched her bridesmaid dress just yet, but the sweatshirt helped.

"I'm not talking about the hoodie and you know it."

Obviously. But with her bruising ankle and needling emotions over all that'd happened earlier, she wasn't exactly in the mood for a lecture from her big sister.

At least she'd managed to put on a peaceful front before Neil and Sydney had finally left for their honeymoon thirty minutes ago. Of course, they'd had to practically force Neil out the door after the incident with the intruder. Even Sydney had suggested changing their plans, leaving in the morning instead, waiting to make sure nothing more happened tonight.

But they'd eventually been coaxed into heading out, and a few minutes later Philip had texted her. *Okay, if you're really serious, we'll take you up on the offer. Sorry I'm just now letting you know. Took a while to convince Holland. Plus, I owed her French fries.*

Three hours after he'd shown up at Muir Farm out of the blue, two hours after he'd driven away once more, Philip West was coming back.

And that, surely, was why Lilian was glowering at her from the doorway now.

"It's not enough that you lied to us about who he is? Now he's coming to stay here? For how long?"

"I don't know." She slung the top sheet over the daybed mattress, smoothed it out, tucked it under at the foot of the bed and then the side.

Lilian plucked the light green comforter from the floor. "How long have you even known this guy?" She flung the comforter over the bed.

"I met him the evening of Maggie's heart attack." She angled to the foot of the bed again and slid the blanket between the mattress and the daybed's brass bars. "He happened to be in the store when you called and he saw me breaking down and he offered to give me a ride." The explanation thrummed from her on autopilot.

"So he was a stranger." Lilian yanked on the comforter. "You let a stranger drive you from one town to another. Let a stranger stay overnight in our house. And now he's coming back. With a teenager. Also a stranger."

"You've made your point, Lil." She bent to pick up the second set of spare sheets she'd pulled from the cedar chest earlier and brushed past Lilian.

"For all the good it's doing." Lilian trailed after her. "I just don't think it's the smartest idea ever to be having company with everything that's going on here."

Indi ducked into Neil's old bedroom. He'd moved all of his stuff up to the new master suite he'd created in the attic days ago. Everything except his old queen-sized bed.

She figured since the daybed in the spare room was only a twin mattress, Holland could have that room and Philip could sleep in here. Except, shoot, Neil had taken his pillows upstairs. Oh well, Maggie probably had a supply of extras in the hallway closet. If not, Indi could donate one of her own.

She began stripping off the old sheets Neil had left on the bed.

"So, you're just ignoring me now?"

"I'm not ignoring you. It's just . . . Philip's going to be here soon and I'd like to have the room ready for him. And this isn't as crazy as you're making it sound. We've always been a hospitable family. That spare room has seen guest after guest over the years. Wilder stays here all the time. Sydney lived with us for weeks before moving to the Carter place."

Lilian threw up her arms. "Yes, because we thought she was Maggie's granddaughter! She wasn't some random stranger."

Indi limped around the bed. "Philip's not a random stranger to me, okay?" And she just hadn't been able to help the offer to let Philip and his sister stay here. Philip hadn't told her much about Holland or even what he expected to happen by bringing her to Muir Harbor, but he'd said enough.

He loved the girl. But something was broken between them and he was desperate to fix it.

Plus, she'd seen the look in his stormy gray eyes when he'd admitted that the past eight months hadn't been easy. When he'd tried to put into words why he'd come back. He'd come for Holland, but maybe he'd also come for himself. Even if he didn't realize it.

And for a moment out there on the shore, all she'd wanted to do was help him the way he'd helped her last fall. When she'd been the one lost and worried and alone. "He's not a stranger," she said again.

"Well, he's not your fiancé either."

She cast the bottom sheet over the mattress.

"*Indi.*" Lilian grabbed the sheet before Indi could begin tucking it into place. "You lied to us. Why would you do that?"

"I don't know, Lil. Maybe because we were in the midst of a crisis and it just didn't seem like the right time—that night at the hospital—to blurt out that Ben had walked out of my life."

"You could've told us after."

"And you could've told me about the gray car. And the footprints. And the treehouse and the machine shed and—"

"I already explained—"

"You could've told me you talked to Trey."

Lilian's arms dropped, the sheet fluttering to the floor. "I'm sorry. I wasn't trying to hurt you. None of us were."

Us. See, that was the word that stung. *Us.* Like they were the strong family unit and Indi was the one on the outside.

Like eleven years ago when she'd finally told them how badly she'd messed up. She'd felt on the outside then, too. Even after, when she'd tried her best to clean everything up, to make all the right and expected decisions. She was still . . . on the outside.

She refused to meet Lilian's eyes. "Could I please have the bedsheet?"

"Indi—"

Whatever her sister meant to say, she didn't get the chance. Not with the sudden commotion from downstairs—a string of thumps and gasps and an actual scream—breaking in.

Their gazes collided for one stunned second, and then the bedding was forgotten as they raced from the room, down the hallway, to the staircase.

It only took a moment on her way down to dissect the scene at the bottom of the steps. Wilder, clenching one fist while Tatum Carter held him back. Philip, standing ramrod-straight on the welcome mat. Maggie, with her arm around a teenage girl with wide, pale blue eyes.

Holland. Had she been the one to scream? Yes, because apparently Wilder had been far too close to clobbering Philip.

Indi barreled down the remainder of the stairs.

"Would you let me go, Carter?" Wilder wrenched away from Sydney's grandfather, but the older man held firm. "I'm just trying to do what I should've done when I first saw the guy earlier."

Indi winced, her ankle throbbing as she reached the first floor. "Wild, calm down. You don't understand."

"I understand this is the jerk who broke your heart."

"No, he didn't."

"I'm close enough to being your brother that it's well within my rights to deck the guy. Neil will thank me. Probably would've done it himself if it wasn't his wedding night." He yanked away from Tatum, but Indi anchored herself between Wilder and the stunned pair on the welcome mat.

"Oh, would you put a sock in it?" Lilian marched to Wilder's side. "He's not who you think he is. And even if it was, we don't need you throwing a punch and breaking your hand. We only have so many bags of frozen veggies to go around."

"But—"

Lilian cut him off. "He's not her fiancé."

"Ex-fiancé," Indi muttered.

"He was just pretending," Lilian finished.

Awkward silence clambered through the group, until finally, a whisper from the teenager huddled between Philip and Maggie. "You pretended to be her fiancé?" Strands of white-blond hair slanted over the girl's forehead.

"N-not exactly. I mean, not on purpose. It was k-kind of an . . . an accident." Philip gave Indi a helpless look. They might laugh about this tomorrow, but right now . . .

Right now all she could see was the way he'd looked earlier tonight when he'd told her about Holland.

"I didn't know what else to do," he'd said.

Except come here.

Philip needed to be here. She *knew* it. Somehow she just knew it. He needed to be here as much as she'd needed that ride to the hospital in November. As much as she'd needed him at her side as she walked into Maggie's room. As much as she'd needed him sitting beside her in the waiting room.

So Lilian could lecture her and Wilder could go into over-protective brute mode, but she wasn't backing down on this.

"Come on, you two. I've got your rooms ready."

"Indi, maybe we should—"

She shook her head before Philip could finish suggesting they leave. "Neil's mattress is old, but it's better than a hotel floor." She picked up what was probably Holland's duffel bag and led them past their onlookers, Wilder mumbling an apology as she passed. "Holland, I think you'll be comfortable in the guest room. The daybed has a pillowtop mattress."

She started up the staircase, Philip and his sister's steps behind her.

And then, another whisper from Holland. "You almost got punched over a fake engagement. And all this time I thought you were a boring nerd."

8

*J*ndi lingered beside her open bedroom window, cold air whispering in and raising the hairs on her arms. Water trickled through old pipes in the walls, as familiar a sound as the creaking of the window's wood frame as she pushed it open another inch.

The radiator against her wall rasped in protest. She'd barely cracked the window open a minute ago, needing the blast of refreshment to chase away the last of her sleepy haze after a night of fitful sleep.

She wished she could blame her restless night on her ankle, but it barely pinched anymore, and though she could feel the toll that fall down the steps had taken on the rest of her body, it wasn't her sore muscles that had kept her awake. It was . . .

Everything. The wedding. Philip. The home intruder. Her confession to her family. That argument with Lil. Philip, again, this time with Holland.

And Trey's text, swarming behind all the rest of it, refusing to let her forget . . . resurrecting her old nightmare. It'd slunk in last night just as it had the night of Maggie's heart attack. No visual, just that eerie crying, just like years ago.

She took another breath, gaze raking over the backyard, where the marquee tent still stood, a gleaming silver luster quilting the ground around it and curling like ribbons over the birch trees. Streams of tangerine sunlight pushed through woolen clouds.

You have to go downstairs, eventually. She had guests, after all. And it was Sunday, which meant church, which meant wedging into a pew and attempting to focus on a sermon when all she really wanted to do was hide away in her workshop and lose herself in something therapeutic. Like painting the antique dresser she was restoring as a wedding gift for Neil and Sydney.

The icy wind tangled with the colorful array of scarves tied around her bedpost, their edges fluttering and brushing against the backs of her knees, until she reached for the window and pulled it closed.

Enough stalling. She'd promised Neil she'd take over his morning chores while he was on his honeymoon and she only had so much time before church.

She stood, tugged her same zippered hoodie from last night over the paint-speckled overalls she'd thrown on a few minutes ago. Sunbeams fell over her vanity as she stopped in front of it and opened a small drawer, feeling around for a hair band. She looped the band around her fingers and started to close the drawer.

But froze when it was almost halfway shut.

And knew in the next moment she shouldn't have let herself look down. Because she'd known it was there. Because she'd never been smart enough to throw it out.

And she wasn't smart enough now to look away. Slowly, she pulled the drawer the rest of the way open and slipped the scrap of paper from underneath a tangle of hair ties. How was it the note hadn't yellowed or curled by now? The handwriting had faded, but she could still read it. Though why she was reading it now when it'd burned into her memory long ago, she didn't know. Just two names and a phone number. *John and Sandy Holmes.* She'd only met them once, but she could still picture them. John with those thick, Clark Kent–like glasses. Sandy's bobbed hair a reddish color that reminded Indi of Maggie's before it'd gone prematurely white. *"If you change your mind, please feel free to reach out to us."*

She swallowed and stuffed the note back in the drawer, closing it with a thud. She lifted her hair and twisted it into a knot, glanced once more at her closed drawer. And suddenly, all she wanted to do was throw open her window again, stick her head into the wintry morning, and gulp and gulp and gulp the fresh air. As if filling her lungs might push out all the rest . . .

Instead, she hurried from her room, every memorized groan of the old wood floors sounding exactly as she knew it would.

Eleven years. Why hadn't it been enough? Would there ever be enough? Enough time, enough space to forget.

Stop thinking. Go do Neil's chores. Get on with the day. Get on with your life.

She'd been trying to. For so very long.

Voices drifted from the kitchen as she moved through the dining room, along with the creaking of the oven door and the smell of blueberry coffee cake. Maggie, then.

She moved into the kitchen. "Good morn—" She broke off at the sight in front of her. A man sitting at the table in the corner, one foot propped comfortably on the chair next to him, empty coffee mug in front of him. "Oh. Hi."

Tatum Carter dropped his foot to the floor and stood, dipping his head in greeting. The web of creases in the man's sun-bronzed skin stretched as he grinned. "Morning, Indi."

Indi nodded, her gaze flitting from the older man's face to Maggie, standing by the open oven, apron tied at her waist. "I didn't know we had company." Er, well, company other than Philip and Holland.

She had the vague memory of Sydney's grandfather being a part of that scene in the entryway last night. He'd helped Philip avoid a black eye from Wilder's fist. But what was he doing here now, lounging in their kitchen, looking casual as he pleased?

Tatum must've sensed her unspoken question. "Just stopped by to see if Maggs needed any help cleaning up from yesterday's shindig," he offered. "Figured I could come back after church, if so." He rose and picked up his cup.

Maggs?

Maggie closed the oven door and tugged off her mitts. "What he means to say is his curiosity over what happened after he left last night was killing him. But I've assured him there were no more unnecessary dust-ups." Her hazel eyes, dancing with flecks of green and golden-brown, shone with mirth. "Sit back down, Tatum. You've been eyeing my coffee cake since you walked in the door."

"Don't have to ask me twice." He stopped at the coffeepot to refill his mug, then took his seat once more.

Maggie pulled a cup from the cupboard, filled it with coffee, and handed it to Indi. "Would you like a piece now? Or do you want to wait for your young man?"

Philip? Indi sputtered on the hot coffee. "He's not—" She coughed. "Not my young man."

"Oh." Maggie flashed her a sweet smile. "Guess I was mistaken, then. You did invite him to stay."

"I was being nice."

"He's handsome."

Tatum snorted behind her.

"Sheesh, you're as bad as Sydney with Cecil's nephew."

Maggie's smile widened. "Hmm, I'm not hearing a denial. And what's this about Cecil's nephew?"

Indi set her mug on the table. "I've got chores to do." She gave Tatum a stiff nod and crossed the room, stopping at the back door to pull on a pair of work boots.

Brisk air nipped her cheeks the second she stepped outside, the noise of breaking waves reaching around the house to join the sound of the tent's flapping.

"Wait a second." Maggie ducked out the back door.

"Maggie, seriously, Philip's just a friend. I'm only two months out of a relationship. Not just a relationship, an engagement. So please don't think—"

"I wasn't going to tease you, dear." She tossed her long white braid over her shoulder. "I just wanted to ask if everything's okay with you and Lil. There was enough tension in the house last night to fuel a fire."

"She's annoyed I didn't tell her about Philip sooner. I'm annoyed she didn't tell me about everything that's been happening here." *And about Trey.*

"That wasn't just her. It was all of us. So if you're going to be mad—"

"I'm not mad. I'm just . . ." She huddled into her sweatshirt. "In a hurry to get the chores done. Be back in a while."

Before Maggie could argue, she turned and made for the grove, escaping into the tangle of weathered trees and bushes. The hardened ground, coated with twigs and flattened leaves, crunched underfoot, none of last night's paltry snow having made it through the night.

She reached the end of the grove in minutes, emerging into the clearing and bypassing the machine shed, making her way to the smaller of the two barns on the main farm grounds. The large one housed the air blower and packing equipment for Neil's annual blueberry harvest. The small barn sheltered their animals. Indi set to work. Milking Melba came first, then a quick trip to the chicken coop to gather eggs and toss feed. She saved the goats for last.

Her goats, according to Neil. He loved to pretend the small herd was nothing but a nuisance. But while she might've been the one to purchase their first goat years ago on a complete whim, he was the one who'd built the pen beside the barn. She'd even caught him talking to the animals once or twice when he'd thought no one was around.

Knees digging into the barn's dirt floor, she dug a scoop into the feed bag, the musty scent of hay sinking from the rafters above. "He loves all of you, even if he won't admit it." With her free hand, she reached out to scratch Sunny's white and brown peach-fuzz head, their youngest goat bleating in happiness.

Most of the herd scampered around the barn this morning, few braving the January cold. Sunny dipped her nose into the feed bag, but Indi nudged her away. "At least it feels like winter now. We even got a few flurries last night. I'm still holding out for actual snow, though."

"When I talk to myself, I usually pick a more exciting topic than the weather."

At the surprise intrusion of a voice behind her, Indi dropped her scoop and attempted to whirl around. But she bumped into Hezekiah, who bleated his annoyance and knocked his head into her waist. She landed on her backside in the dirt a moment later.

Philip's sister stood in the barn doorway, silhouetted by the morning sun.

"Holy cow, you scared me half to death." Indi stood, swiping her hands over the dusty front of her denim. "And I wasn't talking to myself. I was talking to my goats."

Holland only stared at her.

Loose curls tickled Indi's cheeks as she stared back. "How did you even get out here? It's a trek from the house."

"Trailed you." Holland moved farther into the barn, seemingly unbothered by the fact that her pristine white shoes wouldn't stay that way for long in here.

Where had she been lurking while Indi tended to Melba and the chickens? "Does your brother know where you are?"

Holland didn't reply, apparently distracted by the patter of goats' hooves as they flocked around her. Yeah, those shoes would be goners in seconds. Hezekiah, of course, went straight for Holland's coat, clamping his teeth to its hem and tugging.

"Hez, give her some space." Indi grabbed the open bag of feed and dragged it to the wall, curling the top over to close it.

"Half brother."

"What?"

Holland peered at Indi over the goats. "Philip. He's my *half* brother. Same mom, different dads."

An important distinction, apparently.

"Nice overalls, by the way," Holland added. "You look like Rebecca of Sunnybrook Farm. You just need braids."

That was a smirk if she'd ever seen one. "Laugh if you want, but at least I'm dressed appropriately."

Holland folded her arms. "Maybe I'd be dressed appropriately too if I'd had any warning at all this is where we were coming. But no. First I get dragged to a tiny town that probably doesn't even have a movie theater and then suddenly we're staying at a farm. And it's super awkward and super weird."

"You're very blunt, Holland, you know that?" And she looked more like Philip than Indi had realized last night. Same peculiar gray eyes, though hers were a tad lighter. Same high cheekbones. Different hair color, but her smug grin a moment ago had revealed dimples reminiscent of the ones that framed Philip's smile.

It was more than that, though. The pair of them shared

something else—something she wasn't sure she could fully put her finger on. A sort of unspoken longing, maybe. She'd noticed it in Philip that morning in November when he'd said goodbye. And again last night along the shore.

She caught a glimpse of it in Holland now as the girl shrugged and reached down to pet Sunny. This girl—who'd followed her out here and spoke her mind with a frankness that was as refreshing as it was amusing—was still living through a loss Indi couldn't imagine having gone through as a teenager.

And yet, she could understand the complete unmooring that happened when someone who was a part of you was suddenly just . . . gone.

"It's not that weird. You being here. You and Philip."

Holland straightened. "We must have different definitions of weird. People don't just invite strangers to stay with them overnight."

"We're used to different people staying with us," Indi explained as she moved to the nearby water tank and picked up a hose. "And people tend to like it here."

"It's a *farm*."

She swallowed a grin and carried the hose to the trough. "Yes, but we have adorable goats."

"Goats have demon eyes."

"Sunny, Hezekiah, all the rest of you—pay her no mind. She doesn't know what she's talking about. And for the record, Holland, we have an ocean outside our front door. We have gorgeous, rugged land that stretches on for acres. One of these days it's going to snow and it'll be the prettiest thing you've ever seen. You've landed in one of the best places on earth, whether you realize it yet or not."

Holland folded her arms. "Seems like an exaggeration."

"Anyway, Philip said you're obsessed with home renovation shows. That true?"

Holland only nodded.

"Good. Then I've got something you can help me with."

———————

"I can't believe you actually did it."

Philip barely registered Connor's incredulous tone through his cell phone, his gaze glued to the sight ahead of him on the sidewalk—Holland laughing at whatever it was Indi had just said. They'd been on this walking tour of Muir Harbor for almost fifteen minutes now. Felt like a long time considering how little there was to the town square.

Not even a square, technically. Muir Harbor's downtown consisted of an oval lawn and a cobblestone roundabout. They'd only covered half the non-square town center so far, Indi stopping every couple of minutes to point out one fixture or another.

But if this tour took hours, he wouldn't complain. He could stay out here all day if it meant Holland kept smiling. He just hoped Indi's ankle wasn't bothering her. She didn't seem to be favoring it.

"She hasn't glared at me once since church, Connor. Didn't even argue about going to church in the first place."

"Uh, you lost me."

Philip shoved his free hand in his jacket pocket, wishing he'd been as smart as Indi and bundled up before this outing. She wore a floppy maroon beret that matched her mittens and scarf, along with furry boots that looked fit for Alaska. Still hoping for an outpouring of snow, from the looks of it.

Holland was properly attired, too. Indi had raided the entryway closet before they'd left the farmhouse after lunch. He'd thought for sure Holland might balk at the bright pink color of the fleece hat and gloves Indi had handed her. But no.

"It's Holland. She's . . . in a good mood. Has been all day."

Of course, he'd had a moment of panic that morning when he'd first realized Holland wasn't in the guest room at the end of the second-floor hallway. Or in the bathroom. Or in the living room or dining room downstairs. But then he'd walked into the kitchen just in time to see Indi and Holland tromping in the back door.

Holland had walked straight to the coffeepot, poured herself a steaming mug, and turned to him. *"I guess it's okay if we stay here a while. Indi needs my help with something."*

He'd had to stifle the urge to laugh and to remind her their stay at the farm wasn't exactly up for debate. Holland had promised him two weeks, after all. Still. Something inside him had eased just a little in that moment.

And then even more so when Indi had given him a small smile. Asked if he liked blueberry coffee cake. And how he felt about taking a tour of the town after church.

"See?" Connor's voice was full of gloating. "Aren't you glad you took my advice and got out of Dodge? How long are you staying for? Where are you staying? Also, why am I hearing Christmas music?"

Because apparently Muir Harbor kept Christmas music gliding from the speakers in the square well past the holiday. And it wasn't only the music. The ornamented evergreen in the center of the square, the bright red bows decking out the gazebo, the garland and lights trimming nearly everything in sight—it was like this odd little town existed in a bubble where Christmas wasn't over until they said it was over.

Tabby's muted voice reached through the phone. "Stop asking the boring questions and ask the good ones."

"You could've told me your wife was on the call." Up ahead, Indi and Holland had stopped again and Indi was pointing across the street toward Bits & Pieces with its yellow shutters and sign that perfectly matched the one outside her Augusta store.

"Why?" Tabby must be leaning closer to Connor, because her voice came through clearer now. "It's not like you've gotten to the juicy part yet."

"There is no juicy part."

"Give me the phone, Connor." Tabby's demand resounded over the line.

Philip chuckled. "Tell your wife I don't know how many more ways I can say no to ghostwriting for Grandfather."

"I don't want to talk about ghostwriting." Apparently Tabby had made a successful claim to the phone because now her voice was loud and clear. "Actually, scratch that, I do. But first, I want to know about the woman."

The woman. His gaze sought out Indi.

"Shy, bookish Philip West finally has the first crush of his life."

"I guess Connor opened his big mouth. Whatever he said, it's not true."

Indi's hat flopped farther to the side as she laughed at whatever snide remark Holland had just made, her rosy cheeks and lit-up eyes radiating a delight he found himself wanting to bask in.

Wind chimes. Her laugh was like wind chimes.

"Philip West, you've never done a single spontaneous thing since the day I met you. To pick up and run off to a tiny town on the coast for this girl? She must be something else."

"I did not—" He cut himself off, lowered his voice. "I came here for Holland. I did not come here for Indi Muir."

"Just tell me one thing: Has she seen you in glasses yet?"

"Is this what counts as fun for you and Connor on Sunday afternoons? Calling up your friend and heckling him?"

"I'm just saying, you look really good in your glasses. Wear them around her sometime. She'll like them. She'll think you look smart."

He scraped his cold fingers over his stubbled chin. "I'm hanging up now."

"No, wait. The ghostwriting thing, just hear me out, Phil—"

"Sorry, can't talk anymore. Holland's heading my way." And she had perfect timing. He pocketed his phone and blew out a puff of white air.

"The post office is a library," she blurted when she reached him.

"Say again?"

Holland pulled on his coat sleeve and pointed across the cobblestone street to an aged building on the corner next to Indi's store. Cement slabs formed walls of chalky white-gray that surrounded stately windows. Above the hunter green double-door were stenciled letters etched into stone—*United States Post Office.*

"It's not the post office anymore. Now it's the library." Holland grinned. "The town square is circular. The Brunch Barn serves all three meals despite its name. And the owner of Trinna's Teatime is always, in Indi's words, in a tizzy because no one ever orders tea. Just coffee. So basically nothing is exactly what you think it is in this place." Holland took a breath. "This might actually be the weirdest town in the world." With that, she took off across the street and minutes later had her nose pressed against the glass of the post office —er, library—like a five-year-old looking in a candy shop.

"Too bad it's closed on Sunday." Indi reached him. "It's actually pretty cool inside. They use old PO boxes as a card catalog."

"The card catalog isn't digitized?" He waited for a car to pass, then started across the street.

"You're in Muir Harbor, Philip. Technology is not our thing. Do you know how town meeting agendas are posted?"

"You have town meetings?"

"A flyer is tacked to the bulletin board by the gazebo, that's how we see the agenda. No website announcement. No email blast. Cecil, our newspaper editor, would stomp on his own spectacles before even considering putting out a digital edition. And I'm pretty sure my store is the only downtown business that has a functioning website."

He stopped at the base of the cement steps leading up to the library entrance and leaned on the iron railing. "So we've landed in Mayberry, then."

"Oh no, we've got much more in the way of intrigue than Mayberry."

"Intrigue, huh?"

"Yeah. Have Maggie tell you the Legend of Muir Harbor sometime. For now, I want to show you the project I have in mind for Holland. And you. And me." She nudged him forward and started for her store.

"You really don't have to come up with some way to entertain us."

"I'm not trying to entertain you. I'm trying to help you. You came here to connect with Holland, right? I think working on something together might be a good way to do that. And, selfishly, it'd help me, too."

She captured Holland's attention with a wave and motioned her over, then unlocked her store's front door.

"Yeah, but what you're doing—letting us barge into your world and stay at the farm, showing us around town . . . I'm just really grateful." Freckles. Why hadn't he noticed Indi's faint dusting of freckles before? Because of her eyes, he guessed. Because they tended to distract from all else. The only good word for them was dazzling and they were enough to make a man consider . . .

Consider that, fine, maybe his best friend wasn't entirely

off base. Maybe for the first time in a long time, he might be a little, well, interested in a woman. *This* woman.

The one whose smile lit up her face as Holland reached them. "I'll make sure you get to see the post-office-turned-library another day, Holland. And the harbor, too. You have to see the harbor. It's just around the corner. But I want to show you my place first." She held the door open for Holland to enter.

But instead of following, Philip peered down at Indi. "You're ignoring my gratitude."

She laughed. "Yeah, well, your gratitude might not last once you see what I'm about to ask you two to help me with."

"It'll last." He said it with assurance. Because right in this moment, he was pretty sure she could ask him to jump into the ice-cold Atlantic and he wouldn't mind.

"You still have Christmas decorations up in here, too?" Holland called from inside.

Indi flashed him one more grin, then nudged him inside. A gingerbread aroma—and, hmm, something else he couldn't quite place—wrapped around him. Huh, Holland was right. Christmas lingered in every corner of the store, from white icicle lights in the front windows to the wreath with a burlap bow hanging on the cash register counter to what looked like an antique wood Nativity scene on a pedestal stand.

"Muir Harbor is known for our seasonal festivals," Indi explained as she entered behind him. "Our winter one is at the end of January, so most of us leave up our Christmas stuff until then."

His gaze bobbed from item to item filling the store floor—bookshelves and benches, wall décor and knickknacks. No two items looked alike. Holland was studying the Nativity set, picking up one wood piece after another. "It's like a mirror of your Augusta store." He turned back to Indi in time to see her flinch. He raised a brow in question.

"I had to close that store. Just the other day, actually. I didn't have enough customers to justify keeping it open." She shrugged before he could come up with something commiserating to say. "It's for the best. It felt inevitable in the end. Like the choice was made for me."

"Even so, it had to have been a hard decision."

Another lift of her shoulders. "The thing is, I think I'd actually feel relieved about the whole thing if it didn't feel so humiliating at the same time. I was getting tired of the constant treks back and forth between towns, beginning to wonder what had possessed me to open a second place. It's just people knowing I've failed that I don't like. Especially right on top of a failed engagement." She glanced over at him. "And, um, not my first."

That revelation settled around him. Not her first engagement. Not her first *failed* engagement.

Well, that raised questions. The nosy kind. But the caring kind, too. Because her honesty tugged on his heartstrings.

"Come on, my workshop is upstairs." Indi tugged off her beret and nudged her head toward the curtain at the back of the store. "That's what I want to show you guys. It's in need of a major makeover and with Holland being into home reno shows, this might be a project she can sink her teeth into."

"Your workshop." Something was falling into place— something he hadn't picked up on until just now. He looked around the store again, eyes landing first on a trio of painted, wood-shaved birds perched on the cash register, then a display of colorful fabrics beside a pair of chairs, a handwritten sign on one of the seats. *Pick your fabric, then pick up your reupholstered chair within a week.*

"Coming?"

He faced Indi again, finally recognizing the other thing he'd smelled when he walked in here. *Sawdust.* "You make all this stuff."

"Well, yeah." She shrugged out of her coat and draped it over her arm.

"I assumed you had vendors or whatever. But you do all of it. The painting and the sanding and the designing."

"I don't know about design. I don't actually build the furniture. I just spiff it up a little."

He caught sight of a painting on the wall behind the cash register. The harbor at the edge of town, the one he'd driven past last fall—unmistakable. "You're an artist." Behind Indi, Holland disappeared through the curtain.

Indi let out a light laugh. "I wouldn't say that. I mean, sure, when I was younger, I dreamed of being an artist—going off to Paris and sketching Notre Dame, painting the Seine. But the truth is, I wasn't ever actually that good at any one medium. And trust me, I tried them all. It's why I ended up with a business degree instead of art."

He glanced at the painting again. "If that's your definition of not good . . ."

She followed his gaze. "Actually, that painting isn't even finished. Which is why there's no price tag on it. I'm not even sure why I have it hanging up."

"Looks finished to me."

She shook her head. "There's no definition to the waves and the coastline needs to look rockier, more rugged."

"Clearly you're your own worst critic. I would buy that painting right now and . . ." He didn't even know how to finish the sentence. He was too startled by . . .

By everything, really. The new knowledge that Indi Muir might be the most talented person he'd ever met. The craziness of not just returning to Muir Harbor, but finding himself actually staying at Muir Farm.

The reality that just twenty-four hours ago he was driving away from Grandfather's house praying for a miracle, and maybe he'd actually gotten one. Because Holland had shown more enthusiasm in this one day than in all the past eight months combined. And he . . . he felt *happy* in this moment. Happier than he'd been in so long.

"I'm honestly kind of speechless right now." He dropped onto a bench. "You sanded this, didn't you? That had to take hours, especially with all the ornamental pieces and little grooves—"

"Actually, that bench is more for decoration than sitting."

He jumped back up. "Now I can't wait to see your workshop. Holland's probably already found it by now and—" Jingling bells cut him off, but only for a moment. "But how do you have time to create all this and keep a store running? Being relieved about the Augusta store closing makes total sense now . . ."

He finally stopped rambling when he realized Indi wasn't looking at him any longer. Was looking past him. And those freckles he'd only just noticed, they were more pronounced now, the rest of her face having gone completely white.

He threw a glance over his shoulder to where the store's front door was only just clanging closed, a man now standing inside.

From behind him, Indi's voice was weaker than a whisper. "Trey."

For just a little while there—as she'd played tour guide for Philip and Holland, kept them out in the cold and dragged them around her sleepy hometown on a Sunday afternoon— she'd actually managed to forget.

The text she hadn't responded to. The man who'd sent it.

The man who was . . . here. Wearing a hunter green stocking cap pulled low over his ears.

"Looks exactly like I would've expected in here. Just like your garage back at the farm used to." Trey had followed her up the back stairway after she'd awkwardly asked Philip a few minutes ago if he'd mind waiting to see her workshop until later.

Thankfully, he'd taken the hint, fetched Holland from the backroom. He'd said something about continuing their tour on their own, stopping by the harbor. She'd seen the questions in his eyes, though. The concern.

She'd nodded to let him know it was okay to leave her here with Trey. To let him know she was all right.

Except obviously she wasn't. And clearly Trey sensed it because he'd barely moved a muscle since first taking up residence beside a card table crowded with sponges, rags, and bottles of paint de-glosser and liquid sandpaper.

"Or, well, maybe it doesn't look exactly like the garage."

He meant the garage she used to call her art studio. Back when she was still a high school student with her sights set on a scholarship and an art degree and then who knew what. Maybe that trip to Paris, like she'd mentioned to Philip. Or an internship at a fancy art institute somewhere.

She sidestepped an old piano bench waiting to be re-stained and reached for the light switch on the wall—not that they needed it, not with that huge window at the back of the room letting in streams of sunlight. But she needed to move. She needed to do something. So she turned on the lights, then bent to flick on a small space heater, wishing the familiar smells coasting over her—paint and varnish and sawdust, woodsy and pungent—would do what they usually did.

Make her feel at home. Make her feel capable. Imaginative.

All she felt right now was dread.

"The garage walls were always covered in acrylic paintings and charcoal sketches. This place has better lighting." Trey pointed to the long counter tracing one wall. "Along with a hardware store's worth of paint and varnish, apparently."

He traced the top edge of a card catalog she'd nabbed from the library a couple towns over when, unlike Muir Harbor, it'd finally gone digital last year. She still needed to sand away a few nicks, stain the thing a nice mahogany or walnut. Or maybe paint it a distressed white. It'd make a cool piece of home décor for someone somewhere.

"Switched up my medium," she finally said, feet rooted in place. "Less drawing and more restoring. I still paint." The flecks on the walnut floorboards attested to that. "But usually on wood instead of canvas."

Except for that lone painting downstairs, begun so many years ago, the one Philip had admired.

I'm not even sure why I have it hanging up. That hadn't entirely been the truth. She kept it behind the cash register because, well, even unfinished, the painting reminded her of a simpler time. A time when she'd created for the sheer joy of it. When the emotions that came from pouring herself into her art still thrilled her.

When giving herself over to hours in front of a canvas or bent over a sketchbook had still felt like a lifeline to a God who saw her, inside and out. When had distance and discouragement so thoroughly frayed her faith?

Trey finally moved farther into the room. "You're still wearing those old overalls."

She dipped her chin. "This is a newer pair." And she'd only thrown them back on this afternoon because they were still sitting on her bed from when she'd changed before church. And because she'd wanted to make Holland laugh again. *Rebecca of Sunnybrook Farm, indeed.* "The ones you're remembering—I eventually had to throw them out. They were threadbare and so covered in paint you couldn't even see what color they were originally."

Trey stuck one hand in his coat pocket. "Yellow. Bright yellow. Like, you could stand on the coast and guide ships into harbor."

"They weren't that bright."

"They were an eyesore, Muir."

Muir.

He'd called her by her last name in high school, too, ever since he'd sat down behind her in Algebra II and read her name off the back of her JV cheerleading uniform sophomore year. Only year she'd been a part of the squad. Hadn't been her thing.

But being called by her last name by one of the popular kids? And a basketball player, at that? *That* had been her thing. They'd been an on-and-off couple at first but by senior year it'd gotten serious. More serious than either of them had been ready for.

Her gaze sank to the floor. *Why are you here, Trey?* In the strained minutes since he'd walked in her store's front door, somewhere between her shock and confusion, she'd scoured her mind for the crumbs of information she knew about his life in the eleven years since she'd seen him last. In high school, they'd both talked about going to Bowdoin College, but he'd changed course. Went to the University of Maine, didn't come back to Muir Harbor on breaks. At some point, she'd heard he'd eventually ditched school altogether and joined the Navy instead. There'd been an article in the paper once—something about honors he'd received while in the service.

"I'm sorry I didn't answer your text. I . . ." She swiped her palms over the front of her overalls. "I don't know what to say. With everything that happened . . . I know how much I hurt you when I called things off. I've wished so often that I'd done it differently, that we—"

"That's not why I'm here." He motioned to the piano bench. "Maybe you should have a seat."

"I'm fine standing."

"Okay. It's just . . ." He looked away again as his shoulders dropped with his exhale.

"You're worrying me, Trey. What is it?"

He pulled off his hat and leveled her with a look that didn't do a thing to prepare her for the blunt force of his next words.

"We need to find our child, Indi. As soon as possible."

All the oxygen leaked from her lungs. She couldn't move. Couldn't think.

Our child. It shouldn't be possible for two tiny words to feel so foreign and familiar all at once. Two tiny words she never let herself think about.

The two words she only ever thought about.

"Trey, we can't—"

He took a step nearer. "I have a heart condition. It's serious and . . . it's genetic."

9

The muscles in Indi's hand and arm and shoulder all moaned at once as she scratched the pad of steel wool over a waist-high dresser. Back and forth. Back and forth. She was pressing too hard, pulling off too much paint.

And doing nothing, nothing at all, to quash the tremors left in the aftermath of the earthquake that had shaken her world minutes ago. Or maybe hours. How long had it even been since she'd asked Trey to give her time to process what he'd told her?

Long enough for the space heater in her workshop to roast her. For the steel wool to irritate the skin of her palm. For her lower back to groan when she finally shifted.

"We need to find our child, Indi. As soon as possible."

The scraping of the wool against the wooden surface just wasn't enough to drown out Trey's words. Wasn't enough to keep her heart's relentless *ba-bump* from feeling like a constant echo: *Our child. Our child. Our child.*

Those two horrible, heart-wrenching, still somehow beautiful words . . .

"Indi?"

At the sound of her sister's voice, she spun, bumping into

her workshop counter, knocking over a jar filled with paint brushes. "Lil, what are you doing here?"

"I'm meeting someone for dinner tonight. I got to town early and ran into Philip and Holland."

Oh. Philip and Holland—she'd all but forgotten them. No, she'd downright abandoned them. They'd driven into town together earlier this afternoon, which meant the pair of them had been waiting on her all this time.

Waiting while Trey shattered the wall she'd put up in her heart so long ago. A glass wall that had probably never done any good anyway. Because she'd always been able to see through to the other side. Had never fully managed to turn her back or pretend away the past.

The baby she'd conceived and carried and birthed.

The baby she'd given away. To the John and Sandy Holmes from that scrap of paper in her vanity drawer back home.

Her stomach churned as her hand clenched around the steel wool pad, its rough ridges scraping her palm.

"Philip said you were here." Lilian moved farther into the room. "He said someone showed up here at the store and . . ." Her words drifted, a prodding in their wake. But not an overly curious one.

Which confirmed what Indi had assumed. "You knew, didn't you?"

Lilian stilled a few feet away. She met Indi's eyes. "I knew some."

"Because Trey's mom cleans your office."

Lilian nodded. "I was working late the night Trey called her. I heard her gasp. I stayed to make sure she was okay. She told me about the diagnosis."

The diagnosis. The one that had brought Trey north from Florida. That had prompted him to call her and text, and when neither of those had worked, to seek her out in person. His words echoed through her mind all over again.

149

"*It's called hypertrophic cardiomyopathy. It's not fatal if you take care of yourself and take the right medication. But if you don't know you have it and you exert yourself too much . . .*"

Foggy desperation had clouded Trey's eyes at that point in his story, and that's when Indi had finally made herself sit, sagging onto a plastic tub that held her collection of hand sanders. "*But it's not just my life, Indi. This thing is hereditary. Turns out I should've been tested for it years ago because both my grandad and uncle had it, too. If there's a chance I passed it on . . . Look, if I could do this by myself, I would. But I don't know how to find her. I was . . . out of the picture by the time you gave her up.*"

That's when he'd started bulleting questions. What agency had she used when she put their baby up for adoption? Was it an open or closed adoption? Did she have any contact with the adoptive family?

And all she could think as the questions whizzed past her, one after the other, was that this must be what it felt like when the past finally forced you out of hiding. When it shoved you under its bright lights and refused to be ignored. This tremble that seized every muscle and squeezed.

And forced you to remember what you'd been trying so hard for so long not to. To relive it. To be right there again, in that gut-wrenching summer day between her senior year of high school and her freshman year of college.

Propped on a hard hospital mattress, arms empty.

Slumped in a wheelchair on the way out to Maggie's car, arms empty.

Returning to the same childhood bedroom she slept in now . . . arms empty.

And everybody saying the same thing: that she'd done something good and noble. That she hadn't just stepped off a cliff.

She closed her eyes now, turning away from Lilian, leaning over the counter, and drawing in a ragged breath.

"Gloria said Trey only found out about it because he collapsed at a gym?"

With her back to her sister, Indi set the jar she'd knocked over upright again and gathered the spilled brushes. "Yeah, he joined a basketball league a while back. Passed out during the first game. Woke up in a hospital. Had to get some tests, an EKG."

"And it's a genetic thing, right? That's why he's back?"

Wow, Lilian really did have the full scoop. Indi angled toward the dresser once more and absently went back to scratching her wool pad against its surface, only a stiff nod in acknowledgment of her sister's question.

Lilian's soft steps moved closer. "This is a cool piece. I like how you're distressing it." Lilian ran her fingers along one edge of the dresser. "The white and navy blue plus some of the dark wood showing underneath—it's looking really good."

"Thanks. There's a trick to it when you're distressing with two colors. After you put on the first coat, you take a candle or a piece of wax and rub it over sections here and there to keep the second coat from sticking. Makes it easier to sand later."

"I've always wondered if it's hard to sell a piece after you put this much work into it."

She wiped away a layer of chalky dust. "I'm not selling this one. It's for Neil and Syd, for the new master suite." She moved her hand again, still pressing too hard as she sanded, yesterday's soreness and today's tension colliding in her aching muscles.

Until Lilian stilled her with one palm on her arm. "It's going to be okay, Indi."

She dropped the wool pad. "You don't know that. I have a daughter out there somewhere." *Not my daughter. Not anymore.* "She might have a congenital heart disease she doesn't know about. What if she's, like, some major child athlete? If she's super active . . . it could be really bad."

"But you can reach out to the family. You've got names. The agency gave you contact information, didn't they?"

Yes, but she'd never used it. Sandy Holmes had left the door wide open the only time they'd met, months before Indi had gone into labor, but she'd known she'd never walk through it.

It was better this way. Her baby and the lovely family who'd adopted her deserved a fresh, clean start—no complications. They didn't need a teenage birth mom messing things up.

She should've just chosen a closed adoption from the start. Like her own biological mother had done. If she'd been stronger, she would've. If she'd been stronger, she wouldn't still have that scrap of paper with their phone number, one last flimsy link.

Lilian squeezed her arm, her familiar orchid perfume hovering in the air around them. "Maybe there's a gift in this. Sometimes it seems like you've never quite moved on. I think we've all sensed it."

"We've all sensed it." We . . . as in the rest of the family.

As in the rest of the family who'd gone stone-cold silent back in the kitchen at home when she'd confessed during Christmas break eleven years ago that she was pregnant. Who hadn't quite been able to hide their doubt when she'd told them in the next breath that Trey had proposed and they planned to get married the next summer. That they'd figure out how to raise their baby while going to college.

She'd happened upon one too many whispered conversations after that. Had known she and Trey and the pregnancy were the subject. Had hated that feeling of being on the outside of her own family.

Same feeling she'd had just yesterday, sitting in the living room, ankle throbbing, while an eddy of realization swirled around inside her. They'd all known for months something strange was going on at Muir Farm. For months, they hadn't told her.

She took a step backward, out of Lilian's hold. "This isn't a gift, Lil. Not when Trey is dealing with the reality of a heart disease." Not when their child might have the same thing.

Her breath caught all over again, just as it had when Trey had brought up their baby. *Our child. Our baby. My daughter.*

No. There was no "our" or "my."

She turned away from the dresser now, doing everything she could to swallow her emotion, to calm her racing thoughts. She paced to the window, the battering sunlight together with the stuffy warmth of the heater turning her skin clammy underneath her clothes. She shoved her sleeves to her elbows.

"I didn't express that thought well," Lilian said behind her. "And trust me, I wouldn't say this in front of Trey. Although, from talking to Gloria, it sounds like their whole family is grateful the diagnosis came when it did. She said he's got a great cardiologist, that he's going to make whatever lifestyle changes he needs to." Lilian moved to Indi's side. "But for you . . . what if this is a chance to connect with the adoptive family? Or even meet your—their—daughter."

"No—"

"I never really understood why you weren't open to that before."

"Because it wouldn't have been the best thing for her. Or them. Or . . ." *Me.* "Closure was better for all of us."

"Except I don't think you ever got closure. You changed so much that summer."

"How could I not? I had a *baby*, Lil. I made a whole series of decisions—breaking up with Trey, choosing adoption, choosing to let her go—because I was trying to do the right thing." The thing she'd been convinced God had wanted her to do. "So of course I changed. I grew up."

Lilian fiddled with the thin silver bracelet on her wrist. "But you stopped painting and drawing. You stopped talking about Paris and your art. You stopped—"

"Oh, wow, look at this place." Holland's voice and the clunking of footsteps nearing the top of the stairs cut Lilian off.

Indi turned in time to see Philip's sister emerging into the room, Philip on her heels. A mix of relief and regret skidded through her at the sight of them. Relief for the reprieve from this conversation with Lilian. Regret at how long she'd kept them waiting this afternoon.

But neither feeling was a match for the sense of helpless dejection holding her mind, her heart, her whole body captive. Trey was sick. Her little girl might be sick. Her little girl who wasn't her little girl. And the pain of that truth was too much. It was just . . . too much.

"This is the room you want me to help make over, right?" Holland took a sip from a covered cup with the Trinna's Teatime logo on its side. "It's cool, even if it does look like a crafty hoarder has taken over."

Somehow, a strangled laugh pushed free. "I'm sorry I deserted you two earlier."

From across the room, Philip gave her a look of apology. "We're clearly interrupting. We should've waited—"

"No, you're fine," Lilian said. "I need to be on my way anyway. Peyton's probably waiting for me already."

"Peyton?"

"Peyton Cornish. Cecil's nephew."

Indi knew who he was, but Lilian was meeting him for . . . a date? Guess Cecil had turned his matchmaking attempts on her, too. And why hadn't Indi realized earlier how dressed up Lilian was? Tight pants and ankle boots, a loose light-gray scoop-necked sweater that showed off her long neck and dangly earrings.

"We're having dinner at the Cobalt Pier."

"You're missing Sunday dinner?" Sunday evening dinners were a Muir family tradition.

Lilian nodded.

"Well, have fun."

Lilian's smile was tight, the tension of the minutes before still lingering. But she nodded and turned, boots clomping as she moved past Philip and Holland and down the stairs.

"So explain your project." Holland started right in. "If I'm going to make use of my HGTV obsession, I want to know what I'm getting into."

Indi's gaze was still on the stairway, the sound of her sister's retreat still echoing. "I'm sorry, I'll be right back." She hurried after Lilian, down the stairs, through the curtain leading into her store. "Lil, wait."

Already to the front door, Lilian stopped, flashing Indi a questioning glance as she shrugged into her leather jacket.

"What else did I stop doing? You said I stopped painting and drawing. Stopped talking about Paris. And you started to say something else."

Lilian pushed open the door, the chiming bells colliding with her voice. "You stopped talking to me."

A thirty-four-year-old man probably shouldn't feel this fascinated by a simple Sunday evening meal.

And, really, it wasn't the meal. The spaghetti and meatballs were delicious, no doubt, but Philip's taste buds and quickly filling stomach couldn't account for the contentedness feathering over him just now. He liked the homeyness of the dining room, lavender walls and a dated brass fixture over-head that shook every time someone left the table to refill the water pitcher or basket of buttery garlic bread.

But the setting wasn't the highlight either.

He might say it was the company, except everyone—Indi, Maggie, Wilder—they all seemed a little too quiet. Not that he had any way of knowing for sure, but he had a feeling most Sunday evening dinners here at the farmhouse were noisy, rambunctious affairs. A joyful clashing of voices and passing dishes and clinking silverware.

And that's probably what was doing it—the picture in his head of a family gathered around a table, laughing, talking, eating. Together.

Holland elbowed him. "You going to eat that or what?"

He blinked, realized he'd been holding his fork and half a meatball in midair for who knew how long, dripping sauce on his plate. He shoved it in his mouth, savoring the explosion of flavor and the grin Indi sent him from across the table.

Was she amused more by Holland's snippiness or the fact that he'd taken way too big of a bite and now his cheeks were bulging? *Probably both.*

Either way, it was perhaps the first real smile he'd seen from her since earlier today. Since that man who'd made her face go white had interrupted a perfectly nice afternoon. Wasn't Ben the Buffoon. He'd seen enough of that guy before the infamous wardrobe-hiding incident to know. So who was he? *Indi called him Trey.*

She'd mentioned having been engaged twice. Maybe Trey was Fiancé #1.

"I'm just going to say it." Wilder tapped his fork against his plate. "It's weird without the rest of the family here. I like it best when the whole gang's around and the table's full."

Indi reached for her water glass. "If Lilian were here, she'd have some snide reply to that."

Wilder chuckled around a bite of bread. "Yeah, she would. She'd say, 'And sometimes the table's a little *too* full' and glower at me. Classic." He swallowed. "But no, she's out with a guy with a total Ivy League name. Peyton Cornish."

Philip lifted the water pitcher and leaned over the table to refill Indi's glass. "Who's Peyton Cornish?"

"Someone who probably wears sweater vests and plays tennis."

Maggie laughed at that. Indi, too. But there was something strained about it. Didn't sound like wind chimes tonight. And her smile wasn't entirely natural either. What had happened with the mystery man after he and Holland had left her store? He'd wanted to ask hours later as Indi showed them around her workshop, but he hadn't felt like he should. Not with Holland there.

Not with Indi keeping up a steady stream of words from the minute she reappeared after following her sister. She'd spent the next half hour talking about her plans for her workshop, telling them how she wanted to turn the space into something profitable. She'd kept Holland engaged, saying she hoped Holland would have good ideas for how to renovate the room.

"But don't you need to know what you're going to turn it into before you start renovating it?" Holland had asked.

Indi had shrugged. *"I suppose so. But I'm hoping that becomes clear while we're cleaning it out."*

"So it's not really my creativity you want as much as my physical labor. Nice."

Sarcasm might've coursed through Holland's voice, but Philip hadn't missed the spark of interest in his sister's face as she looked around the workshop. He'd relished it even as he'd been unable to stop himself from wondering about Indi and that man.

"By the way." Wilder leaned back in his chair. "I got all the locks on the doors changed this afternoon. "Took a walk around the farm, too. I think last night's intruder kept to the house."

Maggie sighed. "I wish that made me feel better."

Wilder's chair bumped into the wall behind him. "I'm stuck on the fact that he didn't take anything. Just like every other time. All he did was look around."

"And push Indi down the stairs." Philip heard the edge in his own tone. She could've been hurt so much worse.

She was. She is.

The thought pricked like a bee sting. Yeah, she'd been hurt last night, but not just by the intruder. He stuffed a forkful of spaghetti noodles in his mouth. Something had happened this afternoon, too, and she was still hurting. And suddenly all he wanted was to find some excuse to leave the table and take her with him. Ply her with questions and then take whatever steps necessary to fix what was causing her pain.

And probably somewhere in there, pull her into his arms too. Hold her until he was certain she was going to be okay. And maybe while she was there, he'd let himself run his fingers through her hair, just to see if it was as soft as it looked—

He coughed, sputtered, noodles clogging his throat. He choked them down with a gulp, Holland snorting in amusement at his side.

"You okay, dude?" Wilder's chair tipped to the floor once more.

Philip gave a sheepish nod. Even though, no, he probably didn't classify as okay. He classified as a man who'd let his friends get way too far into his head. Heck, he'd almost worn his glasses down to dinner tonight, just to see if there was anything to what Tabby had said. *"She'll like them. She'll think you look smart."*

But it shouldn't matter to him what Indi thought about how he looked or whether she liked his glasses or if she'd noticed how often he looked her way tonight. What mattered was Holland. What mattered was he only had two weeks to convince her to give up on the idea of going to live with Bryce in Texas. What mattered was—

Indi had been pushing the same meatball around her plate for five minutes. Had anyone else noticed?

"Anyway, it's pretty obvious the intruder's looking for something specific," Wilder went on. "Just wish I knew what."

Maggie pulled her napkin from her lap and wiped the corners of her mouth. "It's not up to you to figure it all out, Wilder. The police are involved now. And we're getting a new security system installed this week."

Indi's head popped up. "We are?"

Maggie nodded. "With everything that's happened, I think it's a good idea. Tatum said he'd come over tomorrow or Tuesday and get the cameras set up."

Tatum—another name Philip didn't know. But he knew Indi wasn't loving this conversation. She wasn't even pushing the meatball around anymore. She'd abandoned her fork altogether, both hands disappearing under the table.

"So, um, do you all do this often?" He blurted the question, caught Holland's raised brow beside him. Probably should've put a little more finesse into the segue. "Eating in here like this?"

Maggie leaned over and patted his shoulder. "Sometimes we eat in the kitchen, dear."

"No, I mean all together. Do you eat all together every night?"

Indi's eyes met his from across the table. "Not every night. Lil works late most weeknights. I spend half the week in

Augusta—well, used to. Wilder's not always here. And anytime Sydney's not here, it's a sure bet Neil isn't either. Although now that they married and will be living here, they'll probably be here most nights."

"About that," Holland said. "Why *do* you all live here? You're grown adults."

Philip cleared his throat. "Holland—"

"What? They all have jobs and stuff. Shouldn't they have their own places?"

He looked to Indi. "Sorry." Was Holland forgetting their own mom had lived in Grandfather's house for a chunk of her own adulthood?

It was a relief to see Indi laugh. "No, it's a logical question. Neil runs the farm, so it makes sense that he lives here. Lilian's working on paying down her law school debt, so living here allows her to save on rent. And me . . . I don't know. I guess when you grow up with the ocean outside your front door, it's hard to leave."

Maggie nodded. "It's the house I grew up in, too. So if you think they're too old to still live at home, then who knows what that makes me."

"I think it's nice." Another abrupt interjection from him. But at least Indi was looking a little more relaxed. "That you're a close-knit family. That you eat meals together. After my dad passed, I mostly ate alone as a kid. My grandfather was always holed up in his office. Deadlines always came first. And Mom just wasn't around that much. I got pretty good at making mac 'n' cheese from a box."

He took the last bite of his spaghetti, chewed, swallowed. Then looked up. Realized everyone was looking at him.

Well, not Holland. But everyone else and . . . *Oh.* Maybe he'd said too much. "I didn't mean to make that sound so . . ." *Pathetic. Lonely.* "To this day, I honestly love any cheap, generic brand of boxed macaroni. It's good stuff. So there were benefits to—"

Holland slapped her balled-up napkin to the table. "I'm full." Her chair scraped the floor as she pushed back.

"Holl—"

She hurried from the room before he could even get her name out. Her footsteps lumbered down the hall, turning into a run as she pounded up the staircase.

Mouth gaping, he slowly turned back around in his seat. "I'm sorry about that. I don't know what—"

Holland's door slammed overhead.

He pulled his napkin from his lap and stood. "Again, I'm sorry. I should . . ."

Indi nodded. Mouthed *Go.*

He left the room, embarrassment twitching through him, though it wasn't nearly as unsettling as his concern over Holland. He took the steps two at a time, reaching her door quickly. He tapped it lightly with his knuckles. "Holl?"

No answer.

She's a fifteen-year-old girl. You can't walk in on her. He kept his voice low. "That was kind of rude down there. Everything okay?" He almost jumped when the door flew open. "Hey, are you okay?"

"You didn't have to make it sound like that."

Um, what? "Make what sound—"

"Like she neglected you. Like she was some terrible mother."

Oh. "I didn't mean—"

"Why are we even here?"

"Could we talk in your room?" So everyone downstairs didn't have to hear this whole thing?

But Holland didn't budge from her doorway.

"I thought we had a fun day today. I thought—"

"Why are *you* here? You never were before. Obviously

there was always something more important than your family." Tears filled Holland's eyes now—and fury, too, her smoky-gray irises disappearing into dark borders as her voice rose. "You were never here. So why are you now? Why?"

"Holland . . ." He tried to find words, but his throat had gone completely dry.

"I didn't need you then, and I don't need you now. I want to be left alone." She slammed the door a second time, the clamor echoing into the hallway, his thumping heart punching his rib cage.

He leaned forward, letting his forehead rest against her closed door. He'd thought they'd come so far today. He'd thought she was enjoying herself.

Or maybe he'd just been so busy enjoying the day himself that he'd missed something. Too caught up in his own thoughts, distracted by Connor and Tabby's heckling, by his growing attraction to Indi.

He groaned. He was failing. Still.

"Philip?"

At Indi's soft voice, he turned. "I'm sorry. You probably all heard that. The yelling, the slamming door . . . sorry."

Where he'd seen pain in Indi's eyes earlier, now he saw compassion. Only he wasn't sure he deserved it. *You were never here.*

He glanced over his shoulder at Holland's door once more. Should he try again or give her space?

As if she could read his mind, Indi touched his arm. "She said she wants to be alone. It might not be a bad idea to respect that. At least for now."

He raked his fingers through his hair. "I'm worried she didn't so much mean 'for now' as 'forever.'"

Indi must've known arguing the point wouldn't do any good because, wordless, she only watched him for a moment, sympathy hovering in her scrutiny. Eventually, she offered him a half-smile. "Want to go see Neil's treehouse?"

"You said treehouse and I pictured . . . well, not this."

At the awe in Philip's tone—a perfect match for the admiration in his eyes—Indi knew this had been a good idea. Back in the hallway outside Holland's door, the man had been in need of a rescue. She didn't know what random whim had entered her brain and resulted in the notion to bring him here, but she was glad it had.

And she was thankful to be thinking about anything other than Trey and his diagnosis and their daughter. And that conversation with Lilian. And the torrent of emotions she'd been trying to outrun ever since. Because if they managed to catch her, she wasn't sure she'd ever break free again.

Don't think about that now. You're here for Philip.

Philip, whose cheeks and nose were ruddy from the long, cold walk through the grove and fields. He blew air into his hands as he took in the structure above. The winter breeze rattled through the branches around Neil's masterpiece, and dusk flirted with the horizon, hazy tendrils of pale pink curling through the sky.

Philip glanced her way. "I thought it'd be smaller."

So had she. When Neil had first told her what he was building last fall here on the far edge of the west field, she never could've imagined the actual thing, not until she'd seen it herself. The treehouse was a marvel, really—larger than any of the second-floor bedrooms back at the house, impressive and inviting with a winding wood staircase that led up to a landing outside its door.

After erecting the main dwelling, Neil had started building a smaller structure at the base of the tree, what would eventually be a modest but functional bathroom. He'd shifted his focus to renovating the attic after Thanksgiving, but he'd likely be back at work on this thing soon after his honeymoon. The first guests would arrive in April.

"You have to see inside." She led Philip to the staircase, sturdy enough it didn't make even the barest creak as they moved upward.

As soon as Philip stepped through the treehouse door, he began oohing and aahing all over again. And she could admit to being a little happy about that, considering she'd helped Neil outfit the spacious room. She'd picked out the grayish-blue comforter on the queen-sized bed and painted the headboard in a distressed white. She'd supplied the simple picture-frame decorations that adorned two walls and the sheer gray curtains on both windows. A bistro table and chairs took up one corner and a counter nearby held a Keurig, microwave, and mini-fridge.

But Philip hadn't seen the best part yet. Indi tapped his arm and pointed to the ceiling, where a long skylight welcomed in the blushing sunset. "Pretty incredible, right?"

The pinkish-orange glow of the sky grazed over Philip's face as he craned his neck. "I'll say."

"Sydney posted it on Airbnb in November and it's already booked almost every weekend this spring. Some weekdays, too. Neil wants to build a second one as soon as he's saved up enough for materials." She glanced around. "I'm glad our repeat intruder didn't do any lasting damage in here."

Philip lowered his gaze. "Of all the places to trespass, why Muir Farm?"

"Who knows." Wilder had said the trespasser must be looking for something specific. But what? She shook her head. "Let's not talk about that now. Otherwise my imagination is going to go into overdrive every time I hear the crunch of a twig outside."

Philip was back to looking around the treehouse, but every couple of seconds, his focus scooted to her. Probably wondering why she'd brought him out here. Or how to apologize for the tenth time about Holland's outburst earlier.

Frankly, she had no idea what'd made her think of the treehouse. Or why she'd felt the impossible-to-deny urge to follow him up to Holland's bedroom in the first place when he'd left the table. It wasn't even so much Holland's abrupt disappearance that'd rattled her.

No, it was earlier—that question he'd asked about whether they often ate dinner together. And what he'd said afterwards about eating so many meals alone as a child, offhandedly revealing his father's death. Her heart had only gone out to him all the more when Holland had slammed her door in his face.

Philip's gaze found her again, only this time he didn't send it skittering away. "So this must be what inspired you to start thinking of ideas for the space over your store."

She blinked. Not what she'd expected him to say. "How'd you know?"

He shrugged. "I can see your touches around here. You probably sewed those curtains, right? And the picture frames obviously came from your store." He knocked on the headboard. "And don't try telling me Neil's the one who painted this."

Genuine pleasure wriggled past the chill of the night, settling in her bones. "You're right. This place inspired me. I've got this gorgeous space above my store that could be something really cool and I want to bring it to life the way Neil did with this. It's like staring at a blank canvas, though. I haven't found the specific vision for it yet."

"You'll find it, Farmgirl."

"Farmgirl?"

He didn't say anything to that. Just smiled and looked

away while she looked down. Right. She still wore her ratty overalls over her cotton Henley, and any attempt to tame her curls earlier in the day had been lost to the rowdy wind on their walk through the barrens to get here. She'd grabbed an old fleece-lined plaid jacket from the coat tree before they'd left the house. Why did she feel the sudden, self-conscious need to button it up? As if that would hide her current shabby state.

Philip walked to the window and traced its wood frame with his fingers. "It must be a Muir family thing."

"What must?"

"Creativity. Vision and big dreams. Neil building this tree-house. You with your art and stores and now your ideas for the workshop. I haven't figured out your sister's big dream yet, but I haven't been around Lilian much."

Indi sat on the bed. "Pretty sure her big dream is to eventually get Wilder to lose it. It doesn't matter how many scowls or snide comments she throws at him—it just never, ever bothers him."

Philip turned and leaned against the wall, grinning as he cocked his head. "What's the story there?"

"He gave her a bloody nose once in grade school. A game of dodgeball gone wrong."

"That's one long grudge."

"Actually, if I had to put money on it, I'd bet Lil has an unspoken dream of discovering who left her on Maggie's doorstep when she was a toddler."

Philip straightened. "Oh. Wow."

"Yeah. Neil came to live here when he was a teenager, and Maggie adopted me when I was a baby. It was a closed adoption and I've weirdly just never been that curious about my biological parents. But Lil? She doesn't talk about it, but I think it's always been hard for her. Not knowing. Not understanding how or why she ended up here." It's probably why

Lilian had never understood how Indi hadn't jumped at the chance to stay connected to her daughter's adopted family.

"So what's your big dream, Philip?"

"Right now it's getting Holland to accept that I'm not trying to destroy her life." He looked up to the skylight once more. "I used to want to write books, though. My grandfather's an author. Like, a best-selling one. He writes mysteries. I was a bookworm as a kid. I used to think following in Grandfather's footsteps might be fun . . . well, not all his footsteps, but . . ." He abruptly snapped his gaze back to Indi. "Actually, I have to tell you something. About my grandfather. Well, not exactly about him. But kind of."

It was all she could do not to let an amused grin creep its way onto her face. She liked it when he got like this— awkward, incapable of full sentences.

"Back in November when I first walked into Bits & Pieces, it was because of Grandfather. See, I saw your name on the storefront window and . . ." He gave a huff, scratched his head, then pulled a chair from the bistro table and sat. "Let me start at the beginning. When I was a kid, I used to sneak into my grandfather's study sometimes. He used to write his books by hand, which is crazy but it was convenient because it meant when he wasn't around, I could get my hands on his half-written manuscripts."

Now she did grin. "I've got the best picture in my head of little gap-toothed Philip West creeping around where he's not supposed to just for the sake of *reading*."

"If I wasn't in the middle of a story, I'd chide you for making fun of the gap in my teeth."

"I wasn't making fun of it!" No, that little gap almost added as much charm to his smile as his dimples.

"Anyway, when I was fourteen, he was writing this historical mystery that I was really into. So I snuck into his office one day, but I couldn't find the manuscript. Instead, when I was looking through his desk drawers, I found an old letter. Really old. Written in 1969." He eyed her. "Written to Maggie."

Indi straightened, the mattress underneath her creaking. "My Maggie?"

He nodded. "It was a love letter. I thought Grandfather wrote it, but just last fall I figured out it was actually his brother who wrote it. Robert. Robert Camden."

"You're saying . . ." Her mind spun. "Your great-uncle is the Robert I've been hearing about for my whole life? Your great-uncle used to be engaged to Maggie?"

"That's why I walked into your store that day. Because I saw your name on the window and I suddenly remembered that old letter and the name Maggie Muir and I knew I was being impulsive, but I had this crazy thought that maybe the Indi Muir who owned the store would know a Maggie Muir and . . ." He took a breath. "But it turns out it wasn't that crazy of a thought at all because you actually did. Do. Know Maggie. The Maggie from the letter."

She could only stare at him.

"I should've told you back then but there was so much happening and I didn't think my being related to someone your mother once knew mattered all that much in light of everything."

She finally found her voice as she jumped off the bed. "Philip, you have to tell Maggie."

"I will. I just haven't had the chance yet." He propped his hands on his thighs. "I wish I'd snuck into Grandfather's office again before coming here to see if the letter is still there. I asked him about it when I found it back then. He was, uh, not pleased. Actually, he ended up collapsing that same day and going to the hospital. I honestly thought at the time it was the shock of me approaching him with the letter and his displeasure that caused it. But no, apparently he had a really terrible case of walking pneumonia."

So many questions chased each other through her mind. What had the letter said? Had his grandfather ever met Maggie? Did he know Philip was here right now?

But for all her questions about the letter and Philip's grandfather and great-uncle, the ones that echoed the loudest were the ones about *him*. This man who'd walked into her life twice now, once as her rescuer and now . . . in need himself.

"Philip?"

"Hmm?"

"How old were you when your father died?"

His feet were hooked around the base of the tall chair, hands sliding toward his knees. "Six."

"How did he die?"

"He worked for the railroad. It was a train accident—a bridge, faulty rails."

"Oh my word. That's . . ." So horrible she didn't know what to say. And now he'd lost his mom, too, and was struggling to fill a parental role in Holland's life. Indi moved closer to him. "Holland does need you. No matter what she says."

He sighed. "Just wish I knew why Mom thought I was the right person to sign those guardianship papers. I feel like I'm failing on every front. I don't know how to be what she needs."

"Maybe just . . . do what you're already doing. Just be the guy who's there, who stays. Even when it annoys her. She'll come around. She'll eventually see what I see—that she's really lucky to have you in her life."

He just stared at her for a slow, quiet moment, the pastel shades of sunset passing over his face once more.

Then he was moving toward her in long, determined strides. And in the next instant, she found herself pressed against him, his arms coming around her, holding her tight. His whisper against her hair, in her ear. "Thank you."

She was too stunned to move at first. But it didn't take long for her senses to awaken. An enveloping warmth, the rhythm of his heartbeat, how perfectly she fit right here.

How much she'd needed this. All day. All weekend. The intruder. Trey's news and all it meant, all the memories she couldn't avoid any longer. Her baby. Her *baby*. There'd just been so much and . . . and . . .

Philip released her too quickly, maybe as startled by the sudden embrace as she was.

Or if not that, then by the sight of the tears pooling in her eyes. "Indi, are you okay?"

She squeezed her eyes closed. "Yes." *No. Not even close.* "But we should probably get back." Before she lost it and did something insane. Like fling herself back into Philip's arms and start sobbing.

She couldn't do that. Because once she started, she didn't know how she'd make herself stop.

*B*right sunlight was a waterfall at the window, flooding Indi's bedroom with light. With a moan, she slid from underneath her covers and her bare feet hit the chilled floor.

What time was it anyway? She reached for her phone, tapped the screen to life. Gasped. Eight ten? The store opened in fifty minutes and—*chores!* Shoot, she'd promised Neil.

She sprang from her bed, lunging for a long orange cardigan hanging from the back of her closet door. She threw it over her shoulders and cinched the belt over her pajama bottoms. There was no way she'd make it into town to open the store by nine, but if she hurried, she wouldn't be opening her doors too late.

She found a scrunchie and swept her hair into a wreck of a bun, stuffed her right foot into one of the tennis shoes she'd kicked off last night, scouring her room for the other. She was still hopping on one leg, trying to shove the second shoe on, when she pushed through her bedroom door.

And collided with a body in the hallway.

That smell. *Coconut and something woodsy.* She dropped her shoe and looked up into Philip's smiling face and . . .

And it all came rushing back at her—last night, the tree-house, how close she'd come to breaking down in those moments after Philip had embraced her, their quiet walk back to the house. And yeah, that embrace—how good it'd felt to be held, even just for a few seconds.

"Morning," Philip said. His hair was damp at the tips, his cheeks unshaven, and a bundle of clothing and a toiletry bag was tucked under one arm. He was barefoot. Must've been coming from the shower. He was wearing dark jeans and a Seattle University T-shirt.

And glasses. Those were new. They made him look smart. And handsome. But then, he looked handsome without them, too.

And she in her purple pajamas and orange sweater and one bare foot. Lovely. "I need to do chores," she blurted, as if that explained her bedraggled appearance.

"No, you don't. Maggie took Holland out to do them. I think it was a mission of mercy times two. Letting you sleep a little longer, giving me a reprieve from Holl's surliness." His lips spread into another slow grin then, revealing that tiny gap between his front teeth.

"What?"

He slid past her, through her open bedroom door, and moved to her bed, lifting her stuffed llama from the foot of the bed. "Do you sleep with this?"

She nabbed it from his grasp, holding the yellowed old thing against her. "Don't laugh at Mister Trousers." Even if he did have a missing eye and a rip in one leg that revealed his cotton stuffing.

Philip's eyes fairly twinkled. "I wasn't going to but then you told me his name. Mister Trousers? Where'd you come up with that?"

"Oh, go put some socks on or something, Philip." Her messy bun flopped to one side.

"Don't feel like I should have to if you're going to be running around like that. The PJs-and-sweater look is interesting, but I like it."

She harrumphed. "Keep teasing me and I'll tell Holland about the time you hid in a wardrobe. I have a feeling she'd enjoy that story."

He laughed, but in the next moment his grin faltered. "She's giving me the silent treatment this morning."

"She'll come around. Bring her to my workshop later. I'll goad her into a good mood. It's a particular skillset of mine."

"I know. It's what you did for me at the treehouse last night." He shifted his bundle to his other arm. "Speaking of last night . . ."

His voice trailed, but she knew exactly where his thoughts had gone. To the tears she hadn't been quick enough to hide. Her silence on the way back to the house. Philip might be perceptive, but he wasn't pushy. It'd be easy enough to say something breezy now and pretend he'd never gotten that brief glimpse into her pain. He'd take the hint, she knew, and let it drop. He wouldn't ask about her tears.

But then, Philip had given her more than a glimpse into his own pain. He'd told her about his grandfather, his childhood, his worries about Holland. For as brief a time as she'd known this man, it was possible she already knew him more than she'd ever known Ben.

The thought startled her. Enough that she turned away from Philip for a moment. But just as quickly, mind made up, she turned back. "I got pregnant when I was in high school."

Now Philip was the one to appear startled. Because of how abruptly she'd spoken or what she'd said?

"The guy who came to my store yesterday—Trey—he was —is—the father. There was a short while where we were going to get married and keep the baby, but in the end, I called off our engagement and gave our baby up for adoption.

But now Trey has this heart condition and it's hereditary and we need to let the adoptive family know and . . ." She dropped her stuffed animal on the bed.

Philip gave a small cough, clearly unsure of what to say. He set his bundle of clothing and toiletry bag on her bedside table. "So, um, you know the adoptive family?"

"Somewhat. Legally, it was an open adoption. I picked out the parents. Met them briefly. But after giving birth . . . I didn't see them that day and haven't talked to them since. I just . . . couldn't."

His nod surprised her. "I get that."

"You do?"

"I've spent almost my entire adult life avoiding my grand-father's house, not really being a part of my family. You're talking to someone who understands the need for distance." He let out a sigh. "I'm guessing a therapist or psychologist or whoever would say it's self-preservation. An attempt at not getting hurt. Again."

Talk about self-aware and emotionally in-touch.

And insightful.

Because Philip had it exactly right. Indi could tell herself all she wanted that she'd never called the number on that scrap of paper because it was what was best for her daughter. But really, she was protecting her own heart. Shielding its already broken pieces from any more hurt.

The kind of hurt that would come from seeing the beautiful child she'd created and knowing she didn't have a place in her life.

"So, um, anyway, me getting emotional last night . . . that's what that was about."

"I'm a little relieved, to be honest. I would hate to think I'd driven you to tears by accosting you with a hug."

How was it so easy to laugh after all she'd just shared? After a night of tossing and turning and wondering what to

174

do about Trey? "You didn't accost me. And the hug was . . ." Surprising and perfect. "Nice."

"Well, it's a particular skillset of mine." He lobbed her own words back at her with a dimpled grin. "Thanks for telling me all that, by the way. I like getting to hear more of your story. I like getting to know you more."

There was enough warmth and sincerity in his tone, his eyes, she nearly went in for a repeat hug. Only the realization that she was still wearing her pajamas held her back. And that she hadn't brushed her teeth or her hair, and how long had they been standing in her bedroom? "Why don't you stammer anymore?" Where the question had come from, she didn't know. Nor why her voice had gone just the slightest bit breathless. "You used to, but you don't now."

"Well." He coughed. "I'm comfortable with you now."

Suddenly, he didn't look comfortable. Suddenly, she was pretty sure that might be a flush working its way up his cheeks. "I'd ask why you were uncomfortable in the first place, but I'm pretty sure the whole hiding-in-a-wardrobe thing accounts for it."

Another cough. And the flush deepened. "Sure, that's the reason. Anyway, I should probably see if Holland's awake."

"Didn't you say she's doing chores with Maggie?"

"Oh, yeah. Sure. I-I forgot."

"You just stammered again. Don't tell me you're back to being uncomfortable. If anyone should be uncomfortable, it should be me. I just told you all my secrets."

"Not all your secrets. I still don't know Mister Trousers's origin story."

She laughed and rolled her eyes, then picked up Philip's toiletry bag and clothing and shoved the bundle at him. "Go away, Philip. I have to get ready for work."

He grinned and moved to her doorway. "See you later." He glanced past her. "Bye, Mister Trousers."

She reached for a throw pillow to chuck at him, but he was already halfway down the hall when it hit the doorframe, the echo of his chuckles lagging behind him. She couldn't help her own laugh as she pulled the useless scrunchie from her spilling hair and tossed it atop her vanity.

Maybe she could make it to the store by nine, after all, if she hurried through a shower, kept her hair and makeup simple, and . . .

She paused in front of her vanity mirror, met her own eyes in the reflection. Took a breath. Then opened the drawer and pulled out the scrap of paper. She had something else to do before getting ready. And thanks to Philip, thanks to his willingness to listen, his surprise understanding, she felt ready. Or, well, maybe not ready, but at least capable.

She crossed the room, picked up her phone from the bedside table, and opened her text messages. It took her less than ten seconds to tap out the message to Trey.

Hey. Meet at the store? 9:30ish? Mondays are usually slow, so it's a good time to talk.

She was halfway to the bathroom when her phone dinged with a reply.

Still do Americanos? I'll stop at Trinna's on the way.

⸻

Philip shouldn't be eavesdropping on his sister.

But Holland had said more complete sentences to Maggie Muir in the ten seconds he'd been standing outside the kitchen than she'd uttered to him since they'd left Augusta on Saturday.

"My mom didn't really like to bake much, but she was, like, weirdly good at beverages. She'd make this slush stuff at Christmas. Basically just mashed-up bananas and pineapple juice and crushed ice with 7-Up poured over it all. So good. And she always had a pitcher of sun tea outside in the summer."

He allowed himself a peek around the corner, caught a glimpse of Holland stirring something at the stove. The berry-sweet aroma drifted into the dining room, tugging on his stomach. He hadn't had breakfast yet. Maggie and Holland must've finished the morning chores sometime when he was upstairs with Indi.

What an interesting start to a morning. First had been the complete and utter amusement of seeing Indi in that sweater and pajamas, her ponytail or bun or whatever it was flopping from side to side as she tried to hop her way into a shoe . . .

And then the unexpectedness of her telling him about her past. A teenage pregnancy, an adoption, an ex-fiancé back in her life.

Whatever beginning of a crush he might've felt yesterday had been blown away by what had rushed in since—an overwhelming surge of protectiveness, an undeniable demand to be anything and everything that Indi Muir needed right now.

Except that hadn't been his only desire. He'd also wanted to keep teasing her about her pajamas and her stuffed llama. He'd wanted to linger in her bedroom and ask if she'd refinished that antique vanity herself and just how many pieces of furniture and wall art in this house were the result of her talents.

And he wanted to find some way to prod for more information about Trey and Ben and whether she still had feelings for either one of them.

He'd wanted all kinds of things he probably shouldn't. Which is surely why he'd started stuttering again.

"Keep stirring the berries. Sugar can burn pretty easily." Maggie's voice drifted toward him. "And beverages—that's a fun forte."

"Yeah, Mom also made the best hot chocolate in the world."

He shook off thoughts of Indi and made himself focus on the conversation he was eavesdropping on. So he'd guessed right the other night in Holland's bedroom. Mom's specialty hot chocolate hadn't gone entirely out the door when Dad had passed away. She made it for Holland.

"We'd have it every Sunday night," Holland went on. "Mom and me and Grandpa while watching old westerns. Or sometimes musicals when Mom could talk Grandpa into it. A tradition, I guess. Like your Sunday night dinners."

Grandpa? It was all he could do not to let out some grunt of disbelief. He was supposed to believe there was a point in time when Grandfather came out of his study long enough to drink hot chocolate and watch movies? *Musicals? No way.*

"Did I hear your brother right last night? Did he say—"

"Half brother," Holland interrupted.

Philip winced. If he'd needed confirmation that he'd made very little headway with Holland in the past two days, it was dragging like a load of bricks in that one word.

"Right. Half brother. You can take the pan off the burner now. We'll let it cool some before filling the crust. Want to help me crimp the edges?"

He glanced in the kitchen again, saw Holland place a steaming pan on a potholder, then tuck her hair behind her ears. She moved toward Maggie's side, and he flattened himself against the wall lest she catch a glimpse of him.

Creeper.

Yeah, well, maybe he was a little gun-shy after getting a door slammed in his face last night.

". . . my favorite method for crimping the crust. Sure, if

you want to get fancy, you can use a spoon or fork or what-
not, but I say your thumb works just as well."

Philip leaned against the wall, grinning at Maggie's
words.

"Oh, but I was going to ask—last night Philip mentioned
something about your grandpa's deadlines. Is your grandpa a
writer?"

Philip straightened.

"Yeah, he's famous, actually. You've probably heard of him.
Ray Camden."

Silence. Sudden, pounding silence.

So then . . . Maggie recognized the name. And was probably also making the connection.

Go in. Explain. You owe it to her. He made his legs move and
rounded the corner. Had no more stepped a foot into the
room than Maggie's bugging eyes flashed to his. *Yes, she definitely knows.*

"Oh. You're up."

He tried not to feel slighted by Holland's less-than-warm
greeting. Tried not to feel the guilt pooling in his stomach as
he watched the realization play over Maggie's face. *Yes, there
was a reason you thought I looked like Robert Camden.*

"Making pie at nine in the morning? It smells amazing."

"It's not for you." Holland pinched a piece of crust too
hard and it tore. "It's for Tatum Carter. To thank him when he
installs the new security system."

He still didn't have a clue who Tatum Carter was. But he
wasn't really interested in that at the moment.

And Holland, clearly, wasn't interested in being in the
same room as him. "I'm going to go see if Captain needs food
and water." She was out the back door in seconds.

Maggie gestured toward the coffeepot. "Help yourself."

He pulled a mug from the cupboard, filled it up, then
turned to face Maggie. "I was hoping there'd be a . . . a right

time to mention it. My connection to . . . the Robert I think you knew. My grandfather's brother."

Maggie rested her palms on both sides of the pie plate. "I don't understand. How did you . . . when did you realize . . . this can't just be a coincidence, can it? That you're here and you just happen to have a connection to *my* Robert."

He gave Maggie the same explanation he'd given Indi last night. Told her about finding the letter years ago, remembering her name, seeing Indi's last name on the store window. "So no, it's not a coincidence that I'm here. Unless you count me walking past Indi's store in the first place." Except that hadn't felt like a coincidence at all. It'd felt . . . strangely preordained. "I came back to Muir Harbor for Holland, but I'll confess, I've been curious about the great-uncle who wrote that letter." And the woman he'd written it to. "Sorry I didn't mention it sooner."

Maggie repaired the tear Holland had made in the crust. "When would you have fit it in? Between the wedding reception and the intruder and all, it hasn't exactly been peaceful around here lately."

"I'm sure Holland and I aren't helping with that."

She disagreed with a wave of her hand. "That girl is a delight and so are you."

"That girl is not my biggest fan." He finally took a drink of his coffee. Hazelnut. Heavenly. "I'd love to hear about Robert. Grandfather doesn't talk about him."

"Robert was . . ." She gave the pie crust one last crimp and pushed it away. "He was the great love of my life. Proposed to me only three weeks after we met."

Whoa. Three weeks?

"He was sunshine and sweetness and charm."

"Huh. So the opposite of Grandfather."

Maggie laughed and moved to the counter, sliding a Tupperware container from the corner. "It's interesting to me that you call Robert's brother Grandfather and Holland calls him Grandpa."

"Yes, well, I'm realizing more and more that Holland's relationship with our grandfather and mine are two very different things." Hers had apparently involved hot chocolate and movies. His? Mostly just . . . silence. Distance.

Maggie pulled what might be the biggest blueberry muffin he'd ever seen from the container and plopped it on a napkin. "I met Robert's brother, actually. Same time as I met Robert. He seemed nice enough."

"But he's not the one who stole your heart."

"No, that was all Robert. Stole my heart and took it with him. A pretty big piece of it stayed with him after he died. The truth is, Philip, I spent a lot of years—decades, really— holding on to a picture of what I thought my life should've looked like. So much so I think I sometimes missed out on the beauty of what it did look like." Her back to him, she closed the Tupperware and pushed it back against the tiled wall. "Sometimes I think it's why things with my oldest daughter were so tumultuous for a time."

"Lilian?"

She turned to him. "No, not Lilian. Indi must not have told you. I had another daughter, also adopted, long before the others came along. Diana. She died in a car accident twenty-eight years ago. Almost twenty-nine now. My grand-daughter was in the car as well, though her body was never recovered. I still hold out hope . . ."

He lowered his mug to the counter. *A fiancé. A daughter. A granddaughter.* It was more loss than one person should have to face. "Oh . . . no, Indi didn't mention . . . I'm so sorry."

"In a way, I'm glad she didn't mention it. Diana's death and Cynthia's disappearance have been the sad backstory of this farm for so long, but I've never wanted Indi or Neil or Lil to feel like I think Diana might've once felt. Overshadowed by the past." Maggie sighed. "When Diana was young, Robert's death hung over me like a storm cloud. Looking back, I'm sure she sensed that. She would do these outlandish things sometimes. Her teenage years were such a struggle and then she ran away after high school. For the longest time, I didn't even know where she was and it was pure torture. Then one day she shows up on my doorstep with a granddaughter I hadn't known a thing about. And that same weekend . . . the car crash."

He couldn't find words to respond to her story, the tragedy of it too much to comprehend.

Maggie shook her head. "I'm convinced her acting out was an attempt to get me to *see* her. But I was hurting so much myself, missing what I could've had with Robert."

"That's completely understandable."

"Oh, I know. But at the same time, I wish someone had taken me by the shoulders during those years, given me a solid shaking, said, 'You're so blinded by what you've lost you can't see what you have.' I needed a reminder that love isn't a single flower, once plucked and gone forever. It's the soil underneath, rich and ready to grow a whole garden of living color. A lost bloom leaves a gap, no doubt, and mourning that is only right. But there's still watering and tending and nurturing to be done. There's joy and life and love still waiting for us."

Joy and life and love—they seemed to be in abundance here in this yellow farmhouse by the sea. "You said you've never wanted Indi to feel what Diana might've felt. From what I can see—from what I saw the night of your heart attack—Indi feels your love deeply."

"Thank you for saying that."

"Do you mind if I ask . . . it's not my place to be curious, but being the grandson of a mystery writer and all . . . oh, never mind."

"You want to know about Cynthia. Why I still think she's alive. Believe me, I wish I could explain it. It's just this feeling, this *knowing*. Which I'm sure sounds ridiculous."

"No. Not at all." Because hadn't he had a peculiar feeling when he'd first come to Muir Farm? Hadn't there been some uncanny knowing deep down that he needed this place? That Holland did?

"There's still an active investigation into Cynthia's whereabouts. The prevailing theory has always been that Diana ran off with an out-of-towner she met at the bar connected to The Lodge—that he's the father of Cynthia and that if she is still alive, he's the key to finding her. But no one's ever been able to identify the man." Maggie moved to Philip's side, picked up his free hand, and set the napkin and muffin he'd forgotten about in his palm. "Breakfast."

"Thanks." He paused for a moment. "Maggie? I'm glad Holland and I landed in your garden for a little while."

She surprised him by reaching up to pat his cheek. "I'm glad too, Philip West. Now, have a seat."

"Actually, if you don't mind, I might take this outside. Bring Holland a coat since she went out without—"

A chirruping phone cut him off. Maggie pulled it from the pocket of her apron as she smiled and waved him toward the door.

He would've been out the door in a second if he hadn't heard her gasp behind him. And then, "Oh, Indi. Have you called the police?"

———•—— ——•———

Red and blue pulsing lights reflected off the back wall of Bits & Pieces as waves of unbarred frigid air pushed their way in.

Indi burrowed her chin deeper into her collar, grateful she'd grabbed her thick winter coat instead of her lighter jacket on the way out of the house this morning. But if she would've known what she was going to find when she arrived at her shop, she'd have taken the time to wind a scarf around her neck, made sure her gloves were in her coat pockets.

No, if she'd have known, she'd have stayed home altogether. Saved herself the blow of seeing shattered glass all over her storefront floor.

Why? Why would someone have done this? Broken one of the windows and, as far as both Officer Tompkins and Wilder could tell, did little more than tramp through the place, riffling through her backroom and the workshop upstairs. She'd done one quick walkthrough with the pair of them, confirmed that nothing had been stolen, at least that she could see at first glance. The cash register hadn't even been messed with.

Officer Tompkins tucked his small notebook in his front pocket. "What I don't understand is how no one in town even noticed this until you arrived this morning. Would've thought we'd have gotten a call long before now."

Wilder toed a piece of glass with his boot. "Awning blocks some of the view of her front door. Sun's behind the building in the morning. Turns it into a silhouette." He shrugged. "Plus, downtown's always a little sleepy on Monday mornings."

Officer Tompkins only grunted.

Wilder went on. "I think we need to consider that whoever is behind this might be the same person who's been causing trouble at Muir Farm. It's the same deal all over again —trespassing and scrounging—"

"Not just trespassing." Officer Tompkins poked a thumb over his shoulder toward the front window. "We got an actual B&E this time."

"Right. But once again, no theft."

"We don't know that for sure. Give the girl the chance to look around a little more before settling on a theory."

Indi had seen that expression on Wilder Monroe's face plenty of times. The one that said he had a gut instinct and he trusted it. Generally, they all did. Everyone knew about Wilder's gut instincts. Correct, more often than not. Probably why there'd never seemed to be any doubt he'd follow in his father's PI footsteps.

But he wisely kept his mouth shut. Most likely because he knew if he pushed too hard, Officer Tompkins would remind him that he was the authority figure here and politely or not-so-politely usher Wilder out the door.

Another voice slid in. "So, um, should I come back later?"

Oh. Right. Trey. In the commotion she'd nearly forgotten him.

Well, no, she hadn't. It wasn't really possible to forget his presence. Or why she'd asked him to meet her here. He'd just been walking out of Trinna's Teatime when she'd driven into the town center. She'd caught sight of his same green stocking cap from the other night, recognized his bow-legged walk.

He'd spotted her at the same time and waved. By the time she'd parked in front of her store, he'd made it down the block, two covered coffee cups in hand. And then she'd seen the broken window.

Even through the shock of the discovery and the phone call to the police, the scrap of paper had burned in her pocket. She might've pulled it out while they waited for an officer to arrive, but Wilder had shown up on the scene in minutes, had heard the report on his father's old police scanner, recognized the address.

For twenty minutes now, Trey had been waiting around. Patiently or not, she didn't know. She couldn't read his expressions anymore. Not the way she'd been able to in high school. "Sorry. I didn't mean to ignore you."

Officer Tompkins and Wilder continued talking, so she steered Trey away, reaching for the Americano he'd brought her as she passed the cash register counter. Probably luke-warm by now, if not just plain cold. But he'd been nice enough to bring it, so she took a swig.

He followed her through the curtain at the back of the store, stopped just inside, leaning one hip against the wall. Like her, he still wore his coat, though his stocking cap now stuck out from his pocket. He wore his dark blond hair longer now than he had in high school. He still wore the same minty cologne he used to slather on back then, although apparently he'd learned to pull back sometime in the years since.

"I feel like I should apologize for yesterday," she said. "I was shell-shocked at seeing you and then with your news . . ."

"I know the feeling." There was no smile accompanying his words. But not a grimace either.

"Yes. Of course. I'm sure getting the diagnosis was—"

"Wasn't actually referring to that. I mean, yeah, it wasn't great learning I've got a heart thing going on, but by the time I was given a name for it, I'd been through enough appoint-ments to be prepared." He set his coffee cup on her counter. "So it wasn't actually the biggest shock of my life."

Oh, maybe she could still read him. Because his brown eyes said the rest—that his biggest shock had come eleven years ago. Spring break their senior year. When she'd handed him his ring and told him they didn't have a future.

And then dropped the second bomb. *I'm choosing adoption. It's the best thing for the baby.*

"Trey, I—"

He held up both palms. "I shouldn't have said that. There's really no point in rehashing things. We've both moved on."

Not according to Lilian. Indi's gaze wandered to the stairway that led upstairs, to where she and Lilian had talked yesterday. *"Sometimes it seems like you've never quite moved on."*

Maybe she hadn't. But she'd sure tried. Wasn't this store proof? Wasn't that crowded workshop upstairs proof? Wasn't a second location and a year's worth of running back and forth between towns proof? Wasn't Ben proof?

Was that what the past eleven years of her life amounted to? Just constantly trying to stay one step ahead of the pain and regret that would pull her under like quicksand if she gave them half a chance?

Oblivious to her roiling thoughts, Trey went on. "All that matters now is making sure the adoptive parents get the information they need. I can make the call, I just need to know who or what agency—"

"I thought maybe we could make it together." She pulled the paper from her pocket. "I have their names and a phone number."

His mouth hung open for a moment. "So you know . . . so you're in contact—"

"No, I've never had contact with them. That is, other than one short meeting that spring after I picked their photo and bio out of a binder. I didn't even see them at the hospital when . . ." She paused. Swallowed. Willed her composure to hold. "I thought it was better to make a clean break."

Trey turned away from her, lifted both hands to his head, gripped the hair at the base of his neck. When he turned to face her again, he was back to being unreadable. "Okay, let's call them."

"Right now?" With Wilder and Officer Tompkins' voices drifting from up front?

"I just want to get this done, Indi. I want to get back to Florida and get back to my life. So yes, we're doing it now."

He plucked the scrap from her hands and jabbed the numbers into his iPhone. Lifted it to his ear.

And everything else fell away then. The voices out front. Any cares about the broken window or her rummaged store. The cold, the coffee in her hand . . . everything save the thumping in her heart and her lungs pushing in and out too quickly.

Until that stopped too when Trey lowered the phone. Growled. "Disconnected."

Oh. *Oh.*

He shoved his phone into his pocket, knocking his hat to the ground in the process. "All this time you've had this number. And you've never once tried it?"

She could only shake her head.

"Geez, you didn't even care to stay in contact with them? Make sure you'd given her away to people who deserved her?" He bent to pluck his hat off the floor. "Though why am I surprised? In one spring night, you took away my whole future. Called off the wedding, made a decision about our child, didn't give me any say in it at all."

She could feel the cold again. It was needling through her, icing her veins, freezing her ability to speak.

Trey yanked his hat over his head, then folded the scrap of paper she'd guarded for eleven years and stuffed it in his back pocket. "At least I have names to go on."

She finally found her voice. "I'll help find them. I'll call the agency. Agape Adoptions—that's who I went through. They have an office in Bar Harbor. And we can Google—"

"Don't bother. I can take it from here." He stalked toward her back door.

"Everything all right back here?"

Philip? He poked his head through the curtain at the same moment Trey threw open the door and disappeared into the alley.

No, no, everything wasn't remotely close to all right. But she'd stopped herself from falling apart last night. Somehow she had to do it again now.

"Maggie's here. Lil, too. And I brought Holland."

She blew warm air into her numb hands. "I hope everyone's being careful. All that broken glass."

Philip pulled a pair of gloves from his pocket. He lifted one of her hands and fitted a glove over her fingers. Did the same with the second. "Tell me how I can help."

She should thank him for the gloves. She should find some kind of comfort in the warmth. But with Trey's anger, something had detached inside of her. And she needed to let it stay detached because if she started thinking too much, if she let her emotions loose, if she broke down . . .

She didn't know if she could ever put herself back together. So she wouldn't think. She wouldn't feel. "You brought Holland?"

He nodded.

Good. Okay. Then she knew how he could help. He could distract her. They'd go upstairs. They'd start cleaning up and hauling boxes of supplies and she'd return to her efforts to engage Holland. She'd be too busy to feel.

Perfect.

11

*H*e'd thought the seaside view mere steps from the farmhouse's front door was beautiful, but this . . . this was nothing short of majestic.

Philip breathed in the piney air, completely and fully captured by the quiet of this cliffside haven. The ocean rippled, cobalt and calm far below, down a slanting stretch of weathered, craggy rock. Morning sunlight splashed over their lofty perch, not a single feather of white trailing in the sky after two-and-a-half days of rain.

Two-and-a-half days that had left him feeling antsy and restless. A cloud every bit as weighty and gray as the ones that had rolled in on Monday afternoon and hung around until Wednesday night had seemed to hover over Muir Farm this week. The break-in at Indi's store, so close on the heels of the one at the house over the weekend, had left everyone on edge.

But it was more than that. In the few times he'd seen Indi and her sister in the same room, it was clear they were practically tiptoeing around each other. Holland wasn't avoiding him any longer, but the best he could say of their time together over the past couple days was that she'd tolerated him. Worked alongside him as they'd helped Indi clear out her workshop.

And as for Indi . . . he didn't know this Indi Muir. This full-speed-ahead version who'd turned her workshop transformation into some sort of therapeutic race. Only the long hours she'd spent packing up boxes of art supplies and unfinished projects, loading them into Neil's truck—on loan while he was on his honeymoon—didn't seem like they were having a restorative effect on her.

Maybe that's why, when she'd mentioned last night that her store would be closed today due to the new window going in, he'd found himself making the nervy request that she play tour guide again. *"What sights or landmarks do Holland and I need to make sure we see while we're here?"*

Indi had suggested a winter hike and now here they were, standing at what felt like the edge of the world. Tall cliffs and the bottomless sea. Evergreens and unadorned birch silent and still on the breezeless day, as if holding their breath to gauge his reaction.

"So tell me, was this worth the little drive? The short hike?" Indi's voice might've broken the hushed moment if it wasn't filled with an awe that matched his own. "I know you weren't excited about this outing, Holl, but I think even you have to admit this is wondrous."

Not excited? Holland had complained the entire five-mile drive down the coast and the whole half-hour walk up the rocky terrain. *"Philip and I aren't outdoor people."*

He'd found a laugh through his panting breaths. The hike wasn't overly arduous or steep, but Indi had kept them moving at a steady pace. *"Speak for yourself. I wear flannel now. I haven't shaved since Sunday. I'm practically a lumberjack and lumberjacks are outdoor people."*

Holland was nodding now, her wide-eyed gaze gulping up their surroundings. "Still doesn't mean I'm into hiking."

"Neither am I, really." Indi pulled out her phone. "But even so, this is the place I always come when I need to get away. Come on, let's take a selfie."

He easily predicted Holland's rolling eyes, and yet, she didn't pull away when Indi draped an arm around her.

"Philip, get in the photo." Indi waved him into place on Holland's other side. "Hunch down, otherwise your head will get cropped out."

"All right, Bossypants."

"Holland, please tell your brother nicknames aren't appreciated. And then both of you, smile."

He waited for Holland's inevitable correction—*half brother*—only it didn't come. Which was why he probably grinned a little too wide when Indi held up her phone. Yes, this hike had been a good idea. Made him think even though they hadn't had any big moments or brother-sister talks in the past few days, perhaps he was doing an okay job following Indi's advice. *Just be the guy who's there, who stays.*

Indi glanced at her phone screen and gave an approving nod. "Now I'll show you the chapel."

"The chapel?"

"Yes, Alec Muir built it back in the late 1700s. Maine wasn't even a state yet and Muir Harbor still several years away from becoming a full-fledged town." Indi led them to a slim trail that reached into a wooded patch, Holland just behind her and Philip bringing up the rear.

Holland glanced at him over her shoulder. "Alec Muir is Maggie's ancestor. He built Muir Farm and founded the town."

Doubtless it was silly how much satisfaction he took in the fact that she'd offered up that bit of information of her own volition. No snark in her voice.

"And he's the subject of the legend, too," she added.

"What legend?"

Now Indi was the one to twist her head toward him. "You still haven't heard the Legend of Muir Harbor?"

"I've been a little busy helping someone move a thousand boxes from her workshop to a barn."

"The barn *is* my workshop now."

Yeah, and if you asked him, it was a shame. That space above her store was airy and open and bright. The barn loft might be spacious, but it was also dirty and dim and smelled like hay. She shouldn't be relegated to working in there. But apparently the garage had become too crowded over the years and there weren't any other spare rooms in the house.

"Maggie told me the legend." Holland bent to pick up a long stick from the side of the trail, proceeded to use it as a staff. "Back in Scotland centuries ago, the Muir clan had a feud with another clan. Before the Muirs sailed away to America, Alec Muir stole the other clan's prized possession— a cup the Bonnie Prince Charlie once drank from during some rebellion or something. Only he didn't realize until he got to America that there was a bag of gold tucked into the cup. He used some of the gold to start his new life, but then he buried the rest of it and died eventually and now no one knows where it is."

Indi's laughter floated from the front of their line. "You're supposed to tell it with a Scottish accent, Holl. And you left out a few details."

Well, Philip was just fine with the Spark Notes version considering it was the most Holland had said to him in days. They emerged into another clearing then and there it stood. A chapel—tannish-yellow walls and a foundation of rock, aged and somehow grandiose despite its relatively small stature. Perhaps it was the way it perched at the edge of another cliff, its steeple piercing the sky.

Or maybe it was simply the reverence in Indi's glowing green eyes as she slowed her steps.

A chapel . . . a chapel on a cliff.

That letter Grandfather's brother had written to Maggie—it'd mentioned a chapel on a cliff, hadn't it? It'd been twenty years since he'd read the thing, but its contents were still uncannily clear in his head. Could this be the place where Maggie and Robert first met? Grandfather had been there, too, according to both the letter and Maggie.

Indi halted entirely now, but Holland strode past her and disappeared into the chapel.

He stopped beside Indi. "It's picturesque."

"This whole area used to be a part of Muir land. But over the centuries, parcels were sold off one by one when times got tough at the farm. It's technically a state park now, has been since the 1940s or something, but I like to pretend it's still ours."

"Too bad no one ever found that cup filled with gold."

She laughed and started moving toward the chapel. "The correct term is chalice. It was a pewter chalice, according to the legend." She lowered her voice and added a lilt reminiscent of her brother's accent. "'Tis said that somewhere on Muir Farm, a chalice filled with gold still rests in its hiding place. And that some nights at the harbor, you can still hear the flapping of Alec Muir's cape in the wind."

Those must be lines straight from the legend. "Okay, now I'm going to need to hear the whole thing."

"Oh no, Maggie tells it way better than I can. And Neil would laugh his head off if he heard my poor rendition of a Gaelic brogue."

"Sounded good to me." If by good he meant charming and delightful. But then, it was probably about time he admitted to himself that he found most things Indi Muir did charming and delightful. Well, except for her workaholic frenzy of the past days. That he found . . . concerning. "So is there any truth to the legend or is it just a story?"

"I don't know, you tell me, Mr. History Professor." She flashed him a smile. An actual smile, not the pinched variety he'd been seeing lately.

At the little stoop outside the chapel's arched wooden door, Philip reached for the handle, but its metal latch refused to give at first. He pulled harder and it creaked open, a waft of musty air releasing in a plume.

"We do know Alec Muir was a real person," Indi said as they stepped inside. "His voyage across the Atlantic is well-documented, but did he bring a pewter chalice filled with gold with him? Who knows. It hasn't kept treasure hunters from stopping by the farm through the years. Maggie says when she was younger, it was a rite of passage for Muir Harbor teens to prowl around looking, too. Oh, and Lilian went through a phase as a kid when she obsessed with the legend. She talked me into helping her dig for the treasure a few times."

Holland turned a slow circle up front. "Maybe that's what your intruder's looking for," she mused as she leaned over a wood altar.

Indi passed by the rough-hewn pews filling the uneven floor. "That would be hilarious. If we had a bag of gold at our disposal, trust me, our harvester wouldn't still be sitting in the machine shed waiting for a new part and Maggie's medical bills wouldn't have added another wrinkle to Neil's forehead."

Oh, huh. So money was tight at Muir Farm. Maybe another reason for the cloudy tension he'd noticed this week. And . . . *oh.* Indi's former workshop. All those ideas she'd been tossing around for turning it into a revenue stream. He had a clearer picture of her motivation now.

Even so, he had to think there was more to her long hours and bustling work this week than a desire to help out with Muir Farm's financial situation. He'd heard just enough of her conversation with Trey on Monday to know the guy had only added to the hurt and regret churning around inside her.

What was it with buffoons and backroom conversations? First Ben, now Trey. Indi deserved better. She deserved better than old love interests causing her pain. She deserved better than a barn for a workroom.

She deserved better than the ache he'd seen glimpses of too often this week even as she tried so hard to befriend Holland, to make their days in Muir Harbor meaningful.

"Not really much to see in here," Holland announced now.

"I know it's rustic and simple, but I love it." Indi lowered onto the front pew. "It's always felt like a hallowed space to me." Sunlight streamed through stained glass, painting her in patches of colorful light. "I used to beg Maggie to bring us here when we were kids. So much so that she eventually extracted a promise from me that I wouldn't come out here on my own."

Philip sat down beside her. "Did you keep the promise?"

She only shrugged.

"Indi Muir, you broke your word."

Her laughter echoed off the walls. "Only once and for what I really thought was a good reason at the time. I was ten and it was almost Christmas and I wanted snow. Prayed every night for days, and eventually, I got it into my head that maybe God would be more likely to pay attention if I was in a church. I rode my bike to the cliffs, hiked to the chapel, and started praying my little heart out. And then . . ." She gave a dramatic pause. "I fell asleep and proceeded to freak out my entire family when they couldn't find me."

At some point during her story, Holland had passed by the pew and lugged open the heavy door, light passing over the warped boards of the floor before disappearing again as Holland returned outside.

"So did the prayer work? Did it snow?"

"Actually, it did. The next day we got a full-on blizzard and I was in heaven, even if I was facing the longest grounding of my young life." She turned her gaze to the stained-glass window at the front of the church. "Maybe it's silly, but I honestly think that was one of the happiest days of my life—that day when it finally snowed. I was fully convinced it wasn't a coincidence. I prayed and God answered my prayer." She let out a quiet sigh. "I wish I could have that kind of faith again. Childlike, untarnished, innocent. Free and full of wonder."

"Wonder," he mused. "Maybe that's it."

"That's what?"

"Ever since the morning I first woke up at Muir Farm, back in November, I've tried to put my finger on what I felt. I thought at first it was peace, but it's something more. Something that makes me feel . . . I don't know. Like a child again, I guess." Like how he'd felt when Dad was alive. He leaned back in the pew, legs stretched out in front of him. "I think Muir Farm might be to me what this chapel is to you."

"Then I'm glad you came back, Philip."

"I just hope it's doing something for Holland, too." Today was a good day, but he still couldn't help feeling like the clock was ticking. Tomorrow would make one full week in Muir Harbor. Holland hadn't brought up going to live with Bryce again, but he wasn't naïve enough to assume she wasn't still thinking about it.

"Let me show you something." Indi pulled her phone from her pocket, tapped the screen, and handed it to him.

It was the selfie they'd taken earlier. Three faces filled the screen. Except Holland's wasn't pointing at the camera. She was looking up to him, her lips caught between a grin and a laugh, her gray eyes lit by the sun.

"It was right after you called me Bossypants."

Holland looked so much like Mom. She looked so . . .

happy. He had to blink, clear his throat. "Gonna text this to myself." Reception was spotty up here, but he'd give it a try. He tapped the screen to open Indi's texts, but before opening a bubble to send the photo to his own phone, he caught sight of her previous messages.

He cleared his throat again, sent a message to himself. Hoped she hadn't noticed his pause when he'd observed Trey's name in her messages. But when he handed her phone back to her and met her eyes, he knew she'd seen.

"I've texted him a few times since Monday. Finally tried calling yesterday. He's angry with me."

"In one spring night, you took away my whole future. Called off the wedding, made a decision about our child, didn't give me any say in it at all."

Indi's stricken expression in the seconds after Trey had hurled those words had burned itself into Philip's brain. Which was why he definitely shouldn't ask the question on the tip of his tongue now, but it scrambled out before he could stop it. "Why did you choose adoption, Indi?"

Her gaze dropped.

"I just wonder because . . . you said the other day you originally planned to marry Trey and raise your baby together. Why did that plan change?" He inched closer to her on the pew. "Or if I'm being rude and insensitive in asking, just ignore me."

"I highly doubt you've been rude and insensitive a single day in your life, Philip West."

"Some people would call crashing a wedding reception rude."

"Well, others of us would call it a nice little surprise."

He barked a laugh. "You did not consider it a 'nice little surprise' that night. You were so vexed when you saw me. You chased me into the house, hauled me up the steps, and demanded to know what I was doing there half a dozen times."

"Okay, yes, I was vexed. But I've had time to reconsider. Didn't I just say I was glad you came back?"

Yeah, and he'd already tucked that comment away in a spot in his brain where it'd be easy to pull out later—probably more than once—and ruminate on it. Most likely with an idiotic grin on his face. Like the one that was surely there right now. "I'm glad you're glad."

Indi shifted in the pew, twisting to face him, her knee bumping into his, the light in her eyes dwindling away until she spoke again. "I chose adoption because I was too scared to be a single mom."

Her confession lingered in the air between them like dust particles hovering in sunlight.

"I knew I couldn't marry Trey. It seemed right when he first proposed, but in the months after, it just got clearer and clearer. He was into the high school party scene. I was an emotional, unstable wreck. I had this flash of clarity that getting married wasn't going to solve anything." She pushed a strand of hair from her face. "But I couldn't do it to my family. I couldn't have my baby and try to raise her on my own and inevitably need their help and their money and their time."

She paused, her gaze drifting as memories seemed to carry her back in time. "There was this one night in March of my senior year. The pregnancy had me falling asleep at the most random times and that night I must've conked out right after dinner. I woke up in the living room and heard voices in the kitchen. It was Maggie, Neil, and Lil—talking about financial struggles at the farm, the need for new equipment, Lilian trying to save for law school. And then one of them brought up me and the baby, something about how they hadn't seen that complication coming.

"It's so strange. I can't even remember who said it, but I remember that word so clearly—complication. I'd had no idea the farm was struggling, but I realized the last thing they needed was me underfoot with a baby. So, standing there outside the kitchen eavesdropping, I made the decision. Could've sworn I even heard some kind of divine whisper telling me what to do."

She knotted her hands in her lap. "Plus, I wanted her to have a better mom than what I felt capable of being. I wanted her to have someone more mature, more stable. Less of a mess and more of a guiding light. Someone like Maggie."

At some point while she was talking, he'd propped his elbow on the back of the pew and they sat close enough that his fingers brushed her shoulder. "You are a lot like Maggie. And you've been a guiding light to Holland this week." *And to me.*

He wanted to say more. He wanted to find the right words to express what he felt with such conviction. That while Indi might look back and see a young woman who'd been scared to be a single mom, he saw someone who'd made a hard but brave decision. She might look back and call her past a mess, but he saw so many ways it'd shaped her into the soft, compassionate person sitting next to him now.

Not everyone would take Holland's sarcasm and shifting moods in such easy stride. Not everyone would welcome a random sibling duo into her life without any warning and make it her mission to help them hobble their way toward some kind of family bond.

No one had ever stirred his heart the way Indi Muir did. And now, as his gaze traced the angles of her face, moving from the wispy curls around her forehead down the slope of her nose toward her parted lips, he suddenly *didn't* want to say anything more. He wanted to do something instead.

Something impetuous and probably a little reckless.

Something Indi might not mind. Because her green eyes had traveled his face, too, coming to a stop near his lips. Because she'd gone still all of a sudden.

"Indi—"

His husky voice didn't get a chance to finish his words. Because in the next instant, Holland's scream tore through the air and ripped into his heart.

———•———•———

Indi didn't have a hope of catching up to Philip. Not with his long legs gulping up the ground as the frantic fear she'd seen on his face drove him in the direction of Holland's cry.

Still, she raced after him, her heavy breathing, the pounding of her steps over the hard ground nearly drowned by the hammering of her heart. And the pulsing realizations, one after another.

The jagged edge of the rocks. The ground still slippery from yesterday's rain and last night's frost. The fact that she couldn't see Holland . . .

"Holland?" Panic—no, terror—vibrated in Philip's yell.

Her feet skidded against pebbles and dust as she finally reached Philip. He dropped to his knees at the edge of an outcropping of rocks.

"Philip." Holland's voice, distant and weak, rose from somewhere below.

Indi lowered to the ground beside Philip, pebbles and sand scratching her flattened palms as she peered over. There, a clump of color on a jutting stone amid a rolling descent of brown rock. Holland must've slipped somehow and gone sliding down the slant of the bluff. At least it wasn't a straight drop.

"Are you hurt?" A tremble threaded Philip's question as he shrugged out of his coat.

"My wrist," Holland called back as she sat up. "My knee."

Indi reached over to touch Philip's arm. "She's talking. That's a good sign." She pulled her phone from her pocket, fruitless hope lost in an instant when she saw her screen. No bars.

"I'll be down in just a second." Determination darkened Philip's gray eyes and he bolted to his feet, tossing his jacket to the ground. "I should've been out here. I can't believe I let her wander a mountainside on her own."

This was hardly a mountain, but now wasn't the time to correct him. Not with panic clobbering every inch of his features as he surveyed the distance to Holland, probably attempting to mark out a path.

She hurried to stand. "What if you get down there and can't get back up?"

"I'm not leaving her there alone." He started forward, but she pulled on his sleeve.

"Maybe I should go. That way if she can't climb, you can pull us up."

"How, Indi? We don't have ropes. We don't have a harness." His eyes locked on her phone. "No reception?"

She shook her head.

"Then run back toward the car and call 911 as soon as you get a bar."

"But—"

"Go." Grim lines bracketed his mouth and then he turned away, moving to the edge of the rocks once more and lowering until he sat. His legs dangled over the edge for only a moment before he pushed himself away.

Her heart slammed into her rib cage as she watched him land a few feet below, rocks and debris loosening underneath his boots and clattering toward the sea. *Oh God, please . . .*

It was the most she could manage to pray before adrenaline pummeled her into action. She spun, cold air scuffing her face even as perspiration trickled down her spine. *Run.* She moved as fast as she could, cutting through the cover of the trees toward the path that would lead back to the car. A branch snagged her coat, ripping fabric, but she yanked free and kept moving.

Holland was hurt but alive. Philip would make it down to her. She would call 911 and someone would come.

She lifted her phone as she jogged. One bar. She slid to a halt and punched in the numbers. Relief washed over her like a warm rain when a dispatcher answered. It didn't take long to relay the details in spurted sentences.

"All right, Ms. Muir, we'll have emergency responders to you as quickly as possible." The woman's voice came through the line in broken rasps due to the poor reception. "In the meantime, I'd like you to stay on the phone with me and—"

"I can't. I'm out in the middle of nowhere. I had to run halfway back to the car just to get reception. I need to get back." Or maybe she should race the rest of the way to her car? Didn't she have a first aid kit in the trunk?

"Still, I'd like you to . . . with me . . ."

"I think I'm losing you."

The phone beeped, letting her know the call had dropped. But at least she'd gotten through. Someone knew where they were. Someone was on the way. And she could still help while they waited.

She started moving again, letting her feet carry her to where they'd left her car on the other side of the trees. Lungs heaving, she threw open the trunk and scoured the space until her focus landed on the small plastic container shoved along one side. Thank God for Neil and his big brother tendencies, his insistence on regularly checking her oil and checking her tires and, yes, outfitting her SUV with a first aid kit.

She closed the trunk and rounded the side of the vehicle, grateful she'd filled her water bottle before leaving the house. She tucked it under one arm, kicked her door closed, and lurched toward the trees once more.

By the time she reached the bluff, she guessed she'd been gone nearly half an hour. Still, she'd made it to the car and back in the same amount of time they'd originally hiked to the chapel. Muscles fatigued and breaths coming in quick pants, she dropped to the ground at the edge of the outcropping.

"Philip!"

Relief clouded around her again as her anxious gaze settled on him, now crouched on the jutting rock with Holland, the girl's body half sprawled in his lap. Had Holland passed out?

"I'm coming down." She shrugged out of her coat.

"Don't," he called up. "It's even steeper than it looks."

"I've got a first aid kit and water. I'm coming."

"Indi—"

"EMS is on the way."

"Then wait up there."

She ignored him, copying his move from earlier and pushing herself up to the edge of the rock, letting her feet hang over. *Don't look down. Don't think about what you're doing or what could happen if you slip. Just focus on where you need to land.*

A moment later, her boots met the hard ground, her water bottle pinned under one arm and the first aid kit under her other.

"Be careful," Philip called.

There was a bite to the oceanside air she hadn't felt earlier and it butted up against the heat racing through her veins.

With cautious steps, she crept over a rounded boulder, hands scraping on its coarse edges, then lowered herself over another rock.

Her landing wasn't as smooth this time, though, loose sand skidding under her feet and sending her sprawling onto her backside. Her water bottle rolled to the side but she managed to catch it before it slipped over the edge.

"Indi." Frustration had worn Philip's tone ragged.

"I'm fine. I'm almost there." And she'd almost gotten the assurance out without her words wavering. But surely Philip heard her voice crack on the last word. Could he hear her heart thundering too? The sea was still calm, no crashing against the shore, but it might as well have been for all the roaring in her ears.

Almost there. You're fine.

She picked her way across a blessedly flat stretch of land before once again reaching a slanted drop. No way could she navigate the final descent while balancing anything under her arms. "Catch my water bottle?"

Philip nodded, carefully moving Holland to free his legs, then standing.

She tossed him the water bottle, then the first aid kit.

"I went sliding on this part. Be—"

"Careful, I know. I'm not exactly being reckless, Phi—"

She started skidding then, her feet scrambling, one thigh banging into the sharp edge of a rock as she tried to stay upright, a shriek tumbling free . . .

She crashed into something solid and warm. And moving. Philip's chest rose and fell with heavy breaths as his arms closed around her. "Got you."

For one fleeting moment, she let herself stay there, encompassed and safe from the barraging fear present in every minute since they'd heard Holland's scream. Until she realized Philip's hands had moved to her arms in an attempt to steady her. On shaking legs, she backed up. "Holland?"

He lowered to his knees once more. "I'm pretty sure her wrist is broken. I think she fainted from the pain. She said her knee throbs, too, but it only looks banged up to me, not broken." He brushed a piece of hair from Holland's pale face.

"But she was talking to you. And moving around, right?" They could rule out a broken back or neck?

He gave a miserable nod. "She said she slid most of the way. Said her side hurts, too. What if she has a broken rib? What if it's poking into her lungs? She could have internal bleeding—"

"Philip."

"She fell down a cliff."

"She's alive and breathing."

"She's unconscious!" He flung the words, one fist balling even as his other hand gently moved Holland's head onto his lap once more.

She didn't know what to do. A little first aid kit wasn't going to fix a broken wrist or do anything to dispel the dismay clinging to every inch of Philip's rigid body. But then he unclenched his fist and she saw the scrapes on his palm, his knuckles. From his fevered climb down to Holland, no doubt.

With soft, careful steps, she moved to where he'd set the kit and opened it. She found the tube of Neosporin and retrieved her water bottle, then sank to her knees beside Philip. "Let me see your hand."

He shook his head. "There's a cut on her cheek."

Okay, then. She scooted nearer to Holland's head. She untucked her shirt from her jeans and wetted its edge using her water bottle, then dabbed it over the small laceration. Once it was clean, she smoothed it with antibiotic cream, then covered it with a Band-Aid.

She turned to Philip. "Now you."

"I'm fine."

She ignored him, took hold of his hand, and lifted her water bottle. He didn't put up a fight, didn't say so much as a word as she tipped the water over his hand and used another section of her shirt's hem to clean his scrapes. She repeated it with his other hand and dabbed Neosporin over his cuts.

"Now your own," he finally said.

She glanced down. She held his left palm between both her hands. She hadn't even noticed her own scrapes, not nearly as many of them as Philip had. "I was in the chapel with you, too, Philip."

She heard his sharp intake, felt him try to slide his hand free. But she held on.

"So if you're sitting here blaming yourself for lingering in that pew for three, four, five minutes—whatever brief amount of time we were in there while she was outside—thinking this is all your fault, then you better blame me, too."

She waited for him to argue, to pull away. But instead, his fingers curled around hers as he bent to kiss Holland's forehead.

He couldn't stop staring at her.

Holland rested on the daybed in the guest room, encased in a mound of pillows, her casted wrist propped on a bunched-up blanket on her lap, eyes closed.

He moved to the foot of the bed, pulled a pillow with a lacy sham from the floor, and gently slid it under her elbow to help out the blanket. Then went right back to staring, one hand closed around the bracelet he'd found on the rocks beside Holland earlier. Mom's old charm bracelet, now with a snapped clasp. Holland's face was still pale, a fresh bandage covering the cut on her cheek. Her hair was damp from the shower she'd insisted on taking when they'd finally arrived back at the farm after three hours at the hospital.

He'd lingered on the staircase's top step while she cleaned up, close enough to the bathroom door to hear her call if she needed anything.

"This is gonna get old real fast," she mumbled now, barely opening her eyes. She was awake?

"The cast?" At least his worries about broken ribs or punctured lungs had been for naught. She'd bruised her side, but the X-rays hadn't shown any other damage.

"No. You. Hovering."

For once, he was grateful for her testiness. He'd take a grouchy Holland any day over an unconscious one. "How are you feeling?" Voices drifted through the register near the foot of her bed. Must be suppertime by now. Or maybe after. Honestly, he hadn't a clue.

"Well, I slid down a mountain today. So I'm not really at my best." She turned her head. "You're a wreck."

"What? I changed." Spent all of three minutes a couple rooms down, throwing on clean sweatpants and a sweatshirt. But he could still feel the dirt in his hair, the grime on his face, the antiseptic smell of the hospital on his skin. "Are you comfortable? Or, at least, as comfortable as possible, all things considered?"

She lifted one shoulder, the one not weighed down by a cast. "I'd be more comfortable at home."

Home. Grandfather's house, she meant.

He slid a rocking chair from the corner to the side of Holland's bed. She lifted one eyebrow. "Promise I won't sit here all night. But give me a few minutes, okay? You did give me a good scare today, so you owe me."

She rolled her eyes, and he felt another feather of relief.

Breathed in the hint of normalcy like a swimmer breaking the surface after too long under. He'd just stay here until she fell asleep.

"It's not the same for you there, is it?"

His gaze returned to Holland's face. Her eyes were fully open now, fully alert. "Huh?"

"Home. Grandpa's house. It's different for you there than it is for me."

"Well . . . yeah."

"I've lived there since I was three. I've always liked it. I like how huge it is. I don't really even remember when we lived in a condo with Dad." She shifted slightly and he leaned forward to readjust the pillow under her arm. "There was a while when Mom was dating this guy a few years ago. I was so worried she was going to marry him and we were going to have to move out of Grandpa's place."

Had they given her some kind of medication at the hospital to make her talk like this?

"Why's it so different for you? Why did you stay away so long? Was it really so bad living there when you were a kid?"

He flattened his feet on the floor to keep his chair from rocking, fidgeting. For days—no, months—he'd been wishing for a real conversation with Holland. But this one . . . it wasn't the one he'd wanted. He gave a useless cough. *Stalling.* "Well, Grandfather and I . . . we aren't exactly close." *He didn't drink hot chocolate with me. We didn't watch westerns and musicals together. I don't call him Grandpa.*

"You weren't close to Mom either."

It wasn't a question. So maybe he didn't have to respond. He slid his thumb over the bracelet in his palm.

"Because she was different with you, too, wasn't she?"

He placed the bracelet on her bedside table, then scrubbed his palms along his sweatpants, stopping at his knees and letting his fingers curl. Medicine—they had to have given her something at the hospital. Or that fall down the cliffside had loosened something inside of her. And he should be basking in it.

But he couldn't. He couldn't answer those questions honestly. If he did, he might stain her memories of Mom. He might taint her current relationship with Grandfather. *Grandpa.*

"I just want to know why it was so different for you. Because if I did, maybe then I'd know why you were never around. I'd understand. I wouldn't be so angry at you all the time."

"You're right. Things were different for me. But to be honest, I don't really want to dredge it all up. It's in the past."

"No, it's not. If it was really in the past, you wouldn't act like moving back to Grandpa's house was like taking up residence in an igloo wearing nothing but your underwear."

"I haven't acted like that." Or been that obvious. Had he?

"Please. You'd have been on the first plane back to Seattle if not for me and those papers Mom made you sign."

"She didn't make me—"

"What's so great about Seattle? A silly Space Needle that just looks like an oversized spinning top?"

Was she actually smiling? At him? "You're kind of punchy right now. I like it."

Another eye roll as she sank farther into her pillows. And then, "I don't know why you didn't know the same Mom I did. But I'm sorry you didn't. Because she was really great."

He almost thought he saw tears in her eyes just before she closed them. On purpose? An effort to end this conversation? Or was she drifting off to sleep? He leaned forward, hoped she wouldn't jerk away when he reached for her un-casted hand. *I'm sorry too, Holland. Sorry I didn't come home sooner. Sorry I missed so much.*

She didn't grasp his hand, but she didn't pull away either.

Nor did she open her eyes again, slowly falling asleep under his watchful gaze. Only after her breathing had settled into a steady cadence did he finally slip his hand free, quietly slide the rocking chair backward, and stand.

He turned off the lamp on the bedside table and gently closed the door, letting himself lean against it for a long, tired moment, before stopping in Neil's room to grab a few things.

The bathroom was humid when he walked in, fog and droplets on the mirror, leftover from whoever had been in here last. Finally time for a shower.

Maybe the water would wash away more than the dirt. Maybe the residue of this day would wash away too—the terror he'd felt at the sound of Holland's scream, the memory of the sight of her sprawled too many feet below, every thwacking notion of how much worse it could've been . . .

He set his toiletry bag down—or tried to. He missed the counter and it clattered to the floor, contents spilling around his feet.

And those questions she'd just asked him, the things she'd said . . . *"You weren't close to Mom either."*

"Philip, is that you in there?" Indi. "Everything okay?"

"Because she was different with you, too, wasn't she?"

Yeah, Holl, she was. Because for the most part, Mom wasn't *with* him at all. Because she'd left him. Left him in that huge, dreary house with a grandfather who hadn't wanted him.

He gripped the edges of the counter, breathing too fast. Why was he breathing so fast? Gulping swaths of air that didn't make it to his lungs like they were supposed to. Just kept evaporating before they could do any good, disappearing . . .

Like everyone who'd left him. Dad. Mom. And Holland, she could've left him today, had come so close.

He tried to loosen his grip on the counter, back away, but

he stumbled on the stuff he'd spilled, knocked into the edge of the shower.

"Philip? Is something wrong?"

He couldn't breathe, that's what was wrong. Didn't know what was happening to him. Why his vision was going blurry all of a sudden.

Vaguely, he was aware of the bathroom door opening, a blast of cooler air marching into the mugginess around him. A palm landing on his back. "Philip?"

"I don't . . ." He could hardly speak through the panting. "Don't know what's . . . happening."

"I think you're having a panic attack. Sit down, okay?"

Indi had him by the hand now, leading him like a child. And then her other palm was pressing against his shoulder, pushing him down until he sat on the closed toilet.

"Just focus on breathing. I'm right here. In and out—one breath after another."

He didn't know how long he sat there. Heart and lungs trying to find a rhythm, eyes squeezing shut and then opening, trying to focus only to close again. His palms sliding over his thighs over and over . . .

And Indi, speaking quiet, gentle words that glided over him until finally the buzzing was gone from his ears. And maybe his heart wasn't going to staccato out of his chest. And he could breathe again.

"I'm sorry. I don't know . . ." His head still hung, neck and shoulders tight, sore.

Indi was on her knees in front of him, one hand on his leg. "Has this ever happened before?"

"Maybe once before. The night my mom . . ."

She nodded. "The night she died."

"No. The night she left."

Yeah, this is exactly what'd happened that night. He'd been

in a bathroom that night, too. Trying not to cry. Didn't want Grandfather to hear him. Didn't want him to know . . .

"S-she just left me there. I was only seven years old. I wasn't over Dad. I was terrified of that huge house and how dark it was at night and . . . she just l-left me there." Hot tears started a slow crawl down his face.

No. No, this was ridiculous. It was twenty-seven years ago. He wasn't a child anymore. He wasn't abandoned and alone. He pressed his eyes closed before any more tears could pool, swiped the back of one hand along his cheeks. "Sorry. After everything that happened today, I guess I just . . . freaked out or something."

Sitting back in a crouch, Indi simply looked at him. She wore light gray joggers now and a white T-shirt under a long green sweater. She was probably the one who'd been in here before him, left the mirror foggy, because her hair was wet, hanging loose around her face. She'd washed off her makeup.

"Sorry," he said again.

But instead of responding, she rose up higher on her knees and leaned closer, circling her arms around his neck. She pressed his head to her shoulder, fingers in his hair, and just held him there for a moment. He drew in the strawberry scent of her skin, or maybe her hair, felt the last creases of his breathing smooth out.

Home. That's what this moment felt like. So much so he almost groaned seconds later when she finally began to pull away. "Indi, I—"

She touched one cheek with her palm. "Philip, if you apologize one more time . . ."

And then he did groan. Because he couldn't stop himself. Because though this might be a terrible mistake, he just couldn't not lower his head until the inches between them disappeared and he kissed her.

The moment his lips touched hers, he felt the jolt of her

shock. Or maybe that was all him, every nerve flaring to life inside him. And then sparking into full-on flames when he realized she was kissing him back, still with one hand on his cheek, the other now clutching at his sweatshirt.

His arms went around her, lifting her to his lap, his fingers finding their way into her damp hair. He drank her in, deepening his kiss until finally, lungs still raw from earlier, heart galloping all over again, he had to breathe.

He inhaled. Whoa." It was the only word he was capable of getting out.

There was no getting around it—she was a coward.

Indi's shoes slapped against the dock, still slick from another overnight frost. Chunks of ice bobbed in the unsettled water of the harbor, the dock wobbling under her boots. White clouds crowded the sky and she could almost taste the promise in the crisp stillness of the air. *Snow.* It was coming. Finally.

A happy foreshadowing that should have her picking up her pace, practically skipping toward Wilder's houseboat at the end of the dock. But what were the chances he was even awake this early?

Her steps slowed as she neared the boat. It nodded up and down, *The Marilyn* painted in hunter green on its hull. *At least I brought coffee.* She knocked on the sliver of a door that led to the boat's small living quarters.

No answer.

A brutal wind scraped over her cheeks, the barest sliver of a white winter sun to the east doing little to cast any warmth at all into the air. She knocked again and, thankfully, this time the squeak of rusty hinges met her ears and then Wilder's confused tone. "Indi?"

He was pulling a hoodie on over a T-shirt with faded letters as he opened the door. He wore shorts. No socks. Did the man remember it was January? "Were you sleeping?"

"Uh, yeah. Is it even six yet?"

Only just. She'd been out of the house by five this morning, had Neil's chores done by five thirty. Was driving down the lane by 5:45.

Because you're a coward.

Fine. Yes. Because last night Philip West had kissed her and she had no clue what to do with that fact. Or with the fact that she was pretty sure she'd heard music. Like, actual melodies ringing in her ears that wouldn't quiet down enough to let her sleep last night.

And then there'd been that sizzling warmth. It'd started sparking through her in that potent, magic moment right before Philip's lips had touched hers and had already heated every inch of her body by the time the kiss ended.

Good grief, she could still feel the balmy perfection now. Could probably melt the icicles dangling from the overhang above Wilder's houseboat door just by looking at them. Philip's murmured *"Whoa"* had perfectly summed up her own thoughts.

Of course, then she'd practically run away from him in the aftermath. She'd slid off his lap, mumbled something inane about hoping she hadn't used up all the hot water when she'd showered, then fled to her bedroom and spent the rest of the night trying to convince herself not to march right on back and demand the man kiss her again.

You barely know him. Only two months ago, you were engaged to someone else. And another guy you were once engaged to just walked back into your life. Plus, Philip needs to focus on Holland. And besides, there's just too much else all happening at once.

The break-ins. Her plans for her workshop. Trey's disease.

Yes. And that last one was her purpose for being here now.

Standing on Wilder's doorstep. Er, well, his dock. Holding a Thermos filled with coffee and a bag with two of Maggie's blueberry muffins, trying and failing not to relive that kiss for the millionth time since last night.

Wilder waved a hand in front of her face. "Did you sleep-walk here?"

She blinked. "Sorry." He waved her in and she ducked under the doorway. "Apparently I'm not fully awake." Or probably the opposite was true. She'd never actually fully slept last night. No REM-cycle rest for her. Not after—

Indiana Joy, put it out of your head!

Right, like it was easy or something. Like she couldn't feel her cheeks heating all over again at just the thought . . .

Or, wait. Maybe it wasn't just the memory of Philip's kiss hitting her like a tropical breeze just now. "Holy cow, Wild, it's like ninety degrees in here." Guess that explained his shorts and bare feet.

"Blame Junie Smalley. She was out to look at my heater yesterday and swore she fixed it. Instead, it went from Siberia in here to a sauna."

She set her Thermos and bag on a small oval coffee table and shrugged out of her coat. "You should've come out to the farm last night."

"You guys gave the guest room away to a kid."

"You've spent plenty of nights on the couch before."

He shook his fingers through his shaggy hair. "True. And I might reclaim the spot tonight." Wilder swept a pair of discarded jeans off the small sofa in the living quarters' main room and motioned for her to sit. Through a narrow doorway only a few feet away, she could see the bed that took up most of his sleeping area, its sheets a twisted mess and his comforter in a pile on the floor.

"I'm sorry. I totally woke you up."

"It's fine." He yawned on the heels of his words. He

dropped onto a cushioned storage cube across from the couch and reached for the bag she'd brought. He took out a muffin and chomped into it. "Wait, this was for me, right?"

She laughed. "Yeah. And the coffee, too." She'd already downed the contents of a tall travel mug on the way into town, desperate, on the one hand, for caffeine to make up for her restless night, and pretty certain, on the other, that she didn't need anything else adding to her jittery-ness. In the end, the hazelnut aroma had won out.

"Good. I'll eat and drink. You tell me why you're here."

"I was hoping maybe you could help me locate someone. A married couple. I have their first names and an old phone number. I know that at one point, at least, they lived up near Rockport, but I don't know if they do anymore."

Actually, she was pretty sure they didn't. Because on Monday evening, she'd Googled about a thousand combinations of John and Sandy Holmes's names together and separately, Rockport, and every other town in a fifty-mile radius and had come up empty.

On Tuesday morning, she'd called Agape Adoptions first thing and had been relieved to discover the social worker who'd handled her adoption still worked there. She'd left a message, then texted Trey to let him know she'd done so.

But he hadn't answered that or any of her other texts. And there'd been no return call from the agency, despite the second message she'd left yesterday. When she'd tried Googling the Holmeses two more times, she hadn't had any more luck than the first time. Shouldn't she at least have been able to find a social media profile for one or the other of them?

Wilder took a long swig of coffee straight from the Thermos. "Sure, I can help with that. Shouldn't be hard. Text me the names and the phone number and I'm on it."

She let out a relieved exhale. Not that she'd expected

Wilder to refuse her request, but maybe she'd needed to take this step more than she'd realized. Of course, for all she knew, Trey had resources of his own and had already located the couple. But surely he didn't expect her to just sit back and assume it was over—that he'd spoken to the adoptive family, passed on his news, and everything was fine.

Surely he didn't think she didn't care?

"You didn't even care to stay in contact with them? Make sure you'd given her away to people who deserved her?"

She'd been trying to fight off the severe impact of those words ever since Monday.

Wilder finished off his muffin, eyes stuck on her. "For the record, it's not imperative I know why you need to find whoever it is you're wanting to find. But as your friend and honorary big brother, I at least have to ask if you're okay right now. Because you don't look okay."

"Gee, thanks."

"Lil told me Trey's back."

"She did?"

He pulled out the second muffin. "Every once in a while, she's civil long enough for us to carry on a conversation. Surprising, I know. Almost as surprising as the fact that she went out with that Peyton guy a second time."

"Really? Where've I been?" *Holed away in your workshop. Hiking to the chapel.*

Kissing Philip West.

She might as well stop trying not to think about it. "Huh, well, Lil must like the guy. She goes on plenty of first dates, but second ones are few and far between."

Wilder only grunted. Took a too-large bite of the muffin.

"Anyway, you're right." She lifted her phone and opened a text. "The names I'm texting you now are the couple who adopted my—the—baby. Trey found out about a hereditary heart disease and we need to inform the parents, make sure they know to get our—their—child tested."

After several days, it was getting a little easier to lay out the facts, line them up one after the other. *Trey has a disease. The family needs to know. So we need to find them.*

But if she thought about it, *really* thought about it . . . if she even considered something might be wrong with the baby she'd carried inside her . . . if she pictured the tiny heart inside that bundle of pink, puckered skin . . .

A bundle she'd forced herself to turn away from when the nurse had asked if she'd like to hold her baby, no goodbye. And she had to turn away from her feelings and fears now. *Just don't think about it. Recite the facts when you have to but nothing else. Nothing more.*

But how was she *not* supposed to feel when Wilder turned his dark, assessing eyes on her. He was far too skilled at reading people. It's what made him a good PI. "Indi, if you need to talk—"

"Have you learned anything more about the break-in? At the store? At the house?"

He waited a beat, then set down the muffin. "No. Not that I haven't gone over all the details a hundred times."

She glanced around the houseboat-turned-sauna. She'd done what she'd come to do. She should leave the man in peace. Before he turned that private-eye-and-pseudo-big-brother stare on her again. But when she stood, she caught sight of the crate packed with files on a tiny table wedged between the couch and the kitchenette.

She'd seen that crate before. Wilder's father used to bring it to the house before he died, back when he'd met regularly with Maggie to talk about his ongoing search for her missing granddaughter, Cynthia. "Any progress on that one?"

"I wish." He gave a sigh and folded his hands together behind his head. "You know, around the time of her heart attack, Maggie started remembering some additional details about the night Diana died and Cynthia went missing."

"Really?" Another thing she'd missed in that tumultuous season.

"Thought maybe it might get us somewhere new but I dunno. I go to sleep every night with the facts plaguing my brain. Diana runs away after high school, supposedly with someone she met at The Lodge's bar. Two years later, she shows back up on Maggie's doorstep with two-year-old Cynthia. Dies in a car crash that same weekend. So what happened in between? All we know is she was in Atlanta for a time, but who was she with? Was it really some guy from a bar, and if so, we should've been able to identify him. I have a guest list of every person staying at The Lodge that night, but none of them lead anywhere. And what brought Diana back to Muir Harbor the night of the crash?" Another sigh, and he dropped his hands. "Here's the thing, though. I can't let go of the feeling that the two things are linked. The old case and our current friend, the mysterious intruder."

"What? How? Cynthia went missing twenty-eight years ago. The intruder only started coming around last fall. Don't tell me you're thinking the intruder *is* Cynthia. Like, she's been out there all this time, waiting to be found. Only she found us first and . . ." Okay, so a night of little sleep had done a number on her imagination.

"Nah." Wilder stood. "Wild as that'd be, I'm convinced it's a male. Shoe size, for one thing. And I saw just enough of him as he jumped in his car last weekend to be pretty sure it's a dude we're looking for." He took another long drink of the coffee, then capped the Thermos. "Just wish I could land on what he's looking for. Or maybe he's not looking for anything. Maybe someone's just trying to taunt us. Breaking in, but never taking anything. He's not exactly covering his tracks. But why?"

"Holland thinks he's looking for Alec Muir's treasure."

"Ha!" He grinned. "Although, actually, that's not as outrageous of a thought as it seems on the surface. Not like Muir Farm hasn't had treasure hunters come calling before." He rubbed his chin and stared at the crate full of files. "Don't know. Just can't get past the idea that it's all connected. What happened then, what's happening now."

"Another famous Wilder Monroe gut instinct."

"Something like that." He gave her a tired smile. Only it seemed as if more than the early morning was wearying him. "But don't worry, I've got plenty of time to find your—" He reached for his phone and glanced at the text she'd sent. "—John and Sandy Holmes."

"I'm not worried. And I'll pay you for the work, of course."

"Don't be silly. Like I'd take a cent." He walked with her the few steps to the door. "I'll call or text when I've got something."

She stopped at the door. "Hey, if you're my honorary big brother, then that makes me your honorary sister. So it's totally normal for me to do the asking now. Everything all right with *you*? You seem . . . weighed down."

He only shrugged and opened the door for her. "Don't worry about me, Indiana. I'm just fine."

She knew a pretense when she heard one, but who was she to argue? Neil was Wilder's best friend, not her.

Then again, something told her not even Neil knew everything that went on in Wilder Monroe's head.

"You're being extra weird this morning. And I so did not ask for breakfast in bed."

Philip waltzed to Holland's bedside, her glare only illuminating all the more what already felt like a flawlessly bright day. Never mind the wan sun and the white sky, the wind shouldering into the house, sending enough of a draft scrambling through the walls and windows that the radiators were having a hard time keeping up.

No, his good mood didn't have a thing to do with the weather. Had everything to do with the woman he'd kissed last night and the teenager flashing him a withering scowl just now.

"Morning to you, too, Sleepyhead. I'd remark on the fact that it's almost nine thirty already, but you did do the whole sliding down a cliff thing yesterday, so I'll cut you some slack." .

"Seriously, why are you smiling like that?"

He set a tray on the bed beside her, careful not to bump her broken wrist. "I made hot chocolate. Homemade, this time. Probably won't be exactly what you're used to, but I found this recipe on the internet and the person who posted it spent, like, twenty-eight paragraphs talking about how amazing it is and how it's a Christmas tradition in her family and then felt the need to list every other family tradition before actually getting to the recipe—" He took a breath. "So either she's just insanely ebullient, or this stuff should knock your socks off."

"Speaking of insanely ebullient . . ." Holland's voice was a full-on grumble.

A glorious grumble. So glorious he leaned down and kissed the top of her head.

"What the heck was that?" She swung her good arm, nearly knocking over the tray he'd brought her. It was crowded with toast, homemade blueberry jam—courtesy of Maggie, of course—bacon, and a banana. Barely ripened, mostly green, just the way she liked. "Did you just *kiss* my *head*? I'm fifteen not five. And you're my brother not my father or, like, the mall Santa."

"The mall Santa kisses the top of kids' heads? That seems sketchy. Try the hot chocolate. I need to know if the time I spent on that recipe website was worth it."

"Not until you tell me why you're being weird."

"I'm just glad you're alive, okay?" And that underneath her frown, he was pretty sure he saw something like amusement. Maybe even the tiniest smidge of happiness at seeing him.

Or . . . or had last night left him so rattled that he was imagining things?

Well, for sure he hadn't imagined that kiss. And how wonderfully, unbelievably perfect it'd been. Sure, Indi had jumped out of his lap after he'd had the dumb need to come up for air, but the fact remained: She'd kissed him back.

Of course, a scorching kiss hadn't been the only thing that'd happened in that bathroom last night. He'd sort of fallen apart beforehand, hadn't he? Indi had said it was a panic attack.

Indi had seen it all.

Not really his most dignified moment, and twelve, thirteen hours later, the whole thing was kind of a blur. Overshadowed, he supposed, by that kiss. Or maybe . . . maybe just whittled down in his memory because of Indi's comforting presence. When she'd wrapped her arms around his neck, he honestly could've wept. Maybe did. He didn't even know.

He dropped into the rocking chair beside Holland's bed.

The one thing he was certain of—that panic attack had been coming for months. Looking back, the garish signs were all there. The anxiety he'd felt on his first night back in his old room at Grandfather's. The stress and pressure he'd experienced when he'd been so sure he was failing Holland.

Losing Mom—the grief mixed in with a confusing blend of decades-old emotions.

He wasn't foolish enough to think one breakdown was some kind of magic breakthrough that would erase all the angst of the past eight months. Or the past twenty-seven years since Mom had carried her suitcase out Grandfather's front door. Or the twenty-eight since Dad died.

But *something* had happened last night. And he felt lighter for it this morning.

"Listen, Holl." He leaned forward in the rocking chair. "You asked me some questions last night. I don't know if you remember, but I didn't really answer."

"Of course I remember. I was two doses deep in ibuprofen, not hopped up on morphine." She bit into a piece of toast. "Is that why you're being weird now? You're going to finally reveal some big secret?"

"No, there's no secret." He nabbed a slice of bacon from her plate and took a bite. "I guess I just wanted to say you're right. I didn't know the same Mom you did. When I was seven, about a year after my dad died, she left to go live with Bryce—your dad. And I stayed with Grandfather." He swallowed another bite, hoping he was setting the right tone with his words. He wasn't trying to be accusing, just honest. "On an intellectual level, I can understand why she made that decision. Bryce lived in a one-bedroom apartment. Grandfather had a huge house, was paying for me to be in private school. And it's not like Mom disappeared from my life. She came to all my school events, spent time with me on weekends. Picked me up for holidays or brought Bryce to the house."

He finished the bacon and gripped the rocking chair's armrests. "But on an emotional level, I really struggled to understand it. And to adjust. I think some of those feelings just . . . stayed with me. Maybe deeper than I realized for a long time."

Holland had stopped eating sometime in the past few seconds. Her glare was gone.

"So, no, I didn't know her the way you did. And I guess that's why I didn't come back from Seattle very much."

Holland shifted against her pillow, settled her cast on the breakfast tray. "You used to come more. When I was really little. I remember you being around more often."

Sure, because he'd been closer then. He'd wanted to go farther away than Thornhill for college but with Grandfather tenured there, he'd had a full ride. He'd had more opportunity then to see Holland. "I felt more like your uncle than your brother back then. You were a pretty cute baby, for the record. And toddler." That'd been difficult, too, though— seeing Mom with Holland in those first few years. Realizing this new child might share something with his mother that he no longer did.

It'd made the decision to move to Seattle for grad school easy. And then staying there . . . well, it'd made more sense than coming home.

Home. No, Grandfather's house hadn't seemed like home to him. And it didn't now.

But it did to Holland. His *sister.* Who he'd already missed out on too much time with. So when this two-week bubble burst, when it was time to say goodbye to Muir Farm, he would try harder. He would stop seeing only the shadows in that big house in Augusta, and start looking for the light.

The brightest of which was sitting right in front of him. "I love you, Holl. And I'm really sorry I wasn't around before."

She was looking down at the plate she hadn't touched in long minutes. She didn't say anything. And that was okay. It was enough that she'd heard. That he'd said the words he should've said long ago.

He leaned over the edge of the mattress to give her shoulder a small squeeze, then stood. "Enjoy breakfast. And make sure you report back on the hot chocolate." He moved toward the doorway.

"Philip?"

He stopped under the doorframe, leaned against it as he faced her once more.

"I almost called you."

He straightened.

"Right after Mom got the diagnosis, when I realized how bad it was, I almost called you."

"I would've come. I hope you know that."

She nodded. "I should've called. She should've told you sooner. I'm sorry."

"You don't have any reason to be sorry, Holland. I'm just glad I'm here now." He waited in the doorway just in case she might offer a "Me too." And maybe she did. Not verbally. But in the way she lifted her mug of hot chocolate and sipped. In the quiet, half-smile she offered after she swallowed.

Yes, he thought as he left the room and moved down the hallway, this was a good day. One that was only destined to get better after he saw Indi. Told her about the conversation he'd just had.

And then maybe he'd kiss Indi again. Because all of this had happened because of her, hadn't it?

"Philip!"

He stopped at the entrance to the kitchen, surprise and then confusion and then a whole new burst of cheerfulness settling over him. "Tabby? I have no clue what you're doing here, but you have to try this hot chocolate I made."

"I can admit it, this town is pretty adorable. Even on a day as gray as this one."

Connor's wife leaned forward to turn up the heater in Philip's Honda, apparently not at all in a hurry to tell him why she'd driven almost an hour to talk to him when she could've just picked up the phone.

Decorative storefronts and brick buildings lined both sides of the cobblestone street, awnings alternately sagging and billowing with the wind. Indi just might get her beloved snow today. Speaking of, he pointed to Bits & Pieces, the sign in the front door flipped to *Open* and the new window reflecting the pale glint of the sun. "The building with the white exterior and bright yellow shutters—that's Indi's store." Where he'd probably be right now if Tabby hadn't tracked him down at the farmhouse.

He glanced over at her as he drove. A new dash or two of color usually streaked Tabby's blond pixie-cut whenever he saw her. Pink and blue, this time. She was still sipping the hot chocolate he'd reheated and poured into a travel mug. Did Connor know she was here?

"And you're right—it's a fun town," he said. "I like it, and though I doubt Holland would ever admit it, I think she does, too. It's the sort of place where it feels like Christmas every day." Of course, that was probably because there was still Christmas music playing in the square. And a tree lit-up in Maggie's living room.

He turned his car toward the harbor and found a spot to park overlooking the waterfront, surprised to see more than a few boats bobbing in choppy waters away from the docks. Portside lights cut into the tepid day, glowing yellow and casting their floating reflections upon the bay.

"So you going to fill me in on the purpose for your surprise appearance or keep me waiting another fifteen minutes?" If he'd had his way, she would've spit out her reason for being here back at the farmhouse. But Maggie had been in the kitchen with her, having opened the door when she'd knocked, and then Lilian had shown up.

So he'd decided maybe a driving tour of Muir Harbor was in order.

"You're wearing your glasses. Got plans to stop by that 'white exterior, bright yellow shutters' building or something?"

"Don't even start, Tab. Not even you would make an hour's drive just to heckle me."

"Okay, fine." She reached down into the messenger bag at her feet, came up with a stack of papers at least an inch thick. "I brought you some reading material."

"But I don't need—" Oh. *Oh.* Of course. He cut the engine. "Right. You're not here as a friend. You're here as Ray Camden's literary agent. Sorry you wasted a trip."

"Just hear me out."

"Why should I when I've already told you no a dozen times?"

"All I'm asking is that you read what he's written so far. Your grandfather wrote these pages nine, ten months ago. The full manuscript was originally due in June, but I don't think he's written a page since your mother died."

"Can you blame him? It was his daughter, Tab. If his publisher can't understand that and give him some deadline grace, maybe he needs to find a new one."

"This isn't the publisher sitting beside you right now. It's me. Not as an agent. As your friend. And as your friend, I'm telling you I really think you need to read these pages, Phil."

"Because you want me to ghostwrite the second half of the book. Because Connor opened his big mouth and told you I used to want to be a writer."

"No. Because your grandfather told me you used to want to be a writer. He gave me this." She held up a flash drive and, wait, he recognized that. Hard to forget a flash drive shaped like an alligator.

"Is that . . . tell me you didn't . . ."

She nodded. "I opened every doc. Read every word."

He clicked his seat belt and leaned back in his seat. "Wow. Talk about an invasion of privacy." He wanted to sink from his seat and disappear under the floor mat. How many novels had he started writing as a teenager and saved on that flash drive? All juvenile and ridiculous, surely. And where had Grandfather even gotten it? *Apparently that's what he does— hold on to other people's stuff.* His brother's old love letter, Philip's old flash drive. "I have no idea why he'd give that to you."

"Probably because he read everything on it, too, and realized the same thing I did. You are a writer, Philip."

"I'm not."

"Deny it all you want, but I know good writing when I read it." She set the stack of papers on the console between them. "It wasn't my idea to float the possibility of ghostwriting. It was Ray's."

He twisted in his seat and stared at her.

"Actually, scratch that. He brought up co-writing first. But I think he's aware he's not in a great place creatively. Thankfully, he already has the book plotted out. He's a meticulous outliner. So ghostwriting might be more in order than co-writing."

"I'm sorry, I'm still back on the part where Grandfather— my grandfather, Ray Camden—had the idea of pulling *me* into this thing." The grandson he'd never seemed all that keen on.

She nudged the papers onto his lap. "Just read it. Please? This book is incredibly different than his others. There's time travel and history and . . . and you just need to read it for yourself. If the answer's still no, I promise not to bring it up again."

He glanced down at the cover sheet, empty save the title in capital letters and Grandfather's byline underneath, the rubber band holding the stack together cutting through his last name. *The Centuries Between Us.* Interesting title. It really had time travel in it? "Okay."

"Really? You'll read it?"

"I'll read it if you tell me why you're really here." He strummed the manuscript's rubber band while he eyed her, unwilling to let her off the hook. "You could've emailed the document."

"Yeah, but the effect wouldn't have been the same. Plus, I really liked seeing the surprise on your face when you saw that alligator flash drive."

"Please. I don't even want to think about what you read in those files."

"There was one story about an archaeologist on a quest to find dinosaur bones that particularly intrigued me. I could just picture little Philip West plunking away at a keyboard—"

"Tab."

"Okay, you're right. I have another favor to ask you. Well, not really a favor so much as . . . there's something I have to tell Connor and I've been trying to figure out how to get it out for days and . . . I just need advice or . . . or something."

"You're scaring me a little. Tell him what?"

She let her bag drop to the floor and took a breath. "We're going to have babies."

Babies. Not one but . . . "Did I just hear you right?"

Tears filled Tabby's eyes. "There've been so many miscarriages. I couldn't make myself tell him this time. Not until it was . . . until I was sure . . . I mean, I guess we won't really know until . . ."

"*Babies?*"

Her tears overflowed. "Three of them. We're having three

babies. We're having triplets." A sob caught in her laugh. "I'm so freaked out."

"Triplets. You're having triplets. You're having triplets and you decided to talk about the next Ray Camden bestseller first? Holy cow, Tab, if it wasn't all of twenty degrees outside, I'd make you get out of the car and give you a hug. But Connor would pound me into the ground for making his pregnant wife get out in the cold. Oh my gosh . . . triplets. Congratulations." He couldn't stop his shocked jabbering. "I suddenly have the intense need to be there when you tell Connor. He's going to keel over. I can already see his face going white. He's going to . . . why can't I stop talking?"

"Because it's *insane*. Triplets."

He reached over her to open the glove compartment and pull out a napkin. "Here."

She wiped her cheeks, dabbed her eyes. "I can't believe he hasn't figured it out. I'm totally showing. But he's been distracted." She rotated in her seat. "How do you think he's going to take it? You're his best friend. You've seen him at his best and his worst."

Oh. That's what this was about. "You're worried about his drinking."

"He's been distant lately. I've wondered . . ."

"I think if he's been distant, it's because he's worried about you. He was telling me last week how hard the holidays can be for you, how badly he wished he could fix things—"

"Oh, he fixed it, all right. And the holidays this year were hard for a whole different reason. I knew I was pregnant but couldn't stop thinking it was only a matter of time until another miscarriage. I didn't know whether to tell Connor or wait longer." She sniffled. "I keep imagining him opening the calculator on his phone and trying to figure out how we're going to afford three cribs, three car seats, three college educations, and oh my word, all those diapers." She blew her nose. "It's not even really the drinking I'm concerned about. He's been sober for four years. He still goes to meetings every week. He's got me, you, his faith. He's doing the work. I'm more worried he's going to be as scared to hope as I am."

"That's why you need to tell him. So you can be scared together. And I bet you'll even figure out how to hope together." He pressed another napkin into her hand. *Together.* He was really beginning to like that word. "Tell him, Tab. Connor's going to be over the moon. And you'll be in it together, like a family should be."

Like maybe he was finally learning to be with Holland.

He flattened his palm over the half-written manuscript in his lap. Maybe, someday, he could get there with Grandfather, too. *Maybe.*

Except for the paint splatters on the floor and the scent of sawdust still tarrying in the air, a person might never know this open space had once been Indi's workshop.

"Wow, you said you'd emptied it out, but this is *empty-empty.*"

"Maggie?" Indi spun around from her spot in the middle of the room. She'd come up here right after turning her door sign to *Closed*, hoping maybe if she stepped into the hollow space, the fresh vision she'd been waiting for would sing its way right into her soul.

Are you a coffee shop? An apartment? An extension of the store?

"It's after six, dear, and your front door was still unlocked. Remember? We're all about safety and security right now."

Locking her door hadn't kept someone from shattering the front window on Monday. But that probably wasn't a reminder Maggie would appreciate. "What are you doing here?" Their voices were near-echoes in the barren room.

"Oh, I was just in town for a bit." She wore slim black pants and a light pink shirt, topped with a cream-colored cardigan. No braid in her hair this evening. She'd left it loose and wavy, reaching halfway down her back. She looked, well, young tonight. Not that she looked old on other days, but there was something extra bouncy about her this evening. Those were Lil's gold hoops in her ears, weren't they? She almost looked like she'd dressed up for . . .

"Maggie, were you—"

"Oh, fine, yes, I was on a date. But I didn't come here to discuss that."

"I'm sorry, but my mother who, to my knowledge, has not dated—" Why did that word sound so wrong in this context? "—anyone in my lifetime, does not get to casually drop that she was out on a date and then not follow up on it. Who with? And where'd you go? It's only . . . ?" She checked her phone. "Six ten. Is the date over already?"

"Well, when you're in your sixties, you do early evening dates, I guess. I don't know. We went to Trinna's. We got decaf coffee. We had a nice time."

"We *who*?" But just like that, she knew.

Of course. Hadn't she seen them laughing together at Neil and Sydney's wedding? Hadn't he stayed long after the other guests had begun departing? Showed up again the next morning to see if Maggie needed help with post-wedding clean-up? Installed their new security system? "Wow. My mother and Tatum Carter."

"There's something about the way you keep saying 'my mother' that's irking me. And don't start planning a wedding or anything. Like I said, we had a nice time. But this is new for me." She let her purse slip to the floor. "Tatum's become a good friend, but I'm not sure it's meant to be anything more than that. And that's okay with me. Anyway, he was about to drive me home, but I saw the light on up here and asked if he'd mind dropping me here instead."

"Because you wanted to talk to me?"

She nodded.

"If not about Tatum, then . . . ?"

"Anything. I would be happy to talk to you about anything, Indi. I've missed you lately. You're around but . . . not around." One corner of her mouth tipped up. "And if I thought it was only the sweet and handsome man currently sleeping in Neil's bedroom that had you distracted, I wouldn't push the point. But I know it's not."

Just twenty-four hours ago, Indi would've at least made an attempt to argue about the reference to Philip wedged into Maggie's words. But tonight—after last night—neither her heart nor her conscience would let her.

Truthfully, that "sweet and handsome man" hadn't left her mind all day. When he'd texted her late this morning to let her know about the friend who'd stopped by for a brief visit and his plan to stick around the house for the rest of the day and hang out with Holland, she hadn't known whether to be relieved or disappointed. In truth, she was both.

Relieved because she had absolutely no clue how to act around him after that heart-stopping kiss. How to display any shred of normalcy. Disappointed because, well, she missed him. And it'd become clearer with every hour that passed that she didn't *want* normalcy anymore.

And it wasn't just because of the kiss. After all, it wasn't as if she hadn't been kissed before. She'd been engaged twice. Gotten pregnant, for goodness' sake. But this kiss . . . it'd been different because Philip was different. He was kind and compassionate and sensitive. No, not the kind of sensitive that wrote poems and spoke in Hallmark card phrases.

But sensitive to what others were feeling. Good grief, he'd

been in Muir Harbor for all of a week, and how many times already had his patience and thoughtfulness drawn her in until she was spilling her heart and sharing her secrets? She'd laughed with him. She'd sobbed in his arms. She'd let him see so much more of her than Ben had ever known, and probably Trey, too.

She'd loved Trey. Of course she had. But it'd been a puppy love that'd never had a chance to grow up.

What she felt for Philip, it was a grown-up . . . love? *No, you can't love him.* One. Week. He'd only been in town one week.

"Oh my." Maggie's grin widened. "Maybe it *is* Philip we need to talk about."

Maggie shouldn't be smiling. Couldn't she see that this was impossible? Nonsensical.

"I can't believe I'm doing this again. Jumping in too fast again. Making a mess again. I did it when I opened the second store without being ready. When I said yes to Ben after only six weeks." She combed both hands into her hair. "When I slept with Trey. I knew it was happening too fast, but I let my heart run on ahead and didn't think about the consequences. Oh my gosh, I'm being the messiest Muir all over again."

"Indiana." Maggie said her name on a sigh. "Don't do this to yourself. And you are not the messiest Muir."

"I am. I always have been. I'm the reason all the rest of you have hushed conversations in the kitchen and—"

"What are you talking about?"

"I need to be focusing on the store. And creating something up here that can be profitable." She wetted her lips. "And Trey. Poor Trey. I hurt him so much more than I ever realized. We have to find the Holmes family and then . . . I don't know. There's just so much right now."

Maggie closed the gap between them and took hold of both her arms. "Whoa, Indi, take a breath."

She listened to her mom. Made herself breathe the way she'd told Philip to last night—*in and out.*

"That's better." Maggie peered at her for a moment. "Can I tell you something? It's something I think about a lot, actually. I think about how when you were younger, you'd spread out at the kitchen table with a sketchbook and colored pencils. Or, oh, the paints. I was forever finding splatters on the floor or the cupboards. But the charcoals were even worse —all those black smudges on the tabletop."

Where was Maggie going with this? "Guess you must've been glad when I moved out to the garage."

"Not really. I loved watching you. I loved seeing you get completely lost as you worked. You'd sit there for hours some days. Sometimes I'd stand in the doorway and peer over your shoulder. I remember so many times seeing all these lines on your paper and wondering what your creative little mind was seeing that I wasn't yet. And you were never in a hurry. Whatever you were seeing, you were never in a rush to make the lines come together before it was time."

She slid her palms down Indi's arms to grasp her hands. "It's okay if the lines haven't come together yet."

Indi felt the prick of tears as she swallowed.

"You are not a mess. God sees what you're becoming. He sees the beauty you already are. He's not in a hurry and you don't have to be either." She squeezed her hands. "And if there's a new line in the picture now, one you didn't see coming, you don't have to be scared of it. Not if it's supposed to be there."

She couldn't not think of Philip's gray eyes then. Of his dimples and his glasses. Couldn't not think of the way the light of the setting sun had spilled over him in the treehouse Sunday night. The way he'd teased her about her stuffed llama or how he'd called her Farmgirl. How he'd rushed over the side of a cliff to get to Holland yesterday.

And kissed Indi last night.

And before the kiss, when he'd let her into his pain, panicked and panting for breath, he'd crawled right into her heart and was waiting there still.

"It's only been a week."

"A lot can happen in a week." Maggie pulled her into a hug.

She returned the embrace, maybe for the first time today feeling a simple sense of . . . freedom. Freedom to feel. To hope.

To wonder if maybe all the reasons she'd come up with last night for why she shouldn't have kissed Philip were as insubstantial and fleeting as flurries that melted before they touched the ground.

Clambering footsteps cut into their moment, soon followed by the voice she'd missed all day. "Hey, Indi, I saw the light on when I was driving past and—" Philip bumped his head on the too-short doorframe when he appeared on the top of the steps. "Oh, hey, Maggie. I didn't realize you were here."

He was wearing another flannel shirt again. He'd finally shaved at some point since last night, but a day's growth shadowed his cheeks and chin already. She might have to start calling him Farmboy soon.

"And I didn't realize you were just taking a random drive through town." Maggie's eyes twinkled as she teased.

"Well, I mean, it wasn't a random drive. Okay, actually I was coming here. Lilian's with Holland and they're watching some home reno show and we were talking about getting pizza." He looked back and forth between them. "Anyway, I just wanted to see if Indi . . ."

"Wants pizza, too?" Maggie finished for him.

Philip only nodded, his cheeks going as red as Indi's felt.

"Well, I'll leave you to have that very vital and apparently impossible-to-have-via-text conversation without me." She wasn't even trying to hide her amusement now. "Indi, could I trouble you for your car keys? I'm sure Philip will give you a lift home. Once you sort out your pizza plans and all."

"You're so subtle, Maggie," Indi muttered. "Or should I say *Maggs?*" She lifted her eyebrows as she handed Maggie her keys.

Maggie laughed. "Touché." And then she was patting Philip's arm as she passed and disappearing down the stairs.

Leaving Indi to watch, hopelessly anchored to her spot by the window, as Philip crossed the room.

He stopped in front of her. "Hey."

"Hey." She swallowed. "So . . . pizza?"

"Actually we already ordered. I remembered you said you like vegetable."

She nodded. "Philip, I—"

"Indi—" he started at the same time.

She gave a nervous laugh. "Go ahead."

But instead of talking, at first he simply let his gray eyes glide over her, drinking her in as if . . . well, as if maybe he'd missed her today, too. And then, "Okay, I'll just say it. I know there's probably a hundred reasons why this is a little bit crazy. I know you have so much going on. And I have Holland to consider. And I've only been in Muir Harbor for a week."

He stepped closer to her and suddenly she realized her back was at the window, the cool glass a palpable contrast to the warmth sliding through her.

"But it's been more than a week for me, Indi. That night in November, the next morning, you'd just gotten un-engaged, so I wouldn't admit it to myself, but . . . I think I thought about you every single day after that. And so while I would never pressure you and I'll understand if last night didn't mean to you what it did to me . . . well, the point is, it did mean something to me."

He finally stopped. Finally met her gaze.

"Your eyes are changing colors again."

His forehead wrinkled. "My eyes are gray. It's a family trait."

"I know but they turn a little blue sometimes. A little green other times. Right now—it must be the sun—they've got streaks of amber or something."

He'd been looking for an answer on her face, hadn't he? And he must've found it. Because she was pretty sure his eyes changed color all over again as he flattened one palm on the window behind her. "The sun went down an hour ago, Farmgirl."

And he probably would've kissed her then if she hadn't tugged him down by the collar to kiss him first. She twined her arms around his neck, letting him back her the rest of the way against the window.

"By the way," he whispered against her lips. "You're going to want to turn around and look outside. It's snowing."

13

"This is going to take a whole lot longer than I thought, isn't it?"

Indi couldn't contain a laugh at Holland's grumble as she bent over the dining room table, Holland's casted arm stretched out in front of her. "You brought this upon yourself, my friend. You asked an artist to sign your cast and that's what I'm doing."

Except that she wasn't just signing it. She'd started with her name, yes, but couldn't leave it at that. She'd added a few snowflakes around her name, then branched out to add trees that somehow turned into a full landscape.

Holland started humming the Jeopardy song.

"If you think that's going to distract me, think again." The smell of breakfast—Maggie's homemade maple-blueberry syrup over buttermilk pancakes—still lingered in the air, even as they approached lunchtime.

They'd woken up this weekend morning to a mantle of sparkling white stretching every direction, draping the hills and garnishing the trees. Hours ago, Indi had hurried down the stairs before she'd even brushed her teeth, bursting through the front door, her window view from upstairs not good enough. Oh no, she'd needed to stand in the same dazzling sunlight that rippled over frothy waves and breathe in the magical sort of hush that'd hovered over the wintry landscape. The wind had calmed somewhat overnight, though not enough to stop the faint keening of her favorite hickory tree, its aged branches bending under the weight of the snow.

And that's where Philip had found her earlier, her fuzzy socks and comfy cotton pants no match for the blast of frigid air that'd wrapped around her, nor the dusting of snow that skimmed off a leaning drift near the porch. He'd eventually coaxed her inside with promises of coffee.

But not before bending down to kiss her cheek and ask if she had evening plans. Gosh, he'd looked cute just then, a few stray snowflakes from the porch ceiling salting his hair, the cold fogging his glasses.

"I had this idea of a double date with a couple of my friends. But I have to warn you, they're ridiculously nosy. The second they meet you they'll start prying into me and you and us and . . ."

She'd almost stopped listening at that point, too caught up in the delight of that word—*us.*

Indi finished off one final snowflake with a flourish, then capped her Sharpie.

Holland looked at her cast. "Huh, not bad. Maybe kind of worth sitting here for fifteen minutes while I had to pee."

Indi burst out laughing again. Honestly, this girl . . . "Bet you're glad it was your left hand. You're right-handed, right? You can still write, at least. Will you still be able to play your violin?"

Holland's expression sharpened. "Philip told you about that?"

"He likes talking about you. He's proud of you." He'd also said Holland had refused to bring her instrument when they'd left Augusta. That she hadn't shown up for a concert last week at which she was supposed to have been the star soloist.

"I'm not really into playing lately."

"Nothing wrong with that. Even with stuff we love, sometimes we just need a little break. Although if you play as beautifully as Philip says, I kinda hope the break doesn't last forever."

"You stopped painting and drawing. You stopped talking about Paris and your art."

Lilian's voice had found her at the strangest times all week long. They were overdue for a conversation, a redo of that heated exchange in her workshop last weekend. But she hadn't seen much of her sister in recent days.

Holland stood from the table. "I do play beautifully. I know it sounds arrogant to say, but it's the truth." She shrugged. "I'm actually crazy-good. My instructor thinks I could get into Juilliard early. I'm ahead with my homeschooling. Could technically graduate at the end of next school year."

"Seriously?" Wow, so she could be heading off to New York when she was what? Sixteen?

"But just because you're good at something doesn't mean you're supposed to do it forever, right?" Holland reached into her cast to scratch her arm.

Wait, she was asking for advice, wasn't she? There wasn't any snark in her voice. She wasn't trying to escape a conversation early. She genuinely wanted to know what Indi thought. "Well . . . no. I haven't heard you play, but Philip says you have a gift. And I think . . . that's probably what it's meant to be—a gift, not a burden. If it feels more pressuring and stressful than it does joyful, then no, I don't think you're required to do it forever. I think you have the freedom to walk away if you want. As long as you're walking away because you truly want to." *And not because you're running away from something.*

Is that what Indi had done when she'd stopped painting and drawing? When she'd decided against an art degree in college and had opted for a business one instead?

No, because you're not Holland. You weren't a prodigy. It was the truth. She'd loved her art, but she'd never truly been that immensely talented at it. She might have been a bit of a standout in high school, in a small town. But early on in college, she'd known she wasn't an artistic genius.

Why, then, as Holland walked away, was she feeling a sort of convicting niggle now? Repeating the thought that, yeah, she had been running away from something when she'd folded up her easel and put away her sketchbooks. But what?

"If you just want to wait here, I'll run upstairs and change into something warmer." The voice drifted in from the entryway. *Lilian.*

Indi hopped up from her chair and hurried down the hallway. But she stopped at the sight of the man waiting just inside the front door, Lilian already halfway up the steps.

Oh. Peyton. He looked as debonair as he had on the night of Neil's wedding, his sandy-blond hair parted at the side, no evidence of the wind in its settled state. His warm brown eyes were taking in his surroundings as Indi neared. Whatever he might think of their cozy house—nothing as up-to-date as the homes on one of Holland's HGTV shows, but well-loved and lived in—didn't show in his expression.

"Oh, um, hi. Good morning, Peyton. I'm Indi, if you don't remember."

"I remember." He held out one hand covered by a leather glove. "Nice to see you again."

"So you two are . . ." She shook his hand, glancing behind her at Lilian, who'd paused on the stairs.

"Going for a snowy walk," Lilian supplied. "Peyton's from

Georgia originally. He's almost as fascinated by the snow as you."

The man grinned. "I spent plenty of summers with Uncle Cecil, but New England winters are still a novelty."

"We had brunch in town earlier," Lilian offered.

Right. She hadn't been at breakfast. Indi had assumed she was at the office—not unusual for Lil, even on Saturdays.

"Be down in a sec, Peyton." Lilian started up the stairs once more.

Indi gave Peyton a quick smile and nod before following her sister to the second floor. "Hey, before you leave, can we talk? Just for a minute?"

Lilian moved through her bedroom door. "Sure, if you make it quick. What's up?"

"Oh, well . . ." Actually, she hadn't really thought this far ahead. "I don't know. It's just ever since Sunday, things haven't been . . . I haven't really seen you much. I didn't know about Peyton and—"

"There's not really anything to know at this point." Lilian pulled a crewneck sweater over the thin shirt she wore. "We've hung out a little. He's a good conversationalist."

"A good conversationalist. How romantic."

There was a hint of playfulness in the glare Lilian sent her. Seemed like a good sign. "I just want to make sure everything's okay between us, Lil."

Her sister bent over to pull off her socks and replaced them with a thick, wooly pair. "We're good."

"Really? I'm imagining the distance?"

Lilian straightened. "Hasn't there been a distance for a long time? It's not really anything new, Indi."

"You stopped talking to me." Was that really true? If so, when had it happened? When had they stopped talking like sisters? "I'm trying to talk to you now, aren't I?" But apparently she

was making a mess of it. Really, she didn't even know what to say. "Wilder texted this morning. First thing."

Lilian pulled on the parka she'd removed when she first came in the room. "Can't believe he wasn't *here* first thing. Would've thought between the broken houseboat heater and the snow, he would've freeloaded on the couch."

Lilian knew about his broken heater? "He found the parents. Took him less than twenty-four hours."

Both the Holmes work for Core-Tec. Sandy's high up in the company. They do security work for the government, all very hush-hush. It's why you weren't finding them with a quick Google search. Lucky for you, I have my ways.

Wilder's second text had included an address, two phone numbers, and an email address. All of which she'd forwarded to Trey. Once again, he hadn't replied, but at least she could tell from the tiny gray notification under her text that he'd read it.

Lilian finally stilled. "Wow. So what are you going to do?"

"I passed everything on to Trey. I'm sure he's going to call—"

"Wait, that's it? You're just going to let him make the call on his own? Indi, he's contacting the parents who adopted your baby. *Your* baby. He's probably going to find out how she's doing. What they named her. Heck, who knows, maybe he'll get to meet her. And you're just going to what? Sit it out? I don't understand you sometimes."

"I know you don't. You can't."

"So tell me. Talk to me." Lilian threw up her hands. "This is what I'm talking about. You don't *talk* anymore. Look, I know it was really upsetting for you when you realized stuff had been going on around here that we didn't tell you about. And I am truly sorry about that. We thought we were doing you a favor, but we were wrong. And I'm sorry." She pulled her gloves out of the pockets of her parka. "But you got engaged to a man last year that none of us had ever met. We didn't even know you were dating someone."

"Ben was a mistake. It was . . . I don't know what it was, but—"

"The point is, it'd gotten serious enough for you to accept his ring, but you never even told me—your sister—there was someone in your life. And then when things went south, you didn't tell us that either. Not for weeks. And after you finally did, you still wouldn't let any of us in."

"I just needed time—"

"Or maybe you needed your family." Lilian started for her door. "But you've gotten too good at pushing us away. You've been practicing for eleven years now."

She hurried from the room then, her wool socks keeping her steps from thumping, yet Indi heard their echoes all the same.

⎯⎯•⎯ ⎯•⎯⎯

"If you think I've forgiven you for getting to hear the news before me, you've got another thing coming, West."

At Connor's exaggerated rancor, everyone at the restaurant table burst into laughter—even Connor himself. With his arm draped across the back of Tabby's chair, Philip's best friend radiated joy. *See, Tabby, I told you he'd be over the moon.*

"I'd defend myself by pointing out that it was your wife's decision to track me down and tell me about the triplets first, but I'd rather not cause a rift in your marriage. So go ahead and blame me all you want."

At his side, Indi had long since finished her pad thai. When he'd asked her on the double date this morning, he'd briefly wondered if he was making a mistake. His friends probably already had them mentally married off by now, but beyond that, he'd kind of hated the thought of leaving Muir Harbor. With last night's snow, the world he'd spent the past week in had morphed into a winter wonderland. He could've taken her to that restaurant he'd spotted yesterday—Cobalt Pier—overlooking the harbor. That place probably had candlelight and cloth napkins.

Or he could've planned some kind of romantic thing in that empty room over her store. It overlooked the harbor, too, after all. He could've laid a blanket on the floor and prepared a whole spread of food. An indoor picnic.

Or they could've simply hung out at the farmhouse with everyone else, played Scrabble and snacked on the cookies Maggie had made this afternoon, watching a movie with Holland.

All great options, but for the tiny inkling at the back of his head telling him maybe it was important to introduce Indi Muir to his world the way he'd been introduced to hers. Augusta might not feel like home, but if he was going to make a life with Holland here—where she already had friends, a seat in the orchestra, and apparently a better relationship with Grandfather than he did—then he needed to start seeing his life here in a different light. See it as something to embrace, to claim as his own.

So here they were, at the little hole-in-the-wall Thai restaurant he and Connor had probably singlehandedly kept in business throughout their college years. Even with his plate empty and his stomach full, he savored the aromas of ginger and peanut sauce. The orange booths lining two walls, the clanging of dishes in back, the music that always seemed to be playing a little too softly, making a person feel like their conversation was being broadcast to everyone else in the room—all of it was delightfully familiar.

Maybe it wouldn't be as hard to start thinking of this city as home as he'd thought. Maybe there was more of it stamped on his heart than he'd realized.

Or maybe his friends' elation, together with the thrill of having Indi Muir at his side, was all swirling together to make tonight perfect. Just . . . perfect.

While Connor went on, teasingly nagging Tabby about the fact that she'd told Philip about her pregnancy before him, Philip leaned closer to Indi, voice low. "I'm really glad you said yes to this."

He'd never get tired of watching a slow grin spread over her face. It was like watching a sunrise—no two the same. He was glad, too, that she appeared to be legitimately having a good time. He'd worried a little, considering the tension he'd sensed when they'd left the farmhouse earlier this evening. When he'd asked if everything was okay, she'd mentioned a difficult conversation with her sister but hadn't elaborated. She seemed looser now, though. Cheerier.

And she confirmed it with her, "I'm glad, too."

"Even with the whole twenty-questions thing earlier?" Connor and Tabby had taken Indi captive with their inquiries when they'd first been seated. They'd wanted to know every-thing—had she lived all her life in Muir Harbor, where did she go to college, what about her siblings?

"It was twenty-six questions, actually."

Even without candlelight, her emerald eyes glowed. If not for his friends sitting across from them, he might just get lost in them. "You counted?"

"Impressed?"

Yeah, he was lost already. A full-blown goner. "Everything about you impresses me, Farmgirl."

"They've started whispering." Tabby pulled her purse from behind her chair. "I think that's our cue."

"What?" Indi's voice was charmingly close to breathless. "Oh, sorry—"

Tabby interrupted her with a laugh. "Please don't apologize. Tonight has been so fun, but this pregnancy has me wanting to sleep around the clock. I'm about ten minutes from nodding off here at the table."

"Right, time to get you home." Connor stood and pulled out Tabby's chair while Philip did the same for Indi. They'd already paid the bill, and it didn't take long for everyone to bundle up and bustle out the door.

Soon they were standing at the corner where they'd part ways, Philip's car halfway down the block at the curb, Connor having parked in a parking garage across the street. Tabby was busy hugging Indi when Connor nudged him. "So, do I say I-told-you-so now or wait until you've proposed?"

"Uh, maybe lower your voice, or better yet, don't say anything?"

The streetlamp overhead created a circle of light over their group, highlighting the smile that hadn't left his friend's face all night. "I'll hand you this. When you finally fall for a girl, you fall fast."

"You're making me regret inviting you guys tonight."

Connor slapped him on the back. "Too late now."

"You do know I'm so ridiculously happy for you and Tabby, I could burst, right?"

"Might just be the panang curry speaking, man." The tease left Connor's voice, but the grin stayed. "Yeah, I know. I'm happy for us, too. Also a little freaked out. Ever since she told me, it's basically been all I could do not to start worrying something will go wrong, but yeah . . . mostly I'm just happy."

Philip wanted to offer an easy assurance that nothing would go wrong. That might not be what Connor needed from him, though. "I'll pray every day you two have three healthy babies this time next year, keeping you up all hours of the night."

"Lose the second part and I'll forgive you for getting the news out of Tabby first."

Tabby pushed her way in then. "He did not get the news out of me. I offered it up of my own accord." She gave Philip a side hug. "A bribe, really. So he'd make sure to keep his promise to read Ray's manuscript." She lifted her eyebrows at him.

"No, I haven't started it yet. But I promise to keep my promise. Just been a little busy."

Tabby glanced at Indi, grinned. "Of course."

Philip rolled his eyes. "We'll be going now."

Connor and Tabby were still laughing behind him as he laced his fingers through Indi's and tugged her down the block.

"I really owe you for putting up with them."

"You don't owe me a thing. I loved meeting them. They're hilarious. And adorable. And Tabby's going to make one cute but feisty pregnant lady."

He slowed his steps, pausing altogether when they reached his car at the curb, angling until he faced Indi. "Hey, I . . . I should ask . . . I didn't realize until just now . . ."

She tipped her head, her curls tangling in the nighttime breeze. "I don't know why I enjoy it so much when you struggle to finish sentences."

He felt the corners of his mouth lift, but pressed on. "It just didn't occur to me until this moment that maybe being around Tabby and hearing her talk about the pregnancy . . . I mean, with everything you've had happen this week . . . Trey coming back and all it's brought to the surface . . ."

She leaned up on her tiptoes and kissed his cheek. "I'm just fine, Philip. But I love you for asking." She jerked away at the next moment, her mouth dropping open. "That is . . . I didn't mean . . . of course I didn't . . . it's just a phrase . . ."

Gosh, he loved it when her eyes got this wide. "Now who's the one who can't finish a sentence?"

A drop hit her cheek and she swiped it away. "I think it's starting to sleet. I-I guess we better h-hit the road and get home."

He could keep teasing her, but she was right—it was beginning to sleet. He wasn't anywhere close to ready for the evening to end, though. "Or we could make a quick stop first. I could show you one of my other old favorite haunts. Say yes and I promise not to bring up the fact that you just told me you love me. Not even once."

"Philip, I did not—"

He cut her off with a laugh he felt deep in his bones, then reached behind her to open the car door.

Indi was a winter girl, but even she, lover of snow and all, might not be up for whatever nighttime adventure Philip was pulling her into. Another stinging drop, half-ice, half-liquid, landed on her cheek and slid to her chin. Her boots sank with every step, made more for fashion than tromping through two feet of powder.

"Are you going to tell me where we're going before my extremities start freezing off?" She knew where they were—partially. She'd seen the Thornhill College sign when they'd parked. But then Philip had started leading her through what could've been a football field, it was so big. Shadowed buildings rose up around them, but apparently none of them marked their destination.

Philip's grip on her hand was sturdy and sure. "You've

spent too much time around my sister, Indiana. You're picking up her sarcasm."

She might like when he used her full name almost as much as when he called her Farmgirl.

"And I swear we're almost there."

And then, thank goodness, they were. He pulled her to a stop outside a brick building that looked like it could pass for Pemberley with its stone cornices and oversized cement steps and—she craned her neck to look up—wow, three stories? Rows of rectangular windows reached both directions from the set of doors in the middle, a half-circle of frosted glass ornamenting the space above the entrance.

A black lamp with a globe top let off enough light for her to make out the gold letters on the glass doors. *Thornhill Academic Library.*

Of course. Of course Philip West the professor and bookworm, who'd fit the mention of a favorite childhood book into their very first conversation, would bring her to a library. But it was after nine on a Saturday night. "How are we going to—"

Philip had already pulled out his wallet and now he held up a white card. "My faculty badge. Also a key. And our way in."

The building might be old, but clearly its security was up to date. Philip slid the card through the slot near the doorknob and she heard a telltale click.

"You might have a key, Professor West, but I highly doubt we're supposed to be here right now. If my first arrest is for breaking into a library—"

"This isn't breaking in." He opened the door and nudged her inside with a palm on her back. "And what do you mean your first arrest? You're planning on getting arrested more than once?"

She would've expected the gaping space inside to be pitch-black, but instead, tiny dots of faint light lined the floor along the walls and rows of bookshelves. Not enough to read the titles on spines or the plaques on each endcap. Barely enough to make out the carpet's maroon color.

"I really don't think we're supposed to be here."

"You don't have to whisper, Indi." Philip walked ahead of her, stopping in front of a long desk. "Mmm, the smell of books."

Hmm. She smelled stale coffee. And maybe dust. She tugged off her gloves, sneezed. *Yeah, dust.* Another sneeze tickled the back of her throat, but after the overloud echo of the first one, she held it in.

Philip chuckled. "Let yourself sneeze, silly girl. We're not going to get in trouble for being here. I work here. I've got the badge and everything. Plus, my grandfather is Ray Camden—best-selling author and former chair of the history department basically since the dawn of time. He's a celebrity around here so that gives me extra sway."

Yeah, his grandfather. The author. She had questions about that. "What'd Tabby mean about you reading his manuscript?"

"Oh, she has this crazy idea that I should ghostwrite the rest of his next book. Or co-write. I'm not clear on that anymore. But I promised her I'd read what he's got so far." He reached for her hand again. "Come on, I'll show you the spot where I hung out as a kid."

He tugged her toward a spiral staircase and led her upward, their steps clanging past the second floor. She was out of breath by the time they'd twisted their way to the third floor, yet Philip picked up his pace as he towed her forward, past one bookshelf after another.

He halted in front of a tall window that let in just enough silver moonlight to trace his profile. He was clean-shaven tonight, dimples on full display, long lashes framing the pleasure in his eyes. He tapped the bulky window frame with his hand. "This was my favorite perch. Holed up here for hours at a time."

"You sat in a window."

"It'd be a tight squeeze now, but it was plenty comfortable then. Probably read all the Narnia books right here."

Cold rolled off the window in waves, but despite the lack of heat in the building, the climb up the spiral staircase had begun to thaw her. "I have so many questions. What were you doing hanging out in a college library when you were a child?"

He shrugged. "Grandfather taught a lot. And sometimes he stayed on campus when he was on a tight deadline. He couldn't just leave me at home alone all the time."

But he'd left Philip in a massive library? "I guess it's only natural you became a professor after spending so much time on a college campus. Whatever happened to your old writing dream, though? You said the other night you used to want to write books."

He shrugged, then leaned over the tall frame, peering out into the dark night. "I decided pretty early on in college to focus on history instead."

She scooted into place beside him, propping her arms on the window's ledge. "Why?"

His breath fogged the windowpane. "A lot of reasons, really. For one thing, I took this creative writing class my first semester in college and I swear, half the students in the class were aspiring novelists. All very literary-minded and hilariously serious about it. All I could think was, yeah, this isn't me. I didn't feel some intense calling to be a writer. I was just a kid with a big imagination who loved stories. But I wasn't the 'writing is my lifeblood' type."

Huh, she'd just been thinking about her art in similar terms earlier today. But whereas she'd felt a bit of a sting when she thought back, wondering if she'd run away from something she was supposed to do, Philip seemed entirely regret-free about his decision to pursue teaching instead of writing.

"Maybe the bigger reason is I didn't want my life to mirror my grandfather's that closely."

She let her gaze slide over his profile once more before returning to the window. Outside, the light of the moon made the falling sleet look like shimmering diamonds. *We really need to leave soon.* With as cold as it was, the sleet could freeze quickly, coating the roads, turning them slick or even treacherous.

But her mind and heart worked traitorously together, begging her to stay right here, getting to know this man who'd so unexpectedly wandered into her life twice now. And this time, she couldn't stand the thought of him ever wandering out.

"It's only been a week."

"A lot can happen in a week."

Yes, like an epic discovery that a woman could make it through two engagements without understanding the life-changing fullness of what a relationship should be. This one was so very new. Probably even a little fragile.

But the richness of it put her time with Ben to shame. It emphasized how little she'd been ready for something solid and lasting with Trey.

"Your voice always goes a tone lower when you talk about your grandfather." Not that he talked about him much. Anytime the man came up, Philip changed the subject quickly. Would he change it now?

"We just aren't close. Truthfully, I think . . . I think I've had a pretty big chip on my shoulder when it comes to him for a long time. A lot of resentment."

She waited, wondering if he'd go on. Hoping he would.

He did. "The same day Mom told me I wouldn't be living at Bryce's with her, I heard the two of them arguing—Mom and Grandfather. I couldn't really hear what they were saying, but I caught the gist. Grandfather was upset she was leaving me behind. He didn't want me there."

She couldn't help scooting closer to him, winding her arm underneath his, reaching for his hand and lacing her fingers through his on the windowsill. "Anybody who doesn't want you around is crazy."

"I appreciate your defensiveness."

"It's not defensiveness. It's just the truth. You are . . . well, I just really like you, Philip." It sounded so trite and so simple. She leaned her head against his shoulder.

"Hmm, but you said earlier you loved—"

"Don't." She tried to scold him but giggled instead. Then stilled. "I'm sorry your childhood was filled with so much hurt."

"It wasn't all bad."

Maybe not, but it'd been lonely. That much was obvious. Whereas she'd been surrounded by siblings, so nurtured by Maggie's tender, ever-present love she sometimes forgot they weren't biologically related. Unlike Lilian, whose adoption hadn't come as early or as smoothly as Indi's.

Lilian, who'd accused Indi of pushing the entire family away.

Did I really?

Maybe. Yeah, probably. Even Maggie had said last night that Indi didn't talk to her enough anymore.

"Indi?"

"Sorry. I let my mind wander."

He tilted toward her. "Were you thinking about . . . her?"

Her daughter, he meant. She shook her head. Although, truly, there had rarely been a moment in the past week when her daughter hadn't been on her mind.

"She's out there somewhere, Philip." Not some unknown somewhere. She was at 4326 Orchard Lane in Lewiston, only forty-five miles west of Muir Harbor. "There's an eleven-year-old girl out there who might have my eyes or my smile or my impossible-to-control hair. She might love art like me or she might have some entirely different hobby. She might be into chess or dance or . . . I don't know, basket-weaving."

He twisted a strand of her hair. "Are kids into basket-weaving these days?"

"I don't know. I'd rather it be that than sports, though. Every day since Trey told me about the hypertrophic cardiomyopathy, I've been praying she's not one of those superstar athletes who's destined for the Olympics by sixteen. Because if she has it, too . . ."

Holding her hand, Philip turned her just that quickly, gently steering her toward a nearby corner with a pair of reading couches. He sat down first, then nudged her down beside him, creating a cocoon around her with his arm.

"Lil doesn't understand why I'm not jumping at the chance to talk to the parents now. I think she thinks I don't have feelings or something. Trey certainly thinks that." She took a tattered breath. "It's not that I don't have feelings. I have feelings. So many of them I think they could drown me. They did drown me the summer I let her go. I had nightmares for weeks. My whole first semester of college is this dark blur in my head."

But then, during her second semester, she'd gotten the idea for what would eventually be her store. She'd started paying more attention in class. Thinking ahead, even creating a business plan. She'd thrown herself into her studies.

And then her store.

And then another store.

And then Ben.

And . . . maybe . . . maybe for eleven years she'd been

throwing herself into anything and everything but the feelings that terrified her. And maybe it was in pushing her feelings away that she'd also pushed her family away.

That was probably why she'd quit drawing and painting, too. Because it was too easy to feel too much when she lost herself to her art. Better to sand and stain than let a paintbrush or charcoal pencil carry her away. Carry her too close to the truth of what lay in her heart.

The truth that slipped out now. "I can understand the resentment you've been carrying around, Philip. When I decided to give my baby up, I thought it was what God wanted me to do. So I did it. But then . . . it just hurt so much and the hurt didn't go away and . . ." And that was likely another reason she'd backed away from her art. Because it'd always been the thing that made her feel close to God.

Until it didn't. Until the pain and disappointment were too much. So yeah, she could understand resentment.

"But it's not just God. As much as I love my family, as much as they all tried to support and encourage me through that whole ordeal, as many times as they told me I was making a noble decision . . ." She lifted her hand to where Philip's rested by her shoulder, gripped it like a lifeline. "To me, it's only ever felt like the worst decision I ever made. And all I really wanted back then was to hear just one of them tell me I could do it. I could be a mom. An amazing mom—with Trey or without him. I wanted someone to see what I couldn't see in myself."

"I see it." Philip's voice was soft and low.

She released his hand and lowered her legs to the floor. "I didn't tell you this so you'd say something nice."

"I'm not saying something nice, I'm saying something true." He shifted on the couch cushion and then slid off altogether, coming onto his knees in front of her, just like she had with him two nights ago in the bathroom. "I see it. I see *you*. I saw you the night of Maggie's heart attack—I saw the depth of your love pouring from every inch of you. I've seen you all week long with Holland—putting up with her moods, drawing her out, making space for her grief, making space for her. For both of us. I saw you Thursday night, helping me through a panic attack, understanding exactly what I needed in that moment."

He pressed his palms into the cushion on both sides of her knees. "Indi, I see not just the mother you could've been to your baby, but the mother you are. A mother who made a sacrifice out of love. Who made a hard, good, best, worst decision."

She blinked away her tears. "You're ridiculously good at saying the right thing, you know that?"

"Better than Mister Trousers, I'm sure."

"Phil—"

His lips were on hers before she could finish his name, the passion in his kiss reinforcing every heartfelt word he'd just said. She wound her arms around his chest underneath his coat, pressing into him and pouring every tender feeling she had for this man into kissing him back.

Only when he moved his kiss to her cheek and then to just below her ear could she make her voice work again. "H-he used to have pants."

His lips stilled against her skin. "What?"

"Mister Trousers. He had these felt pants on his back legs when I first got him. That's where I got the name."

He was still laughing as he found her lips again, and oh, she could stay here, secure in Philip's arms, forever.

"This is a real heartwarming scene and all, but you folks don't belong here."

14

*J*ndi awoke in a cocoon of warmth, a hazy contentedness summoning her eyes to open, one and then the other as her senses took lazy, languid stock of where she was.

The smell of leather. The cotton weight of a blanket. The taste of chocolate still on her lips.

She stretched and rolled to her other side, a leather cushion creaking underneath her as scarlet sunlight met her eyes and awareness trickled in. Oversized furniture. Eggshell walls. Heavy blue curtains only half-drawn. Thick wood trim.

The den in Philip's grandfather's house was unfamiliar in the light of morning. They'd whispered their way into the house sometime after eleven, Philip leading her through dark halls into this room. *Philip! Where . . .*

She sat up, the blanket she didn't remember covering up with sliding to the floor as she looked around, and an unhurried smile found its way to her lips when she spotted him. He slouched in a king-sized armchair, both legs sprawled in front of him, one arm flopping over the side and the other propping his head.

She had exactly zero memory of him moving to the

chair, nor of falling asleep herself, all stretched out on the couch. But she remembered the rest. How a security guard had caught them in the library last night. How Philip had stuttered an explanation about who he was, showed the man his badge, endured a lecture about how just because he was faculty didn't mean he had free rein of buildings after hours. How both the sleet and the wind had picked up by the time they made it back to Philip's car, and the realization that they wouldn't be driving back to Muir Harbor just then.

And then, Philip's sigh when he'd said he knew where they could spend the night. *"Grandfather's house has about a million bedrooms."*

Only they'd never made it past this den. They'd been too keyed up after the drive on icy roads. Instead, Philip had told her to get comfortable in the den and had disappeared, only to return ten minutes later with two mugs of decaf coffee and a box of chocolates leftover from Christmas.

And then they'd talked into the early morning hours. She didn't know when she'd nodded off, but she must have been the first to fall asleep. Philip must've covered her up before moving to the chair.

His hair was adorably disheveled now, his clothing wrinkled, and one pant leg rode up his ankle. She bent to pick up her blanket and gently laid it over him, her movements slow and quiet, but enough to make her aware of the headache lurking at the back of her head. Probably a result of the short night of sleep.

She needed aspirin. And water. And to leave this room before the temptation to wake up Philip for the sole purpose of seeing his smile and hearing his voice got the better of her.

She padded from the room, closing the door behind her as quietly as she could, then glancing both ways down a dim corridor. Nothing looked familiar—not the wood paneling on the walls, not the long, narrow rug underfoot, none of the closed doors.

"Nothing for it," she whispered into the quiet. "Just pick a direction and start walking."

If she was lucky, she'd find the entryway where she must've left her coat and purse last night, which was where she'd find aspirin. From there, she'd go looking for the kitchen and a glass of water.

She wasn't wearing shoes, but it didn't matter—each step was a thump echoing into the yawning silence. This sturdy house didn't creak and moan the way the farmhouse did. A strapping wind probably wouldn't even be enough to rattle its windowpanes. Instead, the hush was a din all its own, unnerving even in daylight.

She turned a corner, hoping to see something she remembered from last night. Maybe the dining room they'd passed. It hadn't been too far from the entryway, had it? But no, around the corner was only another stretching hallway, more doors—one open at the end.

Maybe that leads to the dining room?

She trekked forward, slowing as she reached the open door, the warmth of the library entirely missing here. Instead, a brisk heaviness drooped in the air. She took a breath and peeked through the open door.

Not the dining room. Not the entryway. Not another hallway.

Not empty. A man with salt-and-pepper hair, his back to her, sitting in a chair by the window—the only window in the room, thick drapes drawn, letting in little more than the barest wedge of light.

Philip's grandfather?

She shouldn't disturb him. For all she knew, this man didn't even know Philip had brought her here.

She took a step backward, began to turn—

"Who's there?" The voice was a mere scratch, small and crackling.

She stood, immobilized, uncertain. What should she do now? Why hadn't she just waited in the den until Philip had awoken? Instead, she'd gone and disturbed his grandfather.

Curiosity fluttered in.

"Philip? Is that you?"

"Uh . . . no." She stepped into the room. "I'm, um, I'm a friend of Philip's."

Dust blanketed almost everything in the room—the desk, two wingback chairs, the accent table in between. The faint scent of tobacco hung in the air. Shelves lined one wall.

The man in the chair turned.

"I'm sorry to barge in on you like this. I was looking for my purse. Or the kitchen. Or . . . well, Philip hasn't really shown me around yet. You must be Philip's grandfather. I-I'm Indi. Indi Muir. It's nice to meet you."

He stood then, nearly as tall as his grandson. His salt-and-pepper hair was probably a picture of how Philip's would look one day. Wow, same gray eyes, too.

Only Ray Camden's seemed so much more . . . tired.

"Indi . . . Muir?"

"Yeah, I'm from Muir Harbor. Maybe you've heard of it. Little town basically the size of a postage stamp down on the coast. I met Philip last fall." She couldn't find the mental spigot to turn off her uncomfortable rambling. "He drove me to the hospital the night Maggie had a heart attack."

"Indi?"

Philip's voice was breathless behind her. Oh, thank goodness. He could save her from making a fool of herself in front of his grandfather. If it wasn't too late for that already, that is.

But when she turned to him, he wasn't looking at her. His gaze was pinned on his grandfather.

And then, finally, his grandfather spoke again. "It's nice to meet you, Indi Muir. But would you mind giving us a moment?" His jaw tightened. "My grandson owes me one heck of an explanation."

The look in his grandfather's eyes could turn back a raging ocean tide.

And Philip didn't deserve it. "You didn't have to toss her out of the room like that."

The granite in Grandfather's expression only hardened. "I didn't throw her out. But maybe you could be so kind as to explain who she is and what she's doing in my house."

He didn't know what it was. Maybe it was the crick in his neck from spending a night upright in a chair. Maybe it was his immediate irritation at the way Grandfather had dismissed Indi. Maybe, most likely, it was too many years of feeling like an interloper in this house when he'd never once asked to be here.

Whatever it was, it churned through him like liquid steel, hardening as he met Grandfather stare for stare. "She's Maggie Muir's daughter. Yes, that Maggie Muir. The one from the letter you used to keep in that desk drawer."

"That letter was never yours to read."

"I'm sorry. I'm sorry that twenty years ago I did a dumb thing and snooped in your desk. And you know what, as long as I'm apologizing, how about I apologize for years of taking up oh so much space in this oversized cave of a house? And if you want, I'll find somewhere else for Holland and myself to live as soon as we're back."

Grandfather only stared at him for a moment before moving to the chair behind his desk and slowly lowering. "I don't want that."

Wow, so he was capable of sitting somewhere besides that chair by the window?

"Well, I sure don't know what you do want."

Grandfather didn't say a word. No, he wasn't going to let the man go back to his usual stony silence. He stalked to one of the wingback chairs in front of Grandfather's desk, but instead of sitting, he gripped its back, posture still rigid.

"I know Mom's death had to be shattering for you. She was your only daughter. I don't know what you've been feeling all these months but I know it has to have been terrible for you to hole up in here like this." He heard the scratch of the fabric under his fingers. He didn't even know what he was trying to say. "I'm finally starting to get through to Holland. She's opening up and I can't stand the thought of her closing down again. I can't bring her back to a house that's as . . ."

As hollow and lonely as the one he remembered as a kid.

"Sit down, Philip."

"Indi—"

"Will survive for five minutes without you. Sit."

He rounded the chair and sat, feeling suddenly small. Too much like the child he'd been when Grandfather had brought him into this room to tell him about Dad's accident.

"You've been in Muir Harbor all this time?"

He nodded.

Grandfather waited.

Okay. "I met Indi last fall. A chance meeting." Except no, because something so significant, something that breathed new life into his anxious, exhausted spirit, couldn't just be chance.

A line from that old love letter, somehow still embedded in his brain even all these years later, found him again. *I'm still an unspoiled believer, unwilling to credit to coincidence what my soul insists is from the Divine.*

He probably couldn't call himself an unspoiled believer like a young Robert Camden had. Not when he was only recently beginning to realize how many years he'd ghosted through his life, letting old pain, old rejection keep him from holding on to anything too tightly. It's why Seattle had never felt any more like home than Augusta.

But he was changing. Just like Holland, he was opening up. Having Holland in his life, getting to know Indi . . . no, none of this had been chance.

All of it had been a gift from the God who was teaching him how to wonder again. Teaching him through the beauty of a seaside farm and a tiny town at the edge of a lit-up harbor. Through all the ups and downs of finding his place in Holland's life.

Through the surprise of falling for a woman with liquid green eyes and wild, curly hair and a heart he already treasured.

"We've been staying at Muir Farm," he finally offered. "Maggie's house."

The man still didn't have anything else to say?

Philip leaned over his knees, ready to spring from the chair, go find Indi—

"She had a heart attack?"

Philip stilled. "Who—"

"Indi, your friend, said . . . she said Maggie had a heart attack."

He only nodded.

"But she's . . . okay now?"

"Yeah, she's okay."

And there was the silence again, far too familiar, clinging like cobwebs to what might be the strangest conversation he'd ever had with his grandfather. Maybe, honestly, the longest. At least since he'd moved back from Seattle.

Finally, Grandfather pulled open a desk drawer, pulled

something free. He laid it on the desktop and stared at it for a moment before sliding it toward Philip. "Go ahead and deliver it to her, then."

Oh. Philip took hold of the envelope's crinkled corner, yellowed from age, Maggie's scrawled name fainter than he remembered.

"Grandfather, I never meant . . . I didn't go to Muir Harbor to pry into your brother's past. I wasn't trying to nose in where I didn't belong."

"You have so many ideas of where you don't belong, Philip. I don't know where you get them."

His head jerked up and he met Grandfather's eyes.

Grandfather only nudged his head toward the door. "Go on. Indi's waiting for you."

A minute ago he couldn't wait to leap from this chair and escape this room. But now . . . "Why did you tell Tabby about my writing? How did you even know?"

"You lived here until you were eighteen. You think I don't know some things about you?" The faint traces of a smile were so foreign on his grandfather's face, he wasn't entirely sure what he was seeing.

"You'd seriously want to work on a book together? You didn't just throw out the idea to, I don't know, get Tabby off your back and onto mine for a while?"

"I'm a novelist, Philip. We get wild ideas from time to time."

He didn't know how to respond to that. How to feel or even process any of this. So instead, he rose. "We'll be home next weekend."

Grandfather nodded and Philip turned to walk away.

"Wait, Philip."

He stuffed Robert's letter in the pocket of his jeans and turned again. "Yeah?"

"You should ask Holland about Bryce. I think she might already be in contact with him."

Every confusing moment of the past few minutes shriveled with that revelation, leaving disbelief to rise up in its place. "Why would you think that?"

"Bryce called. A few days ago. He asked what I thought about him coming to visit."

"*What?*" His voice had gone black and heavy as an anvil, his dread a pounding that was growing louder with each second. *She would've told me if . . . She said she'd give me two weeks!* "Did Bryce say they've been talking or something?"

Grandfather stood behind his desk. "Not exactly. But when I said that if he should be asking anyone, it should be you, as her legal guardian, he said something about giving you a call when you were back from your trip. How would he know you were out of town unless . . ."

"He could've looked at Holland's social media. She's posted some pics."

"Maybe." But the look on his face told him Grandfather didn't think that was the case.

"Why would he want to come now? When he didn't even come for the funeral? When he hasn't been around for years?"

"Believe me, I asked him the same thing. And not politely. To his credit, I guess, he said he knew he'd made mistakes. Had regrets. Wants a second chance at being a part of her life now."

This couldn't be happening. Not now. Not when he'd made so much progress with Holland. Not when she'd burrowed so deeply into his heart.

When he'd first come home from Seattle, first signed those guardianship papers, he'd felt a sense of responsibility, maybe even some hesitant obligation. But then she'd sat beside him in that hardback pew at the front of St. Mary's,

Mom's casket in front of them. No tears, hardly any expression at all . . . and something in his heart had cracked.

And it'd kept on cracking through eight months of living in the same house with her. Listening to hours and hours of her playing that violin. Trying so hard to push past her barriers.

This past week in Muir Harbor, he'd felt the light finally begin to fill in all those cracks.

"And you believe him?"

"I don't know what to believe." Grandfather's sigh was long and weary. "Except I really think you need to talk to Holland."

Indi laid the wrinkled paper on her lap, angled, faded handwriting facing up. "Wow, that's some love letter."

Philip only nodded, the car's heater chafing against the labored silence that had been a third passenger all the way from Augusta to Muir Harbor. Indi glanced through the windshield, the farmhouse's yellow siding standing out like a beacon against blankets of white as they moved down the lane. At some point, last night's sleet had changed to snow and now fresh layers covered the landscape.

She tried to muster up her usual delight. But Philip had been so quiet on the way home. Agitated. Neither of them had gotten enough sleep last night, and though the roads were plowed and salted, it still hadn't been the easiest drive.

But she guessed—no, she knew—it wasn't the lack of sleep or the road conditions that had Philip's knuckles white against the steering wheel for the bulk of the trip. It was whatever had gone on behind the closed doors of his grandfather's study.

She'd hoped he might share when he was ready. But then the lights of Augusta had faded behind them and the miles had stretched and they'd been nearly home when she'd finally lost patience and asked.

He hadn't answered—not really. Just handed her that fifty-year-old letter and said his grandfather had asked him to deliver it.

She glanced down at the letter once more, gaze landing on the scribbled lines in the middle of the letter.

I know we're young, Maggie. I know we only talked for a few hours this afternoon (and let's be honest, my brother did most of the talking). I know this timing is awful. I ship out soon. Who knows when I'll return. Or if . . .

Robert Camden hadn't returned. The ring he'd given Maggie all those years ago was now on Sydney's finger. But oh, what beautiful words he'd left behind.

"I'm glad Maggie will finally get to read this. I wonder why your grandpa never gave this to her."

The tick in Philip's jaw made her think he didn't have a response to that. But then, a moment later as he pulled into the driveway, he said, "I don't know. I don't know why he held on to it all this time. I don't know why he had it in the first place. And I'm beginning to think I don't really know anything about that man at all." He jerked the gearshift into park.

"Philip, what did he say to you in there?"

"Too many things that didn't make sense, that's what. And sorry, by the way. I meant to say it sooner."

"Sorry for?"

"The way he made you leave the room." He cut the engine and yanked the keys from the ignition.

This . . . was a different Philip than she was used to. "I didn't mind. Really. It was awkward of me to go wandering around the house and straight into his study anyway." And then the way she'd attempted to introduce herself—pure rambling inelegance.

"I just don't get him. As long as I've known him, I've thought he was cold and unfeeling. And for the most part, I still think that. But then . . ." He shook his head.

"Trey called me unfeeling." She folded the letter and slipped it back into its raggedy envelope. "But you see the truth. You put it into words last night. Maybe your grandpa—"

"Grandfather." He must've realized how bleakly the word had come out. Because he dropped his shoulders, pivoted to face her, reached for her hand. "Sorry. Last night was supposed to be a fun night—"

"It was a fun night."

"I just wish it hadn't ended the way it did."

"Are you kidding me? I got a great deal of enjoyment out of watching you just about melt into the floor when that security guard told us to find some other place to, and I quote, 'canoodle.'"

He finally cracked a smile, enough that one of his dimples peeked through, and if it wouldn't be such an awkward reach from her passenger seat, she might just reach up to trace one with her finger. "I meant this morning. The way *that* ended."

"I know you did, Professor."

At the nickname, the creases around his smile deepened. And actually, if she twisted in her seat just so, she probably could reach—

A pounding at Philip's window broke the moment. And a muted voice. Lilian. "Good, you're finally back. You need to come in."

Philip tapped the button to slide open his window, but with the engine off, it didn't work. So he opened his door instead. "Everything okay?"

Lilian still wore her church clothes—a black woolen skirt

and gray leggings, matching sweater on top. Without a coat, she hugged her arms to herself. "I don't know. All I know is Wilder came barreling in five minutes ago and said he needs to talk to all of us." She looked past Philip to Indi. "Especially you."

Whatever Wilder needed to say would have to wait at least long enough for Indi to hug her brother.

Somewhere in the back of her mind, she'd known Neil and Sydney were coming home from their honeymoon today, but not until she'd seen them perched under the arched entry to the dining room had she remembered.

"Oh my goodness, you're both so tan." She moved from Neil to Sydney.

Sydney laughed. "Which is extra funny because Neil made such a big deal about how he's not a beach guy. Then we get to Mexico and to my surprise, I discover the man can relax in the sand all day and not get bored."

She had a feeling her brother could relax anywhere all day as long as Sydney was there with him. Over Sydney's shoulder, she saw Philip leaning down to give Holland a side hug. She might've thought Holland would roll her eyes and pull away, but instead, for once, Philip was the one with the strained creases at the corners of his eyes.

"I still say we should've gone to Scotland," Neil grumbled, pulling Indi's attention back.

"We will." Sydney pecked him on the cheek. "Soon as we get the Airbnb up and running and save up a little and can be gone for longer than a week."

"Hey, you okay, sis?" Neil eyed her with concern. "When Lil texted about the break-in at the store—"

273

"She did? I told everyone not to bother you with it. I was worried you'd hop on a plane and come home early."

Neil folded his arms. "Well, I didn't."

"Only because I talked him out of it." Sydney gave a smug grin. "I can be very persuasive."

Indi groaned at her sister-in-law's suggestive tone. "I really did not need to hear that."

Wilder clapped his palms together. "Okay, is the family reunion over? Can we get down to business now?"

Lilian dropped into a chair beside Maggie. "It's Sunday. Do we really have to?"

Wilder plopped a manila folder onto the dining room table. "I'm *so* sorry to have interrupted whatever Sunday dinner plans you probably had with Mr. Ivy League—"

She narrowed her eyes. "Peyton went to Georgia State, Wild, so you can knock it off with the Ivy League digs. And excuse me for having the audacity to enjoy the company of someone who has manners and even manages to get a proper haircut once in a while."

Indi's gaze shot to Wilder—to the shaggy hair he'd be able to pull into a ponytail soon if he didn't get a trim. *Sheesh, Lil.*

"That was unnecessarily pointed," Neil muttered.

But if Wilder was bothered, he didn't show it. Still standing, he opened his folder and leaned over the table, palms flat. "I've got a lead on the intruder. I think. It's a little out there, but my gut's telling me not to ignore it."

A collective pause settled over the group. Indi glanced at Lilian again—and she wasn't the only one.

Lilian tossed up her hands before folding her arms. "What? I wouldn't mock Wilder's gut instincts. They're usually annoyingly correct."

"So very magnanimous of you, Miss Muir." Wilder didn't even look at her. Turned instead to Indi. "I couldn't get what you said the other day out of my head. About how maybe all the repeat trespassing had something to do with the Legend of Muir Harbor."

"Hey, that was my idea," Holland piped in from Philip's side.

Wilder nodded at her. "I think it was a good one. For one thing, there's precedent. Back in the day, you used to have trespassers all the time looking for the treasure, right, Maggie?"

"Yeah, but that was way back in the day. Decades ago, when I was a kid. And even back then, it was kind of dying out. I think it was a bigger thing in my grandparents' day."

Wilder shrugged. "Well, it was a good enough jumping off point for me. I started wondering what would make someone search now, after all this time. Then I started digging, scouring the internet, looking for any recent hits that mentioned the legend. Didn't take long to find this."

He glided a paper free from his folder. Indi was close enough to see it was a printout of an article, the bolded headline reading *Buried Treasures and Unsolved Mysteries: New England's Favorite Folklore.*

"Published eight months ago. It's a list of old legends or stories, all of which have some kind of lost fortune or hidden cache at the center. The Legend of Muir Harbor is number six on the list."

Indi lowered into the chair beside Wilder. "So that's the theory? Someone saw this list and now you think whoever it was is searching around for Alec's chalice?" She tried to keep the doubt from her voice.

But even if he heard it, Wilder was nonplussed. "Not just someone." He slipped the paper toward Indi.

She read the byline under the title. Ben Foss.

Wilder waited until Indi looked up and met his eyes to clear his throat. He was all PI now, no tease, no carefree jauntiness. "Indi, how well did you know Bennington Foster?"

She could only stare at him for a moment. Then back at the paper. *Ben Foss.* Then back at Wilder. "No, that's impossible." She pushed her chair away from the table.

"It's not." Wilder pulled out more pages. Printouts of . . . social media profiles? Even as her vision blurred, she realized what she was seeing. Identical profiles, identical photos. Two different names. Ben Foss. Bennington Foster.

"Ben Foss owns an antique store in Rhode Island. But he's also an avid treasure hunter. He's been on multiple digs. He's written for archeological journals. Last year he was part of a group that uncovered a shipwreck in the Bahamas that'd gone undiscovered for thirty years."

She couldn't stop shaking her head. "No. It doesn't make sense. *No.*"

"From what I can tell, every trip he's been on that's included a discovery, someone else has gotten the credit. He's been part of the team, but never the name out front. So maybe this time, he went on a solo hunt."

Under her chair, her legs shook. In her lap, her hands did the same. "You think he used me. You think—"

"Did he ever ask you about the legend?" Lilian interrupted.

"No, maybe, I don't know." She couldn't look at her sister. Couldn't look at any of them. *This can't be happening.*

And then it came pouncing into her brain, one little memory. One little comment she would never even have given a second thought if not for Wilder's horrible, impossible suggestion.

"You're from Muir Harbor? I've heard of that little hamlet. There's a legend, isn't there?"

Her first conversation with Ben. That day he'd walked into her store. Said he was looking for a gift for his mother. Then laughed and admitted that truthfully he'd seen her in the area once or twice, looked in her storefront window now and then, and was intrigued by a woman who could turn an old shutter into an eye-catching wall display.

No, no, *no.* "It doesn't make sense. Even if Ben was trying to use me to find out what I did or didn't know about a legend, he would've realized right away I didn't know anything. So why keep dating me? Why propose only to break up with me? And if he really wanted to search our place, why not stay engaged to me—even if he was faking the whole thing—for the sake of getting closer to all of us, worming his way onto the property? And for the record, he doesn't drive a gray sedan."

Wilder closed the folder. "I'm not saying it's an open-and-shut case, Indi. But we've got two big, bold facts staring us in the face. One, the guy lied to you about who he is. Two, he's a treasure hunter, plain and simple. To me, that's reason enough to pursue this."

Okay. But even if there was something to this, why had Wilder had to break the humiliating news this way? With everyone—literally everyone she cared about most—in the room?

Everyone who already knew how many times she'd messed up in her life. It was bad enough she'd had to confess to her family that her whirlwind engagement had come to an end. But now, for everyone to know that not only had the guy dumped her, but duped her, as well?

All she wanted to do was flee from the room, escape every gaze she knew was glued to her, but Neil and Sydney were blocking one doorway and Philip and Holland the other.

"The regional airport charters trips to Providence. I nabbed two seats for tomorrow."

Lilian whistled. "Whoa, that has to be expensive."

"Not really. I traded Jorge Diaz two spots in his puddle jumper for the use of my houseboat on his anniversary. He wants to plan a romantic weekend with his wife sometime."

Lilian scoffed. "Your houseboat? Romantic?"

"Yeah, and don't give me any grief about crashing on the couch here whenever said anniversary rolls around. Or however many days after it takes me to burn the old mattress and buy a new one."

Indi barely registered his comments. "You want to fly to Providence to confront him?"

Wilder nodded. "If I call, he can hang up. If I show up on the doorstep of his antique shop, on the other hand . . ."

Antique shop. He'd told her he was an accountant.

She was a fool.

"I thought maybe you'd want to come with," Wilder offered. "If not, maybe Neil—"

"I'll go." She pushed her chair away from the table, stood. She couldn't stay here. Couldn't handle seeing all their faces, knowing what they must be thinking. She squeezed past Wilder's chair and then pushed in between Neil and Sydney.

She was down the hallway and out the front door in seconds, no stopping to pull on the coat she'd discarded earlier. What'd it matter if she froze outside? She'd rather go numb than feel what she was feeling right now.

Stupid. Pathetic. Pitiful.

At least she was still wearing her shoes. They crunched into the thin layer of ice and snow on the porch, the salting someone had given it not having fully melted the results of last night's weather.

Bennington Foster is Ben Foss. And Ben Foss is a treasure hunter.

Also, a liar. Also, possibly the same man who'd wrecked Neil's treehouse, rummaged through their house, broken into her store.

And she'd just thrown open the door to her life and let him right in. Given him easy access to the people she loved.

Steps sounded behind her. "Indi?"

"Please, not now, Lilian. I'm not done mentally kicking myself."

"You didn't have any way of knowing."

Maybe that was true. Maybe it wasn't. Maybe if she hadn't let herself get swept up in the whirlwind of his attention, his swift proposal, she might've realized something was off.

"Did you have a nice time in Augusta?"

She let out a tight breath, white against the cold. Nodded. Not quite ready to accept Lilian's show of mercy in her abrupt change of topic.

"You and Philip must be . . . well, I saw you in the car. You looked . . . close."

There wasn't any accusation in Lilian's voice, but she could only imagine what her sister was thinking. *Really, you're already with another man? Isn't it kind of odd that you're dating the guy who walked into your life on the same night your lying fiancé walked out? Isn't that a pretty quick switcheroo?*

"I don't know what Philip and I are, Lil. And this isn't really a good time."

She heard her sister's retreat. Heard her own words replay in her head. She was shutting down. Shutting Lilian out. Exactly like Lilian had said she'd been doing for . . . for years.

She spun. "Lil, I—" But the form she saw then in the doorway wasn't her sister's. Philip. "Oh, hey."

He stepped onto the porch, her coat in his hands. He held it up, waiting for her to slip inside. She turned in front of him, sliding her arms into the sleeves, then angled to face him. And that's when she noticed the dejection in his eyes.

Heard her own words a second time. *"I don't know what Philip and I are."*

"I didn't mean that."

"It's okay. We haven't really talked about what we are or aren't."

No. But they were something.

"I'm scared, Philip." The words scraped up her throat. "What I feel for you is . . . I don't even know how to put it into words. It's . . . so much. But it's also so fast. And after what I just learned about Ben—"

"I'm not Ben, Indi." Philip's voice was firmer than she'd ever heard it.

"I know you're not." Although anybody hearing her say it —well, she guessed she wouldn't blame anyone who wondered how she could think that after little more than a week, she knew this man more than she'd known Ben. She'd had five more weeks with Ben, after all, and hadn't come anywhere close to suspecting the truth.

Still. This was Philip. Philip whose boundless gray eyes let her into his soul. She *knew* him.

"I'm not Ben," he said again. "I'm not a creep who's lying to you. You've met my family. You've met my friends—"

"You don't have to convince me."

"This is real." He motioned between them. "Even if it's happened quickly. Even if we haven't picked out a silly label. It's real."

"I know it is. I really do know that. I'm just reeling a little here. I feel like a fool and . . . I just maybe need to slow down some. Just so I can, I don't know, catch my breath. Recover from feeling like . . ." Like she'd stepped right into her same old role. Flighty, messy Indi Muir—accepting a ring from a man who wasn't who he said he was.

She could see the disappointment written all over Philip's face, the cold biting his cheeks and nose, turning them red. But all the same, he gave her a soft smile. "I can do slow, Farmgirl."

*P*hilip held his grandfather's half-written manuscript in both hands, staring at the man's name underneath the book title. He'd promised Tabby he'd read this thing.

But he hadn't made any promises as to how quickly. He tossed it on Neil's old bed, and it landed in a puddle of sunlight atop the quilt. Same sun that had roused Philip from sleep at the crack of dawn. After such a short night of sleep Saturday, he would've thought he'd have slept like the dead last night.

But yesterday's double-blow had rebelled against his slumber. Holland—very possibly in contact with Bryce. Indi —backpedaling out of their relationship.

He pulled on a dark blue sweater over his T-shirt. Okay, Indi hadn't exactly "backpedaled." And as for their "relationship," it was the truth that they'd never put an actual definition on it. But it was still new—really new—and, heck, *he* was new. New at this, that is. He didn't know what the rules were for dating in your mid-thirties. Maybe he was supposed to have some kind of "will you be my girlfriend?" talk with her.

But he'd sort of thought baring his heart to her multiple

times, spending an insane amount of time together last week, and going on a pretty fantastic date if you asked him, never mind how it'd ended, had gone pretty far in cementing their status, even if it was without a label at this point.

And then there were those kisses . . .

He could think of some pretty good labels for those. *Magnificent. Mind-blowing. Pretty much perfection.* He huffed as he sat on the bed and pulled on his socks. Yeah, he could go on and could probably even keep the alliteration going too. But then he'd have to think about how he definitely hadn't kissed her goodnight last night.

And that while maybe *backpedaling* wasn't the right word, Indi *had* crept at least a little ways away from him. And he didn't love that.

Hmm. Had that hole always been in his sock or had he let his frustration jam his foot in so hard he poked the hole just then?

He stood, tracking the door, then stopping and returning to the dresser where he'd stored Robert Camden's letter last night when he'd remembered it was still in his pocket. He'd find the right time to give it to Maggie today. But first . . . Holland.

He glanced at his reflection in the small mirror over the dresser. Over the past week, he'd started letting more days pass in between shaving. Saturday was the last day he'd run a razor over his face, before his date with Indi, which meant by today, his cheeks and chin were plenty bristled. His hair wasn't nearly as long as Wilder's, but he definitely normally would've had a trim by now. He hadn't worn a tie in weeks and not on his life would he ever wear jeans this faded into the classroom.

Or jeans, at all, really. Thornhill had a faculty dress code.

In a way, he was looking at a completely different person in this mirror than the one who would've stared back at him even just two weeks ago. He'd been so weighed down for so long and yet, he'd held to the standards expected of him. Not just appearance-wise, but in pretty much every way.

The Philip of before couldn't have pictured himself wandering into the Thornhill library after nine on a Saturday night with a beautiful woman at his side. That Philip couldn't have fathomed how right it would feel to hold that same woman in his arms. Or how easily the wind could bleed from his sails when she metaphorically stepped out of them.

But if Indi needed space, of course he'd give it to her. So even though he couldn't get over the irrational thought that she shouldn't be going to Providence with Wilder today, that she might only get hurt worse by confronting the man who'd lied to her, he couldn't—wouldn't—interfere.

As for yesterday's other blow . . . he couldn't put off talking to Holland any longer. He opened his door. Maybe if he was lucky, Holland would laugh and tell him Grandfather didn't know what he was talking about.

He collided with a body in the hallway, Holland's screech filling the air. And then his own yelp as scalding liquid splattered on his chest and pooled around his socks.

"Ack, sorry, Holl. I didn't hit your arm, did I? Or your bruised side. Are you—"

"I'm fine." She held a now-mostly-empty coffee mug away from her casted arm. "Except I was trying to do something nice for once and you ruined it."

He backed away from the puddle. Guess he'd be changing out of the holey socks after all. Same with the sweater. "Something nice?" He lumbered to the bathroom and plucked a towel from the storage closet.

"Yeah," Holland called after him. "The coffee was for you."

Oh. He emerged into the hallway once more. "Thanks."

"Thought that counts, I guess," she mumbled.

"You're sure I didn't hurt you?"

She shook her head. He wiped up the spill, then returned to the bathroom and tossed the wet towel in a hamper. Huh, she'd brought him coffee. It *was* a nice gesture.

Or a guilty gesture. Because she'd been hiding something from him for who knew how long.

She moved toward him now. "I can go get you another cup—"

"Actually, stick around for a sec, will you?" He nodded his head toward his bedroom and she followed him in. He shucked off his socks, then reached for the edge of his sweater.

"Whoa, you're not going to change in front of me, are you? We're not *that* close."

"Got a shirt underneath, Miss Prim and Proper. Relax." He pulled off the sweater, then gestured for her to sit on the bed.

"I have to sit? Wait, you're going to tell me about you and Indi, right? How you're a couple now and she's amazing and you hope I'm okay with it. Let me just put your mind at ease because I am. She's cool. Go for it, bro."

Any other time and he'd get a ridiculous amount of gratification at her sudden chattiness. No, it wasn't even sudden. Ever since the accident on Thursday, she'd begun to talk to him more. To actually initiate conversations. Even when she'd complained about how much he was hovering on Friday, he'd gotten the distinct feeling she wasn't just tolerating his presence, she was enjoying it.

She called you bro.

And he was going to go and ruin it. But what choice did he have?

He pulled a fresh pair of socks from the dresser drawer and turned. "I guess I'm just going to say it."

"Oh man, you asked her to marry you already."

"Holland." He was tempted to chuck his balled-up socks at

her. Probably would've if his stomach wasn't churning so much right now. "Have you been talking to Bryce?"

He could practically see her playfulness slough off. It pressed her shoulders down. But she straightened them the very next instant. "Why would you ask me that?"

"Can we skip the sidestepping? Please just answer the question honestly. Have you been in contact with your dad?"

She looked him square in the eye. "We've emailed a few times. Talked on the phone once."

"How did you even get his—"

"I'm fifteen, Philip. I keep having to explain this to you. I'm not a child. I'm capable of figuring out my own dad's phone number." Despite her stony posture, she seemed to sink into the mattress. "Besides, I still have Mom's old phone. His number was on there."

If he let himself, he could trip on the crack in her voice when she'd mentioned Mom. But he had to push through with this. He was her legal guardian. If she was talking to Bryce about leaving Maine and moving to Texas—if Bryce was somehow on board with making it happen—he needed to know.

"So the night of your concert, when you first said you wanted to go live with him, had you already been talking to him?"

She looked away, nodded.

"When I asked you for two weeks..."

"I haven't brought him up. Well, not since the car ride here."

He could feel himself flagging as he leaned against the dresser behind him.

"Look, I'm not going to run away and ditch you without warning or anything. But he's my *dad*. I have every right to talk to him. And . . . he's made a lot of changes in his life over the past decade."

"Just not the kinds of changes that would bring him back here when Mom was dying, not even for her funeral." He shouldn't have said it. The hardening in Holland's eyes all but shouted that he shouldn't have. "Forget I said that—"

"No. I know what you think of him. And I don't even blame you. Yeah, he ditched me and Mom. But so did you. And if I've forgiven you for that, why can't I forgive him?"

She had a point. She had several points. Bryce *was* her dad. And no, it wasn't impossible that he could change. Philip should've had a different reaction the first time Holland brought him up. Why hadn't he figured out some kind of compromise then instead of coming up with a crazy plan to bustle her off to Muir Harbor as if that would uproot any ideas she'd formed about going to Texas?

She can't go to Texas.

"I think it's great if you've forgiven Bryce or you're on the way to forgiving him. And I know I shouldn't overreact to the idea of you communicating with him." He set the socks on the dresser and moved to sit beside her. "But Holland, there's a reason Mom asked me to step in as your guardian. Bryce isn't—"

"You don't know what he is." She vaulted from the bed. "And I don't care what papers Mom got you to sign. It doesn't mean you get to control me."

Just that fast, the too-familiar helplessness that'd dogged his steps for months before coming here budged its way in again. "Holl—"

She was out the door before he could blink. And of course, the slam of her door echoed down the hall a moment later.

Déjà vu. Great, just . . . great.

Indi found Wilder already waiting for her in the entryway after she made her way from the kitchen.

She'd thought to fill a travel mug and grab something for breakfast to eat on the way to the little airport on the other side of Muir Harbor, but roiling nerves were having a heyday in her stomach and then there'd been the fact that her entire family had already been gathered in the kitchen, a little too reminiscent of other times when she'd walked in on them all talking together, and, well, food and caffeine hadn't sounded so great anymore.

Besides, who knew what Jorge's puddle jumper would do to her? Maybe it was better to have an empty stomach anyway.

"Ready?" Wilder said as she reached him.

"As ready as I'll ever be, I guess."

"Wait!" Philip came bounding down the steps just as she was winding her scarf around her neck. "I was going to come down earlier, see you off, but Holland . . ." He was out of breath by the time he reached the bottom, his gaze darting back and forth between Indi and Wilder. "I have to ask one more time, are you sure you should be doing this? We can't just let the police handle it?"

She leaned into his side, relished the feel of his arm going around her.

Wilder had started to open the front door, but he scooted it closed with a flattened palm. "I get the concern, West, but if I could've handed this off to law enforcement, believe me, I would've. But Tompkins doesn't think there's anything to this, and I don't even blame him. We have no evidence Foss was ever in Muir Harbor. Everything is circumstantial. He agrees it's creepy the guy lied to Indi about his identity, but unless she wants to press charges for fraud, there's nothing he can do."

Philip rubbed her arm. "So maybe you should do that, Indi. Or we take a little more time, look for evidence."

A frustration she didn't usually see in Wilder's eyes took his gaze captive now. "Or we save a lot of time and I ask him outright if he's our guy."

She could feel Philip's rising tension beside her.

"And you're expecting him to just roll over and admit everything? What are you going to do then? Make a citizen's arrest?"

"Philip, please." She slipped free of his hold. "I need to do this. I need to look him in the eye and ask him why he lied to me. Nothing dangerous is going to happen. For all we know, we'll get there and Wilder's gut will turn on him and he'll realize we followed the wrong instinct."

Wilder obviously didn't believe that for a moment. But he didn't say anything. Even had the grace to look away when Philip surprised her by pulling her against him.

"Hugs can still be included in the slowing-down thing, can't they?" he whispered.

She breathed in the scent of him, so familiar now. She loved it even more than the smell of paint. "If Wilder wasn't three feet away, I'd say slowing down could include even more than hugs."

"Then kick him out already, will you?"

Wilder moaned. "Hurry it along, Indi. Jorge wants us off the ground by nine, which means we really should've been on our way ten minutes—"

A sharp rap on the door interrupted him and he pulled it open. "Oh, hey, Trey."

Trey?

Indi untangled herself from Philip's embrace and turned. Trey stood on the porch, stocking cap in his hands, snow dusting over his boots and onto the welcome mat. "Hey." He nodded at Wilder, then looked to Indi. "Can I talk to you?"

Wilder looked to the ceiling. "We're never going to make it out of here, are we?"

"Jorge can wait a few extra minutes, can't he?"

Wilder sighed, but he already had his phone out. He glared at Trey. "Keep it short."

"Ignore him." Indi motioned Trey inside. "We can talk in the living room."

Trey nodded and stepped past Wilder, moving toward the living room. She started to follow him, but Philip reached for her hand as she passed. Squeezed. Because he knew, of course, that Trey would only be here if he had news of some kind.

News about her . . . their . . .

It shouldn't still be so hard, after all these years, after the slew of conversations she'd had in this past week, to just *think* the words. *My baby. Our child.*

But even now, as she brushed her fingers free of Philip's and trailed Trey into the living room, her heart, her soul, her whole being could weep if she let it linger in those painful words too long.

Trey stopped in front of the couch but didn't sit. "I talked to John Holmes," he blurted.

In a flash, her heart was thundering. "O-okay."

"I called him Saturday right after you texted the contact information. I explained who I was, gave him the basic facts, asked if I could email him some of the information about hypertrophic cardiomyopathy my cardiologist gave me."

"Okay." It seemed to be the only word she was capable of.

He twisted his cap in his hands. She recognized an old Muir Harbor Marlins football tee under his open Army surplus coat. And for just a moment, he was the kid behind her in class again. The one who called her Muir and then flirted with her in the hall outside her locker. The one she'd been so sure she loved.

"I was going to hang up then, but I don't know, this impulse just got ahold of me and suddenly I was asking if I could meet him. I said I had some questions and I knew I was catching him off guard but could we meet. And he said yes. And I'm driving over today. Now."

"You are?"

"They'll both be there—John and Sandy. I couldn't believe he said yes. But he did and we're meeting at a café and . . ." He stuffed his hands in his pockets. "I think you should come with me."

"Trey, I . . . I can't. I'm supposed to be going with Wilder—"

"The things I said last week—I was wrong. I know you made the right decisions back then. I was drinking and partying all the time, and you were right not to marry me. I signed those adoption papers willingly. I've been telling myself the lie for over ten years that you forced me into it, but you didn't."

"I'm sorry, Trey. I'm so—"

"You aren't hearing me. I'm not here for an apology. I'm here because you need to come with me. Neither one of us has moved on. We both know it. And we both need this."

She was shaking her head. Backing away from him. "I don't . . . I can't . . ."

"Indi." It wasn't Trey's voice. She didn't turn, but Philip covered the distance anyway, coming up behind her, placing his hand on her back. "Please go. Please let yourself go."

Eleven years. She'd had that scrap of paper with the Holmeses' names sitting in her vanity drawer for eleven years. Eleven years of taking it out, reading the number she'd memorized long ago. Thinking about calling. Thinking about opening a door in her heart she'd forced closed when she'd turned away from the nurse who held out her daughter.

Or maybe it was never really all the way closed.

Maybe there'd always been a crack in the door. And if she could just gather the courage to push on it now . . .

She turned to Philip. "What about Wilder? Ben Foss. The plane—"

"I'll go with Wilder."

"But . . . Holland."

"Trust me, she'll be happy to have a little space. And Wilder said it's only a twenty-minute plane ride. We'll be back in the afternoon." She didn't know what the cloud in his eyes meant when he looked away momentarily. But when he looked back, they held an earnestness she couldn't ignore. "Please go with him."

"You're not just telling me to go so I won't make the trip with Wilder? The one you were just trying to talk me out of?"

"I'm not telling you to go at all. Encouraging you, maybe, but not telling you. Because you, Indi Muir, don't need anyone to tell you what to do. You've made hard, good decisions before. I just can't help thinking this might be another one. I can't help thinking . . . that it might be healing to meet them. To find out what her name is."

There was a line she'd read in that letter Philip's great-uncle had written. *Love and bravery go hand in hand.* Never had she stopped loving the child she'd given away. But never had she been brave enough to take a step toward her, one that had been available to Indi from the beginning. The door was inching wider now. *Just one step.*

"Actually I already know her name," Trey offered.

She spun back to face him.

His eyes bore into hers. "John said it once on the phone. It's Olivia."

Olivia.

She inhaled. Exhaled. Reached toward bravery and pushed on the door. "Okay, Trey, let's go."

16

*O*f course the buffoon's antique store was called The Buried Treasure. Just about the least surprising thing in the world.

Philip matched Wilder's impatient strides as they crossed the street in Providence and neared the red metal building that looked more like a warehouse than the mom-and-pop shop he'd imagined.

"I'll do the talking." Wilder shook his longish hair out of his eyes as he walked.

"Right. You, Batman. Me, Robin."

Wilder halted on the sidewalk. "We're not playing super-heroes here. We're here to ask questions. In, out, that's it."

Okay. Couldn't say he'd seen this side of Wilder Monroe yet. From what he'd observed, the man was generally as carefree as a spring breeze. Easygoing, too. But the man who'd tapped his foot incessantly their entire cramped ride in that hunk of metal was someone else altogether. And he'd only grown more focused and serious once they landed.

"Got it. Best-case scenario, we find out he's nothing more than a lying jerk." Apparently Wilder had already set up a meeting with the guy, had pretended to be a high-end antique collector.

"I'm not so sure that's the best case. If he's our guy, then at least we have the comfort of knowing it's over. Once we out him he'll probably just slink away. If this isn't our man, then it means there's someone else out there. Someone who's already had a field day with both Neil's treehouse and Indi's store. So who's to say he won't hit Lil's office next?" Wilder's fists were clenched at his sides.

Yeah, this definitely wasn't the man Philip thought he'd gotten to know a little over the past week. But he didn't have time to dwell on the observation. Not with Wilder hauling open the door and marching toward the counter in the middle of the store.

A metallic smell permeated the air, probably from the rows of steel shelving, or maybe that gigantic collection of rusted silver watering pots gathering dust near a display of trunks. This place pretty much *was* a warehouse. Made him think more of a giant rummage sale than any of the cutesy antique shops he'd been in before. The horizontal windows along the front of the store didn't let in nearly enough light.

Wilder had already made it to the counter, where a woman with chin-length gray hair was working the cash register, and Philip two-stepped to catch up.

" . . . have a meeting with the owner. Ben Foss. He's expecting me."

The woman offered a pleasant grin. "Of course, you're the collector. Just walk on to the back until you hit a set of stairs. It's the first and only door you'll see at the top."

"Thank you kindly." Wilder eyed Philip and mouthed a *Let's go.*

Seconds later, they were climbing metal stairs, painted the same red as the building's exterior, that clanged with each step. Wilder didn't waste a moment, rapping his knuckles against the door as soon as they reached it, twisting the knob on the heels of a muffled, "Come in."

And there he was—the buffoon. Ben Foss aka Bennington Foster aka the man Philip had overheard breaking up with Indi. Dark, almost black hair. Eyes a greenish-brown. *Like swamp water.*

"Good morning, gentlemen. Which one of you is William Morton?"

He shot Wilder a glance. Wilder gave a barely imperceptible shrug that suggested turnabout was fair play. Then he jutted out his hand toward the creep behind the desk. "That'd be me. Nice to meet you."

"And you." He turned to Philip. "And you are?"

"Uh, Philip." *Sorry, Wild. Not really into the alias thing.*

They all sat. So did the questioning begin now?

"You mentioned on the phone you collect antique boat paraphernalia," Ben started in. "I can't say that we have much in the way of that here, but I've got connections all over the place, so I can probably be of some help."

"I think you'll be of some help, all right." Wilder leaned forward. "And you can start with telling me about Bennington Foster."

Ben's chair squeaked though he didn't appear to move a muscle. "Excuse me?"

"I'd like to know who Bennington Foster is. And why he felt the need—the very idiotic need—to mess with my friend Indi. And while you're at it, you can tell me what your interest is in the Legend of Muir Harbor."

Ben started to rise.

But Wilder was faster, on his feet with his palms flat on Ben's desk before he could so much as push his chair back. "There's really no need to get up. None of us are leaving this room until Philip and I have answers. So you might as well start talking."

Ben almost looked like he might argue.

But Wilder's glower darkened. "Now."

———•—————•—————

"Maybe I had the time wrong."

It was the third time Trey had said it in the minutes since they'd slid into the booth at the Lewiston café. It might've been straight out of Muir Harbor with its eccentric décor—a spindly faux evergreen in one corner, still decked out with Christmas lights; loose twine tacked up around the cash register counter with coffee mugs hanging by the handle every few feet; a chalkboard on the wall covered with customers' doodles.

Beside her, Trey wouldn't stop fidgeting. He'd already rearranged the salt, pepper, and sugar shakers a dozen times. She'd lost count of how many times he'd cracked his knuckles. "If they said they'll be here, they'll be here."

"You're right. I don't know why I made us leave so early anyway. Except I thought the roads might still be slick."

"Trey." She stilled him with a hand on his arm. "I'm nervous too."

"It's weird, you know? I'd actually gotten pretty good at going months at a time without thinking about her. Then I get this diagnosis and . . . she's all I can think about. Her and Cecily."

"Cecily?"

"Girlfriend. Met her two years ago. I think I would've married her by now if it wasn't for you."

Wait, what? "Um—"

"I don't mean it like that. I've just never been able to get over the feeling that I've got unfinished business here. Cecily can tell. I brought her home for Thanksgiving last year and she kept saying I seemed different here. *Broken*, that's the word she used."

"I didn't realize you were home in the fall."

He lifted one shoulder. "It's always been weird anytime I've come back. I usually keep it on the down-low. Anyway, when I got the diagnosis, Cee was the one who insisted I come up and tell you in person. Figure out how to notify the family. Get closure." He reached for a packet of Splenda and tapped it against the Formica tabletop. "You ever wonder, though, if closure's even possible? Or do we carry our mistakes with us forever? I mean, do you have any idea how many times, especially before I met Cee, I thought, 'Man, if only you'd have quit going to the keggers senior year. You might be married right now to your high school sweetheart with a daughter—maybe even more kids— instead of sitting alone in a condo in Miami.' Only there's no redos, right?"

"It wasn't just the partying, Trey. And it wasn't just you. I wasn't ready either. I was immature and scared and . . . somehow I knew even then we weren't the kind of teenage sweethearts destined for forever. We could've tried, but that's not what I wanted for our baby. I wanted her to have so much more." She paused. "I know you said you don't want an apology but I really am sorry I hurt you."

She waited for his response, but it never came. Because seconds later, twin shadows fell over the table. And she looked up into the faces of her daughter's parents. For one feeble, foolish moment, Indi had almost expected to see her with them.

Olivia. Her child.

Their child.

But of course not. Of course they wouldn't unexpectedly bring their daughter to this meeting. The fact they were even having this meeting—that she and Trey were now standing and shaking hands with John and Sandy Holmes and then sliding back into the vinyl booth.—still didn't seem real.

Why had she agreed to this?

Why had *they*? Sandy Holmes still had the red hair Indi remembered, but it was shorter now, not quite reaching to her shoulders. Though her sole meeting with the couple had been brief, she'd studied the woman's face enough in the photo from the adoption agency binder to know she had a few more creases around her eyes now and her cheeks were a little rounder.

But she had the same kind, cornflower eyes. A kindness mirrored in the face of the man at her side. He had a goatee now, a mix of russet and hints of gray. His cheeks, nose, forehead—all bright red.

He must've noticed her noticing. "Family ski trip last weekend. Late Christmas gift for the kids. Turns out the sun can get ya pretty easily on the side of a mountain, even if it is the dead of winter."

Family. Kids. Olivia had siblings.

Their first bread crumb of information. She glanced at Trey at the same moment as he reached for her hand under the table. "Um, well . . ." he started, perhaps assuming he needed to kick things off since he'd been the one to request this meeting. "I guess . . . thanks so much for being willing to meet. So quickly, too. I mean, you probably have work and stuff."

Understanding threaded John's expression as he nodded. "This was worth rearranging some things."

Trey kept tapping his thumb against the back of her hand, his nerves only feeding hers all the more. She squeezed his hand and then, blessedly, he released hers. She should probably say something, but she couldn't find words. Anything she'd rehearsed on the drive had long since scattered to the recesses of her flustered brain.

Finally, John Holmes took mercy on them all, waving at a waitress, asking for a carafe of coffee and a pitcher of water. And then, probably because he felt bad about their paltry order, said they'd also take a plate of cookies.

"Well, first of all," John said as the waitress moved away, "thank you, Trey, for your phone call. For letting us know about your condition and the possibilities for Olivia. We've already got her an appointment this week with our family doctor and he should be able to get us into a cardiologist from there."

Family. That word again.

"Has she had any symptoms?" There, she'd done it. Finally spoken.

Sandy shook her head. "Not that we've noticed. And I've asked her a few leading questions since Saturday. She's not in any sports, hasn't really ever shown an interest in athletics, so thankfully that's not a concern. From everything we've read ever since you called, this disease doesn't tend to make itself known in kids unless they're pretty active."

Trey nodded. "So . . . you haven't mentioned the disease to her?"

John shook his head. "Not yet. We're praying about that. She'd probably have more questions than we could answer at this point, so we're not sure what the best course is."

Trey nodded again.

Sandy glanced at her husband before picking up where he'd left off. "We were also happy to meet with you today because we never had the chance to thank both of you for the incredible gift you've given our family." Her gentle gaze found Indi's. "I don't know your full story or all that led to the decision you made. But that decision changed our lives forever and we'll be grateful always. I'm sure it wasn't made easily. The fact that you're both sitting here right now tells me it's not something you did and then simply moved on from."

"Sometimes it seems like you've never quite moved on." Lilian.

"Neither one of us has moved on. We both know it." Trey.

Everyone had seen it, she supposed. Everyone had seen the haunting that wouldn't go away no matter how much she threw herself into her stores or her workshop or relationships that moved too quickly. *Ben* . . . Foss, not Foster.

And Philip? Was she doing the same thing all over again? Had Trey's return only stirred up her ghosts to the point that she'd run into the arms of another man?

"I'm not Ben."

No, Philip wasn't Ben. Philip was a safe harbor. He was a starry night, a snow-capped landscape, a crackling fire. He filled her with wonder and warmth and if she could just lose herself in him . . .

But that was the thing. Even when she lost herself, the ghosts always found her. In her old nightmares. In her latest messes. In a baby's cry in a hospital corridor.

In a café where she looked at this nice, stable, praying couple and saw the future she'd given away. Unless . . .

"Y-you said you weren't sure about telling . . ." *Say her name.* "You weren't sure about telling Olivia about Trey's condition and what it could mean. What if . . . ?" She couldn't ask this. Couldn't make this suggestion. It was too abrupt. Too big of a leap.

"Indi, I see not just the mother you could've been to your baby, but the mother you are."

Philip's words had been with her for almost two days now —deep, beautiful words like coral on an ocean floor, swaying but rooted as a storm raged on the surface. What if it wasn't too late? What if she could reclaim just a tiny part of what she'd given away?

"What if Trey told her himself? What if he explained . . . if she could see how healthy he looks and get an in-person understanding of what she's getting tested for and . . . We could both tell her. Together."

Trey had gone still beside her. John and Sandy, too, save for a quick meeting of their eyes. A husband and wife silently communicating, considering her suggestion.

Or . . . or not considering. Because the moment Sandy focused her gaze on Indi, reached across the table to take her hand, she knew. They'd been prepared for this. They'd seen it coming. They already had an answer.

"Indi, in the beginning, we were obviously receptive to the idea of an open adoption. You wouldn't have our names otherwise. But it's been eleven years and Olivia's a pre-teen. We know our daughter. She's studious and focused, and she's got a determination that can be both amazing and frustrating." She squeezed Indi's hand. "But she's also got a lot on her plate right now. She skipped a grade this year and though it was a good move academically, it's been a difficult social adjustment. Now she's got a doctor's visit that's probably going to lead to a cardiology appointment, and we're going to have to figure out how to talk to her about this." Sandy sighed. "To add one more element on top of that, meeting birth parents that, to be honest, we haven't talked much about . . . well."

However gentle Sandy's smile, it just couldn't soften the blow of her next words. "It's not a no forever. But we need to give you a firm no for now."

Indi pulled her hand away, let it drop to her lap. "That makes sense. I understand."

John looked uncomfortable. "I hope you truly do. We both hope this can stay, er, informal. That we don't need to worry about legalities or—"

"Of course," Trey interrupted. "We didn't come here to complicate anything for Olivia or you. Her family."

Her family. As in, not them. Not Indi.

"We just both needed a little closure, you know?" Trey rushed on. "So it's just real nice to have met you and know that our—your—Olivia's in a good place with good people. And hopefully this heart thing is a non-factor in her life."

Even as Trey clearly tried to steer them out of the hole Indi had nose-dived into, she could feel Sandy watching her. John, too, in between nodding along with Trey's rambling.

It's better this way. It's better this way. The gonging refrain she'd been stuck in for over a decade clanged on now. *It's better this way.*

Because hard and horrible as this was, wouldn't it be worse to actually see Olivia? Once, twice, didn't matter how many times. Every time she'd have to walk away. Every time she'd have to accept all over again that she might be Olivia's mother, but she wasn't her mom.

It's good they said no. You never should've asked. It's better this way.

So why could she feel her heart shattering all over again?

———◆———◆———

"I'll allow it was thoughtless, but everything else you're accusing me of—trespassing and break-ins and searching through bedrooms—no. Just no."

Twenty minutes Wilder had been hammering this guy and getting nowhere and Philip had had enough. "Thoughtless? *Thoughtless?* That's what you call making up an entire identity?"

Wilder put his hand out but Philip knocked it away.

"That's what you call lying to a woman who trusted you? No, buddy, that's not thoughtless. That's putting way too much thought into a callous, selfish plan to deceive someone just so you could dig for information about a so-called treasure that probably doesn't even exist."

Wilder angled in his chair. "Philip, calm down."

He yanked himself from his chair, sending it tumbling behind him. "No, I'm not going to calm down. It's bad enough he lied to Indi, but to get romantically involved with her? To go as far as proposing?" He wrenched his ire back in the direction of Ben. "You were just being downright cruel by that point."

"I wasn't." Ben slapped his hand on his desktop as he rose, sloshing soda from a can. "Believe what you want, but I actually cared for her. I got carried away, and yeah, I got stupid. And when I realized I'd gotten in too deep, I turned tail and ran. But I wasn't out to hurt her and I sure as blazes didn't break into her store or her family's house or whatever else you think."

"Okay," Wilder barked. "That's enough. Sit down, Foss. Philip, maybe you should let me finish this."

No, he wanted to finish this guy. Hurt him the way he'd hurt Indi.

"If you're not going to leave, at least sit," Wilder groused. "And shut up."

Why should he? Wilder wasn't the only one capable of a gut instinct. This guy didn't have a thing to do with the trespassing and the break-in at the store. So they might as well put him in his place and get out of here.

But at the harsh demand in Wilder's eyes, he conceded and plucked his chair from the floor, plunked it back down— loudly—and sat.

"Explain again," Wilder said slowly, "why I should believe that if you'd go so far as to lie about your name, make up a whole persona, for the sake of a two-hundred-and-fifty-year-old legend, you wouldn't then go traipsing about Muir Farm and playing intruder."

Ben crossed his arms. "Yes, I made up a name. Because, yes, I didn't want Indi or any of her family members searching my name on the internet and figuring out who I was and what I do." He flicked a sullen glance at Philip. "But I got to know Indi. I liked her. I got the idea into my head that maybe I could get two good things out of this at once. I could marry her and then take my time searching the farm at my leisure."

Buffoon was no longer a good enough designation for this man. *Creep* didn't do it either. The only other words that marched through Philip's brain weren't the kind he usually said out loud.

"But sanity set in—I mean, it's not like I could marry her using a false name and if I told her the truth, that'd be the end of things anyway. So I called time. I let her go. Let the whole thing go."

"We're supposed to believe you just had a lovely little change of heart?" Holland would've been proud of how forcefully he rolled his eyes.

She wouldn't be proud. She can't stand you at the moment.

Not a reminder that made him feel any less like getting into the first physical brawl of his life. But Wilder would probably tackle him before he could throw a single punch.

Ben spoke slowly, hostility in his voice and in his refusal to cower. "You can believe whatever you want. But I'm not the person you're looking for."

Philip opened his mouth but Wilder kicked his leg and spoke first. "And you don't have any information about who that person might be?"

"No."

Wilder stood. "Then we'll say goodbye for now."

"Good." Ben leaned back, his chair bumping into the wall behind him. But he jerked forward just as quickly. "Wait. Why for now?"

"Because I'm real hopeful Indi will decide to sue you. I asked her lawyer sister and she's got all kinds of legal grounds —fraud, intentional infliction of emotional distress, you name it. Which means we just might see you again. Could even be an arrest in your future. A guy can hope anyway, right?" He motioned to the door. "Let's go, Philip."

They were down the steps, past the counter, and halfway to the door when Philip couldn't hold back any longer. "That's it? We're just going to let him off the hook?"

"You need to take a long, deep breath. Just trust me."

"What, you mean your magical gut instinct is telling you something new now?"

Wilder pushed through the door. "What happened to the agreement that I'd be the one asking the questions?"

The winter cold blasted him in the face as they crossed the parking lot. "Like I was really just going to sit back and—"

A voice rang out from behind them. "William, hold on."

Philip kept walking, but Wilder stopped. *William.* Right, Wilder's alias. He paused, turned in time to see Wilder flash a grin with just enough smugness to know that, okay, maybe he did have some kind of inside track to reading situations. Because Ben Foss was jogging from the building, his blazer whipping in the wind. He was panting when he reached them. "I remembered something."

Wilder folded his arms. "Thought you might."

Ben narrowed his eyes but went on. "Look, the circles I run in—"

"Con artists?" Philip inserted.

From the look Wilder gave him, he'd never be accompanying the man on a case again.

"Archeologists, adventurers, treasurer seekers." Ben glared. "Call us crazy, but everybody has a thing."

Wilder nodded. "Go on."

"It's a small circle. A lot of us know each other. We end up on the same digs, searching for the same things." He pulled his phone from his pocket. "I was in Muir Harbor around Thanksgiving—"

Philip gaped. "What? You said you never—"

"I said I never set foot in Muir Harbor when Indi and I were dating. I went there once later in November with the idea of apologizing to her. Got cold feet and never did. I was in town all of twenty minutes, but it was long enough to see someone I thought I recognized." He held his phone out to Wilder. "Didn't occur to me until later that I knew his face from a message board I'm on. His photo's just a thumbnail but even so, I'd swear it's him. Wouldn't have stood out to me, except the only questions he's ever asked on the board were about the Muir Harbor legend. I remember thinking he had a lot of familiarity not just with the legend, but with the area. Figured he might be from around there."

Philip glanced at the screen in Wilder's hand as Wilder tapped the tiny image and zoomed in.

Recognition careened in and Philip jerked his head to meet Wilder's eyes. The man's dark gaze sharpened. "We need to get back. Now."

"*R*eally, Indi, I don't feel good about leaving you here alone."

Indi climbed out of Trey's car. Well, his mom's car. She'd recognized the silver Taurus this morning as easily as she recognized most cars in Muir Harbor. She'd never even asked him if he'd flown up from Florida or road-tripped, but considering he was borrowing Gloria's car, she'd guess the former.

This was how the whole drive back to Muir Harbor had been—her brain latching on to any mundane thought, even as mundane as a car model and Trey's travel methods, to keep her from drifting back to that café booth. From reliving the hope that had flooded her heart one minute to the letdown that had parted the waters in the next moment. Like Moses parting the Red Sea.

Only this parting hadn't delivered her to freedom.

The rocky hill that led toward the chapel on the cliff rose in front of her, snow still quilting most of its ridges, but enough of it having melted away to reveal patches of the winding trail she intended to follow.

"I've walked this path so many times I could do it blindfolded." She might not have worn the best shoes for it, but it wasn't an overly strenuous walk. "I just want to spend a few minutes in the chapel. You know me. You know that's always been my spot."

Trey stood beside his open door, tapped the roof with resolve. "Then I'll go with you."

"No, please."

"But how are you going to get home?"

"I've got plenty of family members who can come pick me up." Or she could return one of Philip's three calls over the last couple hours.

None of which she'd answered. She just hadn't been ready to talk to him. Not when she knew he'd ask how the morning went.

It's not a no forever. But we need to give you a firm no for now.

No, it was a no forever.

Because Indi wouldn't be asking again. Because today had proven what she'd known all along. She didn't belong in her daughter's life. Then, now—it was the same either way. She was a complication. A hindrance to the tidy, happy, secure life she'd always wanted for her daughter.

Olivia.

"You go to the chapel when you're upset. If you're upset, you should be with people." Trey tipped his head to where the tip of the chapel poked through the trees. "I just don't get what you're hoping to find up there that you couldn't find by going home."

"I don't know, Trey, maybe Alec Muir's lost gold."

From his grimace, he didn't appreciate the sarcasm.

"Sorry."

He glanced to the trail again. "You'll be careful?"

"I promise. And, um, thanks for inviting me along today." He'd been trying to do something nice. He hadn't known what it would do to her. She should be thankful that one tear in the fabric of her past had been mended.

"Well, I'm going to watch you go up the first little bit. Just to make sure it's not too slick. If you start sliding or something, I'm coming after you."

She did her best to smile. "I'll be fine."

And then she took off, rounding his car, making for the trail. She picked her way along the path, aiming for spots where the snow had sloughed away or someone else's footprints already cleared the way. Within minutes, she was enveloped by the trees, their shadows closing in around her, their pine scent offering her the first comfort in hours.

Maybe, somehow, some kind of miracle would happen up in that chapel. Like when she'd been ten and prayed for snow. Maybe once she got there, pulled open the heavy door, settled into a cold, hard-backed pew, she'd figure out how to be okay with everything that'd happened today. How to pick up and move on again.

Perhaps God would actually answer her prayers this time. Help her no longer think of Olivia. Or the Holmeses. Or her splintered hope. She'd no longer have that scrap of paper in her vanity drawer haunting her, after all.

Even with the snow, it was an easy climb to the clearing where the chapel kept watch over the rugged seaside. See, Trey didn't have a thing to worry about. She knew this place, this path . . .

She knew that sound—the metal-on-metal peal of the chapel door's hinges. She rounded a towering evergreen and emerged into the clearing. Gasped.

"Holland?"

The girl spun around, letting the chapel door clang to a close. "Indi?"

What in the world? "Is Philip here with you?" She lumbered through the snow to reach Holland.

Holland shook her head. "No. He's mad at me. I'm mad at him. What's new?"

Actually, that *was* new. Holland had been warming up to Philip more and more every day. And Philip, well, he was all but wrapped around this girl's finger. Couldn't Holland see that?

"He's texted me like four times, though. He'll be home soon."

"Then why are you here? And . . . how? With a cast and—"

"Yeah, on my wrist. My legs work fine."

"But it's five miles from the farm." She couldn't keep herself from stating the obvious. "You can't drive."

"No, but I happen to know it's an easy bike ride away. I mean, if a ten-year-old can do it on Christmas Eve, I can do it. Even one-armed. I came because . . ." She nudged her head toward the building. "You said this was a hallowed space." Her expression loosened a little. "I haven't prayed in a long time, so . . ." She shrugged.

Indi draped her arm around Holland's shoulder and they walked into the chapel together then sat side by side on a middle bench. Cold seeped from the stone walls despite the sunbeams streaming in through stained glass, painting stripes over their legs and the pew in front of them. And silence edged in.

Except not the peaceful silence Indi used to feel in this place. Not the hushed stillness that invited prayer. No, there was too much of a storm rollicking through Indi today. And, if Holland's unyielding posture beside her was any indication, she wasn't alone.

"If you need to talk . . ." A memory trickled in. Of that night in November on the way to Muir Harbor. Of Philip, getting ready to push her car out of the ditch, but offering first to pray with her. A sweet suggestion from a sweet stranger. *Not a stranger anymore.* Nor was Holland. "Or we could pray together—"

"What's the point?" Holland didn't look over, her piercing focus unwavering from the stained glass. "I know I said I came here to pray, but now . . . What's the point when so many times before, God just kept ignoring me. Or maybe He wasn't ignoring me. Maybe He was just saying a big fat no over and over."

"Holland—"

"I'm serious." The girl ripped her gaze from the window and turned her gray eyes on Indi, a tempest rumbling through them. "He could've healed her."

Indi didn't have to ask who. She inched closer to Holland, tried to slip her arm around the girl again, but Holland wrenched away, jumping from the pew and into the aisle. She jutted her hand toward the altar up front, pointing to the open Bible.

"If I'm supposed to believe that book, then He can heal people. But I asked a thousand times for Him to heal Mom and every time He said no. So . . . what? I'm supposed to just keep praying? I'm supposed to think He's going to fix things between Philip and me? Fix the mess I made by contacting Dad?" A lone tear trekked down her cheek, but she swiped it away with an angry thrust of her palm. "You prayed for snow and you got it. Well, that's nice for you, but I didn't get the miracle."

Indi needed to say something. She needed to come up with something kind and wise and comforting. But she had . . . nothing. Nothing except that stinging realization that she was seeing herself in the girl in front of her. Hearing the clanging echoes of her own fragmented faith.

She and Holland differed in age and life experiences. But she knew—she *knew*—that anguish in Holland's cracking voice. Yes, Indi's ten-year-old self had gotten her snow that long-ago Christmas. But her twenty-eight-year-old self was still waiting on healing. And right here in this moment she was ready to give up on it.

She'd had years to let go of her daughter. Years for the wondering to fade and the regret to dim and the anguish—so much anguish—to loosen its hold. But it hadn't loosened. If there was anything this past week had proven, it was that everyone was right. She hadn't moved on. She hadn't let go. She wasn't over it.

God hadn't healed her pain. What if He never did? What if He just refused to fix her? Like He'd refused to heal Holland and Philip's mom?

You can't do this now. You can't let your own hopelessness spill over to Holland. Not when she's hurting so badly.

But she couldn't seem to dredge up any hopeful words either. They felt too trite. Too . . . untrue. *Where are you, God? We climbed up a hill and came to this chapel to look for you. So why aren't you here?*

Tears were streaming down Holland's face now, her thin frame shaking. Indi rose and reached her in seconds, pulling the girl close despite her resistance. Finally, Holland gave up resisting, wilting into Indi as she cried.

"I'm so sorry, Holland. I wish I could take this pain away from you." If only Philip were here. He was the one Holland needed right now. "I wish—"

She didn't know what she'd meant to say next. But it didn't matter because she was cut off by the noise of the metal hinges screeching again.

Philip? Had her wishful thinking conjured him up?

But no, that wasn't Philip's silhouetted form filling the doorframe when she looked over her shoulder. She couldn't see his face but . . . *Not tall enough.*

And when he spoke, it wasn't Philip's reassuring, low timbre. "You know, I saw the two sets of footprints but didn't actually expect there to be two people here. Thought it would only be Indi." He shrugged. "It's fine. We can still have a nice little chat—the three of us."

He finally stepped into the light of the stained glass.

Confusion muddled through her. "Why are you . . . ?" Her words died then, right along with her bafflement—no match for the instant dread that took over when she saw the gun in Peyton Cornish's hand.

Holland wasn't in her bedroom. The bathroom door was wide open—the bathroom empty. Philip hadn't seen her in the living room or dining room when he'd glanced in before climbing the stairs.

He hurried down the staircase now, trying and failing to shuck off the irrational worry that'd taken hold of him with every mile they'd traveled from Muir Harbor's regional airport toward the house. He needed to find Holland. And Indi. Tell them what he and Wilder had learned. Pray that nothing had transpired in the hours he and Wilder had been away—

"What if she's not just ignoring my texts? What if something's wrong?" Wilder's voice blew through the house. "I've texted her five times!"

Okay, so Philip wasn't the only one beginning to feel a buzzing anxiety in the back of his head. Or the front. Or all over him.

He hurried to the kitchen, found Wilder gathered with Maggie, Neil, and Sydney. No Indi. And according to Wilder's manic voice, no Lilian.

He stopped in the kitchen doorway. "Has anyone seen Holland? Or Indi?"

Maggie's forehead was wrinkled with bewilderment. "Holland's upstairs doing schoolwork."

"She's not."

The buzzing grew louder. *Don't be ridiculous. She's around here somewhere. She's probably out back with the dog or—*

"You haven't heard from Indi yet?" Wilder jabbed one hand in his back pocket.

"No. She should've been on the road home a long time ago. I'm getting worried."

Neil palmed the back of his head. "Yeah, hello, so are the rest of us. You two come barging in here, stomping through the house like madmen, and we're all in the dark. What happened in Rhode Island?"

Philip threw a look to Wilder. "You haven't filled them in?"

"No, I've been a little busy trying to track down—"

A banging at the front of the house cut him off. "Wilder, where are you? I saw your jeep. I know you're here." Lilian's voice echoed through the house.

Relief flooded over Wilder's face. But he didn't have long to bask in it before Lilian burst into the kitchen, holding up her phone. "You have no right—"

"Lil, listen for a sec—"

"You don't get to tell me—"

"Would you just be quiet for a minute and let me explain?"

Neil groaned. "Seriously, Lil, let the man talk."

"Fine, talk. Explain to me where you get off telling me to stay away from Peyton!"

"He's the one. He's the one who's been trespassing, breaking in, looking for a treasure. He's. Our. Guy. Which you'd know if you'd read any of my other texts after the first one or listened to the stupidly long voicemail I left you."

Somewhere in the middle of Wilder's tirade, Lilian's face had gone white. "What?"

"Wait, so Ben's not . . ." Neil's voice trailed off as Lilian dropped into a chair, her voice shaky, quiet.

"*Peyton Cornish* is the treasure hunter. You're sure?"

Mouth tight, Wilder nodded. "Actually I'm almost positive there's much more to this than the legend and Alec Muir's treasure."

That was a surprise to Philip. Wilder must have pieced together something the rest of them hadn't. But he was having trouble figuring out why he should care about that when there were two people vitally missing from this group.

"I'll explain more later," Wilder said. "But for now—"

"For now, we need to find Holland and Indi," Philip interrupted, barely restraining his distress. Or maybe not restraining it all, because he'd said that too loudly, hadn't he? Because the buzzing in his head was almost deafening now.

"I know," Wilder said, glancing at him. And then Philip only felt worse when the man whose gut instincts were rarely wrong added, "I'm feeling it too."

The loamy smell of the chapel rose up to suffocate her with every step Peyton Cornish took down the center aisle.

The door had long since rattled to a close behind him, snuffing out any extra shafts of light. How had Indi never noticed how dark it could feel in here, stained glass and all, even in daylight?

"Um, what's happening?"

Oh Lord, Holland.

And Peyton. Moving toward them. With a gun in his hand.

On instinct, Indi shifted, putting herself between Philip's sister and the man she barely knew, only the barest facts tripping through her brain as she stared at him. *Cecil Atwater's nephew. Works at the paper. Took Lil on some dates.*

He'd come to the house on Saturday. She'd talked to him in the entryway. He'd been friendly, polite . . .

No hint of the sinister aura cloaking him now, despite the half-smile that owned his face. "I expect the gun is having a bit of an impact at the moment." His grin filled out. "Which, I have to tell you, is a nice feeling from where I'm standing. Makes a man feel like perhaps there's a hope he won't be ignored."

"U-uh, Peyton. I'm not sure what this is about but . . . or w-why . . ." Her mind was still whirling, desperate, frantic. She chewed on her lip, hard enough for the pain to keep her from fully giving in to her panic. What had he said when he first walked in?

"You know, I saw the two sets of prints but didn't actually expect there to be two people here. Thought it would only be Indi."

Did that mean he'd come looking for her? Followed her up the hill the way Trey had wanted to? *Trey!* Maybe he was out there somewhere. Maybe he'd stayed parked at the landing long enough to see Peyton arrive and trail her up to the chapel. Maybe any minute now—

Peyton stopped halfway down the aisle. "Before we go any further, I'd appreciate it if you could confirm for me once and for all: there's no hidden gold, is there? The Legend of Muir Harbor—just a bonnie little story, yes?"

She sucked in a breath, tasting the blood from having bitten down too hard on her lip. "*The legend?* You're the one who broke into my store. Broke into our house—"

"Walked right in, more like. There was a nice little party out back for cover."

"You ransacked Neil's treehouse. The machine shed. Left footprints."

"Took a look around the barns too. Vandalized a generator

just so someone would notice but I'm not sure anyone ever did."

A generator? Yeah, she had a hazy memory of Neil's frustration over the thing last fall. Another expensive repair when the farm was bleeding funds.

"You *wanted* us to notice?"

"Do you really think I would've done such a shoddy job covering my tracks if I didn't?" He took a step closer. Another. And another. Until he was close enough she could feel the cool metal of his gun even though it was still inches from her. "Here's the thing, though. I'd prefer not to be the guilty party at the end of the TV courtroom drama who makes a sweeping confession and explains his every motive just so viewers can get a tidy ending. I'd much rather make quick work of this."

She didn't want to know what *this* was. Really, really didn't want to know how the same pair of brown eyes that looked so warm and pleasant just days ago could simmer with such menace now.

"We're going to head outdoors now. All three of us, nice and cooperatively."

"And if we don't?"

"Then I guess I use this thing." He wiggled the gun. "But I'd like to avoid a mess, so . . ."

There it was. The cruel truth of their situation. The reality of his intentions.

"I don't understand why you're doing this. We don't even know you." Was this just a horrific case of wrong place, wrong time?

"Well, I know you. I've spent way too much of my life hearing the name Muir. Listening to that lie of a legend. If it wasn't her putting the baby to sleep by reciting it for the three thousandth time, it was him. Moaning and murmuring and refusing to let her go years and years after she was gone."

Nothing he'd said made sense to her. Nothing made sense at all. Except for the one clear thought she refused to release. *Holland. Get her out of here.*

"I'm sick of it. I'm done." Peyton towered over her now, the gun butting into her thick coat. "So walk, Indi Muir."

18

*I*f Philip didn't know Wilder already had the gas pedal pressed to the floor, he'd have yelled for the man to drive faster.

As it was, it was all he could do not to growl his frustration with a volume loud enough for the 911 dispatcher on the other end of Neil's phone call to hear.

"Yes, the chapel at the cliff. Police and EMS. We might need them both."

The *might* in that sentence must've confused the person on the other end, because Neil spent the next several minutes trying to explain in stops and starts a situation that anyone would admit sounded outrageous.

They were all overreacting, right? *Please, God, let us be overreacting.*

But the facts mocked his attempt at self-assurance. They'd called Trey not long ago, put him on speakerphone, found out he'd left Indi at the base of the chapel hill. They'd plied him for information, for anything he'd seen. No, he hadn't seen any other cars there, but he'd noticed a bike. And, well, yes, actually, come to think of it, a gray four-door had been pulling in when he'd left. One that he'd noticed following them earlier.

Just about the time Philip had been about to throw the phone across the room in frustration, Lilian had barreled in. Said they'd searched every inch of the house, the property at large. No sign of Holland.

But there'd been a bike missing from the rack in the garage.

And now his heart had been lodged in his throat for so long, it was getting difficult to breathe.

"Can't you go faster, Wild?" It was the first thing Lilian had said the whole drive, after shouldering into the car despite both her brother's and Wilder's objections. Surely Maggie and Neil's wife would've insisted on joining them if someone hadn't needed to stay behind just in case Indi and Holland weren't where they all thought.

"I'm already gunning it," Wilder said now.

Neil finally ended his call. "Okay. I think I've thoroughly confused the dispatcher, but they're sending law enforcement and an ambulance."

An ambulance they wouldn't need. They *wouldn't*. Indi and Holland would be fine. Peyton Cornish would be nowhere near the chapel. Everything would be fine.

Please, God.

Neil leaned forward from the back seat. "I still don't understand why you think this has anything to do with the other case—Diana and Maggie's granddaughter."

"I should've figured it out sooner. I knew something was off about Peyton but I thought . . ." Wilder kept clasping and unclasping the steering wheel. "We wasted so much time on that blasted list."

"What list?" Lilian scooted forward like Neil.

"When my dad was originally working Maggie's case, he had

this visitor's book from The Lodge, all these handwritten names. Guests who'd stayed there around the time when Diana first left town right after high school. Because the rumor was always that she'd taken off with someone she'd met at the bar connected to The Lodge, right? So he pored over that list for years."

Philip was struggling to focus, his attention on the landscape out the window, almost as blurry as his brain with as fast as Wilder was driving. They had to be almost there.

"But if someone connected to Peyton—say, his father— was ever in Muir Harbor back then," Wilder went on, "he wouldn't have stayed at The Lodge. He was once married to Cecil Atwater's sister, remember. They would've stayed with family."

"You're saying you think the man Diana ran off with was Peyton's father?"

"I looked the man up on our way from the airport back to the farm. Nicholas Cornish. Divorced his first wife a year or so after Diana ran off. Timing fits." Wilder's jaw ticked. "It should've clicked when I heard Cecil introduce Peyton at the wedding reception. He said he was from Georgia. And remember, the only thing Maggie ever knew about where Diana went after high school was that she'd landed somewhere in or around Atlanta."

The car was quiet for a moment.

"Anybody could say they're from Georgia," Lilian countered, her tone surprisingly gentle. "Hundreds of thousands of people live there. Most of them have nothing to do with Diana."

Wilder didn't respond.

Neil cleared his throat. "It's a pretty big jump to go from Peyton Cornish being in Muir Harbor now, causing trouble at the farm and searching for a treasure that probably doesn't exist, to the assumption that it must be his father Diana ran off with. How would you even go about finding out if the man was in Muir Harbor at that time?"

Philip couldn't listen to this anymore. He didn't care who Peyton Cornish was or what he had to do with anything in the past. All he cared about was that in the present, the man wasn't anywhere near Holland or Indi.

But no matter how hard he tried, he couldn't make himself believe that wasn't exactly where he was.

The sun had begun its slow descent, hiding itself sliver by miniscule sliver behind the bluffs. The cold pierced Indi's face as she stumbled over a mess of ice and slushy snow.

She gripped Holland's hand, trying with every last remnant of resolve to imbue assurance into her voice as she leaned close. "We're going to figure something out. I'm not going to let him hurt you."

Holland had no reply. Oh, what Indi wouldn't give for a slice of the girl's sarcasm right now. Any snarky little comment to convince her Holland was ready to fight to get away.

Behind them, Peyton's boots crunched into the snow and dirt. He'd all but pushed Indi out of the church door earlier after Holland had exited first.

"Please, Peyton, let her go. There's no reason to drag her into whatever this is."

He'd grunted and jabbed the gun into her back. *"Cooperate or it'll only be worse for both of you."*

He'd marched them toward the trees, onto a path, but not the one that led back to the parking lot. She'd realized too horrifyingly quickly where he was pointing them. Up toward the higher cliff, the one where she and Philip and Holland had taken that selfie last week.

God, you can't take Holland from Philip. Too many people have left him already. He needs her. She needs him. Please.

"At some point," she whispered, "I'm going to distract him and you're going to run. I don't know how or when, so just be alert." It was the best and only plan she could conjure. Murky and incomplete, but at least she had a course of action.

"If you think I'm just going to run away and leave you here—"

"I know you're going to. You have to."

Peyton huffed behind them. "Let's stop with the whispering, shall we?"

Holland whipped around, yanking on Indi's hand as she did. "We'll stop whispering when you start talking."

"Holland, no."

"If he's going to kill us, I think we at least deserve to know why. You already know we don't have the treasure and we don't know anything about it, *Peyton*." She spat the man's name. "So what gives? Did Lilian turn you down or something so now you're taking out her family? Huh?"

"Holland," Indi hissed again.

Peyton actually smiled. "No. Lilian didn't turn me down. And she was very helpful in making it clear that if the treasure does exist, the family doesn't know anything about it. I'll admit, I was disappointed. Might've been nice to return to Georgia with that little surprise for Dad. It's why I went looking, after all. Literal decades of him holding on to that story, talking about how if Diana had lived—"

"Diana?" For the first time since this maniac had come into the chapel, something clicked into place for Indi. "Diana Muir?'"

"Yes, Daddy's little sidepiece, come to us all the way from Maine. He kept her tucked away in Atlanta, with the rest of us

clueless over in Savannah. Until he got tired of the charade."
He loomed over the pair of them. "Keep walking. And I'll keep
talking."

Indi swallowed. Turned. Holland did the same.

"Diana Muir is the reason my father left my mother. She's
the reason Mom spent the rest of her brief life drinking and
depressed. And she's the reason Dad has spent decades
ignoring the family he has left. Clinging to his memories of
wretched Diana Muir. Diana Muir from the precious Muir
family who died in a tragic car accident."

Indi's heart hammered against her chest. "S-so . . . so this
is all because . . . because you resent Diana for—"

"Ruining my mother? Splintering my family? For my
father treating me like a cast-off son from the moment he
brought her into our lives? Partially, yes."

They'd reached the bluff where the view had been so
breathtaking only days ago. But now, the sea was a wild,
ominous blue-black. The sky far too endless, far too empty.
The trees too silent.

"I'm sorry you went through that, Peyton, but none of us
were even around when Diana was alive. I wasn't adopted
until a year after she died. Neil and Lil didn't join the family
until later. What happened with your parents is heartbreak-
ing, but why punish us for what Diana did?"

Peyton's steps slowed. "Diana stole my father and mother
from me. But the rest of you stole something else."

Despite her attempt to stay calm, Indi threw up her
hands? "What did we steal? You already know there's no treasure. Is this about Cynthia?"

He scoffed. "No. You took something far more important.
So now it's my turn to take something."

"But—"

"We're done talking. Like I said, I'm not required to tie up
loose ends. And I'm in a hurry."

Indi looked to Holland. *Be ready,* she mouthed. She turned back to Peyton.

"Well, I'm not in a hurry to die. Are you sure there's not some other way to make things right? If you could just put the gun down and—"

"Save yourself the breath, Indi. We're doing this. You're going to take a jaunt up to the ledge and walk right on over. A nice little accident. Some actual news for my uncle to report on for once."

"This is insanity, Peyton. Our family hasn't—"

"Your family took everything from me!"

She knew in that moment, from the darkness of his gaze, the jumping of his Adam's apple, there was no more talking to do. No more stalling.

Please, Holland, do as I said. Don't hesitate.

She lunged for him with a scream that could shatter glass, kicking up snow under her heels, one hand flying toward his face while the other whipped toward his arm.

In the next moment, she hit the ground with him and he was kicking her off before she could catch her breath. Frantic, she looked for Holland, looked for the gun—

Felt a knee connect with her stomach and wet snow slosh under her back as she hit the ground again—hard. And then a hand at her throat, pressing, squeezing, even as she raked her fingernails across skin, tried to kick against the weight holding her down.

His grip tightened, two hands now. She couldn't breathe, couldn't breathe, couldn't breathe.

A shadow rose over Peyton. *No. Holland, you were supposed to run.* She would've screamed the words if her lungs weren't already screaming for air.

And then, suddenly, they got it—air. It scraped down her throat, her neck throbbing as she pushed over and rolled free of Peyton's weight, scrambled to a sitting position, then to her knees. Holland was getting ready to hit Peyton with her cast a second time, her arm lifted.

But he plunged toward Holland before the girl could make contact, his arms wrapping around her waist. *No!* With another scream, Indi threw herself at him, flailing, kicking, begging Holland to pull away, run—

And then someone else was yanking Peyton from her grasp. Wrenching and throwing the man against a tree as if he weighed no more than a pillow.

"Philip!" Holland's shriek pierced the night.

Philip. Indi's hands and knees dug into the cold ground, breaths still ragged and tortured, as she watched Philip bear down on Peyton. But Peyton was too fast. He was on his feet by the time Philip made it to him, his fist already flying.

Indi pulled herself up. "The gun, where's the—"

"It s-slid off the ledge." Holland's voice was shaking, tears streaming down her face.

Philip slammed Peyton into a tree, but his head snapped back the next moment and he stumbled backward, landing on his backside.

"Indi! Indi, are you okay?"

"Neil?"

Her brother came crashing through the trees, hulking toward her, pulling her toward him before she'd even fully registered Wilder racing past the both of them. She sank into Neil's arms as more voices and footsteps echoed around her.

And then it was Lilian, tears streaming down her face, who was towing Indi into an embrace. "Oh, thank you, God. Thank you. You're okay?"

"Yes, but—" She whipped around to see Wilder still advancing toward Peyton, Neil helping Philip up, then the pair of them falling into place behind Wilder.

"Give it up, Cornish. Police are on the way."

Peyton gasped for breath, looking past the men. "Hello,

Lilian." Blood trickled down the side of his face. From Indi's fingernails or Philip's fist or Holland's cast, she didn't know. Only knew the look in Peyton's eyes didn't spell the defeat it should.

Wilder's voice was darker than she'd ever heard it. "We know who you are. We know who your father is."

Oh, *oh*, but then the look changed. Weakened. Slackened. Went black.

Somehow, Indi saw what was going to happen next. Somehow she moved quickly enough, reaching for Holland, pulling the girl toward her, burying her head in her chest.

Protecting her from the sight of Peyton Cornish flinging himself from the cliff.

19

If Philip never saw another hospital again, it'd be too soon.

And if he never had to hear another siren or listen to the scratchy walkie-talkie voices of law enforcement officials as they secured and assessed a scene, that would be more than fine with him.

He held Holland against him in the wide back seat of Maggie's Buick. She hadn't once attempted to pull away, her re-casted wrist propped on her lap. "Only you would break your wrist twice in one week, Holl." He propped his chin on her head, inhaling the sanitary smell of the hospital that clung to her.

Or maybe him. The only time he'd left her side in the two hours they'd spent there—not even a week after the last time —was to get a few stitches on the side of his face, near his eye, where Peyton had taken a crack at him.

"I don't know if I technically broke it a second time since it wasn't healed yet from the first time."

"Either way." He squeezed her and met Indi's eyes as she twisted in her seat and peered at them from the passenger seat.

Such beautiful green eyes. Not that he could see much of them with darkness shrouding the landscape. He had no concept of what time it was. Knew only they'd spent much longer than he would've expected at the scene—answering questions, watching as a search-and-rescue crew arrived to look for Peyton—before finally leaving for the hospital.

They'd left Neil and Lilian and Wilder behind, still answering questions, though he assumed they were back home by now. At some point, someone must've called Maggie. She'd been waiting for them at the hospital when they'd arrived.

"Whether it's a new break or not, you injured it saving me." Indi's voice was still raspy and he could honest-to-goodness throw up if he let himself linger on why. Even if Holland hadn't recounted to him how Peyton had gripped Indi's neck with both hands, he would've been able to picture it from the bruises already beginning to show.

If they'd been a few minutes later . . . if Peyton had managed to fire off his gun before Indi knocked it from his hands . . . if Holland had run like Indi had told her to and there'd been no one to stop Peyton from choking her . . .

The what-ifs could shred his last hold on his emotions.

Indi coughed and spoke again. "Seriously, Holl, thank you."

He couldn't see Holland's smile, but he was pretty sure he felt it against his side. "Anytime. Just wish I'd asked the doctor to check on my eardrums. I think you might've broken them when you screamed as you jumped at Peyton. You were like a raging banshee."

Philip had heard that scream. It'd sliced through the trees when he was still too far away and lanced clean through him.

"Sounds like you took turns saving each other." He'd pulled Indi into his arms the first chance he had after the commotion at the cliff. *"Thank you. Thank you for keeping her safe."* She hadn't responded, had only sagged against him, holding on until someone said her name and pulled her away to answer more questions.

It wasn't enough. He wanted to circle his arms around both Indi and Holland at once, keep them pressed into them until he could convince himself this was all really over, they were really okay, he hadn't lost them. Hadn't lost the two people he loved more than anyone.

Love.

Indi had turned back around now, scooted over into the Buick's bench seat, laid her head on Maggie's shoulder. Yes, he loved her. And he was done counting the days as if he wasn't allowed to admit it until some arbitrary amount of time had passed. He loved Indi Muir and he probably wouldn't be able to stop himself from telling her once they got back to the farmhouse and found a moment alone.

That is, if he could bring himself to let Holland out of his sight. *Doubtful.*

So maybe he'd just declare himself in front of his sister. After all the ugliness she'd seen today, it might do her some good to witness something happy and right.

Holland elbowed his side. "Well, now that we've taken turns lauding each other, we should probably talk about how you just about threw that jerk off the cliff yourself, Philip."

"Not off the cliff. Just into a tree." And yeah, he didn't know where that moment of brute force had come from. But he'd seen the man grappling both his girls at once and he'd gone into some kind of automatic attack mode. He'd probably feel the clash tomorrow in every muscle and bone in his body.

More, he'd probably relive the fear and shock for days.

But everyone's okay. Everyone's alive.

Even, surprisingly, Peyton. They'd gotten a text from Neil just as they were leaving the hospital. Amazingly, S&R had found the man's body washed up a half-mile down the coast-line, battered and unconscious, but alive. If he pulled through, it'd be some kind of miracle.

But this was a night for miracles, he supposed. And at least Peyton wouldn't be going anywhere other than a jail cell if he did wake up. And maybe he could provide some answers for Maggie about the daughter she'd lost and the granddaughter she was still searching for.

"There's something more going on here," he'd heard Indi saying to her siblings and Wilder back at the scene. *"He was mad about Diana stealing his father from his mom, and yeah, he had some interest in the treasure. But that wasn't his main reason for nearly killing me. He said we took something from him. What did he mean? What did we take?"*

No one knew, and maybe they wouldn't until the man woke up.

It didn't take long for the lane that led to Muir Farm to stretch out in front of them, the lights of the farmhouse beckoning into the night, the car's window frosty and cold as he gazed into the darkness. Reminded him a little of that first night when Indi had brought him here after they'd waited at the hospital for Maggie to make it through surgery.

He'd felt such a weird sense of wonder that autumn night as they'd traced the seaside to arrive at the house. And even more so, the next morning, when he'd stepped out onto the front lawn and smelled the salty ocean mist rise up to meet him. Probably, buried somewhere under the ordeal of this day, the wonder was still there.

Holland stretched against him. Indi glanced over her shoulder once more, maybe just to assure herself he was there, like the way his gaze had kept straying to her as they waited with Holland.

Yeah, the wonder was still there. And if he could help it, he'd never let go.

Maggie parked in the crowded driveway, a mess of snowy footprints leading to the porch and into the house. He could imagine Neil's wife flinging herself at the man the moment he got home. Was the unspoken truce between Lilian and Wilder still in place or was Lilian already back to rolling her eyes at everything the guy said by now?

He gently unwound his arm from around Holland and they climbed out of the car. Maggie touched his arm, tipping her head to look him in the eye, the nighttime breeze flitting through strands of her white hair. "Thank you, Philip. I could've lost another daughter tonight."

"You don't need to thank me. From the way Indi was fighting when I got there, I have no doubt she would've taken Peyton."

Still, he let Maggie pull him into a hug, held her tightly.

"There's been an awful lot of hugging tonight." Holland sighed. "I'm okay with it at the moment, but by tomorrow, we all need to pull ourselves together."

Maggie laughed as she turned. "Just for that, come here, you."

If he could, he'd have taken a snapshot of that moment. The full smile Holland shined on him just before she gave in to Maggie's embrace. Then the way she let Maggie keep an arm around her as Maggie steered her to the porch, the way she slipped her non-casted arm around Maggie's waist.

And then it was just Indi and him and the sound of the waves and a half-moon peeking through lacy clouds.

"I keep thinking at some point the shock's going to wear off." Indi's unbuttoned coat hung loose. "Or that I'm going to wake up and find out this was all a dream. A nightmare. I wish that was it. Philip, if you all hadn't figured out where we were—"

He couldn't wait anymore. In one long stride, he demolished the space in between them and towed her to him, wrap-

331

ping his arms around her, burying his face in her hair. "If I'd lost either one of you . . ." *Or both.*

He shuddered, pressing his lips against her cheek, her chin, then finding her lips and kissing her like a man desperate. There was simply no holding back. If there'd been any uncertainty in his other kisses, any restraint, he banished it now—pure, hungry need fueling his every movement, one hand splayed on her back and the other lost somewhere in her hair.

And he might've let the minutes stretch, the heat coursing through him surely enough to ward them both from the cold, if he hadn't slid one hand to her face, the pad of his thumb running over her cheek . . . her cheek wet with tears.

For a breathless moment, he slowed. Allowed himself one more feather-light kiss, then pulled back, leaning his forehead against hers. "You're crying." His voice was the raspy one now.

"No, I'm not . . . I mean, I guess . . . yes." Then she pulled away. All the way. Hands sliding past his waist, feet pressing into the snow as she took a step back.

He felt instantly bereft. "I-I'm sorry if that was too much. You're probably bruised and here I just acted like a Neanderthal and—"

She used the edge of her coat to wipe her eyes. "No, you were . . . you are . . . that was . . . amazing."

Any other time and he might allow himself a smile at that. But the woman he loved was crying. "Happy to give an encore performance anytime you say the word. But Indi, what's wrong?" It was a stupid question considering all she'd been through today.

But whatever he might've expected her to say, it wasn't what came out of her mouth next. "You should probably get Holland back to Augusta."

The heat that'd kindled every ounce of his awareness leached from him now. "What?"

"You said it yourself. She's broken a bone twice. Both times I was with her. Both times she was on that hill because of me. She wouldn't have gone up there today if I hadn't told her stories about riding my bike—"

"Indi."

"It's not just that. Before Peyton got to the chapel . . . she was weeping, Philip. She was crying for your mom. She just cried for so long and I couldn't help her. I couldn't find anything to say. I couldn't be what she needed."

He tried to reach for her again but she backed up more.

"And you're hurt. You've got stitches. You'll have a black eye tomorrow."

"None of this is your fault. You can't think that."

Tears coursed down her face. "I can't lose myself in you, Philip. It's not fair to you. I have too many ghosts. And Holland needs you. I can't be a complication that makes things harder for you two so . . ." She drew in a ragged breath. "I think we just need to step back and—"

"I don't understand where this is coming from. You're not a complication. Holland still might not even be speaking to me if not for you." Why was she shaking her head? Why was she moving backward toward the porch? What did she mean by ghosts and losing herself?

The wind raked over him as a wearying realization trembled through him. "What happened this morning? What happened with the Holmeses?"

She turned away, hurrying up the porch steps, reaching for the front door.

But it opened before she grasped it. She flew past the two individuals on the threshold, and even over his quaking heart and the whitecapped sprays brawling with the rocky shore, he could hear her steps fleeing up the stairs.

He might've gone after her if not for Holland in the doorway. And the person beside her.

Under the dim porch lights, his sister met his eyes. "Uh, look who's here, Philip."

Bryce.

*J*ndi should be reveling in her surroundings. Sheets of powder-white fell from the sky, sparkling flakes catching in streams of lamplight, turning the town center into a real-life snow globe.

Despite cold temperatures and the winter weather advisories that kept dinging on her phone, the Muir Harbor Winter Market was in full swing. This was usually her favorite of the four seasonal markets her hometown hosted each year, drawing visitors from all around the region who wandered from booth to booth, opening their wallets for arts and crafts, homemade goods, and all manner of food.

Usually she loved the twinkle lights wrapped around every tree and the Christmas garland that still reached from lamppost to lamppost a full month after December 25. Holiday music piped through speakers and fire barrels painted red and green did their best to huff warmth into the evening air.

But none of it was enough to pull her from the doldrums.

Twelve days since that gut-wrenching morning at the café and the horrible events that followed at the chapel. Eleven since Philip had finally realized she was serious about taking Holland back to Augusta and had left town.

She wrapped a set of three hand-painted wooden birds in tissue paper, nestled them in a paper bag, and handed the bag to a cheery customer. The market wasn't quite as busy this year, but she'd still had a steady stream of shoppers at her booth.

Just get through tonight. Then you can pack up and go home.

And then what? Spend another night tossing and turning? Desperately missing the man who'd slept just down the hallway up until a couple weeks ago? Hoping Holland hadn't left for Texas with her father and left Philip alone in Augusta.

Reliving that moment with the Holmeses in that Lewiston café. Feeling her heart sink when Sandy said no.

Wondering how that appointment with Olivia's doctor had gone and whether she'd been to see a cardiologist yet and telling herself over and over to stop wondering. Because Olivia wasn't hers.

She could get it through her head but her stubborn heart just wouldn't listen.

A blast of frigid air sent strands of hair scratching against her cheeks underneath her knit hat as she passed a receipt and change to her customer. The woman thanked her. "Now if I can just get back to my car before I get frostbite—and get home before a blizzard sets in, for that matter. It was all I could do to convince my husband to make the twenty-minute drive over to Muir Harbor. I thought for sure the market might've moved indoors."

From somewhere underneath her dejection, Indi willed a friendly grin onto her face. "Around here, we're either too hardy or too stubborn to let the weather drive us inside."

"Or too cuckoo." Lilian entered Indi's booth, a thick blue scarf tucked under her chin and her long coat turning her steps to shuffles.

Indi should've expected her sister's appearance. Up until a few minutes ago, Neil had hovered at her side, and before that, Maggie had taken up residence on a nearby stool. They must be on a rotation, taking turns babysitting her in between manning the Muir Farm booth, where they were selling pies, pastries, and jars of Maggie's preserves by the dozens.

She supposed she couldn't blame any of them for their protectiveness. The bruises around Indi's neck and all over her body had finally started to fade in the past few days. But circles still lingered under her eyes, and certainly they all heard her up at night, pacing across her floor, or padding downstairs to make herself a cup of cocoa.

Which never really helped because all it did was remind her of that homemade hot chocolate recipe Philip had perfected after Holland's first injury and proceeded to make several times in the days that followed.

Until he'd gone and taken his recipe with him. Along with any opportunity for her to take her words back. Tell him the last thing she wanted him to do was leave.

Don't be selfish. Holland needed to go home. Philip needed to go with her.

"Have you been down to the harbor yet?" Lilian straightened her fleece headband over her ears.

Indi blinked. "What?"

"You always say the harbor is one of the prettiest places to be when it's snowing. I'm kind of surprised you're not out on a dock drinking in the view right now."

Indi gestured to the crowd filling the oval lawn. "Can't abandon the booth."

"You've been here three hours and haven't left the booth once. You should move around some, make sure the blood's still flowing in your limbs. Wilder can man the cash register for a few minutes."

Wilder was here? Indi turned in time to see the man slide onto the stool where she'd perched in between customers. "Yeah, take a break," he drawled. "And take Lil with you. I'm not in the mood for her barbs and scowls tonight."

Indi turned widened eyes on her sister. Lilian shot Wilder a frown before tugging on Indi's coat sleeve and pulling her away. "Let's go."

She had to two-step to keep up with Lilian's stride as they wove in and out of a maze of booths, crossed the cobblestone street, and turned the downtown corner that led to the harbor.

"I can't believe you've finally managed to wear Wilder's patience thin," Indi huffed into the cold.

"Ha! He deserves it after years of wearing mine out entirely." Lilian marched toward the largest dock.

"Neil said Wild actually lost his temper with you the night of the Peyton thing."

An amused grin appeared on Lilian's face, but it disappeared just as quickly. "Ugh, I don't want to think about Peyton." Lilian's gaze hardened. "I still can't get it out of my head—the way he looked at me just before he jumped. That 'Hello, Lilian' still freaks me out."

Yeah, what had that been about? What had any of it been about? *What did we take from you, Peyton?*

Unbidden, Indi's gloved fingers rose to her scarf-covered neck. The man still languished in a coma in the hospital. She knew Wilder was champing at the bit to question him. He'd even gone down to Georgia a few days after the cliffside incident, hoping to talk to Peyton's father, Nicholas Cornish—the man they now knew had whisked Maggie's daughter away from Muir Harbor decades ago. The father of Maggie's missing granddaughter.

But Nicholas Cornish had seemingly vanished and Wilder had come home more frustrated than ever. Which might account for his surliness with Lilian just now. And the fact that they'd seen far less of him at the farmhouse than usual.

"What if Peyton never wakes up and we never find out what this was all about? He said Diana was only half the story. I asked him point-blank if it had anything to do with Cynthia and he said no, but maybe he lied. Maybe . . . I don't know." She fingered her scarf again. "But whatever this is, it's not over, is it?"

Lilian shook her head and stopped at the edge of the dock, burying her hands in her coat pockets, her distant gaze hooked on the inky sea and her grimace deepening. Until, with a blink and a turn of her head, she looked to Indi. "That's not really what I wanted to talk about."

Indi lifted her brow. "I thought we were just here to admire the view?" And it was a gorgeous view—the glow of lit-up storefronts casting golden reflections over the water, swirling snowflakes disappearing into windswept ripples, stars peeking through shadowed clouds.

"I can't do it anymore, Indi." Lilian burrowed her chin into her scarf. "I can't stand by watching you withering and sinking into yourself because you're holding everything inside."

"So you're putting me on the stand?"

"I'm doing what I've wanted to do for months. No, years. I'm asking you to talk to me the way you used to. Before Trey and the pregnancy and the adoption. I don't know what you need to talk about most, whether it's what happened at the chapel or with Philip or with Trey and your visit to the Holmeses—" She halted when Indi looked away. "All right, that answers that. What happened with the Holmeses? Talk to me. Please."

"There's nothing to talk about. It's over. They know about Trey's condition. They'll take good care of Olivia." Her voice broke on her daughter's name and she turned away, hunching over the dock's wooden railing.

Lilian's steps sounded beside her. "Her name's Olivia?"

She gave a miserable nod. "I asked to meet her."

Even as the dock swayed under her feet, she could feel Lilian go still beside her. "They said no," Lilian said softly.

Another nod. "I don't blame them. It was the right thing. Just like . . . just like giving her up. It was the right thing to do. I knew it. Everyone knew it." Her voice splintered again and she blinked back tears. "It was the best thing for the b-baby. For Olivia. And me and the family."

"What do you mean 'the family'?"

"I heard you guys talking one night that spring. The farm was struggling. Neil was worried. You were trying to save for law school. Me and the baby . . ." She squeezed her eyes closed, rubbing her fingers against her eyelids. "We were a complication."

When she forced her eyes open and glanced to the side, it was to see Lilian studying her, realization drifting through her eyes. Or maybe a memory. "One of us said that, didn't we? We used that word. *Complication*."

"It doesn't matter." Her gaze returned to the wrestling waves.

"Yes, it does."

"I don't even remember who said it. And anyway, it was the truth. Besides, there's no point in rehashing it because adoption *was* the right decision. Meeting John and Sandy proved it. They're good people."

"Yeah, but so are you."

"I'm an emotional wreck."

"So what? Emotions mean you're alive. They mean you have a heart that's working. You and the things you feel and the experiences you've gone through aren't a complication to our family. I'm so sorry we ever made you feel that way."

She gripped the dock's railing. "You didn't—"

"We did. Even if we didn't know it at the time, even if it wasn't intentional—we hurt you. For all I know, I was the one to use that word. It sounds like something I'd say." Lilian let out a puff of white air. "I just hope you hear what I'm saying now. How sorry I am and . . . how much I care. I know Maggie's better at things like this, and Neil's got the whole big-brother tender-heart thing going on, but I care, too. And I've really missed you."

She couldn't look at her sister, couldn't find her voice beneath her clogged throat.

Lilian must've taken her silence as a cue to leave. Because after a moment's hesitation, she reached up to squeeze Indi's arm, then backed away from the railing. "I'll go make sure Wilder hasn't pocketed all the money from your cash register or anything." Her sister's retreating steps set the dock swaying again until . . .

Indi whirled. "Wait." Hot tears pooled in her eyes. "You were right. About all of it. You were right."

Lilian waited, unmoving and quiet, where the dock met the snow-covered ground.

"I did stop talking to you. I stopped talking to everyone. Because if I told you . . . if I really talked to you . . . you'd see what a mess I really am inside. Worse, *I'd* see it. I'd finally have to see it." Her fingers curled inside her gloves. "And I stopped painting and drawing because that always used to be how I felt closest to God—it was this sacred, emotional thing and I didn't want it anymore. It hurt too much. I was too angry that He asked me to make such a hard decision that left such a horrible, gaping hole in my heart. And it's still there. No matter what I do. I went to college, I opened a store, I opened a second store, I divided myself up into pieces trying to live in two towns and fill two shops with inventory and . . . I got engaged to a guy I barely knew. And none of it helped."

She pulled off her knit hat and used it to wipe her tears. "And neither did meeting with John and Sandy because now I have to let her go all over again. Only I don't think I ever did in the first place."

Lilian retraced her steps until she stood in front of Indi. She hesitated only for a moment before pulling Indi into a hug. "I'm so sorry, Indi. I wish I'd tried harder to understand what you were going through. What you *are* going through."

"You couldn't have fixed it."

Lilian stepped back. "No, but I could've listened. And if it would've helped, I could've told you what a mess I am, too."

Indi wiped her eyes again before the tears could freeze on her cheeks. "Ha! You?"

"There's things I don't know how to let go of either. But we're not talking about me."

Somehow, miraculously, a choked laugh pushed through. "I'd be a lot more comfortable if we were."

Lilian reached for Indi's shoulders with both hands. "The thing is . . . what if you don't have to let Olivia go?"

"John and Sandy said no, Lil. They don't want me to meet her."

Lilian shook her head. "I mean, what if it's okay to let your heart hang on to her a little? You gave birth to her. She's a part of you. You have every right to love her and miss her and feel the pain of her not being here."

"But I'm scared it's going to swallow me up. I'm scared there's always going to be this unfulfilled longing keeping me from being fully happy, being a whole person. From . . ."

Having a future with an incredible man like Philip.

No, not a man *like* Philip but Philip himself.

The truth welled up inside her. "More than anything, I'm scared I'm losing my faith. Because every time I ask God to fix my broken heart and He says no, it's harder to ask the next time. Harder to trust He cares. Or that He's listening at all." It was a fear that had been creeping up on her for years until it'd finally crashed over her in the chapel with Holland.

Lilian held Indi's gaze for a long, quiet moment. "There's this Saint Augustine quote I read once. 'In my deepest wound I saw your glory, and it dazzled me.' I think about it a lot, especially when I try to remember my life before Maggie adopted me. When I think about whoever it was who left me on her doorstep." She met Indi's eyes. "That's the hole in my heart. It's the thing I can't let go of."

Indi's fingers curled her hat as she studied her sister's face, glimpsed the flickering ache in her eyes. "Lil . . ."

"It's okay. Like I said, we're not talking about me."

"And like I said, I'd actually be okay with—"

Lilian interrupted her with a laugh. "Okay, fine, let's talk about both of us. I just wonder if maybe we're better off not trying so hard to let go, not wriggling so fiercely to be free of the ache or the hurt or the wondering or any one of the crappy emotions that come as a result of the wounds we carry. I just wonder if instead of asking God to take the pain away, we invite Him into it, which may sound trite but . . ."

Lilian sighed. "Look at Maggie. She doesn't pretend she doesn't have holes in her heart where Robert and Diana and her granddaughter should've been. But she still has beauty and joy and love in her life. She's figured out how to live in the tension between honest heartache and steadfast hope. She's put her trust in a God who . . . who maybe doesn't make every crack disappear, but who holds all her broken pieces tenderly. Who heals her simply by being with her. Staying with her."

Faint music from the town center drifted on the wind. *Staying.* It's what she'd told Philip Holland needed—someone who stayed. "That wasn't trite at all." Indi stuffed her hat in her pocket. "I want to believe everything you just said. But what if I can't?" What if she couldn't be the child anymore who prayed for snow and *knew* God heard her? Who trusted so innocently?

What if, in her deepest pain, His staying wasn't enough?

"If you can't right now, then you let everyone who loves you believe for you." Lilian nudged her toward the railing once more. "But considering you're the Muir who can stand in the coldest temps of the winter, who can feel the wind stinging her cheeks and the chill creeping under her skin, and still be dazzled by the snow and the stars and the sound of the sea, I don't have any doubts you'll eventually see the light pouring in."

As if lulled by Lilian's words, the night air stilled for a moment. No heavy gusts. No crashing waves. Just the slight bob of the dock and the soft halo of lamplight.

There is still goodness for you, Indi. It was a hushed assurance, whispering its way to her heart, as she tipped her head to the starlit sky. *There's still beauty and joy and love waiting for you on the other side of your pain.*

Or maybe even right here in it as snowflakes landed on her cheeks and mingled with her tears. "Lil?"

"Hmm?"

"Could you do me a favor? Could you help Wilder man the booth for a while? There's something I need to do."

21

*P*hilip turned over the last page of Grandfather's unfinished manuscript and plucked his glasses from his face. He chucked them onto the desk in his closet-sized office on the Thornhill campus, letting them slide across the surface, stopping when they bumped into the stack of papers.

What *was* this story? This wasn't one of Grandfather's usual twisty but familiar mysteries, the ones that earned him spot after spot on bestseller lists. This thing was . . . lyrical and literary, genre-twisting and moving and . . .

And he sort of hated Tabby for making him read it.

After weeks of putting it off, he'd finally forced himself to start reading it after his Monday afternoon Western Civ class, first one of the spring semester, and that'd been over two hours ago. At some point, he'd pulled off his tie, perched his shoes on the desk. He stared at the pages now, trying to make sense of what this half-told story had just done to him, this story of a man time-traveling through history while also journeying through his own past, facing his mistakes and regrets.

His feet clunked to the floor. And what was with the

young man in the story who time-traveled with the older one? He seemed . . . a little too familiar. A little too relatable. And bottom line, the emotional work-in-progress he'd just read might be Grandfather's masterpiece. He'd actually forgotten Grandfather was the one to write it somewhere in an early chapter.

For a time there, he'd forgotten everything else, too. Like Bryce's lingering presence back at the house, how much time the man had spent with Holland. Like the way Philip's gut twisted every time he was alone in a room with him, just waiting for the inevitable *"I'd like to take her back to Texas with me"* conversation.

Like Indi . . . radiant green eyes gleaming when it snowed or glistening when she teared up. Her laugh, her freckles, her smile. The way she could so easily shift from artsy, stylish storeowner to farmgirl-in-overalls and back again.

The way she'd told him to leave exactly two weeks ago . . . no, the way *she'd* left *him*. She'd so thoroughly emotionally retreated that in the end, he hadn't really had a choice about leaving Muir Farm.

And besides, once Bryce arrived, it's not like he could stay anyway. He couldn't let the man whisk Holland back to Augusta on his own or, worse, down to his ranch in Texas. Yeah, apparently Bryce was a rancher now. Had made a nice life for himself after he'd ditched Mom.

To be fair, the guy sure seemed repentant about that—and especially about how he'd failed to be any kind of support for Holland after Mom died. *"Truth is, I guess you could say I had a come-to-Jesus experience over Christmas. Saw my past stretched out behind me and knew I wanted something different."*

Sort of like the main character in Grandfather's book. With a sigh of frustration, Philip lurched to his feet and swept Grandfather's pages into a pile, stuffed them into his leather bag, and headed home.

Yes, home. Things in Muir Harbor might've fallen apart in the end—he might've been forced to walk away after Indi had walked away from him. But he wasn't going to walk away from the commitment he'd made to try to see life in Augusta in a new light, for Holland's sake. As long as she was still living at Grandfather's, he would consider it home.

And if Bryce tried to take her away . . . he didn't know what he'd do.

Or what to do about that *thing* he'd just read. Evocative, emotional . . . exasperating. Because how was he supposed to turn down Tabby now? How was he supposed to just walk away from a story that, even unfinished, could so deftly needle his soul?

He tromped into the house, stamping snow from his feet. He pulled Grandfather's pages from his bag, then started across the foyer to the hallway that led to the man's office.

But Bryce's appearance on the stairs stopped him. "Afternoon, Phil."

Never bothered him when Connor or Tabby shortened his name. But from Bryce, it rankled. "Hey."

"Hear that?" Bryce pointed over his shoulder. "She's playing again."

How had he not heard the strains of Holland's violin drifting through the house when he first walked in? *Beautiful.* He recognized the solo she was meant to have played the night of her concert back at the beginning of the month. Before . . . everything.

"Well, I'm looking for Grandfather—"

"Actually, uh, can we talk first? Just for a second?"

Oh Lord, here it came. The conversation he'd been waiting for. The one he had no clue how to handle, no matter how often he'd rehearsed his possible responses. *I'm her legal guardian. You can't take her. You might be her father, but you've hardly been a dad.*

Yeah, well, he wasn't Holland's dad either. But the lines had gone blurry in his head sometime over the last few weeks. Holland had gone from being the half sister he barely knew to *family*. The kind with roots that twisted and curled around your own until there was no untangling them.

And he didn't want to untangle them. *We belong together. Somehow Mom knew it. She knew—*

"I've been wanting to say this since I got here. Should've said it years ago. I had the opportunity to be a father figure in your life, Philip, and I didn't step up to the plate. I'm sorry for that. An apology might not mean much after all this time, but all the same, I'd like to ask your forgiveness." Bryce held out his hand and Philip was too flummoxed to do anything other than shake it.

"I, um . . . well . . . okay, I guess you have it. My forgiveness, I mean."

At first they were just words, but then Bryce squeezed his hand before letting go, and huh, maybe his forgiveness was genuine. Because as much as it irked him to admit it, this man seemed to be genuine, too.

Bryce nodded and moved back to the stairs, leaving Philip to stand there in the foyer, trying to figure out what to make of what'd just happened. Facing up to the truth that maybe it was time to buck up and admit Bryce's presence here had been good for Holland. She was playing her violin again, after all, wasn't she?

What am I supposed to do with that, God? If she's happy with him, if he wants her in his life, am I really supposed to stand in the way?

He plodded down the hallway to Grandfather's study. Why couldn't he hear God's answers anymore? He didn't know what to do about Holland. About his feelings for Indi. Was he just supposed to forget those?

His fingers curled around the pages in his hand. And,

yeah, what was he supposed to do with the realization that Grandfather wasn't just writing another book—he was pouring out a piece of his heart Philip had never seen. The cold, gruff, distant man he'd known couldn't have penned these words.

The truth of it brought him to a stop just outside the office door: These pages were the words of a grandpa speaking to his grandson.

Without knocking, he pulled open the door and marched in. "Did you write this for me?"

He expected to see Grandfather in his old chair by the window, where he'd sat day after day for so many months after Mom's death. But no. He was seated behind his desk, laptop open in front of him, glasses perched halfway down his nose.

Philip plopped the stack of pages on the desk in front of the man. "Are you the old man? Am I the young man?"

Grandfather nudged his glasses up his nose, closed his laptop, stood. "You didn't have to call me old."

"Did you write it for me?"

Grandfather looked away and sighed, then nudged his head toward the door. "Let's go, Philip."

"Go where?"

"Grab a coat."

What else was there to do but follow the man? Once they were in Grandfather's pristine Lincoln, he tried asking again where they were going, but Grandfather only shook his head and kept driving.

But it didn't take long to figure out their destination. Within ten minutes, they were pulling into the gravel parking lot next to the cemetery behind St. Mary's. "It's not even in double-digits today, Grandfather."

"I haven't been to her grave since the visitation. I doubt

you have either." The man turned off the ignition. "Stay here if you want, but I'm taking the keys."

Which meant no heat. So he could sit here and freeze or accompany his grandfather. And freeze.

He chose the latter, sliding from his seat, stifling a groan at the cold that sliced through him as he closed the car door. He followed Grandfather over the snow-packed path that led into the cemetery, curved past a towering evergreen.

And there it was—Mom's gravesite. The black marble tombstone that looked newer than all the surrounding ones. *Nora Helen West. Beloved Daughter and Mother.*

The wind stung his skin, his lips, his eyes. He swallowed.

"I bought a plane ticket so I could come get you."

He glanced to Grandfather. The man stood with his hands folded behind his back, his black trench coat reaching to his knees.

"I thought she was wrong not to tell you about the cancer. Got a ticket. Planned to buy a second one for you so you could come home with me."

"When?"

"When she first got the diagnosis. They told her right away she didn't have long."

"Why didn't you?" He couldn't imagine what he would've done if Grandfather had shown up on his doorstep in Seattle. Probably would've assumed he was seeing a hologram and closed the door in the man's face.

"She begged me not to. Said it should be her choice. Said she was already going to be asking you for a big favor and she didn't want to disrupt your life before she had to." He shook his head. "I still thought it was wrong, but in the end I chose to respect her decision. I regretted it, though. Still do. You should've had the chance to say goodbye."

They stood in silence for another thirty seconds, the chill eating through Philip's coat.

"The truth is, Philip, you should've had a lot of things through the years. Things I failed to give you. More . . . conversation. Affection, probably. So, yes, I did write the book for you. And for me. And for Nora and Holland, too. And probably even for Robert and . . ."

Philip's dumbfounded speechlessness just wouldn't let go. From being swept away in the pages of Grandfather's novel to Bryce's apology to this, now . . . it felt like someone had picked up his world and slanted it until he couldn't catch his balance.

"I know you think you never belonged in our home. And even, somehow, that I never wanted you there. But neither one is the truth." Grandfather dropped his arms to his sides, cleared his throat. "I'm not good at saying these things. I never have been. It's why I write, I suppose. But I wish I had. Said more, that is. Before."

Philip couldn't find words, couldn't process everything Grandfather was saying. So he just kept standing there, staring at Mom's gravestone. Until finally the older man burrowed his chin into his pulled-up collar and turned. "Shoot, it's Siberia out here today."

Okay. He trailed Grandfather back to the car, lowered into his seat, exhaled his relief when the heater hummed to life. But Grandfather didn't back out of his parking spot.

And it must've been the heat that finally thawed Philip's voice. "You're right. I hadn't visited the gravesite yet. I was too angry with her. For not calling. For waiting until it was too late. Even for asking me to uproot my whole life after not being a part of it in so long. I'm glad about it now, obviously. Holland is a gift. But still." He'd clicked his seat belt into place when he first got in the car, but he unlatched it now. "Mostly, I don't know if I've ever not been mad at her for leaving in the first place."

And anger was only the surface emotion. That panic

attack back at Muir Farm had revealed the deeper strong-holds—the hurt, the rejection, the loneliness that had been woven into his life for so long.

"Yes. She shouldn't have done that. I tried to talk her out of it."

Wait. The day Mom had told him she was moving in with Bryce and that he'd be staying at Grandfather's . . . the arguing he'd heard between Mom and Grandfather . . . he'd always thought . . .

He'd thought wrong. Grandfather hadn't been upset about Philip staying. He'd been upset about Mom leaving. He'd been upset on Philip's behalf. Why had Philip never once consid-ered that possibility?

"Nora was a little too much like me. Stubborn." Grandfa-ther's hands were perched atop the steering wheel, his distant gaze roaming over the cemetery grounds.

"You were always there, though." The words surprised him even as they came out of his mouth.

Grandfather's hands slid down the wheel.

"You gave me a home. Food. Clothes. A really good educa-tion. Books. So many books." Realization, like brushstrokes on a canvas turning into a picture, formed in his mind. "You made sure I was at St. Mary's every Sunday. You kept my old bedroom like it used to be, always ready for my visits." Which had been few and far between. Not just because of his feelings toward Mom, but toward this man who he could see so clearly now he'd never given a chance.

Philip palmed his knees, looking down. "I'm sorry I never saw it. I'm sorry I was so caught up in what I didn't have that I didn't . . . see you." Always there. Quietly providing for him. Asking for nothing, not even Philip's appreciation, in return.

"You're not the only one with regrets, Grand . . ." He almost said it. *Grandfather.* The only thing he'd called this man since he was six years old. But what if he tried something different? Just to see how it felt coming from his lips? "Grandpa."

Grandfather's eyes were still pinned on his windshield, but they'd gone glassy. "I do . . . love you, Philip."

He studied his grandfather. The thin lines etched into his face. The gray eyes he'd passed down. The hands weathered with age spots, fingers that had typed the beginnings of a story that could change hearts.

Had certainly begun to change his. And maybe he was the one with glassy eyes now.

"Nora loved you, too," Grandfather added quietly, finally looking to him. "I know one visit to her gravesite, one conversation with me doesn't change everything that's happened. But she did love you."

"I know." He rubbed his eyes, but the tears only welled again. Maybe the only thing to do was let them spill down his cheeks for a few silent moments. To soak up the heat humming into the quiet and, then, eventually, to meet Grandfather's gaze. "I love you, too."

Grandfather—Grandpa—nodded. Swallowed.

Then sniffed and started the car. "Okay, well, that's settled. Let's go home."

⸻

The farmhouse smelled like heaven when Indi arrived home from work. Like basil and marinara and something doughy and hot.

It sounded like heaven too—voices and laughter and the clanking of dishes. Maggie must have help preparing whatever deliciousness was on the menu this Monday night.

Indi unwound her scarf and tossed it onto the overflowing coat tree, shrugged out of her coat, and rummaged around for a spot to hang it. She finally found a free peg hiding somewhere near Wilder's leather jacket.

Good, maybe he'd finally decided to stop missing family dinners. The man had every right to be frustrated over his lack of progress on his ongoing quest to find Maggie's missing granddaughter, but she had a feeling all he ate when he was buried in work at his houseboat were microwaved freezer meals.

Indi paused outside the kitchen doorway, surveying the scene inside. Sydney laughing with Maggie as they cut up vegetables. Lilian standing in front of the island counter, clearly growing more flustered by the second as she watched Neil and Wilder attempt to shape individual pizza crusts. *Ah, so we're having homemade pizzas.*

There is still goodness for you, Indi. There's still beauty and joy and love waiting for you. The words that had murmured their way into her soul two nights ago hummed in again.

Some of that beauty and joy and love was right here in front of her, wasn't it? Her family. So many times in the past years, she'd remembered standing in this exact spot, listening to them talk, feeling burdened and separate and alone.

But the memory had loosened its hold on her. Because of that talk with Lilian two nights ago. Because of how she'd spent the rest of that night—holed up in the barn loft turned cluttered workshop. She'd unfolded her easel for the first time in so long, propped up the canvas she'd stopped by her store to pick up—the half-finished painting of the harbor. She'd turned on her space heater, pulled out her paints . . .

And in an act of surrender and hope and fragile faith, she'd made the first brushstroke. And then another and another and another, the healing truth wrapping around her with every dab of color. The truth that, yes, Lilian was right. That maybe it wasn't so much about letting go of her daughter as holding on to love.

The love she felt for a child she'd never met. The love God had for both of them. *The God who stays.*

Somehow, as she'd given herself over to the feel of her brush scratching and sliding against the canvas, she'd felt something new. Or maybe something old. She'd felt a little like a child again, willing to believe. Willing to trust.

It didn't erase the pain of the last few weeks or the last eleven years. Or even the pain of right now—of not knowing Olivia, of being separated from Philip and Holland.

But she wasn't so alone in it anymore. And the warm, welcome weight of that understanding had stayed with her ever since Saturday night. And today, it'd helped her take another brave step . . .

"Indi!" Lilian's voice cut into her thoughts. Her sister dropped the lump of dough she'd stolen from Wilder and strode across the room. "We've been waiting for you. You've inspired tonight's entertainment."

"Pizza?"

Lilian laughed, her blond hair bouncing around her face. "No." She moved to the table and reached underneath, lugging out a giant roll of brown paper. Wilder made to move around the counter and help her with it, but she hefted it onto the table before he could.

"I had this random memory the other day of Maggie once asking you what you wanted to do for your birthday. I think you must've been eight or nine. And you said you wanted to take a drawing class, only, this being Muir Harbor—not really the pinnacle of the arts—she couldn't find any nearby. So instead on your birthday, she covered the table with paper and put a bunch of markers and crayons in front of us—"

"And we had drawing class during supper," Indi finished.

Lilian nodded and rolled the paper across the table.

Indi hurried to catch it on the other end. "But, uh, it's not my birthday."

"I know but it just sounded fun." Lilian came up to Indi's side and pulled a pair of scissors from her apron, cutting through the paper. "Besides"—she lowered her voice —"Wilder's been in a bad mood for days. I figured we could throw him a bone. Do something unplanned and different just to get his mind off his caseload."

"You. Concerned about Wilder. I might pass out from shock."

"Very funny. But look at him."

Indi looked. Wilder still hadn't gotten a haircut, his dark hair brushing past his collar now, and the pizza crust he was attempting to stretch had about a dozen holes, but . . . "He looks fine to me." She turned to Lil, leaning her hip against the table.

"Are you kidding?" She held up her scissors and snipped at the air. "I should use these on his hair. He's a mess. He's working too hard on the case."

"You're actually worried. Seriously, get me some smelling salts."

Lilian smirked and heaved the roll of paper back to the floor. "Come on, let's save our pizza crusts from being annihilated by the men."

"Wait, I have to tell you something first. I emailed Sandy today."

Lilian's mouth formed an O. "You did?"

"Just to thank her for meeting with me and Trey, but I also asked her if she'd mind telling me a little about Olivia. I said I didn't want to be intrusive and I'd completely understand if she'd prefer not to communicate. I promised I wouldn't try contacting Olivia. I said I'd just love to hear a little about her but that, again, I'd totally understand if she'd rather not."

Lilian pulled her into a hug. "That's a huge step. Have you heard back?"

Indi shook her head. "No, but I only sent it ten minutes

before leaving the shop. And then checked my inbox like thirty times before locking up."

Lilian stepped back. "Well, I hope she replies soon. And I think it's awesome you reached out."

"Is pepperoni enough for the meat lovers or do I need to get sausage out of the freezer?" Maggie asked from the other side of the room.

"Pepperoni's good," Neil and Wilder said at the same time.

Indi couldn't help it—she just stood there for a second, watching her family all over again as Lilian directed a scowl toward Wilder and told him to surrender the dough. Even after she moved to Lilian's side, her grin stayed in place as she took over Neil's crust and worked it into a perfect oval, as they topped the pizzas and tucked them in the oven, then found their places at the table and started doodling.

Lilian had supplied crayons and markers, but Indi chose a simple black pencil. She gazed at the brown paper like it was a fresh page in a sketchpad or maybe canvas stretched over a frame, waited for the image to form in her mind, then bent over and went to work.

The smell of pizza, the sound of the paper crinkling and utensils scratching, conversation flitting back and forth . . .

No, maybe God wasn't making the hole in her heart disappear, changing all her circumstances, but she had to think He was restoring her. Even now as the lines came together on the paper in front of her.

"Oh, you're drawing the farmhouse," Maggie said at her side. "You're so talented, Indi. It's ridiculously unfair."

"You know, *Maggs*, I've been wondering if we're ever going to have one Mr. Tatum Carter join us for a meal. He could probably get here by the time the pizzas come out. I mean, if someone were so inclined to give him a call or something."

Maggie shook her head as she drew a flower. "Tatum is my friend, Indi. We had one date and it was enough. He's a wonderful man, but I don't think he's meant for me. So you can stop dropping hints."

"Very well." Indi added a chimney. "Guess that letter from Robert must've done a number on you."

"Oh, Robert didn't write that letter."

Indi paused. Dropped her pencil. Slid her gaze to Maggie. "I'm talking about the letter Philip gave you. The one he found years ago. I saw him give it to you before he left two weeks ago. You know, the one Robert wrote on the day he met you."

Now everyone was looking in their direction.

Maggie only shook her head and kept coloring. "I know what letter you're talking about. But I'm telling you, Robert Camden wasn't the one to write it."

It might've been a pleasant Saturday morning—a cup of coffee, a scone Holland had made using a recipe she'd learned from Maggie, only a few papers left to grade—but for the sight of Bryce carrying a suitcase into the kitchen.

Philip reverted his gaze to the double-spaced one-pager on the counter, his first assignment to his students this semester. The muscles in his legs tightened around the stool he perched on. *A suitcase . . . so that means . . . without even talking to me about it.*

He didn't even taste his coffee as he took a drink.

"We need to talk about how you keep making this hazelnut stuff." Grandfather pulled a mug from the cupboard. "Whatever happened to a basic, good-enough-for-the-everyman French roast?"

They did this now, he and Grandfather—had coffee together in the mornings. It'd started Tuesday, the morning after they'd visited Mom's grave together. An accident, really. Philip had wandered into the kitchen before his first morning class, found Grandfather already sitting on one of the barstools. Philip had filled a mug, and then Grandfather had handed him some papers held together with a clip. *"Tried to write another chapter. But it's been months. I'm rusty. Want to read it? Take a pass at a rewrite?"*

Now here it was days later and they'd formed a morning routine. He liked it. He'd gotten used to the kitchen in Maggie's farmhouse being the family's gathering place and he supposed he'd brought the habit home with him. A souvenir of those perfect days when he'd begun to picture a whole new life for himself . . .

But this was a whole new life, too. And it had its treasures. Like his grandpa smiling even as he griped about the coffee.

"Sorry, I developed a taste for the flavored stuff in Muir Harbor."

"Did you develop a habit for not shaving, too?" Grandfather slid onto the stool beside him.

"Didn't realize you had an interest in my hygiene practices."

Bryce still hadn't moved from the doorway, but he'd set his suitcase down at his feet. Seemed to be waiting for the right moment to intrude.

Well, it wasn't going to come. Philip had eased up around the man, yes. Even begun to appreciate that he'd leave his ranch for this length of time to see his daughter. But if he thought he was going to take his daughter back with him . . .

Philip let out a threadbare sigh. *If she wants to go, you have to let her. At least for a visit. And if she wants to stay . . .*

Then he needed to open his mind and be willing to talk about the logistics. Because as she'd reminded him over and over, she was fifteen, not five. She was smart and capable and how could he blame her for wanting a relationship with her father?

So he would stay calm. He would handle this with a maturity and grace he didn't feel. "Good morning, Bryce. Would you . . . like a cup of coffee?"

The man shifted his weight from foot to foot, a brown leather coat draped over one arm. "No, but thank you. As you can see, I'm ready to hit the trails. I realize I should've given you a heads-up earlier, but Holland and I had a good talk last night and since then, things have come together quicker than I thought they would—"

Philip bolted from his seat. Okay, so much for handling this with grace.

He moved to the doorway, apparently with enough bull-headed speed that Bryce knew to step aside.

"Philip?" Grandfather called after him.

But he'd already marched into the foyer. He dashed up the stairs, two at a time, until he spilled into the hallway and covered the distance to Holland's bedroom in long, frustrated strides.

"Holl?" He knocked on her door. "Are you decent?"

"I'm not hanging around in only my skivvies, if that's what you mean."

He didn't have patience for her sarcasm just now. Or for waiting for her to let him in. He twisted the knob and charged in. Holland was sprawled on her unmade bed, laying on her back with her feet on the wall above her headboard.

"Holland, I can't let you go with him. I know you probably don't see what the issue is, being homeschooled and all, but I have to sign off on your schoolwork and I can't do that from half a country away. And what about orchestra? I know you've missed some practices this month, but you're playing again, so I assumed that meant you were going back. And this might sound dumb, but I'm kind of into that one home reno show we've been watching and if you leave, what am I supposed to do? Just watch it without you?"

At some point during his diatribe, she'd lowered her legs and sat up, propping her casted wrist on her knee. Mom's old charm bracelet, the one he'd had fixed at a jewelry store as soon as they'd returned to Augusta, jangled on her other wrist. She was back to wearing it constantly, morning and night. She looked at him through bangs that needed a trim. "How much coffee have you had this morning?"

"You gotta closet the sarcasm for a few minutes, okay? I need you to be serious here."

"I am being serious. You're wigging out."

He anchored himself in the middle of her room. "Yeah, maybe, but I'm sorry, Holl. I can't let you go. And not just because I signed a bunch of legal paperwork but because we belong together. I know that sounds like a line from a Hallmark movie. I know you'll probably make fun of me forever about it. But I don't care—it's the truth. We're family now. And I can't let another person I love walk out of my life."

When had Holland stood up? She crossed her arms over her loose tee, her bare feet poking out from her bright green sweatpants. She spoke slowly, enunciating each word. "Do I look like I'm going anywhere?"

He blinked.

"Do you see any bags packed? Has it registered that I'm still wearing what I wore to bed last night? Does it look like I've even brushed my hair yet this morning?"

"Um—"

"Yeah, I am going to make fun of you about that Hallmark line. For, like, a long time because I don't plan on going anywhere. Okay? Are you happy?" She swiped a hoodie from the floor and pulled it on over her T-shirt.

Okay. So he should probably stop breathing so hard. Could probably loosen his stance a little too. Definitely should say something. "Holl—"

"And for the record, I'm still taking a break from orchestra."

"But you're playing again—"

"Yeah, because it's fun and I like it, but I don't know yet if it's what I'm meant to do forever. I'm not running away from it. But I'm not ready to run full-speed toward it either. I think Indi would tell me it's smart to take some time and figure out what I actually want."

"Indi?" What did she have to do with this?

"And as long as we're having this little chat, I don't want to graduate early. I don't know why, but I like living here with you and Grandpa so I'm not in a big rush to leave—"

"You're not going?" He couldn't handle the force of his relief. He reached for his sister and pulled her into a hug, her groan instantly muffled by his shirt.

She grumbled and slunk one arm around him. "No."

Thank you, God. Thank you. "But Bryce said you two had a good talk last night and . . ." *Stop talking, man. Take the win.*

"We did." Holland pulled back. "I told him I'm really glad he's back in my life. I want to stay in touch, go for a visit sometime, maybe see him on some holidays." She took a long, slow breath, as if working her way up to her next works. "But I belong here."

He couldn't stop a smile from breaking through his heady emotion. "You got the line wrong. It's 'we belong together.'"

"If you start crying right now—"

"I'm not going to start crying."

"Pretty sure I saw tears when you realized I wasn't leaving."

"Well, I'm just so happy I'm not going to have to finish that HGTV show on my own."

He expected Holland to roll her eyes. Or laugh. Or make another sarcastic comment. Instead, she fingered the bracelet on her wrist. "Philip, I really miss Mom."

"Oh, Holl—"

"It's okay. I'm not going to cry or anything. Not like I did back at the chapel, before everything with Peyton." She glanced up at him. "I never told you but, uh, I sort of freaked out on Indi that day. I asked her what the point was in praying for anything when I prayed so many times for Mom and God didn't heal her."

"Did Indi have an answer?"

"Not at the time. I'm honestly glad she didn't. If she'd given me some easy answer, I probably would've gone from crying to full-on ranting." She traced her bracelet's charms. "The thing is, I'm not sure any answer would've helped me then. I just needed to ask the question. Maybe that's what prayer is sometimes—not so much about the answers we get or don't get, but the questions we need to ask."

"Whoa, Holl, that's profound."

"I don't know. I just know I miss Mom. And I wish God had done things differently. And some days I'm still really mad at Him. I guess I'm still working through some stuff."

"Maybe we can work through some of it together. If you want. Trust me, I've had some freak-out moments of my own, also related to Mom, in recent weeks." That panic attack in Indi's bathroom came to mind.

Holland met his eyes. "Just so you know, I think Mom . . . she had a lot of regrets."

He studied his sister's face, heard the words she wasn't saying, the conviction she was trying to convey. Did Mom regret leaving him? There'd been a lot of goodness in this past week. Healing between him and Grandfather. A new acceptance of his place in this house. And now with Holland . . .

But he still had so many complicated feelings about Mom. And mixed in, a grief he knew Holland shared. But the beauty was that now they had each other in a way they hadn't in those first months after Mom's death. They had plenty of time to process their grief together.

Because Holland wasn't leaving. And he could truly say he was content to stay here in this house he'd once hated.

"I have regrets, too, Holl. But I hope you know I've never

regretted signing those guardianship papers. There was a lot of distance between me and Mom, but she gave me a pretty amazing gift at the end." And then, before the tears she'd accused him of could make an appearance, he cleared his throat and ruffled her hair. She huffed in irritation, so he did it again. "Come downstairs and have a scone before Grandpa and I eat them all."

He slipped from her room and into the hallway, using the corner of his shirt to dab at his eyes before she followed him. *She's staying. Holland's staying.* And today felt like Christmas.

Thank you, Mom. If ever there was a cure for the loneliness he'd once felt in this place, it was the joy of having Holland in his life. The surprise of getting to know his grandfather. Why, loneliness was on its way to becoming a stranger.

Except for the piece of him that might always be lonely for Indi Muir. But maybe they'd find their way back to each other eventually, too. He needed to respect her decision now, but that didn't mean . . . well, she could change her mind, couldn't she? He could pray for that miracle, couldn't he?

Maybe. But for now, he'd be grateful for the miracle God had already given him. A cobbled-together family—Holland and Grandfather and him—and it would be enough.

Holland caught up to him before he reached the staircase. "So I guess the facial hair thing is here to stay now. For the record, the five-o'clock shadow look is fine, but you're not going to go full-on beard, are you?"

He attempted to ruffle her hair a third time and she swatted his hand away. "Why is everyone so worried about my appearance all of a sudden?"

"You're just looking a little raggedy this morning. The joggers. The thermal shirt."

"It's Saturday."

"You're wearing a *robe*, Philip. A flannel robe."

"What's wrong with a robe?"

"And the old-man slippers aren't helping any either."

He halted at the staircase. "These aren't old-man slip—"

The trilling doorbell cut him off. He glanced at Holland, but she was already jogging down the steps, flying past where Bryce was just emerging from beyond the foyer, then opening the door. By the time he'd made it to the first floor, she'd already stepped aside to let their guests in.

And . . . and apparently God had decided to give him that second miracle after all. Because a green-eyed, curly-haired wonder was standing on the threshold and she smiled the moment she saw him. "Hi, Philip."

Somehow his feet carried him across the foyer. He was staring. Why couldn't he stop staring? Indi. At his house. With Maggie at her side.

Holland slapped him on the back and finally he spit out the only word he had. "H-hi."

And then, from behind him, his grandfather's gasp echoed in the foyer. "Maggie Muir?"

———•————•———

Indi had almost changed her mind. Had almost stopped Maggie on their way out of the house early this morning and insisted they call first.

But no. Showing up on Philip's doorstep without warning had absolutely been the right decision. The look of pure, adorable bewilderment on his face told her as much. With the front door still open, the frosty morning breeze glided in, tousling his hair and grappling with the loose ends of his robe's belt, dangling unused behind him.

"You're . . . here. A-at eight thirty in the . . . Why? And Maggie . . ."

Ah, the Philip from the wardrobe. The one who struggled

to finish sentences. Good grief, she'd missed him. Except, no, that wasn't nearly a strong enough sentiment. When he'd come to Muir Farm at the beginning of January, Philip West hadn't just temporarily moved into the bedroom two doors down from hers, he'd taken up permanent residence in her heart and mind.

What did it matter if he'd only stayed at the farm a little over a week? It'd been long enough for her to get way too used to his company. And his conversation. And his uncanny knack for looking right into her soul and making her believe he liked what he saw there. It hadn't mattered if they were moving boxes out of her old workshop or feeding her goats or hiking to the chapel—she just liked having him around.

She just liked *him*. Except that once again that word was nowhere near strong enough. And if there wasn't another reunion playing out in front of her right this second, she might just launch herself at the man and finally say the right one. *Love.*

"Hi, Ray. It's been a long time." Maggie stepped off the welcome mat, offering a smile to the older man now standing near the base of the staircase, looking even more shell-shocked than Philip. So much so Indi was halfway surprised he hadn't yet dropped the coffee mug he held.

"Forty-nine years and one month," Ray said. "Not that I've been counting."

"W-what's happening right now?" Philip raked his fingers through his hair. "I'm s-so confused."

Confused enough that he was stuttering. And she loved it. She stepped up to his side, close enough for him to hear her hushed voice. "Well, Professor, you didn't do thorough enough research about that letter you found. Your great-uncle didn't write it. Your grandfather did."

"But . . . Maggie was engaged to Robert . . . she loved Robert . . . not—"

"Which would be why the letter sat in a desk drawer for so long."

Maggie had reached Ray now and, oh, she was nervous, wasn't she? Indi could see it in the way she fiddled with the end of her braid, in the uncertainty threatening to wobble her smile. "You asked me to take a walk with you a long time ago. We were supposed to meet at the pier. I didn't show up."

Ray looked around—trying to find a place for his coffee mug? Apparently so, because Holland moved from her perch near Philip, ducked toward her grandfather, took his cup, then slid out of the way just as quickly.

"It's okay," Ray said. "I-I . . . I know Robert . . . w-well, he was . . ."

Indi leaned closer to Philip. "I see where you get it now."

"What?" He couldn't seem to decide who to look at—her or his grandfather or Maggie.

Holland sidled back in. "Yeah, maybe the whole surprising-the-guys thing wasn't a good idea. I wasn't thinking about the fact that Grandpa could, like, have a stroke or something. And Philip is probably going to faint any second."

"I'm not going to—" He straightened, lowered his gaze. "You knew they were coming?"

"Why do you think I was trying to get you to change out of your robe and old-man slippers?"

His gorgeous gray eyes narrowed.

Holland shrugged. "What? Indi and I text sometimes."

When his gaze reverted to Indi, she mimicked Holland's shrug. Grinned.

And apparently that was Philip's undoing. Because before she realized what was happening, he had her by the hand and was towing her out the open door, into the cold—not that she could really feel it with the warm delight skating through her now—and onto the landing at the top of the cement steps.

"Could you please explain what's going on before my head explodes?" The wind whipped his robe behind him.

And she just couldn't help it. Couldn't help her too-wide grin and the tease in her tone. "You seem flustered, Philip."

"Indi—"

"All right. From what I understand, Maggie met both your grandfather and Robert at the same time at the chapel."

"I know. The letter says as much."

"Before they left the chapel, Ray asked Maggie if she'd like to meet him that night for a walk. She agreed but then in the hours between, Robert tracked down Maggie's address and showed up on her doorstep, because apparently that's a thing men in your family do—"

"Ironic, coming from the woman who just showed up on my doorstep."

"—and he just sorta swept her off her feet. She never took the walk with Ray and was engaged to Robert within three weeks."

"Oh." He rubbed his bristled chin. "That explains some things. The guy pours out his heart in a letter and plans to do the same thing in person but then he gets ditched in favor of his brother and . . . that *really* explains some things. Who wouldn't turn gruff after that?"

"But he held on to the letter all this time, Philip. Isn't that just about the most romantic thing ever? The thought that maybe he's been pining all this time?"

"Well, he married my grandmother and had a daughter, so I'd kind of like to think maybe he wasn't pining the *whole* time."

"Fair enough. Maybe he just kept the letter as a memento or something, but the point is, Maggie has it now. And she's here. And he's here. And Trey's wrong. Sometimes we do get redos."

"What does Trey have to do with—" He shook his head.

"Maggie's here because of the letter. B-but you haven't explained why you're with her."

It was her turn to feel a flash of sudden apprehension. She'd pictured this going so many ways, but in every one of them, she'd pretty much thrown herself at Philip's feet in one way or another, and in every imagined scenario, he'd been happy about it. But what if she'd hurt him too much when she'd pushed him away weeks ago? What if he'd spent the time since realizing he was better off without her in his life?

Well, then she'd just have to convince him otherwise. Because standing here with him now, with the morning sunlight reflecting in his gray eyes, revealing what just might be a hint of hope, she knew—she *knew*—this was her redo.

This was the love that had been waiting for her all along. A gift from the God who'd never once left her side. Who might not clean up all her messes, but who walked with her through them.

Who'd led her right here. "The reason I'm here is . . ." She cleared her throat. "I wanted to ask for your help. And Holland's."

Philip stuffed his hands into the pockets of his robe. "Okay," he said slowly.

"Or rather, to demand it. If you'll recall, both of you agreed to help me transform my workshop. But we didn't get very far. I didn't even know what I wanted to do with the space. To be honest, I still don't entirely."

But ever since that night earlier this week when her family had gathered around the kitchen table, doodling on brown paper, she'd felt a stirring. She tucked flyaway curls behind her ears. "I think it's meant to serve a purpose. Maybe even the same purpose it already was—a home for art and creative expression and . . . I don't know. And I'm somehow okay with not knowing right now."

"It's okay if the lines haven't come together yet."

She smiled and looked up to Philip, then put her hands on her waist, tried to sound demanding. "Anyway, I just think you and Holland owe it to me to help me get it ready for whatever it's meant to be."

Oh, his dimples were beginning to appear. Two very good, very charming signs. "We owe you, do we?"

"Yes." She stepped closer to him, but when that wasn't enough, she threw all caution to the wind and closed in on him, wrapping her arms around his waist underneath his robe and propping her chin on his chest. "Please?"

"Well." His voice had gone husky. "When you ask that politely . . ."

He dipped his head and kissed her then. Lightly at first and then with a growing passion that might actually rival her own. When he lifted her off her feet, she couldn't help a squeal. She lifted her arms and circled them around his neck. "So that's a yes, then?"

"We can come with you right now."

"I didn't mean now."

"It's Saturday. Why not?" He kissed her again and then again, murmuring in between each one.

"You did hear me say I still don't have a perfect plan for the space?"

"So maybe we just start by restoring the hardwood floor. I know all about that now from this show I've been watching with Holland." One last kiss on her cheek. And then, with a whisper somehow firm and gentle all at once, "I don't need a perfect plan."

He was talking about so much more than that empty room, she knew. Even so, she had to ask him. "Are you sure? I pushed you away. I walked out of your life. I wouldn't blame you for not trusting me or worrying I'm just going to freak out again at some point. I . . . I can be such a mess sometimes. Like just this week I emailed Sandy Holmes and when she replied, she attached one of Olivia's school photos and I immediately burst out crying. I was happy and sad and a whole chaotic jumble of other emotions at once and—"

"You have a picture of her?"

She nodded, sliding her hands to his shoulders. "I'd show it to you, except I left my phone in the car, but the point is—"

"The point is, if you're a mess, Indi, then it turns out I was never meant for a tidy life anyway. I was meant for someone exactly like you—vibrant, exciting, talented, and complicated in the best of ways."

Complicated. He was going to turn that word entirely around for her, wasn't he?

"The point is, even if you try pushing me away again, this time I'm staying." When the wind gusted, he reached for the edges of his robe and wrapped them around her, then folded his arms behind her back once more.

Head tucked against his neck, she laughed, then tipped her gaze to his. "The main point is, I love you, Philip West."

Well, it seemed that last kiss hadn't, in fact, been the last kiss. Philip tightened his arms around her and found her lips again. And refused to let her go.

Even when Maggie and Ray stepped out the front door and Maggie said something about finally taking that walk. When Holland's dad cleared his throat and hurried down the steps behind them. When Holland herself appeared in the doorway, then groaned and closed the door.

He just stayed right there and didn't let go.

And that was perfectly fine with her.

*I*ndi leaned closer to the cracked-open window in the room above her store, breathing in the late-March air, fresh and familiar, with hints of the sea and a lingering chill. "The weatherman said it could snow today."

It didn't matter how many times Indi heard Philip's low-toned chuckle. She'd simply never get tired of it. He came up behind her, hooking one arm around her waist. "Only you would be happy about snow on the first day of spring." With his free hand, he tapped her cheek. "Also, you've got paint on your face."

Not surprising, considering the the hours she'd just spent painting walls in her newly renovated space. She looked over Philip's shoulder, taking in the gleaming hardwoods and the champagne gold light fixtures, the new glass wall that portioned off the front part of the room.

"It's looking good, isn't it?"

Philip followed her gaze. "Yep. Any more thoughts on what you want to do with the back half?"

She'd decided to turn the front area into an extension of her store—a gallery where she could display and sell her own pieces as well as others'. But as for the back . . . "I've got plenty of thoughts. Just haven't landed on the right one yet. I want to use it as a studio, but at the same time, I want to share it, too. It's like it was meant to inspire creativity."

She still couldn't believe how quickly they'd gotten the place into shape over the past two months. Philip and Holland had come down to Muir Harbor almost every weekend to help. Some weekends, they'd all worked together. Others, she and Holland dove into a project while Philip holed up in the corner grading tests or, even better, with his laptop, tapping away at the book he and his grandfather were writing.

Oh, the number of pics she'd taken when he wasn't looking—when he was so lost in his work that his glasses slid down his nose and he didn't realize he was mouthing every word he wrote.

Philip turned back to the window and leaned closer. "Are you ready for this?"

"Yes. But also, not at all." She took another deep breath, cool air filling her lungs, along with hope and fear and excitement and . . . awe that this was even happening.

That the email she'd received from Sandy last weekend had really said what it'd said.

Well, the cat's out of the bag. I let Olivia borrow my laptop last night, not realizing I'd left my email pulled up. She saw your last message and, long story short, she wants to meet you.

Oliva wanted to meet her.

Olivia *would* meet her.

Today.

"I can't believe they changed their minds. I can't believe they're bringing her here."

Philip grinned down at her. "I can. Sandy and John got a glimpse of your heart that day in the café. And Sandy's been sharing hers in return for weeks now, one mother to another, in all those emails flying back and forth between you. It makes complete sense they're open to this now."

One mother to another. "You are the sweetest man, you know that?" She tipped upward to kiss his cheek.

And exactly like she knew he would, he turned into her, pulling her to him, never content with just one kiss. He kissed her lips, then her cheek, her temple—

A thump sounded nearby. And then, a familiar groan. "I really shouldn't have to see these things."

Philip smirked and kissed Indi's forehead before turning. "I thought you were at the farmhouse."

Holland's backpack was at her feet where she'd dropped it. "I was, and Maggie and I were having a perfectly good time baking. Except Grandpa kept eating the cookie dough and then he goes and asks Maggie to take a hike to the chapel with him. At least they dropped me off in town first, but still, they abandoned me."

"The nerve."

At Philip's embellished horror, Holland's glower deepened. "I'm getting tired of seeing lovebirds everywhere I go. And it's only going to get worse because I'm pretty sure Grandpa's going to propose to Maggie at the chapel."

"Wait, what?" Indi gripped Philip's hand. "He's going to propose this weekend? Already? That's so . . ." She laughed. "I was going to say fast, but considering it's been almost half a century since they first met, that's not so accurate."

Philip's gaze went her favorite shade of gray when he turned it on her. "Well, I can tell you this, Indi Muir: I won't be waiting half a century." He squeezed her palm, then glanced to the window. "I think your visitors are here."

"Really?" Indi jolted toward the glass, attention hooking on the car parked at the curb in front of her building, the figures emerging from both front seats—Sandy from the driver's side and from the other side . . .

Olivia.

"I should've washed the paint off my face."

"It's just a little streak and it's adorable and you're perfect." Philip gave her a quick kiss. "Go meet her, Indi. Holl and I can slip out the back."

"No, you should wait. I'm sure I'll show her around. If Sandy's okay with it, I'd love to introduce you."

Philip nodded, squeezed her hand a second time, and released her.

"Good luck or whatever," Holland called after her as she hurried toward the stairs.

She clambered down the narrow staircase and wound through the backroom, pausing at the curtain to cinch the belt on her wraparound sweater and push wayward curls from her face. This was it. This was . . .

Everything she'd been so sure she was done praying for months ago. Even as she reveled in the wonder of it, she knew meeting Olivia wasn't going to come without moments of pain around the edges. Just like reading Sandy's welcome, wordy emails hadn't been without an ache here or there.

The girl she was about to meet would still go home with another mother. The girl she was about to meet had lived eleven years already, years Indi had missed.

Honest heartache. Steadfast hope. Lilian's words had stitched themselves into Indi's heart. She would need them—today, probably many days.

Her whole family needed them. With Peyton still comatose in the hospital and Wilder burying himself more and more in an investigation that had only grown more complicated . . . well, there were still shadows mixed in with all the lightness of these past months.

But, slowly, she was learning how to live in the tension between heartache and hope. How to trust the heart of God who stayed even when her own heart drifted, knowing He'd always find a way to draw her back.

The bells over the entrance chimed.

She pushed through the curtain.

And halted in a pool of sunlight as the face she'd seen in pictures from Sandy came in to beautiful view. Olivia had Trey's dark blond hair. It hung to her shoulders in soft waves, framing her heart-shaped face. Green eyes, a light smattering of freckles, a shy smile that revealed front teeth she hadn't quite grown into yet.

"Hi." Indi's voice was a little too breathless. A little too shaky. She moved past the cash register counter, giving Sandy a brief glance, a smile, before her eager gaze returned to Olivia. "I'm Indi. I'm so happy you're here. I'm . . . suddenly at a loss. I . . ."

Olivia bit her lip and looked to Sandy, then stepped forward and held out her hand to Indi. "Glad I'm not the only one who's nervous."

It was all Indi could do to hold back her tears. "Nervous might be an understatement." She took the girl's hand and they shook.

I just shook Olivia's hand. I shook my daughter's hand.

The daughter she'd entrusted to a mother who watched their interaction carefully now. Indi wouldn't blame Sandy for feeling uncertain about this whole thing. And yet, she'd helped make this incredible moment possible.

"So, Mom says this is your store." Olivia looked around. "It seems cool."

Indi had gone back and forth about where to meet with Olivia. She hadn't wanted to suggest a public place, but she hadn't known if Sandy would feel comfortable bringing Olivia to her home. The store had seemed like a safe middle ground. "Can I show you around?"

Olivia nodded and they spent the next few minutes

wandering around the shop, Indi pointing out this piece or that, trying to keep her heart from bruising her ribcage with all its thumping, trying to capture each moment in her mind's eye, to remember there would be plenty of time for deeper conversations, for answering any questions Olivia might have about the decision Indi had made to give her up. If not during this first meeting, hopefully in others.

Please, God, let there be others.

After a while, with a nod of consent from Sandy, she brought them upstairs and introduced Philip and Holland. She showed them the portioned-off front area where her painting of the harbor already hung on one wall, over the newly exposed brick she'd been so happy to discover under the old drywall.

"I'm still trying to figure out the best use for the back part of the room. Although, as you can see from my easel in the corner, I'm already treating it like a studio. But I don't want to keep it all to myself."

Olivia nodded. "I can see why. This place feels inspiring or something. Kinda makes me want to do . . . I don't know, something creative."

Indi's gaze shot to Philip's and the look on his face told her he'd heard it, too—the echo of her own earlier words. *"It's like it was meant to inspire creativity."*

It was getting harder and harder to contain her joy. Harder and harder not to cry.

"You should teach art classes," Olivia offered. "I'd come."

"Not a bad idea." Holland stepped up. "You could give private lessons, too."

She could. Yes, she could see it already. An evening DIY craft class for busy women who needed to unwind. Private sessions with kids like she'd once been—eager to learn every medium no matter her level of talent. There was room for a pottery wheel, a drafting table for sketching and . . .

She couldn't stop grinning as more minutes passed, conversation flowing easily. At one point, Holland pulled a container of cookies from her backpack, offering them to Olivia and Sandy. While they chatted, Philip slid to Indi's side.

"She looks like you," he whispered.

It was the same thing he'd said when she'd shown him the first photo Sandy sent. She'd kissed him for it then. Would now if they didn't have an audience.

"Philip West, have I told you lately how glad I am I found you in that wardrobe last fall?"

"Whatever happened to that thing, anyway?"

"Finally sold it right before closing the Augusta store. To someone who had no idea of its sentimental value."

"Hey, I'm going to show Olivia where the bathroom is," Holland called over.

Seconds later, their steps pounded on the staircase.

Sandy turned to Indi. "I'm going to go with them. I ODed on coffee on the way here."

"Wait, Sandy." Indi stepped toward the woman. "Thank you so much for this. For today. I can't tell you what it means to me. I . . ." For what had to be the hundredth time in the past twenty minutes, she blinked back tears of overflowing gratitude.

Sandy's gaze was filled with understanding. "You're welcome."

When she moved to the staircase, Indi turned back to Philip and he didn't waste any time tucking her against him. Her heart was too full to speak, so she closed her eyes, content just to lean in and feel the tips of his hair against her fingers at the back of his neck and the wisps of cold air from the window still cracked open.

"Are you happy, Indi?"

"The happiest." She melted into him, opening her eyes to

see tiny twirls of white falling from the clouds outside the window, glistening in the sunlight. "And by the way, if you haven't noticed—"

"I've noticed, Farmgirl, I've noticed." He smiled against her lips. "It's snowing."

THE END

AUTHOR NOTE & ACKNOWLEDGEMENTS

This is the book that nearly made me quit writing.

Which sounds dramatic, but it's the truth. I'd expected to spend a few months writing this novel, but instead it took well over a year. A difficult year in which discouragement and burnout, loss and grief hit me hard. I found myself wondering more than once why I was still writing. I have a different career I love, after all. I write in the margins and it feels like the margins are getting smaller and smaller and darn it, I don't need this!

And I'm pretty sure that's the spot where God cracks a smile and says, "Oh yes, you do."

And yeah, I did. I needed this book and these characters because I *am* these characters. I've never been through exactly what Indi and Philip and Holland have, but I have felt their feelings and asked their questions.

When Philip over and over worries that he's failing . . .

When Indi wishes for her old childlike faith or expresses her fear that God won't be enough for her . . .

When Holland asks what the point is in praying when God just keeps saying no . . .

I needed to write those worries and fears and questions because they're my own worries and fears and questions, dredged up from deeper corners in my heart I don't always love exploring. Somehow it's always stories—whether mine or someone else's—that get me to that place of honesty and vulnerability.

Maybe, if you're reading this, stories do the same for you. If so, we're kindred spirits!

And if so, my greatest desire with this and every book I write is that something in it would land in your heart just right, perhaps not answering all your questions, but helping you to, well, simply ask the questions.

Because I think I agree with Holland. Faith and prayer aren't all about having or hearing answers. Sometimes we don't have answers . . . we only have questions.

But maybe that's okay. Maybe that's the point. Maybe God has been gently whispering all along, "Talk to me. Tell me what's bothering you. You can trust me. I'm not going anywhere."

Thank you, reading friends, for letting me ask questions and feel so many feelings on the page. Thank you for taking this latest, much-needed story-journey with me.

My deepest thanks also to:

Mom and Dad—always. I love you both and am so grateful for you.

Grandpa, now healed in heaven, and Grandma—you inspire and bless me in so many ways.

My siblings, nieces, and nephews—for regularly reminding me real people beat made-up ones any day.

Charlene Patterson—please don't ever retire from editing! Thank you for trimming a bazillion words and helping polish the ones that remained.

Courtney Walsh and Lindsay Harrel—thank you for the voxes and texts that encouraged me so often throughout the writing of this book. I'm grateful for your friendship.

Nicole Schwieger and Hillary Lodge—so many times when I was frustrated while working on this book, I'd look at its gorgeous cover and get the motivation to keep going. I adore it!

My coworkers at Hope Ministries—if you guys had any idea how often a fun, busy day spent in your company keeps my writer-brain from freaking out over uncooperative plots and characters, you'd laugh. I'm so thankful my my dayjob is more than a dayjob and that it includes you . . . and that you let me ramble about my "other life" from time to time!

Jennifer Dukes Lee—we've never met but your book, *Growing Slow*, was everything I needed, right when I needed it. Thank you for touching my heart and helping me slow down.

NEEDTOBREATHE—thank you for the song "Child Again." It's the reason this book exists.

Denise Harmer—thank you, thank you for your keen proofreading eye.

And, of course, thank you to God, for the joy of another story, for nudging me over and over to give it the time it deserved even when I wasn't, ahem, so happy about it . . . and for staying.

ABOUT THE AUTHOR

MELISSA TAGG is the *USA Today* bestselling, Christy Award-winning author of swoony and hope-filled small-town contemporary romances. She's also a former reporter, current nonprofit marketing strategist, and total Iowa girl. Melissa has taught at multiple national writing conferences, as well as workshops and women's retreats. When she's not happily lost in someone else's book or plugging away her own, she can be found spoiling her nieces and nephews, watching old movies, and daydreaming about her next fictional hero. Connect with Melissa at melissatagg.com.

facebook.com/authormelissatagg
instagram.com/melissatagg
amazon.com/author/melissatagg
bookbub.com/authors/melissatagg
goodreads.com/melissatagg

Made in the USA
Monee, IL
06 October 2022